West of the Sun

By the same author

Red Branch

G. B. HUMMER

West of the Sun

SINCLAIR-STEVENSON

First published in Great Britain in 1994
by Sinclair-Stevenson
an imprint of Reed Consumer Books Ltd
Michelin House, 81 Fulham Road, London SW3 6RB
and Auckland, Melbourne, Singapore and Toronto

A CIP catalogue record for this book
is available at the British Library

ISBN 1 85619 468 X

Typeset by Deltatype Limited, Ellesmere Port, Cheshire
Printed and bound in Great Britain
by Clays Ltd, St. Ives PLC

In Brueghel's *Icarus*, for instance: how everything turns away
Quite leisurely from the disaster; the ploughman may
Have heard the splash, the forsaken cry,
But for him it was not an important failure; the sun shone
As it had to on the white legs disappearing into the green
Water; and the expensive delicate ship that must have seen
Something amazing, a boy falling out of the sky,
Had somewhere to get to and sailed calmly on.

Acknowledgements

The selection of poetry which introduces the book is taken from "Musée des Beaux Arts" by W. H. Auden. The permission of Mssrs. Faber and Faber to reprint the poem is gratefully acknowledged. The quotation which introduces Book III is taken from *The Red Badge of Courage* by Stephen Crane.

For his wise advice and editorial skill, I am indebted to my friend Marc Miller, who has been my rock of encouragement.

BOOK I

Daybreak with Shadows

1

West Texas at night is a blind man's vision. Stand in the empty dark and let all light be drained away. What follows begins, for a few moments, as a reassuring experience. The earth you stand on is as solid as a foothold. And yet in the dark you feel the wide plain growing away from you as you stand there. The sky, already too big for man or woman, changes even as you turn in an attempt to see if it is ending somewhere behind you, allowing no end and no beginning. It is a pattern of shades of blackness, with no key except the alien stars to reveal that pattern.

What passes for stillness within that dark is actually subdued noises. The land is never still in an aural sense. You don't relax into that darkness, filled as it is with the menace of those sounds. Blind and voiceless snakes, their hungers slaked, cover their fangs and sleep, leaving cruel assassinations to others. Predators whistle or grunt or make chinking sounds to reassure each other, before they kill. The wind whistles a meaningless, unending tune through the dry grass, or it picks out a whining song as it scrapes past the edges and corners of barns and houses.

When the first hint of the violet of dawn shows itself, the sounds multiply as urgency comes upon the wild creatures to kill before they lose the night's opportunity. The sky lightens by the second. And then fear strikes. It comes from that immense, flat, dominating land, black and unfeatured against the sky, merciless and threatening. Drive a car across it. Scrape a plow across it. Light it with electricity that comes from wires strung on poles that are made to march across it. It will win.

The dark shadows of the early morning squatted behind every building and object, including the three men who came out of a screen door at the back of the ranch house and stood looking east at the blaze of light. The faces of the two shorter men were grim and set. The tall man, whose face reflected none of their worry, looked around until he found a stick that was big enough to scrape off some manure that had lumped itself to his shoe.

A woman came to the screen door, hiding herself behind the rusted mesh and whimpering like a small animal that wants to be let out. One of the two men, the shortest, leanest and whitest haired one of the three, turned his back on her and spoke.

"Okay, come on out. Go out to the water trough and stay there. You go anyplace else and I'll whip you, I'm God damned if I won't." He paused to listen as she opened the door and stepped down to the ground one careful step at a time. "Ya hear me?" he barked.

The woman, as white of hair as the men, wailed and ran for the rusty tank at the foot of the skeletal windmill.

Turning so that he couldn't see her, he said to the others, "That's her fixed up. Let's get goin'."

The tall man said, "What do we do first?"

The third man spoke up now, organizing the operation. "We load the truck first," he said, "then we carry everything that's left that the sons of bitches could use out back of the barn, and we burn it, every bit of it. We ain't leaving nothin', not one God damn thing!"

That was the way they did it. The three Whitmore men piled everything they could into the open truck they had bought, and everything else they carried out back of the barn and set on fire. They were damned if they were going to leave anything worth having to the kind of people who would watch the banks foreclose, just to pick up a cheap farm without even thinking about the people who were being thrown out. That done, Henry loaded his family into his Dodge sedan and Karl got into the truck, and they left without a backward glance. Jimmy waited until they were gone, and then waited on even longer so that he knew they wouldn't turn back for anything. Once he was sure, he got his four children into the old square Studebaker and found his wife out near the trough rocking herself back and forth, moaning and crying, her face lost under her long apron. He got her into the car and tied a rope from the door handle to the spare tire that was strapped to the side of the engine panels, securing her in the car.

He went back then and walked through the farmhouse, pulling strips of wallpaper loose and tugging doors back until their hinges sprung, and banging window sashes down so hard the panes cracked and the frames split. He lit a small fire in the kitchen, out in the middle of the floor, then put it out with buckets of water once he was sure it had spoiled the green and white check linoleum and gone through to the floorboards. He went back to the tiny parlor, where he dropped his pants and did a dump on the top of the black, cast iron stove. With a last pull at the curtain tacked over the window in the back door, tearing this last piece of the pink tapestry cloth that his granny had brought with her when she married into the house, he left.

He turned the car west to get out of Texas, making for Albuquerque and Route 66, lighthearted now, happiest always with new beginnings.

"Where we meeting up with them?" the oldest girl asked.

"We ain't," her father answered.

He found a road that went around Lubbock, where they were meant to rendezvous, and kept driving.

*

Jimmy Whitmore stopped the car only occasionally, to spank the three younger children and shout at his wife, who had cried her way through three dish towels before they got to their first night's campsite. Five days later, on the lift of a warm spring wind, he found the little town of Gold Creek in California, where he stopped for a couple of hours of rest. He left the family taking turns washing themselves in the cold, rushing creek at the back of the little town, while he himself stole away from any possible prying eyes to look at his secret, a map that he carried in a silk pocket strapped to his chest. It was a geological survey map of the old, long-abandoned gold mines of the central Sierra Nevadas. He found again the spot on the map he had settled on back in Texas when he had studied the map in secret in the dead of night, away from his wife's whimpers and pleas.

When he had decided how to get to their destination, he pushed the family once more into the car and doubled back east, driving deeper into the lower range of mountains beyond the foothills. Sometime in the night the car stopped moving, and they slept where they were. The morning light showed them far from roads and other people, hidden away in a high, small valley. They were alone and on their own, with some food and a few things to cook it with, candles, some blankets, a good supply of picks and shovels, plenty of matches and a camera.

First Snapshot

There are five people in the photograph, four children with their mother. All five are not merely blond, they are white-haired. The woman is standing awkwardly, with the back of one wrist pressed to her hip and the other hand stopping her lips as if to suppress a giggle, or possibly a sob that has caught in her throat. She is wearing a cotton wash dress that is almost covered by a very long apron that has its strings pulled around to the front and tied there. She is wearing a pair of her husband's shoes and no socks. To her right are a taller girl, then a boy, then two small girls.

The tall girl is very thin and pinched, unnaturally old. She has just pulled her hair behind her ears, so that her right hand is blurred as it is being returned to rest. She looks very worried because she has mistimed tidying up her hair and knows the camera will catch her hand in midair, and she is afraid of the reaction of the cameraman, her father. Her dress is very long, much too long on her, and she is conscious of that. It is one of her mother's that has been taken in at the waist but is too big everywhere else, so that where breasts should fill out the dress below its high neckline, the material hangs limp and flat. In the glare and evident heat of the sun, she is covered almost from neck to ankle by the dress. She looks as if someone is trying to make a little old woman of her, when she is no more than twelve. They are trying to hide her girlhood, which will be very short because she is dying.

The boy, to her right, is wearing long shorts and a long sleeved shirt, and he is barefoot. His shorts, once his best cotton pants, are cut off now and, instead of being hemmed, are bound in a heavy blanket stitch around the legs so that the shorts will last a little bit longer before beginning to unravel. He is squinting hard into the camera lens, trying to see the silver flick of the shutter when it slides across to make the exposure. He is holding his right arm firmly to his side by putting his left arm behind and holding his elbow hard to his side with his left hand. He has been told to keep his hands to himself and stop tickling his sister beside him or he'll get a whipping as soon as his dad has a hand free. In another year he will make funny faces to the camera and his father will give up trying to get a decent snapshot of him, the whipping by then having degenerated into a regular means for his dad to work off energy, with no prospect of improving the boy's behavior.

The two little girls to his right look like twins, but they are not, having been born eleven months apart. For convenience they are treated like twins, and the children obligingly accept it without rivalry. They are dressed alike in dresses made from printed flour sacks, and their hair is cut short and pulled back in the center, fastened back so harshly with bobby pins that the only hair that falls forward is the soft baby down that escapes at the hairline. Like their brother, they also are barefoot. The smallest one has a slight deformity of the left foot. Her foot turns inward and the instep is arched like a porcelain Japanese bridge in an aquarium. Both the little girls are staring intently, their chins pressed down on their wishbones, trying hard not to laugh until their father says they can go back to their playing.

Behind them is a small stand of cottonwood trees and aspens. Otherwise the bowl or amphitheater that they are standing in is carpeted in dry grass, beaten flat in many places, interrupted by a few straggling clumps of brushwood. The trunks of the trees have been used as poles in order to rig a complex of tentlike dwellings among them, and hanging from nails and pieces of wood and lopped branches are all the things that can be hung up that would usually be stowed away in cupboards or drawers. The bedding is hung up on ropes slung between the tree trunks, in order to keep insects and worse from crawling in during the day.

Beyond the border of the photograph at the far end of the cottonwoods is a small creek. This water source is the reason for Jimmy Whitmore's choice of this site. They draw drinking and cooking water upstream, and downstream the children have dug out a bank of the stream and made a small dam with rocks to create a place to wash themselves and their clothes. Except when she comes to the bath place to wash herself morning and night, their mother stays away from the creek and the children. Since their father is two or three miles away, working secretly to try to reopen a collapsed and flooded gold mine that is not his property, the children are left on their own. They have a few chores to do. They carry the garbage, what there is of it, to a place where the creek runs over a rock outcrop and drops into a deep, narrow slice in the rock that an earthquake produced at one time. They dump all their refuse into this, which they call a canyon, and let nature get on with disposing of it. They wash dishes and clothes, what there are of them, when the need arises. The two older children keep a pile of dry brushwood topped up so that the fire, which is an open one inside a circle of stones, can be roused into life whenever their mother wants it.

The rest of the time they keep out of sight of their mother, away from her crying and shouting at the empty space that her mind fills with threatening things. Most of the time they are at the creek, at their bathing place. The reason for this is that each of the children has only one change of clothes. Their mother screams at them and sometimes even attacks them if she sees that an article of clothing is dirty. Being sensible children, they spend most of their time naked with their clothes hung up out of the way of any danger of soiling them, on tree branches or spread over the azalea bushes that grow along the creek. The boy keeps his one pair of underpants on, because he has been told it is a whipping offense to let his sisters see his thing. He washes the underpants most afternoons, getting around the problem of necessary nakedness by washing them while he is sitting in the water of the creek. Annie Evelyn also has to wear underpants all the time. Hers are boys' underpants also, so that Calvin can inherit them when she has to start wearing panties. Her mother says she has to wear underpants because any day she will start to see some changes in what her mother calls her legs. So far, she reports to the other children, there is no sign of any. There is no sign of any change in her breasts either, so she doesn't yet have to wear an undershirt. Sweetheart and Francine, the two little girls, don't know what all the fuss is about. They don't like wearing clothes anyway, and they haven't worn anything around their legs since they were able to go without diapers.

Even up here in the mountains, the heat at midday is

flattening. The children spend long periods quietly making baskets and dolls out of water reeds and sticks, giving the oldest girl, Annie Evelyn, a chance to rest and try to draw breath without fighting the palpitations in her chest. Sweetheart and Francine play with imaginary pets most of the time. They each have a dog and a cat whose names change as the girls think of better ones, and from time to time they claim another animal from wherever they are that day in their play. They had a tiger for a whole week once, which was a long time for one of their casual pets to last, but when they left Africa they left it there.

The boy, Calvin, likes to play tricks, kind ones, to make Annie Evelyn laugh. He has done this ever since he realized during the previous winter that his sister was dying, and that his parents were wrong when they said she would get better on her own once they could stop moving all the time and settle in the mountains for a while. Before that, some of his tricks had been pretty mean. One day, however, he saw Annie Evelyn in a different light, or he looked at her differently, or he saw her before she put aside the dread that had passed through her; however it happened, he understood that she would not be with them much longer. Now he looks at her every night when he goes last thing into her tent, since one of his chores is to take a last look to make sure no rattlesnakes have got in during the day. His parents don't look at her any more, and he keeps his observations a secret from them. He knows from watching her that she will not live past the end of summer. She knows it too, but they don't talk about it. Calvin is eight years old, and he and Annie Evelyn are the only friends to each other, even when they fight.

Second Snapshot

The three girls are standing beside their father at the entrance to the mine he is trying to restore to production so that they can be rich. They are dressed in the same clothes as in the first snapshot, which seems odd because the dress that Annie Evelyn is wearing appears to have got bigger. What has happened is that she has got thinner and smaller and more pinched, and even in this photograph she has put out a hand toward her father, ready to take his arm if it is needed. Jimmy Whitmore is smaller than his wife, of only medium height compared to his wife in the other photograph, and lacking her thick frame. He looks thinned down to muscle. One unusually large hand holds his felt hat, and the other is hooked into the waist of his jeans. He looks as though he is caught between posing as a tough, uncompromising miner of days now long gone, or a benevolent head of this family of blond girls; in the end he manages only to look as if he is posing. Maybe that is because Calvin is taking the picture, and his father doesn't trust him and never will. The hijacked mine in the background is unimpressive, a ragged hole in the hillside screened by pine branches that have been cut from trees higher up the hill and dragged down here where they serve better as indicators than camouflage. The mine itself looks the opposite of what it is, a dream. In October it will be a tomb, but that is after.

Third Snapshot

The three younger children are crouched on the ground, holding back some undergrowth so that the camera can pick up the outline of a large piece of granite, about three feet in height and about two feet across. The children look triumphant but concerned. The two little girls are not smiling or about to laugh or even teasing their brother in order to get him into trouble with their father, the cameraman. Looking at the expressions of all three, it is difficult to know why their father insisted on taking the photograph. What was he recording?

The children had been playing at exploring, which meant tramping across the flank of the mountain in the opposite direction to the mine. They had always before stayed on the open face of the mountain, from where they could see the lower slopes and the foothills and, on a clear day, the huge, flat valley beyond. This morning they had decided to go uphill. Annie Evelyn said she could breathe pretty good, and she wanted to see what was up there where the bigger trees started growing. They walked until they came to a wide draw where in the winter a stream drained the slope, then they turned up the hill. The draw narrowed into a half-rounded corridor that went straight up the hill. They climbed it slowly until it opened into a small bowl only a few hundred yards from the altitude at which the pine trees thickened and began to guard the higher slope. In the exact center of the bowl was a ragged tangle of undergrowth. Emaciated by the summer drought, its leaves failed to conceal a stone at its heart. The children pulled the branches away until they found a crude carving. Judging from the way the granite, lacking a final polish, was beginning to crumble on its surface, the carving had been there a long time.

Annie Evelyn studied it and declared, "It's an angel. It's one of them burial angels, in a graveyard."

Reacting automatically, the girls pulled away and Calvin pressed closer. "It's a angel, all right," he said. "It's all rough, and it ain't very pretty." He got up.

"Reckon somebody's buried here," he pronounced.

The girls backed away and retreated down the draw. Calvin stayed a few moments longer before joining them. They said very little on the way back to their campsite.

When they were in sight of their tents, Annie Evelyn said to Calvin, "You gonna tell Mamma?"

"Maybe," he answered, "but I'll tell Daddy first."

It was almost seven that evening when all six of them went back, Calvin leading the way. Mamma hung back when they got to the place. It was their daddy who verified that the children had found what looked like a monument, hand carved by someone a long time ago into what was just still recognizable as an angel like the ones in cemeteries. He called his wife over, several times, then losing his temper and shouting at her, and she finally came to see it. She crouched down to look closely at it, creeping closer until she could run her fingers over the figure.

"Poor soul," she muttered over and over again. "Poor sad souls." She took a last look and said, "Mountains are closer to God, but they ain't always happy places. I wisht I had some flowers." She turned away and led the little procession down the mountain.

Fourth Snapshot

The mine entrance is at the center of the photograph. A pile of rocks completely blocks it, where the stone from the mountainside above has been deliberately pulled down in a partially controlled landslide. The tree branches have been taken away, and all the undergrowth has been cleared. Instead of a secret place, this is now a monument. The two little girls are posed each side of the rock pile, kneeling in profile, heads bowed and hands stiffened in prayer, deliberately made to look like guardian angels on religious calendars and Christmas cards. A carved wooden board is nailed to a post that is embedded in the pile. It is possible to see that there is a name carved on it, but it can't be read from this distance. Close to, it reads,

Annie Evelyn Whitmore.
12 yrs. d. 1926.
We have to leave her with you.
Amen.

2

"That's all the snapshots I got," Jimmy Whitmore said. "Couldn't afford more film. The children's mother had a conniption fit over one roll of film. I daresent risk another one."

One of the two white-haired men he was talking to said, "She don't seem too good to me, Jimmy."

"She's got worse, Karl," he answered, looking away and closing the subject.

"This here mine, Jimmy," the other man said.

"That there joke, you mean," Jimmy broke in.

The man persevered. "This mine, in the picture here," he pointed, "why'd you think there was gold in it? You must of had a reason to go to all that trouble. You know somethin' the rest of us don't?"

Jimmy Whitmore's face contorted into a bitter, tired smile. "I don't know shit, Henry," he said. "I ain't even got good sense. There wasn't no gold there. I don't know if there ever was, but there sure as hell ain't none now. All that mine has got is Annie Evelyn."

The two other Whitmore men tried to ignore his outburst. Karl pulled out his Bull Durham sack and Rizla papers and rolled himself a dainty, perfectly formed cigarette. He licked it elaborately, sensuously, delicately with his strikingly pink tongue, in a manner that would have been obscene if it weren't for the ordinariness of what he was doing. Henry, the other brother, looked at the ground and seemed to try to draw a map of something with his index finger, using a tuft of dry grass as part of his design.

When Karl had his cigarette constructed and lighted, Henry resumed. "They was other mines up there, wasn't there? Same general area? What do you suppose made them miners go there? It's fifty-sixty miles south of the Mother Lode country."

"I don't know at all," Jimmy answered. "I thought I did. Gold takes you in a funny way. A week away from there, not even that, and I can't rightly remember why we went there at all. I saw them mines marked on that old survey map, and that was it, I was gone. Me and the wife and all the kids. Now I'm down here broke and 'thout my biggest girl. God damn fool, that's all."

He stood up from where he had been sitting on his haunches and stretched the kinks out of his legs. "God damn fool," he repeated. He walked slowly away.

Karl called after him. "Wasn't nothing you could do, Jimmy, nothing at all in the world you could do."

Without turning around, and without pausing in his retreat, Jimmy said, "That don't help none."

WHITMORES

****

KEEP OUT

Whatever their farm had been called before, it wasn't called that any longer. As the sign said, it had passed from agricultural property to Whitmore land. A struggling orchard of almonds and peaches was broken by the road up to the farm, which lay at a slightly higher level than the land down next to the county road. The farm road appeared to be aimed for the side of the barn, until it turned at the last possible moment and skirted the north end of the building close enough to touch. That would not have been a wise move, however, because the untreated, unpainted barn siding was frayed and shattered, offering a handful of splinters at no cost to the donor.

The line of the barn at its northern end had been extended by two long, low sheds, one of which was converted to a bunkhouse. The other was split into two of what the Whitmores called houses. These were the three-room dwellings that were standard issue for the families of the Whitmore clan. Individual houses filled the two flanking sides of a rough quadrangle, with the old farmhouse on the west side. This had been broken up into three units. The wide porch that protected the house on three sides had been filled in to make more rooms, so that everybody could have a kitchen, living room and bedroom. The bunkhouses made this a feasible solution since all the children, from the earliest age at which they could be moved there, slept in the bunkhouses, the boys in the one near the barn, the girls in another that used to be the tractor shed that was concealed from view behind the farmhouse.

The girls had their own ablutions shed, and their detached privy stood a few yards beyond it. The ablutions block for all the others was a large shed in the dead center of the quadrangle, with wash tubs and sinks, the latter divided from each other by hanging sheets and bedspreads so that personal washing could remain personal. The privy for everyone except the girls was south of the quadrangle, just over the ridge that the farm occupied. With the door open, the occupant had the finest view of the valley that anyone could imagine. The door was left open when it was occupied, not for the view so much as a warning to anyone coming along the path that they could save themselves a hundred yards of walking for the time being, because a closed door meant that it was available.

In the farmhouse were the highest ranking Whitmores, the brothers Henry and Karl, and the Donnells and Harveys, the married names of the two oldest Whitmore sisters. Jimmy Whitmore should have been in the house instead of the Harveys, but he had taken the house farthest away from everyone and installed his wife there. His house could be distinguished from all the others by the two-by-fours nailed across all the windows, and the solid door with a sliding bar that fixed the door closed from the outside. It looked like a small jail in one of those cloudy photographs from the old mining camps.

Several of the houses were unlived in for the time being, available for the young people as they grew up and married. The houses, originally shacks for migrant workers, had been bought as one lot from the Ridgeleys when they got out of cotton and converted their entire acreage to orchards. That was what water could do, when you could get it.

The whole place was decrepit but busy, and it had a good feel to it. Curtains flapped at the windows or, pulled outside by the wind, splashed color against the unpainted board siding of the buildings. Wash lines linked the houses like telegraph wires in a more civilized place and, instead of birds, supported sheets, shirts, dresses, underwear, men's socks – the others didn't wear them – wash rags, dish towels, all the windy flotsam of a busy settlement, held to the thin ropes by homemade clothespins. Children, wearing as little as it took to keep them healthy, played complicated games that involved long arguments followed by sudden flights to the far corners of the farmstead, as if they had been influenced by the flocks of sparrows that peppered the quieter parts of the quadrangle pecking for crumbs and seeds. A few girls, in ones and twos, played on their own in their own little worlds, and one child, in imitation of the buzzards that lazily swept the air like the wind's attendants, spread her arms wide and drew curves and circles on an empty patch of field, letting the wind carry her where it pleased.

There were signs here and there of the optimism of the Whitmores. Since the farmhouse porches had been filled in, new porches were needed to keep the fierce sun at bay. Poles from the river banks several miles away had been cut and stripped and used to erect a frame. Pieces of roofing paper and sacking were gradually filling in the frame, first above the windows so that the rooms could be shaded even if not actually cooled. Piles of things that might come in useful, pipes and metal bars and angle irons, lay in a heap beside the big barn door, waiting for storage room to be made for it inside. Beside them was all the equipment and litter that goes with the area where the work is done on cars and trucks and tractors.

The big boy asked Calvin, "You the one with the crazy mamma?"

"Yep," Calvin answered.

"What's wrong with her?" he pressed.

"She's crazy," Calvin answered.

The boy either didn't see or ignored Calvin's embarrassment. It had been the same ever since they got here. Maybe it was because they were all white-haired, all cut out of the same Whitmore mold, every last person at this place. The new farm was smaller than the old one, and the mountains were closer so that you hadn't to wait for a clear day to see them, but otherwise Calvin couldn't see what the fuss was about and why they had to move. There were more Whitmores here, all of them a little bit hungry and all the men worried, the women forever going into corners so they could talk women's talk out of hearing of the children. It didn't seem much different from when they had been in Texas. They were all just Whitmores. It had been different with Annie Evelyn, that was what had changed him. Having last summer in the mountains had changed him. When she died, he went back to being one of the Whitmores, but with a difference from the others.

"What happened?" the boy asked.

Calvin was getting tired of this. "What do you mean?" he said.

"How did she go crazy?" the boy said.

"She didn't like leavin' Texas," Calvin answered. "My daddy and her had a lot of trouble. She started cryin' and later she started seein' things. That's all."

"What's she see?" the boy asked.

Calvin ran away from him, to where the men were building a shed for the implements. He sat watching them for almost two hours, until the men teased Jimmy Whitmore about him and he shouted to Calvin to "Git!"

He found some lunch in Auntie Donnell's kitchen, and then he went hunting for her. Auntie Donnell was the one who had taken him on, since his own mother didn't want anything to do with her children, spending most of her time in the darkened bedroom of the small cabin that was their home now. Auntie Donnell's only child, Harry, was seldom mentioned. He was the one that got away.

There had been three Whitmore men and six Whitmore women, but one of those had died. All the Whitmores, men and women, had married cousins or what they called cousins, except for Karl. They hadn't found him a wife yet, and he always said he didn't care one way or the other. The women carried the name of their husbands instead of a first name. Calvin had an Auntie Henry, his uncle's wife, but the other women were known by their non-Whitmore name. It was a less than subtle form of clan distinction.

The Whitmores had always been a clan. The only piece of family history they possessed was a sampler dated 1697 with the name of the embroiderer, Hannah Whitmore, and the place where she lived, Enstone. They all agreed that sounded like England. The house where Hannah lived looked English also. It was worked in dark wool to show that the house was built of stone, and it had three chimneys. There were windows on three stories, if you counted the ones that were built into the roof. On the rare occasions when the sampler was taken out of its black leatherette folder, the Whitmores gathered around it and stared at the wealth that house represented. Someday they had been important people. A child named Hannah had been taught fine embroidery, not how to work as a field hand. The Whitmores didn't speculate about what had happened to bring them to what they now were. Their speculation was confined to ways to restore themselves to that grand station once again.

Somehow they knew they had once been in Virginia. They also knew they had migrated farther south, because they had helped the South lose the Civil War. They had followed what was left of southern wealth into eastern Texas, then had been pushed on from there to west Texas, which was their Waterloo. They had lasted longer on a cattle ranch than most dirt farmers would have done, but that wasn't long enough. How they were going to find their fortune or restore the family prestige now that they were landed on the godforsaken west side of the great valley, blasted by the west wind and fried to their very marrow by the blaze of the sun, was a mystery to them all. But that was their intention.

Calvin wandered through the three rooms of the farmhouse which were Auntie Donnell's. She wasn't there, but a jug of lemonade was made and waiting in the cooler, and there was a plate of cookies out on the table. It looked as if there was going to be one of her lemonade parties, and he guessed that she was out in the ablutions shed getting herself cleaned up and ready. When she entertained, the ladies would sit at the table for a sip of lemonade, then put their glasses in the cooler and go and lie down on the brass bed. Auntie Donnell would always make a fuss about loosening her girdle, which in her rich speech came out sounding like goidle, letting slip the comment that in her day the ladies and girls always had a little lie-down after lunch to get over having a meal in the heat of the day. It was about the only bit of the Old South left in her behavior, aside from her accent.

After their rest and gossip, when she deemed it time to do so, Auntie Donnell would get up and brush her long hair, wrapping it around her head in a loose swirl of a white bundle, and lead the way back to the rest of the lemonade and, finally, cookies. That was when Calvin was allowed to put in an appearance. Today he was unwilling to wait. He took a handful of cookies and sat down in the corner of the small living room, where he knew he wouldn't be seen. He heard her come into the kitchen, and soon someone knocked at the screen door. He lay down in his corner, dozing until it was time for the cookies. There was nothing better to do.

If he had stayed awake to eavesdrop, he might have heard something to make less difficult some of the confusion, the suffering that was in store. Then again, being a child, probably he would have been able to make as little sense of their lives as the grownups were able to. And if he had made sense of their lives, they wouldn't have thanked him for it. Let him sleep.

"You come along now in here, Pearl," Auntie Donnell said. She worked hard to get the girl's name right, aware that in her dialect the word came out as an unlovely Poil unless she tried to prevent it.

She got down two glasses and took the jug of fresh squeezed lemonade out of the wire mesh cooler box, absentmindedly touching the white blanket that covered it to see if it was satisfactorily damp. Her nervous fingers betrayed her, almost tipping over one of the glasses as she put it on the small table, and she mumbled "Clumsy!" and laughed. "Have a sip, dear, and then we'll go lie down," she said.

Pearl was sixteen and very pretty. She was a daughter of Auntie Harvey, and as the eldest of the Whitmore girls she spent most of her time with the older girls in their bunk-house. No one except the other girls knew her very well, because she was kept away from the grownups except for her mother, and she didn't have anything to do with the children and older boys who, like Calvin, lived and slept in the big bunkhouse.

"I won't have any just yet, thank you," Pearl said. Her eyes ranged around the kitchen and she twisted her going-out handkerchief in her hands.

Auntie Donnell was taken aback. "All right, dear," she said. She returned the glasses to the cooler and led the way to the bedroom without any more attempt at breaking the considerable ice.

"Now make yourself comfortable, dear," Auntie Donnell said. "I'm going to loosen my girdle, and you loosen your belt, take off your shoes now, that's right. You can take that dress off if you worry about creasing it. That's right, just plump up that pillow, make yourself comfortable. There, there, that's better. At least this bedroom's on the cool side of the house."

She chuckled, "Me and my girdle, I guess it's the joke of the Whitmores, isn't it." Still Pearl only smiled and nodded and avoided her eyes, and she pushed on. "The most of them think it's vanity, wearing a girdle." She made a special effort to give it its correct pronunciation. "'Specially in this heat, it's my cross, I tell you. But it helps my back, you see, and I've been wearing it for so long, well this one or another like it, that my stomach would be a sight to see if I did without it. You won't tell, will you?" she asked with a simper.

She cleared her throat noisily. "I seem to have kind of a whisper in my voice today. I expect it's that dry wind again." She turned her face away from Pearl's on the next pillow and concentrated on the ceiling. "You see, Pearl, it's always been given to the oldest of the Whitmore ladies to tell the girls what we grownups call the Whitmore secret, and somebody decided a long time ago it was best to do it as part of a girl's coming of age, I think that's the best way to think of it. Do you understand?" She turned back to Pearl, annoyed at her silence and letting it come into her voice. "How old are you now, child?"

"Seventeen come November," Pearl said. "Likely be Thanksgiving Day this year," she added.

"That'd be nice," Auntie Donnell said. "Two celebrations in one day. You'll have a very nice party that way, won't you." She turned on her side to face the girl, determined to drag her story forward. "It comes from very far back in our family's history, when the Whitmores were somewhere south of Virginia and east of Texas. The Whitmores were very important in the South, the work they did, I mean, they were people who didn't have a plantation but they worked on one, running things for the owners, running the slaves and things like that. That's a Whitmore heritage. That's your heritage, too." She paused until Pearl looked her in the eyes before adding, importantly, "Part of it. It's another part we got to talk about now, why you're here."

Pearl said, "Yes, Ma'am," and looked about to cry.

"I was told the Whitmore story by my Auntie James, and now I'm telling it to you." Satisfied that her audience was now prepared, Auntie Donnell made herself comfortable.

"There were these three Whitmore brothers, this is in your great great grandmother's time, two of them got married and the third was a hellraiser who couldn't settle down because they couldn't find him a wife. The two wives of the married Whitmore boys were sisters, cousins from Savannah, back east in Georgia. They were the only known female relatives of the Whitmores who weren't already married. There wasn't as many Whitmores then as there is now. Until there was a widow, or a daughter in another generation, the third Whitmore brother was just plain out of luck. They let him get on with whatever, with whatever girlfriend he wanted to. Well, they couldn't stop him, I guess."

Pearl said, "If there wasn't any other girls that was Whitmores, why didn't he go ahead and marry one of his girlfriends?"

Auntie Donnell snorted. What in the world had this child's mother been doing when she was supposed to be getting the girl ready for hearing the Whitmore secret? Still, it wasn't the girl's fault if her mother was nextdoor to a simpleton. Some sisters you could stand, and others you hated from the day they were born.

"Oh, I do forget things when I tell this story! I'm sorry, dear. You see, from the time in the south when there was only rich people or slaves and nobody in between except Whitmores, the Whitmores never married out of the family. A cousin, or a second cousin, sometimes an uncle would marry a niece. Never out of the family, that was a rule. I expect they were afraid of colored blood. There's a lot of it down there. Well, anyway, you can guess what happened."

Pearl looked blank and Auntie Donnell sighed deeply. "This unmarried Whitmore boy got a girl in trouble and her father said he was going to have to marry her." She paused. "And the girl had black hair, not just dark hair or brown hair but hair black as black. Whitmores have never had dark hair or black hair or red hair, nothing but this creamy blond hair that we all have, men and women alike." She paused to stroke her own hair, and patted Pearl's. "There's something inside us that's against black hair, I guess."

"I don't like it," Pearl contributed.

"Of course you don't, you're a Whitmore. Well, this black haired girl was going to have a Whitmore baby. The unmarried brother said he thought he might be in love with the girl and he'd be willing to marry her, and her father said he'd agree as long as they got far enough away that his neighbors didn't have an opportunity to keep track of how long it was between the wedding and the birth. But that wouldn't do, not for the other Whitmores. The girl wasn't a Whitmore, and she had black hair. She wouldn't do."

"My goodness," Pearl said. It was a real life romance, with difficulties.

Auntie Donnell appreciated the interest, and her narrative style began to roll and swell. "The three men weren't just brothers, they were always close friends like Whitmore men always are, and they spent days and nights together while they thought about what to do – until finally they figured they knew what they had to do."

Auntie Donnell drawled into a long pause, holding her listener with a rhetorical version of a skinny arm. "You can count on it, Pearl," she said, "when the men call a family conference and it includes the wives, there's something up. We had a conference like that when your uncles found out they were going to have to leave Texas, and we were all going to have to join up together again out here. Well, of course, the Whitmores gathered, back then, I mean, and the oldest brother went through the whole story for them. When he was finished, everybody could see that whatever they did to settle the problem of this baby and its mother, the poor unmarried brother had the same problem at the end of it, and that was that he had no prospect of a Whitmore wife for years and years to come, and that meant no wife at all, period."

Her eyes wide, Pearl nodded her head on her pillow and said, "Mmmm."

"Well, the girl had made things easier for them by refusing to live with the Whitmores as one of the clan. She just flat refused. The girl's father told them he knew of a young man who he'd prefer to be his daughter's husband and the father to the child, and the father and this other young man would be satisfied as long as there was enough money to take care of the stain on their honor, I guess you could say. And that's fair, every family ought to have its own pride. The Whitmores agreed, hard as it might be, to raise the money. That took care of the girl and the baby, but what it did not take care of was the younger brother. He had to have a wife."

Auntie Donnell at this point demonstrated the storytelling skills that had earlier eluded her. "You must put yourself in the shoes of one of those two Savannah women, now, and hear with their ears. And remember that this was with all the family around them, the Whitmore sisters and their husbands, I don't know how many in all." She turned to watch closely the effect of her words on Pearl. "You see, what the cousins from Savannah were told was that since they didn't have any more sisters at home, and the menfolks had run out of other prospects, the girls were being asked to marry more than one Whitmore. The younger brother was going to court one of them and become her second husband, while her first husband was still alive."

Pearl paused in her breathing and opened her large eyes even wider than they had been, staring through the ceiling at a prospect that astonished her. Auntie Donnell got up and brushed her hair a little earlier than she really would have liked to, rattling around in the pin tray until she found the right old fashioned hairpins to keep her long, soft hair in its white twist around her head. Pearl still lay mute. Auntie Donnell adjusted her slip strap and tugged at her girdle, then sighed and lay back down. Finally she said, "It might be easier for you to think about what would happen if it was the other way around, Pearl. Like the Mormons. If the Whitmores were a man short, and you wanted more than anything else to have a safe home and have some babies, what would you do? You couldn't marry outside of the Whitmores, so what could you do? You'd have to share a husband, that's all. I guess if it ever came to that, that's what the Whitmores would decide to do, and I expect you would go along with it. I don't know why but we're the other way around, we've got too many men. So from as far back as your great great grandmother, we share ourselves as wives, that's all. When we need to, I mean, only then."

Auntie Donnell heard what she thought was a giggle from Pearl. Pearl's eyes were on her now, and she smiled. "That's the right idea, Pearl, it's not so bad when you think about it. Well then, this is what happened, the unmarried brother courted both of his brothers' wives, and he and one of the wives made their choice. Which wife it was is something that no Whitmore ever told. Maybe the brother who shared his wife didn't know about it, but I can't think how he wouldn't know, although I suppose it's possible. Or maybe he just didn't bother to know. Children came, and whose they were didn't matter because they were Whitmores, and that was enough. And that's all there is to the Whitmore secret."

Pearl giggled again, biting her lip to keep from laughing. "I can see why the Whitmores keep it a secret," she said. "I've never heard so much as a word about it. None of you grownups ever talk about it, do you."

Auntie Donnell said, "That's right, dear, it's your turn to know, because you're the oldest girl now. It's right you should know, but you see why we keep it a secret until you're old enough to know. None of the other girls is old enough, so you don't tell them, will you. Not the boys, either. Not them ever."

Pearl sat up and said, "Oh no, of course not, it's not something for them to hear, is it." She stood up and smoothed her hair and dress, preparing to leave.

But Auntie Donnell wouldn't let the child get away. "Don't go yet, dear, I just want you to understand, I want to be sure you understand."

"I think I do," Pearl said. Auntie Donnell dragged at her arm and got her to sit down on the bed again.

Auntie Donnell sat very close to her. "It's still the tradition," she said. "Your Uncle Karl hasn't had any Whitmore girl to marry for quite a few years now."

Pearl was very still. Auntie Donnell continued, "He's been a second husband to one of our women for those years, Pearl. You mustn't resent that."

"Why would I resent it?" Pearl asked.

"Well, dear, I thought you'd know long before now that you're the first Whitmore girl old enough to marry Uncle Karl," Auntie Donnell answered. She allowed herself to sound a little scornful of the child's willful blindness to the facts, or her sister's foolishness in not at least hinting to her daughter of her destiny. "And it's my duty to tell you how the Whitmore secret affects you." She paused before continuing with a firmer, a more brutal tone in her voice. "He'll give up his other wife when he marries you, because that's our tradition," she said, "but it's your duty to make him never be sorry he's in your bed, instead of another wife's. Do you understand?"

When Pearl couldn't answer, she continued in a more gentle tone. "The aunties will tell you how to please him, you don't worry about that. And you'll never know who his other wife was, he nor anyone else will tell you who it was. Guess as much as you want, you'll never know for sure. It's better that way."

She lifted Pearl by an elbow and brushed out the folds in her dress once she was standing. Then she led the girl back to the kitchen to conclude the lemonade party.

"I don't know if I made enough cookies," she said. "Doesn't look like there's that many here, and Calvin will be in soon, I expect. Are you very hungry, Pearl? I've got some leftover sponge cake and some nice strawberry jam to go on it. Would you like that?"

3

Mid-September was hot and summery, the only concession to the calendar being that the foliage on the farm's few trees was now hard and leathery in anticipation of fall. It was the time the irrigated farms in the valley were going full tilt. Up here, however, on its arid western edge, they waited for rain.

Karl had come to the boys' and children's bunkhouse to find Calvin. It was a long building on two floors, wide enough only for a row of thin mattresses along one wall and some floor space along the other. He went up the single flight of hayloft stairs, following the sound of voices. Upstairs was where the little girls and the boys under six slept, separated by a blanket hung from one of the low rafters. In what had been a washroom before the men ripped out the useless plumbing, he saw that the children stacked their private belongings in paper boxes and hung their clothes from nails hammered into the unpainted wood walls. Except for Francine and Sweetheart, who were lost in a game about wild horses and warrior princesses, no one was there.

As he came back down the stairs, he caught a glimpse of a face around the blanket that separated the big boys from the younger boys, and the whispery voices that he had heard suddenly stopped. He pushed aside the blanket and found himself looking down on an older boy and two younger ones lying on their stomachs on the floor with arithmetic books open in front of them. The younger ones scrambled to their feet and stood against the far wall.

"Hey, Bobby," he said to the older boy.

"Hello, Uncle Karl," he answered, without looking up from his studies.

"No work to do today? Where's your manners, Bobby?" Karl said. "You kids is supposed to stand up when grownups talk to you."

"Oh, yeah," Bobby said. "I forgot."

"Then why ain't you doin' it?" Karl pressed him. "Is it 'cause your pants would drop down if you stood up?"

Bobby flushed scarlet and hung his head almost on the open pages of the book.

"You little ones," Karl said, "you scoot." The two ran outside and disappeared around the bunkhouse, hightailing it for all they were worth.

"I guess there's one thing good about it," he said. "You showin' it off to them little ones means you big boys ain't playin' the kind of games we oughta worry about. Stand up and let your pants drop, underpants too."

Bobby did as he was ordered, keeping his hands over his privates. Karl stripped the belt out of the boy's pants and lazily, carefully pushed on the boy's shoulders until he was bent over. He brushed the boy's buttocks as if they were some kind of precious cloth, then brought the leather belt across them in a short, full swing of his arm. The boy shuddered but didn't cry out. Karl watched as the red welt grew. "Reckon I'd better even it up," he said, moving around to the other side and whipping him again. "Stand up now," he said, in his quiet, indolent voice, handing over the belt.

"You seen Calvin?" he asked.

Bobby was choking back his tears. "He's out with the diggin'," he said.

"Reckon you'd be better off out doin' some real work,

too," Karl said. "Go find him. Tell him I want him to go to town with me."

Bobby clutched his pants and ran for the doorway.

"What're we going to town for, Uncle Karl?" Calvin asked.

"Couple of things we need from the hardware store," Karl answered. "You got to get you some overalls and your daddy don't look like gettin' around to doin' anything about it. I'd like the company."

As the old truck left the Whitmore farm, Calvin could see across the flat, slightly scooped floor of the great valley, until a gray haze filled the middle distance and obscured any sight of the mountain range beyond. From the arid, brown height of the Whitmore land, which was the last of the flat land before the foothills of the coast range of mountains began to roll westward, the valley to the east was a study in deepening shades of green as the privileged land showed itself nearer the river and irrigation ditches. The Whitmores had bought what they could afford, which was a farm that had defeated two generations of people who thought they could find some way to overcome the lack of water. Down below, what had once looked as much a desert as their land now bloomed wherever the water flowed. They had plans to make a go of it. With their manpower they would scoop out reservoirs close to the fold of the hills, and their profits, when they came, would go to drilling a well, maybe more than one if they could find water. Meantime, the green in their eyes came from the reflection of that rich, fruitful land that broke their hearts with the promises it was making to other farmers.

"What's these, Uncle Karl?" Calvin asked.

"Grapes," Karl answered. "Vineyards, they call 'em."

"Why do they call 'em two different things?" Calvin asked.

"'Cause you make wine from grapes," Karl answered. Calvin was on the verge of asking his uncle to make better sense of it than that, since he didn't know what wine was, but he remembered in time the treatment his father handed him when he asked too many questions.

"Where's this town?" Calvin asked finally.

"Up ahead," Karl answered. "Called Red Branch. You been there?"

"We ain't been anywhere since we got here, end of August," Calvin answered. "Daddy's car don't go."

"Yeah," Karl answered. "Calvin, you thought about school?" Calvin nodded but kept his eyes straight ahead. "What're you gonna do about school now your mamma's sick?" When there was no response, Karl added, "Ain't no Annie Evelyn to help you anymore, son, and your mamma don't seem likely to do your schooling, leastways for a while yet. You got to think about it."

Calvin turned to his uncle then, his face troubled. "Cain't figger out what Daddy wants for me, Uncle Karl. He don't say."

Karl answered as tenderly as he could, "I think he'd be best pleased if you was to figger it out for him, Calvin. Your mamma bein' sick like she is, he ain't doin' too good hisself. I guess you know that, though."

They drove on in silence as the signs of town life began to be seen. There must have been a time when it was important to know that a hotel was up ahead, or a stable could be found for a horse, or even that food and drink were, like some glittering salvation, waiting to be grasped in the moment of extremity. In the valley this had given way to a despoiling, as if you didn't matter commercially until and unless you carbuncled the country around your town with the fact of your existence. Signs for local garages, a feed and grain storage company, the railroad, even a shoestore were nailed up on fence posts beside the road. Calvin didn't know whether to look at the crops or the decorations. There was a sequence of Burma Shave signs also, but having missed the first one, the rest of them didn't make sense to him.

The road passed a turn to a winery, a gray, heavy-looking,

warehouse type of building with a souring smell like a fog around it. Off to the right of the road about a half mile beyond the winery was a dingy blue, tall, old house with huge windows, the whole thing rising like some kind of mirage above mounds of green shrubbery. Calvin asked about it.

"That there is the Atwater Mansion," Karl answered, "so they tell me."

"What is it?" Calvin asked.

"A house," Karl said, "but not the kind you and me see the inside of." He said it without bitterness, since it was merely a fact.

The road turned sharply left around a small grocery store, revealing that they were at the end of a broad street running straight ahead of them like a cleft in the town, or a paved river bed. The spikes of tall, ugly palm trees marked out this end of the avenue, which gaped with spaces between houses like missing teeth. As they drove on the houses increased in number and density, fine houses of an older type set up above half-basements and approached by flights of broad steps, with scattered among them the one-story, newer type of house that looked pleasant but economical. The houses were of secondary interest to Calvin, however. He was dazzled by the green of the lawns. Starved of the closeup look of grass, he stared at it as if looking for a four leaf clover. His eyes detected bright greens where a standpipe leaked and the grass luxuriated, the blue of a stiffer grass that defied the relative dryness of slopes and banks, the emerald green of patches of clover. He stared at the sight of men and women standing on their lawns with rubber hoses in their hands, sprinkling their earth with fans of water as if the precious stuff meant nothing, showing no emotion as it vanished into a silver vapor that they appeared to be offering up to the sun.

"Are they all rich, Uncle Karl?" he asked.

"They are compared to us," was the answer. "This here is a town, Calvin, they ain't like us. They don't hardly know about us at all."

"Why don't we live in the town, then?" Calvin asked.

"There's another part of town for people like us," Karl said. "Even burnin' up and dryin' up and workin' our asses off and cryin' ourselves to sleep is a whole lot better than livin' in that part of town. Don't never forget it."

They were passing large, ponderous buildings now. There was a big, squat school on one side of the avenue that was painted a grayed-over white, with a gray stone, graceless block of a courthouse and county offices facing it. Next to the school was a square, brown, brick built box with windows, which was the library, and opposite that was a park. At the sight of it Calvin shouted, "Looky there!"

Karl pulled the truck up to the curb, then parked it properly and stopped the engine. Calvin was goggle-eyed. The grass was deep, lush, thick, pampered green, gleaming in the sunshine like polished metal miraculously greened. Clumps of shrubs and small trees shaded its edges, and behind these, giant sycamore trees and a few elms darkened the space underneath them like some inviting primeval forest.

Calvin sat in wonder. Karl got out, saying, "There oughta be a men's room someplace in there, we'd best use it while we got the chance."

Calvin followed him as far as the sidewalk and watched in wonder as his uncle walked onto the grass, waiting for the threatening shout to come from its guardian.

"Come on," Karl said.

"You allowed to walk on it?" Calvin asked.

"Well, of course you are," Karl answered. "This here's a park, it belongs to ever'body, you can walk on it, or you can play ball here and have a picnic if you want. Ain't nobody gonna throw you off this grass."

Calvin dropped to his knees and rubbed the palms of his hands on the thick, flat blades of grass, then broke off a juicy blade and chewed it. It tasted what he had always imagined lawn grass would taste like, a flavor he could only think of as green.

"Come on, boy," Karl said.

Calvin did as he was told and advanced to his uncle's side. "Someday I'm going to have me a whole field of grass," he said.

After they had used the men's toilet, while they were returning to the truck, Calvin asked about the buildings around them. A library and a courthouse meant nothing to him, but the school was another matter. He studied the sprawling, heavy building. "If I was to go to school, would I go there?" he asked.

Karl laughed. "Son, you ain't ready for no town school." He laughed again and said, "They'd eat you up and spit out nothin' but the buttons." A thought struck him. "It's a funny thing, you know, you have to be so tough to stay alive and be a farmer like the kind we are, and we can't stand up against these town folks that have everything to make 'em soft and dainty. Never thought about it afore. Let's go up to J.C. Penny's and see about them overalls, what d'ya say?"

They got the overalls in a part of the store that had a small square of carpet laid on the board floor so that people with socks on could try on clothes without having to slip back into their shoes. Calvin rubbed the sole of his bare foot on the carpet when no one was looking. Suddenly he was aware of the feel of the town. The carpet was spiky and resistant. The varnished board floor was slightly sticky when they left with his overalls, and the sidewalks outside were grainy or sandy, hot in the sun and cool under the stores' overhangs, and the oiled boards of the hardware store were rough and felt like dirty moss. In the bank, where Calvin hung back by the glass door while his uncle went up to the teller's window, the stone floor was slick but pitted, and the joins between the gray slabs of granite were wide and deep enough to break a toenail, if you had any left after a summer barefoot. The floor of the diner, where they shared a cheese sandwich and Calvin had his first slice of dill pickle, was linoleum that felt rough where people walked up to the counter but cool and glassy under the stools where their feet seldom dragged.

The space between the stool and the counter wasn't made for boys. Calvin perched uncomfortably on the stool, holding himself up to the counter by putting his elbows on the hard edge of it.

"This here's American cheese," Uncle Karl told the boy. "And this is lettuce, and this is dill pickle." When the girl behind the counter looked at Calvin as if he was to be pitied, Karl told her, "He ain't never been in a place like this before. Ain't never been in Red Branch before, even."

"What do you think of the pickle?" she asked Calvin.

"Fine," he answered, "good." It made him want to spit, and he couldn't think what to say about it, except to lie like he usually did when grownups asked questions like that.

"What do you think of the town?" she asked.

"I like the park best," Calvin said.

"No place for a lady in there after dark any more. Town's going to the dogs," she said. She looked at Karl. "You new here? Don't think I've seen you before. I'd remember if I had."

Karl smiled a lazy smile that got larger and smilier as he realized what she had said. "Got a farm out on the west side. This here's my nephew. I ain't got wife or kids. Not yet."

"Didn't think you had," she said, "from the look of you."

"How do you look if you do have 'em?" Karl asked, playing her along.

"More hangdog than you," she said, "and not so hungry."

"I just had my lunch," Karl said, almost giggling by now.

"That's not what I mean," she said, pausing before adding, "and you know it."

Calvin got down from the stool. Karl followed him, moving slowly and keeping his eyes on the waitress.

"Reckon I'll come here again," he said.

"I'll remember you," she answered. "Thanks for coming. See you again, sonny boy," she called to Calvin as he went out the door.

In the truck Karl said, "She likes you," and Calvin said,

"She don't seem much like somebody who'd eat me up." Karl's response was a laughing fit that reduced him to tears.

They turned back up the avenue and started the long drive back to the farm. The only words that passed between them were from Karl. "We got to get you some shoes," he said, "if you're goin' to come cattin' around town with me again." Calvin didn't answer. He didn't have much liking for shoes, and he didn't understand what cattin' around town meant, and he'd had enough for one day. He put his head into the corner where the hot wind blew into the cab of the truck and went to sleep.

She hadn't been in a town for years and years, for as long as she could remember, she kept telling the three children as they rode into Red Branch. Jimmy Whitmore drove with his hands clutched knuckle-white on the wheel, growling to himself, hating every second of the expedition, hating himself for being so soft in the head that he had agreed when the other women had told him it would help his wife if he brought her into town to see the sights.

It was dark by the time they got to town, and the store windows along Greenfield Avenue thrust their brightness and shine of color into the gloom like so many streetwalkers. The few straggling windowshoppers dragged from one window to the next, sometimes darting back to look again at something that had been passed. Jimmy Whitmore parked the Studebaker in front of the bank, and everyone got out and began their window shopping with the hardware store.

The disparity in the size of Jimmy and his wife was not so marked now. She had lost weight steadily since they left Texas, and her shoulders had taken on a stoop, as if she were ready to duck a blow coming from above and behind her at any moment. When he stood near his mother and father, Calvin, only nine now, showed already that he would grow into the strong stature she had previously shown, and his face reflected too her puzzled apprehension. Jimmy was lean, taut, tightly wound up. His right shoulder was slightly enlarged, and his outsize hands he kept folded behind him and unmoving. He had pulled his greasy felt hat well forward so that he peered out from under it to such an extent that you wondered why he didn't simply turn up the brim and get an eyeful of the world. Sweetheart and Francine, in a world of their own, stood or ran elbow to elbow, sharing private jokes, excluding everything that wasn't theirs mutually. Calvin kept a watch of a sort on them, calling them back when they ran too far ahead, trying to keep a middle distance between the girls and his parents.

When his mother moved close to the lighted window, he could see that she had brought an old black leather purse that Annie Evelyn used to use when she played dressing up. Where Annie Evelyn had worn it slung by its strap over her arm, his mother clutched it to her stomach, her two hands side by side, holding it tightly with fingers as thin and possessive as a bird's claws.

She saw a sugar bowl in the display and moved close to peer at it. It was imitation crystal with a chromium band around the rim and another around the middle of the bowl. Her index fingers relinquished their hold on the purse and shot out in unison to point at the bowl. "Huh!" she snorted, "not near as good as mine."

Calvin said, "They got better stuff up at the department store. About eight windows to look at too."

"Where's that?" his mother snapped, wheeling around from the hardware.

"'Cross the street," Calvin answered.

"Can we go?" she asked her husband.

Jimmy shrugged. "Sure. Okay. Get the girls, Calvin."

They crossed the street and walked past all the windows, turning back when they got to the last of them. "Let's start at the linens," his wife said to Jimmy.

"Linens?" he responded.

"Blankets, all them things," she said. He shrugged again,

and they went to a window at about the center of the store. She went to a cerise blanket hung up by a corner and trailing down in a fan shape. "Ah-hah!" she said, as if she had just detected a mouse in the breadbox. "Looky here, girls," she called. When Francine and Sweetheart got to her side, she pointed to it. "You see that? The sign says that binding is satin finish, and that means it's cheap, and the blanket is cheap too, you can count on that. You got to watch things these days. No quality. More likely rayon than wool. No warmth in it at all." Bored with their lesson, the girls wandered off.

She fastened her attention on a table cloth with inserts that looked like cheap net curtain material. "I'll bet they like to call that French lace," she said. "It's good, but not nearly so good as mine, the one I use when the other ladies come in for ice tea. Not nearly so good. Mine has fern leaves and snowflakes, things that are nice and cool. This is good, but not so good as mine."

Calvin guided the girls away from their mother to a window with toys in it. Behind them, Jimmy stayed as close as it takes for a man to be seen to be in charge without taking responsibility for what is going on.

His wife moved to the next window. "Looky here," she called out. "Silver." Her fingers pointed out a chrome plated coffee jug that glared in the display lights. It was long and wasp waisted, with an oversize pouring spout and blue raffia wrapped around the handle. "That'll be somebody's heir-loom one of these days. That's nice," she declared. "Don't like the tray, though." The jug stood next to a chrome tray of matching metallic intensity. It was hard to look at it in the yellow light. Jimmy blinked at it and looked away, but his wife kept staring at it. It was perfectly round, with concentric circles scored into its surface from the edge to a bullseye center. Instead of feet under it, the tray stood on five or six little balls, like a trophy for a smalltown tennis player. "I think I like that," she said. "Most trays like that have feet, but this one's better. A lot better."

Suddenly she saw the china figurines. She swooped on them with a shout of joy. "Oh, looka these! Oh, Jimmy, don't they just remind you of them of ours!"

Jimmy said "Jesus Christ!" and looked around as if he had escape in mind.

"This little fella here with the guitar," she said, "don't he look good though? Well, maybe his little blue jacket is not as pretty as that there purple one on mine, but he's good, still. You think so?" She was talking to herself now, requiring no verification from her husband.

"I don't know, now. I don't think I like his smile. Looks like he ain't too bright. Well, these china novelties, they don't come up to what they was. Made in Japan, I'll bet. Guitar player looks like a Jap, don't he. All machine work. No hand paintin' anymore. This little dancer here, with her little leg cocked up in the air. Machine made, I bet. Nice little pink ruffles, and all them lace petticoats is nice. But she's not as pretty as mine. Mine's a prettier pink, ain't she, and the lace on mine looks real, not this sort of gauze stuff. Six dollars and twenty-five cents they want for it! They'd wait a long time before they got me to pay that. How much do you think mine's worth, Jimmy, if they want six dollars and twenty-five cents for this? A hundred dollars, I'd think. Wouldn't you?" She didn't look to see the anger in his face.

She suddenly laughed so loudly that people on the other side of the avenue turned to see what was funny. Calvin moved the girls farther away, down to the window where the boxes of candy were on display. "Look at these plates, these here platters, Jimmy!"

"Keep your voice, down," Jimmy ordered. "You want the whole town to hear you?"

"Looka this platter and these plates. I ask you, now, do these look anything like George Washington? It's terrible the things they do to the father of our country. And here! Poor old Abe Lincoln, him too. Oh, there oughta be a law. Look the way these fine men are being used on these plates. You remember how good a picture it was of that French king on that platter I broke? The one we used for the pot roast last Sunday? Did you throw away the pieces already? Maybe we could get it fixed. That picture's so much better than these, Lord knows how much it was worth. It'd still be worth a lot if it was fixed."

She turned around, losing interest in the department store windows, and now spotted the jewelry store across the avenue. Without a glance she ran across, Jimmy following her and shouting apologies to the car that had had to brake hard to miss her.

"You jist get a hold on yourself, Mamma," he shouted at her.

"Looky here," she cried, "rings and jewels. Looky here, quick, Jimmy. A whole box of ruby rings. Real rubies!"

"They ain't but glass," he shouted, "red glass!"

His wife's face was pale with excitement and glistening with sweat, and her eyes popped in her head with each new idea or sight. "I'm going to have my ruby ring taken apart, I think. I'll bring it in here and get them to do it. I want my ruby put in white gold, like they got it there, whattayacallit, platinum. Then I'll get another good stone, something real fine, as good as the ring is, and put that in. A sapphire, I think. I'll have to watch him all the time he's doin' it, though. You won't find another ruby or even a whole ring like those I've got. The color comes through that ruby of mine like the sun through a big old church window. When the sun comes through it, you'd think my hand was bleeding the way that red cuts across my fingers. Ain't no diamonds in this window. Plenty of pearls, though. I think I like pearls better anyhow. They suit me better, don't they. When I come in here with my ruby ring I'll wear that three-decker pearl necklace you give me, that'll make his eyes bug out of his head. I bet they ain't never seen anything like it in this poor little old hick town."

"Shut up!" Jimmy ordered. "You're talkin' crazy agin. I

thought you was over that, and here you're talkin' crazy as a coot. Git back to the car!"

"Shut up, yourself," she said. "You shut up!"

"What're you talkin' about pearls, and rubies, and nice platters, and everything else? What are you talkin' about?"

She screamed at him then, "I've got 'em, and I'm never lettin' you see 'em! That's what! You shut up. You shut your mouth. If you knew all you think you know, you'd be a wise man."

"I know enough," he answered. "Be quiet!"

"Rubies and pearls and things you'll never see. I'll keep 'em hid away forever, too, you ain't seein' my beautiful things, ever!"

"Calvin!" Jimmy shouted. He took his wife's arms and tried to turn her around. She pulled herself free, turning her back as she did. He took her elbows in his big hands and pulled them back until she arched her back and threw her head up and screamed, "Don't! Don't!"

Calvin brought the two girls across the avenue and shoved them toward the car, then ran to help his father. When he tried to lift her at the knees, she kicked out at him. "Leave me alone! I won't! I won't do it!"

Jimmy dragged her onto her knees on the sidewalk, then pushed her face down onto the concrete. "Grab her," he ordered Calvin. "Grab her by the legs."

Calvin held her ankles to keep her from thrashing about while his father pressed her in the back with his knees. "You gonna be quiet now?" he shouted at her. "You gonna shut up?"

In answer she turned her head aside to release her mouth and screeched. Each screaming wail was succeeded by another, while Jimmy shouted, "Shut up!"

He looked up at Calvin finally and said, "I can't take it." Releasing one of her elbows, he took aim with his fist and hit her in the side of the jaw. With the concrete behind to hold her face firm for his blow, it didn't take much of a punch. Her eyes closed, and she was still.

4

Jurgens Elementary School

The school is a single L-shaped building of three classrooms and a very small office. The office is a just-in-case room with a telephone, filing cabinet and typewriter, which is largely unused. The telephone is answered by whichever teacher is free to respond when her pupils shout that it is ringing. The school building is placed about a hundred yards from the street and surrounded by a playground of packed and baked earth that is sanded in wet weather to keep down the mud. Behind the school building is a small, double ended building that houses in one end a storeroom and workshop for the school janitor, Mr. Krafft. The toilet block is in the other part of the building, with a girls' toilet and sink, and a boys' toilet, sink and shower.

The boys' shower hasn't been used in years, partly because country boys won't take off their clothes in front of other boys and partly because they know that if they do, if they have to, Mr. Krafft will come by and have a look. Mr. Krafft is the school legend to the parents of the children who go to Jurgens School. The three teachers are all women, and Mr. Krafft constitutes the male presence. Even though he isn't allowed to do the whipping, the children are frightened of him and don't regard him as a legend, merely a threatening figure for reasons they don't talk about.

If the school board were to fire Mr. Krafft, life at Jurgens School would be much more pleasant, because most of the fifty-eight children, coming from houses that are little better than improved homesteaders' shacks, could use a good shower in place of the rudimentary sluicing they get from a bucket when their mothers can catch them. When delivered by the bucket, water is cold and the children prefer not to have much to do with it.

The toilets themselves are very well used. Only the children from the nine houses in Jurgens itself have toilets that flush. The children from the farms think flush toilets are grand. Mr. Krafft's son Leo understands how they work. He had to learn when he got caught putting tadpoles in the tank of the one in the girl's toilet. Aside from Leo's newly acquired knowledge, the incident had the effect of making Mary Lou Wells now hold her water until she can run home at lunchtime, because it was she who pulled the handle and watched in terror as tadpoles poured into the toilet bowl. Nothing will convince her that the next thing through the water system won't be a watersnake or worse, as the boys predict in order to make her scream.

The Teachers

There are three teachers at Jurgens School, Miss Marty, Miss Thompson and Miss Stoddard. They teach in order all the children grouped into beginners, intermediates and those being prepared to leave the school. Every child of five or six goes first to Miss Marty. The children love Miss Marty because she is the prettiest. The boys are especially devoted to her, since she has a brother who was a state champion high jumper and has been getting ready for the Olympics for the past six years. The boys' favorite activity in the playground is high jumping, with everyone competing to catch Miss Marty's eye so that they can be discovered and coached by Walter Marty to be the next champion after him. Even Leo with his crippled foot tries to high jump. When she joins in, which she condescends to do every once in a while just to keep the boys in their place, Honeygirl Parker can outjump every one of them, and they love her for it even while she spurns them.

When the children can read, write, count and understand at least the terms of basic arithmetic, they go to Miss Thompson to join the intermediate class. Leo Krafft, he of the tadpoles, was in Miss Marty's class for three years with everyone convinced he was mysteriously unteachable because of his club foot. One day his father discovered him writing a love note to Honeygirl Parker, written in joined up letters and spelled correctly. Mr. Krafft took his son out to the janitor's workshop and whipped him until he admitted that he didn't want to go to Miss Thompson's class because he didn't want to watch his father come in and whisper and flirt with the teacher, and even touch her, as the other children say he does.

Miss Thompson concentrates on teaching the children arithmetic, while also trying to take them into more advanced reading. Her favorite reading lesson is her famous introduction to Shakespeare, which concentrates on the scene in Caesar's palace when Brutus says the clock has strucken eight. This gives her the opportunity every year to apologize for Shakespeare's grammar and tell the students that poor Shakespeare wasn't aware that the Romans didn't have striking clocks, or else he was so excited by the discoveries of his own age that he couldn't keep them out of his plays. Two generations of children have passed through Jurgens School believing that Shakespeare wrote unreadable plays that were grammatically and technologically so unsound that even their teacher didn't know what all the fuss was about. Furthermore, most of them will die without knowing that Roman waterclocks struck and that the Elizabethans were not the inventors of the strucken clock as we know it. Since Miss Thompson's errors might indicate to the children that a little knowledge is a poor substitute for blissful ignorance, it is as well they will never know.

The chief attraction for the children in being in Miss Thompson's room, aside from Mr. Krafft's visits, is her famous spelling bees. The children are lined up on opposite sides of the room and each is given a word in turn. One mistake is sudden death. The foregone conclusion is that George Barnton will win, pursued to the wire by Honeygirl Parker, the school's vindicatrix. He won every spelling bee in his seven years at the school except one, when his mind wandered and he spelled column with the n and m reversed. Honeygirl's triumph was engraved on his soul, and she would have paid for the engraving at her own expense. The fun for the other children is in the way that Miss Thompson juggles her list of words in order to give George and Honeygirl some competition, trying to keep the bee going long enough to at least give the impression of an educational activity rather than what it is, a waste of time. When Dewey Wheeler, the worst speller in the school, miraculously came up with mouse as his word, and got it right, the children cheered. Miss Thompson thought their support was a lovely demonstration of innocent loyalty that justified her fraudulent maneuvering, never suspecting that the cheer meant Dewey, who was not well liked, was going to get another pounding by Rafael Gonzalez when they went out for recess. Miss Thompson didn't like Rafael very much because he caused trouble when he was standing up during spelling bees, so he got something like judgment without the e the first time around and spent the rest of his time safely at his seat.

Miss Stoddard once said that she had overheard the comment, "Get to your seats, Old Lady Stoddard is coming," on her second day of teaching at the school when she arrived, as she always does, five minutes after the bell. It indicated that the children could learn her name in a day and that her chances of aging gracefully in her profession were nil, since she was eighteen that very day. Late in life, at the time Calvin was in her class, she was known to the children as Elizabeth, indicating that it had taken forty-two years for the children to learn her first name and that she had devoted her life to a backward profession.

Miss Stoddard's mission is to prepare her charges for the world outside Jurgens. She teaches some ancient history, some American history and some world history. While her pupils seldom have a good sense of historical time, the incidents of man's irresistible rise are successfully implanted in their minds. Thus the Areopagus was the council of state which persuaded Napoleon to levy taxes that resulted in the colonists starting the Civil War by means of the Boston Tea Party. Anything that can be made to end with the Colonists dressed like Indians is very much to the taste of the children. All the children know what to expect in her class, since her routine never varies from year to year. Her most senior students spend their last school year wading through the life of Silas Marner, the weaver of Raveloe, mired in lugubrious prose. The children always stick it out to the end, helped by the knowledge which one child gleaned at the Red Branch Library that George Eliot wasn't a man at all and that he-she had lived as concubine of a man who wasn't her husband. Such perversity earned an audience, if not admirers.

As the longest serving teacher in Jurgens School, Miss Stoddard keeps the purse strings. In her case this is a literal description. The petty cash belonging to the school is kept in a brown leather purse that is attached to a string around Miss Stoddard's neck. The small purse, in spite of its brass fastener, is dropped on the end of its string down the neck of the dress or blouse that Miss Stoddard is wearing that day. When money is required, she fumbles the string into her fingers and then lifts the purse from whatever depths it has been lying in, like pulling up a bucket from a well.

If she had not habitually worn a tight belt around her waist, speculation about where the purse might lodge would have plumbed new depths when Rafael Gonzalez was finally moved up to her class. He was by that time approaching fifteen years of age, having been in the school since he was five. He had learned in that time only one thing, a remarkable ability to subvert the learning process. With Miss Stoddard this became personal. Offended by some remarks of hers about the Spanish-American War, he set out on a campaign of guerrilla warfare that centered on Miss Stoddard's obsession with noise. She was a sensitive woman, especially sensitive of hearing. Rafael's ability to make a dropped protractor into the sound of the mighty blacksmith smiting the anvil with his hammer was little short of miraculous.

Rafael had studied his victim carefully and devised the perfect psychological torture for his teacher. Early one day he got into the school ahead of everyone else by telling Mr. Krafft he had to finish some homework, and smeared a mixture of sand and Karo syrup on the floor under Miss Stoddard's chair, on the runners of her desk drawers, on the ends of the sticks of chalk, even on the faces of the blackboard erasers. When Miss Stoddard entered her room, as always five minutes after the children had taken their seats, she pulled her chair from under her desk to sit down and take roll. The chair scraped and ground, making the pupils squeal as their teeth were put on edge. The process was repeated when she pulled open her desk drawer to take out her roll book. She got up to write the names of the children who tittered on the blackboard. Her shoes felt stuck to the floor, the chalk scratched the board, the erasers wouldn't slide across the board, and each thing she touched felt sticky and dirty, like an all day sucker that had been dropped in the dirt.

She tried sitting down again, and realized she was trapped; everything grated, and what didn't make a scratchy noise or produce a scraping sensation was objectionably sticky to the touch. Starting at 8:15 in the morning, Miss Stoddard bore it for exactly two hours. At that point she walked out of the school and went home. Faced with her ultimatum, that it was to be Rafael Gonzalez or Miss Elizabeth Stoddard but not both, the school board propelled the young man into greater things in the outside world, while Mr. Krafft organized the children in her class into a cleanup crew. Rafael went on to become a respected member of the Los Angeles Police Department, highly respected by the other members of that department.

The Janitor

Oscar Krafft is a short man with one wall eye and a habit of walking sideways. He likes to put his two hands, balled into fists, behind the bib of his overalls and walk in such a way that his good eye, his left one, is looking straight ahead, while the one with restricted vision rakes the right side of his passage with a wild, sheepdog looking gaze, the full white of the eye showing with a piercing stare at its heart. The combination of indirect locomotion and popping eye long ago gave him the nickname Crab, which is doubly unfortunate since his son Leo with his club foot imitates the sidelong approach to forward motion because he has to drag his enlarged foot on its shortened leg.

Each day some excuse is found by Mr. Krafft to visit Miss Thompson. Her invariable response is to tell the children to keep on with their lessons silently, while she retreats to the rear of her classroom and waits for Mr. Krafft to join her. When he does, he stands in the same sideways posture that he uses when he walks, his head turned far enough in her direction to be looking in her eyes with one eye, while the other searches with its strange light for any child daring enough to turn around and look at them. He stands with his left shoulder touching her, his hands pushing out the bib of his overalls like imitation breasts, leaning into contact with her very real ones. The conversation is conducted in a low voice, teasing the children to hear what he is saying, a slight sneer on his lips as much as to say that what he is saying is better unheard by the child being talked of.

Strangely, no one except Miss Thompson knows what he says. Is he plotting the downfall of the realm, or the seduction of the May Queen, or the next meeting of the Jurgens Coven? Or is he discussing the latest purchase of floor mops, sink plugs and toilet paper? The children fear it is all directed at Miss Thompson, that he is saying to her those unknown things called dirty words, and she is so nice and such a lady that she simply smiles and says "I know, yes" repeatedly and lets him say what he likes.

He is capable of improvising when pieces of machinery go wrong or the rope breaks on the swing. He is clean, except for his shoes. He is Leo's father, and the boy is liked in spite of his propensity to bawl when things go wrong for him. But the children don't like Mr. Krafft. He, not the teachers, goes to the girls' toilet when one of the children prolongs her stay, and his method of checking to see if things are all right is to climb on a stool and look through the single, high, narrow window. The same thing is true when more than two boys go out to the toilet at the same time, Mr. Krafft having promoted himself to the role of crusader against illicit smoking. What bothers the children deeply, what gives some of them nightmares, is that the eye that looks through the window is the mad eye, not the good eye. That strange organ, held so close that it seems to rub against the glass, observes them for whom? If not for Mr. Krafft, who receives the image that it records? When Mr. Krafft is on the prowl, visits to the toilet are only as short and as frequent as necessary.

The strangest thing of all about Mr. Krafft is his staying power. Janitor, custodian, caretaker, handyman, he has survived every change in his job description. Children become adolescents, young adults, parents, and then send their children to Jurgens Elementary School without complaining about Mr. Krafft's likely effect on their own children. Leo Krafft married one of the Tauber girls and went to work for her father on his farm. When the time came for his son – perfectly formed, with curly, dark hair and large, perfect, blue eyes – to go to school, the boy was sent to stay with an aunt in Red Branch during the week, so that he could go to school there. Leo explains it by saying that he didn't want his father to feel he had to look out for his grandson all the time.

Calvin was enrolled in Jurgens School by his uncle Karl. When Miss Stoddard realized who he was, she dropped the manner of an efficient schoolteacher and put on the behavior of a gracious hostess. There had been stories of the number of children being collected by the Whitmores at their farm, a large enough number to insure that the school could be kept open when other small schools in the district were being closed down. When Karl said he would give Calvin a try at the school, what he meant was that he wasn't sure Calvin could open up enough to be acceptable to the school as a learner. What Miss Stoddard thought he meant was that the school was on trial. Between the two of them, they made certain that Calvin was going to be treated to the best that Jurgens School could provide.

Miss Marty conducted Calvin to her classroom and gave him a desk near the front, even though he was tall enough to be placed at the back of a row. She spared him and didn't call on him to read when they did the patriotism lesson, and he appeared to know most of the salute to the flag that began her class. She looked at him when they sang "My Country 'Tis of Thee" and found that he could mouth along with most of it satisfactorily. Even when she passed out ruled paper and got the children started on the penmanship lesson, he followed without too much of a struggle. She anticipated an easy transition, until the first recess. When the other children struggled to the door, anxious to be released into a bright October day, Calvin sat at his desk.

"You can go out for recess, Calvin," she said.

"Yes 'm," he answered, and sat where he was, looking out at the playing children and not moving more than his head.

She tried again. "Don't you think you might need the restroom?" When he looked blank, she corrected herself, "the toilet?"

Calvin blushed deeply. "No 'm," he stammered.

She tried to ignore him but couldn't concentrate on her preparation for the arithmetic lesson coming up. Her annoyance flared. "What's wrong, Calvin?" she asked. "Are you afraid of the other children? I'll keep an eye on them, no one will hurt you."

He scorned her offer. "Ain't afraid of none of them kids," he said.

"Well, then," she said, "I guess I'll have to insist, Calvin. You're meant to go out for recess, and I'd like you to leave the room."

He unfolded from the desk slowly and stood up. When he did, his face twisted and his hand involuntarily reached for the lower part of his leg, before he straightened up and prepared to walk out.

"You're hurt," Miss Marty said. "Why didn't you tell me? What's wrong?"

"Cain't hardly walk in these new damn shoes," he said.

Miss Stoddard gave Calvin a letter to take home with him. He hadn't done anything wrong that he knew of, but he was worried nevertheless. All the way to the farm road on the school bus he felt it in his pocket like a hot rock. Walking up the road, he thought of a plan and put it in his empty lunch box. It was addressed to his father, but he would let Auntie Donnell find it. When he got to the farmhouse, he slipped in her door and put his lunch box on the kitchen table, as if he was simply putting it there for tomorrow's sandwiches. He took his books with him to the boys' bunkhouse and did his homework on his own, keeping out of sight.

At six o'clock one of the grownups rang the triangle on the

corner of the farmhouse to call everyone in, and he went to Auntie Donnell's for supper. The letter was out on the table in front of her place. He saw that it had been opened, then turned his eyes away.

Auntie Donnell launched straight into the subject, as soon as the plate of meatloaf and succotash was in front of him. "How do you think you're doing in school now, Calvin?" she asked. "You yourself, I mean."

"All right," he answered. "I'm learnin'," he declared.

"This letter that you brought, it's for your daddy, really, but I thought I'd better open it and see if it was really for him."

They looked at each other, and he understood she had looked first to see if he was going to have to prepare himself for another whipping.

"Is it?" he asked.

"Tell the truth, boy, I don't know who it's for," she said. "They say you're not very happy, and you're not making friends. And I thought about it, and I thought you could say the same for here at home. I guess we haven't really been thinking about you all that much. I hadn't noticed."

He kept his head down, studying each forkful as he gathered and lifted the food. Seeing this, she did the same. "Your Uncle Donnell won't be in until later on. Did I tell you that already?" They ate in silence.

She was clearing away the plates and getting a leftover half of an apple pie out of the cooler before she spoke again. "I know it's your mamma, honey, and there's nothing to do about it. Nothing we can do." She poured a kettle of hot water into the wash bowl, over the supper plates. "Get me some cold water from back of the door, Calvin, thank you," she said. When he came in with the bucket, she added, "Can you think of anything we can do?"

"Can I sleep at Uncle Karl's?" he asked.

"They're botherin' you at the bunkhouse. Is that it? They'd get a whippin' if anybody was to know." She spoke as if the possibility that things would improve with or without punishment was remote.

"Won't let me alone," Calvin said. "It'd be the same if they was to find out at school. Just the same."

"They won't find out, honey, but you can't hide all the time." As if to make a lie of her words, she kept her face addressed to her dishes.

"I'm happier hidin'," Calvin said. "Only time I feel good is when Uncle Karl takes me with him."

"You can't go live with Uncle Karl, though, honey," she said. "He's going to marry Pearl, just as soon as they have a place that's big enough." She turned back to her dishwashing. "He'll have his hands full, gettin' settled with her."

She said nothing more until she came back to the table and put a slice of the apple pie on a plate for Calvin. "I guess either we talk to your daddy, or we go on like we are and you try your best," she said. "Your daddy 'll just take you out of the school, I s'pose. Do you want that?" She looked at him for only a moment for confirmation. "No. Wouldn't do nobody any good. You stay where you are, but honey, you got to try your hardest."

"Don't nobody like me, Auntie," he said. His voice was dull, flat, matter-of-fact. "Don't nobody care. They all got friends and girlfriends, they're all taken care of. Whitmores don't hold with strangers, and Whitmore boys cain't have girlfriends that ain't Whitmores. Even if it was pretend, there ain't no place for me."

"Calvin," she said, "that's just the way of children. They can smell when somebody is pitiful, and they can't put up with it. They got to pity you and pet you, or else they got to drive you out. You aren't the type to be petted, son, you're too proud. You're too much a Whitmore. They don't know what else to do. They have to leave you out. When it comes to bein' people, children aren't very nice, son."

"'Specially Whitmores," Calvin added.

"I think a whippin' might do them boys in the bunkhouse a

power of good," Auntie Donnell said. "But it's not for me to say. The men decide that." She got up from the table again and got some cream she had skimmed off the milk. "Try that on your pie, honey," she said. "I'll talk to Karl. It'll be a while yet before he has to think about Pearl."

The school office was pressed into use for almost the first time anyone could remember. The room had been dusted, the cover was taken off the old, black Underwood typewriter, and a few flowers had been arranged in a milk bottle covered in strips of colored paper stuck on with flour and water paste. Uncle Karl sat beside Calvin in the only visitor's chair while Calvin sat uncomfortably on a stool that had been brought in from the janitor's room by Mr. Krafft, who lurked around the office doorway hoping to hear what was going on.

Miss Marty brought in her roll book and a small folder of records and sat down at the desk next to Uncle Karl. "We'll just wait for Miss Stoddard," she said. "How are you getting along with those fractions, Calvin?" she asked.

When Miss Stoddard came through the doorway, she was already peering over the top of her glasses to see the spectacle of two tame Whitmores in her school at one time. She hoped for many more. "I apologize," she said, "I was born late and I've been running that way ever since." She chuckled at her frailty.

Uncle Karl answered, "I was born early. Maybe between us, we could keep the right time." His slow drawl was charming and his smile was warm. Miss Stoddard penetrated beyond them and found a cold criticism and was shaken out of her composure by the discovery.

"We've asked you here to talk about Calvin," she said. "He's ten now, just last week I believe, and we think it's time we all talked about what is best for him." She smiled again, trying for a fresh start.

"How's he gettin' on?" Karl asked.

"Just fine," Miss Marty put in. "He's a good worker, and he tries hard."

"Whatta we have to talk about then?" Karl asked.

"Well, what do you have in mind for him?" Miss Stoddard asked. "Is he going to help you on the farm?"

"I expect so," Karl answered.

"So you don't really want him to learn more than he needs to do that?" Miss Marty asked. "I mean, you don't want him to go to a college or anything?"

"Don't know anything about colleges," Karl said. "Whitmores don't hold with colleges, 'less there's somethin' about 'em we ain't heard."

"But if you were to give up the farm, let's say, or all you Whitmores to go your own ways, Calvin might need to make a living for himself," Miss Marty said.

Karl's amiable eyes hardened. "What you been hearin', Miss?" Karl said.

"Well," she said bravely, "it's a bad time for a lot of farmers out on the west side, and you haven't put any other children in the school, and it just looks to people like you might not be around for very long."

The wind knocked out of his sails by her frankness, Karl twiddled his hat around in his hands and tried to think what to say.

"Calvin is a bright boy," Miss Stoddard said, "but we need to know how long he is going to be with us. We need to know what we have to try to do for him." She took a leaf out of Miss Marty's book and went on the attack. "Why is it, Mr. Whitmore, that Calvin is the only Whitmore child who goes to school? I'm surprised the county truant officer hasn't been to see you."

Karl said, "He come 'round oncet, but we run him off." He decided to try some frankness himself. "We like to school our kids ourselves," he said. "Mostly, the mothers take it in turn. We got us a school as good as we need. Short of books, but we got enough so we can school 'em."

Calvin braced himself for what was coming. He and his uncle exchanged a look, and Calvin dropped his eyes.

"Calvin's mother's sick," Karl said. "His daddy's all cut up about it, cain't seem to take care of the family. His uncle Henry and me, we talked about it and decided the boy would be better with some schoolin' away from the other kids. Give him a better chance. It'd be all taken care of, no stories 'd get back to his daddy to worry him."

"I'm sorry to hear about your mother, Calvin," Miss Stoddard said. She turned back to Karl. "Does that mean you don't intend to send the other children here?"

"Not 'ntil we can afford the clothes," Karl answered. "We put our money together for Calvin here. Ain't no more for now."

"Oh," Miss Marty said. She looked winded by the blow. "I see."

"Yes," Miss Stoddard said. "I think we see much better now." She softened as they watched. Her face lost its stern authority, and her shoulders and arms became more round somehow. "That gives us a lot more to go on," she said. "When Calvin leaves here, he may never see another school, I think. What we can give him is possibly not the best he could get, but it will be all we can do."

"Can you think that is what you're looking for?" Miss Marty asked.

Karl answered, "That's it."

Miss Marty continued to look at Calvin, frowning slightly and troubled. She sighed, seemed about to say something more, and held her peace.

Karl followed her look. He considered the boy beside him. "You ain't never goin' to make him happy, Ma'am," he bobbed his head to Miss Marty, "Ma'am," doing the same to Miss Stoddard. "They's too much runnin' agin' him, for now anyways. Maybe his daddy 'll come 'round one of these days, maybe he won't." He paused, but then he passed on without a mention of Calvin's mother, leaving the hopelessness as a fact that they all four accepted.

Miss Marty looked at Calvin, who raised his head to face

her as if she had asked him to do so. "Do you hate us here, Calvin?" she asked.

He was hurt that she asked. She should have known him better than that. After all, he loved her. "No, Ma'am!" he said. "No!" He sat forward on his stool, punching the seat of it in between his legs to make his point. "I *like* school. I want to go here." He rocked back slightly. "Don't worry about me bein' happy, it don't count. I want to stay as long as you'll have me. I'll learn real good, I promise."

Karl was moved by the boy's speech and embarrassed by the emotion he felt. He forgot his manners and stood up, taking the few steps that carried him out of the doorway before he remembered to turn and say goodbye. As he did he brushed against Oscar Krafft, who had been standing beside it. Krafft turned and went out the back door to his workshop, and Karl watched him go while he thanked the teachers and said goodbye. He put on his hat and walked out the front door, and Calvin followed him, white and shaking now that it was all over with.

Once outside the building, Karl turned away from the road where his truck was parked and instead walked behind the building in the direction Krafft had gone.

"This ain't the way, Uncle Karl," Calvin said.

"Yes it is," Karl answered.

He went straight to the workshop and pushed the door open. Krafft stood in his sideways stance, his fists balled behind his overalls, a sneering smile on his face.

Karl said, "I guess you heard all that."

Krafft answered, "I know most of what goes on around here. Not much gets past me." His sardonic smile seemed to challenge Karl.

Karl said, "You know who I am then, and you know who this boy is. And I guess you heard about the Whitmores."

Krafft nodded without speaking.

"Then I guess you know I'll be back to bust your ass if you say anythin' about this to anybody, and if that don't work I'll come back and bust your head wide open." Karl lifted his hat as if he was speaking to a gentleman and led the way outside and back to the truck.

5

Three years had made some visible differences to the Whitmore farm. The porch that surrounded the former porch of the farmhouse was completed, and the roof of it looked fairly stable instead of being a handyman's idea of a make-do shelter. The houses looked almost permanent, with porches on the fronts of them and proper steps up to the doors, and awnings of wood laths built above the windows, even a few flowers in tin cans set beside the doors. The girls' bunkhouse had curtains of the same pattern at all the windows, and the path to their privy was laid with gravel and sand brought up from the reservoir project. The main privy had trebled in size, with a separate door, and a separate view, for each seat.

There were now twenty-two children in all. Pearl had become Auntie Karl without too much fuss. As the first wedding in the new homestead, the event deserved more of a celebration than it got; money was too short, however, for much of a party. Auntie Henry had taken the new wife under her broody wing, the bride's own mother being considered to have made a hit and miss job of it up to that point. Karl seemed happy enough at the way things were going in his household.

Auntie Donnell went in to see to Auntie Jimmy every day,

sliding the two-by-four back to unbar the door and peering inside to see if she was near it. If she was, the visit had to be repeated later on, and once again if necessary, until she had retreated, accepting that a rush for the door was useless. None of her three children had seen her since the visit to Red Branch. Francine and Sweetheart tried to talk with her through the barred window once, but she screamed at them and reached out between the bars to get her grimy hands on them, scraping the air with her long, snagged fingernails, so they never went to see her again. Jimmy slept in the living room, not because he wanted to but because unless he did, her screams kept everyone in the homestead awake all night. Sleeping there, he could stumble across to the bedroom and give her a slap if she started one of her fits.

Luck had been on the side of the Whitmores for a change. The winter rain, the days and nights of that drenching rain that thrusts itself out of the heavens as if it is being pursued, had held off until the middle of February, which allowed them to get the first of the reservoirs more or less finished. It not only filled, but held the runoff from the hills so that the rain didn't form little gullies and wash out the lower acres. The orchard down there was no longer struggling as a result but growing and thriving, even the new trees that they had put in. A second reservoir was even more successful. In only a year it looked as settled as a lake. The boys had talked Uncle Karl into an expedition to Las Cruces Slough to bring back live perch and sunfish and crappie; any day now one of them, standing with a willow pole fishing rod along the wall of earth that trapped the water, would catch the first of the fish that had been brought to their lake, they knew they were in there somewhere. The big project now in hand was the system of irrigation ditches which would lead the water gently to their fields and make their desert bloom.

The Whitmores didn't hold with newspapers or radios. They were caught completely by surprise, therefore, when a carload of men dusted their way up the road early that summer and drove up to the barn. There were five men in the black State car. Against strangers, the Whitmores had only one reaction, to close ranks and glare suspiciously. The women came out and gathered all the children in, except for one boy who was sent to find Uncle Henry. The State men meantime were left to stare at the compound of buildings and smile foolishly at the faces that peered out from behind curtains like Muslim women eyeing the infidel from behind their veils.

Henry came in his car from the reservoir, driving as quickly as he could in order to get rid of the visitors in the shortest possible time. He stopped his car next to theirs, pinning them to a narrow platform from which to play out their parts in whatever drama was unfolding. Henry Whitmore wasn't an imposing man until looked at close to. Beefier than his two brothers, with a solid, red face, his blue eyes looked out from under transparent white eyelashes and almost invisible eyebrows. The effect that this produced was to alter him from a poor dirt farmer of average height and build to a man of imperious command with a gaze that would put a basilisk to the test.

The senior official of the five introduced himself and his underlings and, shaken by Henry's silent hostility, gave way to a man of fact.

Mr. Whitmore had been aware of the proposal to construct a canal to carry water south through the valley? "No."

Well, the Government was going to fund a project to build a canal from the Delta down to the foothills of the Tehachapi mountains. "Unh."

The official route of the canal was still being worked on, but the general line of it was getting pretty clear. "Unh?"

Had he seen an airplane, a little light biplane flying around maybe five or six months ago? "Lots of 'em, air's free."

Well, this was doing aerial mapping. "Snooping."

No, not really, taking pictures so the route of the canal

could be mapped against the altitude of land, by sea level height, down in the valley. "What's sea level got to do with it?"

The water at the Delta will have to be pumped to a reservoir up in the hills so it can get a gravity flow, then the canal has to follow a line that will take it as close to the valley floor as it can go, so all you farmers can take it off for irrigation, but still we have to leave it at a high enough altitude so the water can flow all the way south without having to be pumped into another reservoir. "You tryin' to say your water runs downhill."

That's right. "And that means it has to run up close to the hills, this canal, to get your water down south."

Yes, that's exactly right. "And that means you want to run it across Whitmore land."

It looks like it. "Get your ass off our propitty."

We have a proposition to make to you. "Put it in writing. We got us a mailbox. Use it."

We thought you'd be reasonable. (This from a fat man who chewed a dead cigar and stared from eyes that were almost lost in the folds of his fat face.) "Git."

Henry watched the car scramble its way down the rutted road to rejoin the county road. When it stopped there so that the men could have a last look at enemy territory, he turned away contemptuously. The contempt in his face gave way to bleak despair as Karl and Jimmy came to him from behind the ablutions shed where they had remained, out of sight but within reach if he had needed them.

Henry tried a weak joke. "Told ya we got us a prime propitty," he said. "Now the God damn State wants it. Fer a God damn water trough. They wanta put a God damn canal, a God damn ditch, right through us." He turned away from the ramshackle evidence of their dream that lay around him and stared at the sun. "Shit!" he shouted.

His almost inarticulate sorrow at the iniquity of their fate moved his brothers more than their predicament did.

"Take it easy now," "Ain't as bad as all that," "Come on now, Henry, get a hold of yerself," "They's three of us, Henry, don't take on so," the empty assurances spilled from them in a nervous stutter as they realized their rock, their foundation stone, their elder brother, was shaken.

"What'd we come all the way out here for, boys?" Henry asked. "All the way from Texas?" When there was no answer, he said, "For another kick in the nuts, looks like. First the banks, now this God damn State. Why they got it in for us? Huh? Why?" He walked away from the other two, gesturing with a throw of his arm for them to stay where they were, unable to trust himself not to cry.

The big envelope that arrived a few days later was the most expensive brown manila that State money could buy. Inside was a long explanation of the proposed route of the canal, and a detailed map of the Whitmore land with a blue, dotted, double line drawn snakelike across it, cutting right through the buildings as it hung to the edge of the higher ground. A letter explained that there was a proposition in the hands of the attorney who was acting for the State in negotiations for the right of way of the canal. He was keeping office hours in Red Branch, and he would make time for Mr. Henry Whitmore or any representative of the Whitmores to discuss the matter with him fully. He was then empowered to make a firm proposal to the State with every chance that the terms would be accepted.

Henry arranged for clean clothes for the following Monday and discussed it hour upon hour with Karl and Jimmy. They weren't just going to sit there and take this. They were going to fight. They'd need the Army to get them out. What right had the Government taking a free American's land from him? That's what wars were fought about. This was the land of opportunity, wasn't it? They'd come from west Texas for their opportunity, and they were damn well going to get it or know the reason why.

All of this against the backdrop of a firm belief that even the

Whitmores were impotent if the Government was after their land.

Henry set off for Red Branch determined to fight, and convinced he would lose. The attorney had selected neutral ground for the confrontation by hiring offices above the bank. Since the Whitmores didn't believe in banks, the attempt to placate their spokesman misfired from the very start. Archie Hecker was a tall, balding but still dark haired man, heavy and German in appearance. The oversize shirt that accommodated his heavy neck was long in the sleeves, and he wore silver sleeve garters to keep them up. He was the first person Henry had ever seen who wore a bow tie, and Henry wrote him off as a sissy until he got to grips with his handshake. There are two kinds of lawyers who succeed in making a living in this world, those who are going to impress by the power of their legal minds, and those who are going to equal that feat by stomping on the opposition. Archie was of the latter breed. He squeezed the daylights out of Henry's right hand in a real knucklecracker of a handshake. Henry didn't like it and disengaged as soon as he could. First round to Archie, who gloated.

He had, however, reckoned without the appearance of the opposition. Seated across from each other, Archie found Henry's stare at first disconcerting and then sinister. A devout Catholic, he wished he could have found an unobservable moment in which to cross himself. It wasn't that he suspected a simple farmer of outright evil as much as that he superstitiously felt there was a force beyond mere hatred at work in that gaze. Under its penetration, he was reduced to stammering his prepared speech as he greeted Henry. Second round to Henry.

The lawyer's brief was a simple one. Archie Hecker was hired to negotiate a solution to an issue that threatened a group of ordinary individuals who had everything to lose. He had a minimum offer to make and a maximum offer that could be accepted by the State, with his own fee growing larger the closer the accepted offer was to the State's minimum. His job was to grind out a deal that would save the State money, and line his own pocket in the process; either he squeezed the Whitmores, or the squeeze was on him. His brief left no room for humane considerations or for ethics.

As is also typical in such situations, he first delivered a plea to Henry to be reasonable in his demands, because the consequences of unreason were the varieties of animosity of the State. Henry, already regarding the State as an enemy, sniffed at the speech like a well fed dog considering garbage and mentally lifted a leg on it. Archie then set out the benefits of the project to the farmers, who would be able to develop valuable land up to its real agricultural potential. Not so unworldly that he couldn't see that there would be vastly increased tax revenues for the State from the venture, Henry raised a leg on that one too. He turned his gaze contemptuously off the man, letting his eyes wander over the objects and papers on the desk, making it clear that the lawyer was going to have to work harder if he was to get the attention of an audience that found the contents of the desk more interesting than the platitudes on offer. A great deal more interesting.

Finally Archie began to approach the real business of the meeting when he said that the proposals for compensation were, in his opinion, generous. It was an unusual use of the word generous, but it seemed appropriate to him. Not so to Henry.

Henry said, "You're paid to say that. If you wasn't to say that to me, they'da hired the wrong man."

"Look," said Archie, "I'm on your side in this."

"In that case I'm talkin' to the wrong man," Henry said as he got up to leave. "Tell 'em to write me when they got somebody knows what he's doin'."

Archie babbled incoherently and then said, "Here, I'll give you the terms, you figure it out for yourself. It's a good deal."

"I don't want to look at no terms," Henry said. "Can you write?"

"Are you insulting me?" Archie said.

"I'm sure as hell failin' in my efforts if I'm not," Henry answered. "Write this down, and get it right."

He sat back down and leaned forward over the desk, which immediately became Archie's defensive earthworks, Henry's eyes with all their suspicion and menace boring into the lawyer's, demanding to be admitted into his consciousness. Archie pulled a pad of legal size paper toward himself and took the cap off his fountain pen without even looking at what he was doing, his own eyes held by his adversary's.

"You take this down," Henry said. "Here's what it'll take to get us out." All the hatred and bitterness of the experience in west Texas boiled up, and with it came a memory of legal terms and settlement provisions that had been used against him and his brothers. "First off," he said, "I want full compensation, none of this condemnation horseshit. Don't even use the word if you want to get along with me. You're proposin' to run your God damn canal right through our houses and our barn. We'll have new ones, you write down replacement value, not what the old ones is worth. And we'll have 'em on new land. I don't want none of this valuation and payment in lieu. What you take from us is got to be replaced, and that means land that is either right next to what you and your canal is gonna leave us, or a whole brand new spread. I ain't foolin' around with you people, when I say full compensation, that's what I mean. And I want free water rights from the canal. Least you can do is give that when you're takin' my land to run water acrost it. Water rights in perpetuity, I b'lieve you call it. There'll be more, but that's all I can think of right now. You tell them State boys that."

Archie's mouth gaped in astonishment, and he laughed in disbelief. "Do you realize what you're asking?" he said. "You want to be set up for life."

"That's right," Henry said.

"Nobody's going to stand for that," Archie said.

"Do you think I can't read?" Henry said.

Archie answered, "What do you mean by that?"

Henry said, "I mean I come in and sat down and looked at that little map of yours sittin' there in fronta you and figgered somethin' out real quick. Land to the north and south of us is all marked off. That canal's in there in that map, north and south both, in solid lines. You've settled that. Mine's in there in them little broken lines. From here even with my eyes I can read the owner's name of that land both sides of me. No need to try to cover it up, Mister, I already seen it. I see it's changed hands from when I was shoppin' for a farm, and the new owner is the syndicate that owns half the land in the valley, grabbed when nobody wasn't lookin'. Good ol' Cameron and Cox, biggest sharks in the land business. You boys has already done a deal with them. They're all ready to go on this. They prob'ly already got the construction contracts, just to make damn sure nobody else gets a cut of all this free money comin' from the Gov'ment.

"Now you come to little ol' me. You done left me til last, figurin' we're just a little bit of trouble after all those miles and miles of canal you already done settled. But I'm in the middle, with the miles that the canal can't do without. There ain't no way that canal is gonna get dug without my land. Am I right so far? Seems like you lost your tongue, just nod if you get what I'm sayin'."

Archie nodded, and Henry continued. "I'll tell you what you may not know. That there syndicate is goin' to get rich, I mean richer than them bastards ever thought of bein', offa sellin' land that's got irrigation, that they bought for next to nothin'. And I tell you this for nothin', Cameron and Cox don't give doodly squat what it costs to buy me out. I'm peanuts to them. And so are you. If the State don't want to pay it, the syndicate will. One of 'em is goin' to pay, the State or the syndicate, and that's for sure, and I ain't goin' cheap, Mister."

Henry eased the hold of his gaze and switched the attack to sincerity. "I'll tell you what, Mister. I reckon you're new at this, prob'ly a nice young man when you ain't squeezin' people like me. They want their settlement in a hurry. You spend much time tryin' to outdeal me, Cameron and Cox 'll wipe you out of their way like a little bitty bit of bird turd on a brand new car. Be careful."

Henry sat back in his chair, put his hat back on his head like the man who just bought the bank, cocked one leg over the other one, and smiled for the first time. "Tell you what," he said, "if the State don't like my terms, I'll hire you to get it out of the syndicate boys. I'll make it worth your while."

He stood up and held out his hand, prepared to shake the responding hand like a terrier finishing off a rat. "You'll let me know, now, won't ya," he said.

Everything has its price. The land down the hill, with its fine orchards and grass fields and acres spilling potatoes out of the rich soil, all of it irrigated, the place of dreams so recently, was theirs. New houses, real houses this time, barns and sheds and implements and vehicles, they were all coming.

Archie Hecker, now the attorney retained by the Whitmores, brought an architect and a building contractor to see the Whitmore brothers.

"Let's get this straight for a start," Henry told them, "we ain't in the market for a lot of modern stuff. When I say house I mean a nice little box with two three bedrooms, set high up off the ground so's to get the breeze, with one of them shingle roofs that comes together in a point in the middle. Big difference for us is the facilities. We want them houses to have facilities."

The two visitors looked baffled. They turned to Archie for elucidation, but he rubbed his chin and refused to meet their gaze.

Jimmy added, "And a good size porch."

Feeling he had to contribute, Karl said, "The kitchen on

the coolest side of the house, too. It's kinder to the cook that way."

The architect had to ask the question. "Um, what do you mean by facilities, Mr. Whitmore?"

"What ever' civilized man means," Henry snapped, "toilet and a bathtub." It was a momentous statement for a Whitmore, confirming in a sentence their wealth and their confidence. Karl and Jimmy beamed, Karl slapping his knee in delight.

"We'll keep the kids in bunkhouses," Henry said, "just the way it is now, with their ablutions and their toilets outside 'em, separate ones for the boys and girls. When they get growed up, they get to come indoors. Then they get facilities. Like a reward for good behavior."

Karl and Jimmy nodded and looked at each other in agreement. "Might get soft otherways," Jimmy said, and Karl added, "Maybe they could have some more doors, maybe more rooms, sorta walls between the stools." Henry and Jimmy seemed to agree.

"I'll draw you some plans," the architect said, "leave it to me."

"Ain't leavin' nothin' to you, Mister," Henry said. "Like they say, money talks. I'm the one with the money. You hear?"

Karl got hold of a Montgomery Ward catalog and brought it first to the girls, and then to the boys. He made the same speech to each of them. "This here's the Monkey Ward catalog. You got to get yourselves fixed up some. Everyone picks out a new set of clothes, socks, underwear, everythin', and you got to start wearin' shoes, so pick some of them out too. Write 'em down, and we'll get 'em for you."

Three weeks later there was a card in the mailbox saying the packages were in the Red Branch Post Office waiting to be picked up. Karl put the youngsters in his truck, twenty-one in back and Calvin in front, and drove them to the post office in town. They collected the boxes and unwrapped the packages in the back of the truck. Chaos was come again.

When finally he got some quiet out of the children he asked, "Has everybody got the stuff you wanted?"

They all had got what they ordered, more or less, with some colors a little bit wrong and a size or two that might have been improved on.

"Okay, now," he said, "get out one of them pairs of socks you got and put your shoes on."

They all did as they were told, then tried out the shoes with caution, walking back and forth in the back of the truck like people trying to cross a swamp without squishing water up their ankles. "Okay, now hold on," he said, and drove the truck up into the town, parking it in front of the department store. None of the children except Calvin had ever been in the town. They stared at the wonders of it, and the people in town stared back at twenty-one blond, blue-eyed children that seemed to have been created by the same cookie cutter.

Karl walked to the back of the truck and took away part of the tailgate. "Okay," he called, "ever'body out. You're gonna try them shoes on a real sidewalk. C'mon now, lemme he'p you down."

Twenty-one angels paraded up and down in front of the department store, looking at their feet, twirling like tumbleweeds, marching and tiptoeing and goose stepping, innocent of any consideration except that they had just stepped into a new world, and it felt good to be there. Karl and Calvin chuckled together, as men of the world do. Each felt a little as though it would have been a relief to have been able to cry in public.

The earth movers raised plumes of dust north and south now, every day including Sundays. The Whitmores had little to move, so they made a plan to do the whole thing in one day. The night before, while there was just enough light to see clearly, Jimmy led his wife out of the barred house.

The idea was to give her a chance to get used to the idea of going. "You want to see anything, before we go tomorra?" he asked. She was long past answering any questions, but she looked around her and seemed aware of the surroundings.

"Tell you what," Jimmy said, "we'll walk up to the lake. You ain't never seen that, and you won't have another chance."

He led her by the arm up the narrow road that snaked languorously along the foothills, climbing up to the notch that was dammed to make their reservoir. They went slowly, the woman sometimes holding her head as if she were dizzy. It occurred to Jimmy that, cooped up in that house for those years with no exercise, maybe this was too much for her. She pulled him along, however, eager to see where the road led. When they got to the small dam, and she saw the evening sky turning the lake into a great, shimmering, deeply glowing amethyst, enticing stars out of the darkness, she sat down, content to stare and go no further.

The black cutouts of boys doing some evening fishing were just visible in the gloom. Jimmy called to them, "Had any luck?"

One boy had, and the others passed on the news, as if his triumph was all of theirs. "What is it?" Jimmy shouted.

The nearest boy called back, "Chilly says it's a crappie, but it looks like a perch to me. What's the difference in 'em?"

Jimmy laughed. "Fishin' for 'em, and you don't even know what you got? You boys is fine ones. Jist wait a minute."

He walked along the side of the lake to where the boys had begun to gather, to re-inspect the fish with the help of this expert. Jimmy got out a box of matches and lighted one to see by. "Hold on to 'er now," he said.

"That there's a perch," he said, "but it's a funny shape, I declare. Maybe it got hurt when you boys caught 'em down at the slough. It's old enough to be one of them ones, from the look of it."

"Are we usin' the right bait, Uncle Jimmy?" one of the unsuccessful fishermen asked. "Mushed up grasshoppers?"

"Best thing I know of," Jimmy said. "'Course I learned my fishin' in Texas where they wasn't no water."

The boys laughed. "Gettin' dark," Jimmy said. "Time for you boys to get on back, 'fore they's any accidents."

He walked back to the dam where his wife had been sitting. She wasn't there, and that white, silent figure didn't come when he called. Jimmy and the boys searched the margin of the lake, while one boy went back to the farm to bring the men up to search the hills. They brought their long beam flashlights with them, so that the lake and the hills were decorated with a strange, interlocking, dancing pattern of stabs and lengths of light. When the first serious searching was over, the men met together to plan how to continue while the flashlights were handed over to the boys to play them over the hills and make sure she hadn't been overlooked. One of the boys, a seven year old, the youngest child of Uncle Harvey, illuminated what he thought must be one of the shallow parts of the lake. It showed up paler than the rest, and he kept the light on it thinking he might see a fish. When he saw what he had found, he screamed and dropped the flashlight. It was an all weather flashlight covered in rubber, and as it rolled deeper and deeper into the deepest water it went on shining, deep down in the lake like a milky green, subterranean beacon.

Calvin went to Miss Stoddard's classroom as soon as he got off the school bus. She wasn't there yet, but he was content to wait rather than go away and come back later. The children who were in his class teased him as they came in, telling him it was no good trying to promote himself to the leavers' class that way. He knew what they meant, but it didn't hurt. He was still learning a lot from Miss Thompson, and he was amiable about his educational fate. Let it come, whatever it was.

Miss Stoddard came in at her statutory time, which was five minutes late by everyone else's reckoning. Her class needed no quieting down; the children were stone silent to hear what business had brought Calvin Whitmore to see the teacher in charge of the school. They all shared some guilts toward Calvin, and no child was without self interest in this development. Someone's going to get it, they whispered to each other. Ears pricked, eyes came out on stalks, and necks craned when he asked Miss Stoddard if he could speak to her out in the hall.

She cautioned her class on their behavior and gave a reading assignment, then joined Calvin outside.

"What is it?" she said. "Is something wrong, Calvin?"

"No 'm, Miss Stoddard," he stammered, "least I hope not. I got this message from Uncle Karl."

"Let me read it then," she demanded.

"I'm carryin' it," Calvin said. "I got to tell you."

"All right," she said, trying hard to be patient.

"He's put me in charge, you see," Calvin said, "of the schoolin'. Auntie Karl is havin' another baby and he done left it to me to take charge." In the urgency of the message, all Calvin's carefully learned school English deserted him.

Miss Stoddard was lost. Calvin added, trying to explain, "He reckons he's too busy now, and I got to take charge. And the other kids has got clo'es now. Only way I can take charge is to bring 'em along."

"You mean bring them to school?" she asked. "For a day or two, or what?"

"No 'm," Calvin said, "for schoolin'." His face spoke of the hopelessness he now felt in his request. "Crazy idea, I guess. Twenty-one on 'em."

Miss Stoddard was shocked into silence by the idea of twenty-one Whitmores in Jurgens Elementary School.

"Well," Calvin said, "I guess what I come to tell you is that I'll have to quit."

Miss Stoddard collected herself mentally and physically.

"Now we aren't started talking and thinking about this yet, Calvin," she said, unthinkingly dropping into a dialect that he would understand. "Here, come back in my room and let me write a note, and you take it around to Miss Marty and let her read it, then take it back to Miss Thompson. You've got to get to class, she'll wonder what's happened. No, you stay here and I'll bring you the note. Don't say a word to the other children." She saw his face, relief written all over it as bold as scribblings on a notebook. "Stop worrying now," she said. She pulled Calvin's arm until he was close enough to her so that she could kiss him quickly and discreetly on the forehead which he had instinctively ducked when he saw what was coming. It was the first time he had been kissed by anyone except Auntie Donnell.

The Whitmores were added to the school register five at a time each week for a month, except for Sweetheart and Francine who counted as one and came to school the second week. By a swap with Floris school district, Jurgens got a larger bus that made its first stop at the new road to the Whitmore farm. Under Calvin's captaincy, the Whitmore children filed onto the bus each morning and took up the last five rows of seats, with Calvin sitting in the center of the bench seat at the back, the place of honor among the older boys who claimed that seat as their prize. The older Whitmore girls carried tin boxes that at one time had held axle grease but now were stuffed with sandwiches they had made for all of them. By the second week the girls were exchanging some of their sandwiches with non-Whitmore girls, and the younger boys were asking Calvin's permission to sit beside new friends in another part of the bus. Gradually the worry lines eased away from between Calvin's eyebrows, and he looked almost pleased with his brood.

The teachers had a meeting with Calvin when all the Whitmores had been enrolled and assessed and assigned to a teacher.

"I think they're settling down," Miss Thompson said. The others nodded. Calvin nodded vigorously too.

"We've only got one problem, Calvin," Miss Stoddard said, adding quickly, "and that's you. What do we do with you now?"

Calvin saw the smiles on their faces, but he was alarmed nevertheless. "What's wrong with me?" he asked.

"You need your education, but we need your help," Miss Stoddard said. "I think you'd better come into my class, but you'll have to help us with some of your children. We want you to keep up with your own work, but you'll have to help us with some of the teaching."

Without realizing it, the teachers had slipped into calling the Whitmores Calvin's children. At fourteen, he was seen as father to these white-haired, well behaved, educationally backward children.

Miss Marty said, "It's what we call gaps in their preparation. There are funny things they don't know, and we don't pick it up right away. We keep going with a lesson, and all of a sudden we find we haven't carried one of your children along with us. We're leaving them out and we don't know it."

Calvin protested, "That happens to me too."

"There you are, you see," Miss Marty said, "that's where you can help."

Miss Thompson, not to be left out, added, "Maybe you'll even know ahead of time what we shouldn't expect them to know."

Miss Stoddard spoke up in a tone that established that she was speaking as the teacher in charge of the school. "We have a plan. We need you to stay on, and there are still things we can teach you, lots of things."

"I know that," Calvin said, "I'm pretty dumb."

"No, you're not, Calvin," she said, "and you know better. Let's be serious. You stay on here at Jurgens for as long as your family will let you, your father or your Uncle Karl, whichever it is that can say yes or no. We'll teach you everything we can. Part of your time we'll need you in the classroom with Miss Marty and Miss Thompson, helping with your children that we think need help. You'll be the big boy of the school, and you'll be like a helper to the teachers. Will you do it?"

It was in this manner that Calvin got his education, remained in elementary school until he was sixteen, and earned the deadly hatred of Mr. Krafft for replacing him as the dominant male in the school.

6

Jimmy Whitmore lived on his own in the smallest of the houses on the new farm. He said he didn't want more than a roof over his head. He wouldn't marry again, he said, and hadn't any interest in "that sort of thing," by which apparently he meant wife, home and family. This was a relief to the older girls of the clan; Jimmy was nobody's idea of a catch.

He and Calvin hardly saw each other any more. It was a surprise, almost a matter of alarm, when he came to the older boys' bunkhouse one morning looking for Calvin. When he could get free of that morning's emergency, Calvin took time off from rounding up the boys for the school bus to speak to his father.

"You're gettin' to be a big boy now," his father said. "Sixteen now?"

"Fifteen," Calvin corrected him. He did it politely, afraid of any spark that might light Jimmy's fuse. "Sixteen at Easter time."

"Oh, yeah," Jimmy said. He looked around him, uneasy about being a visitor. "Kids behavin' theirselves?"

"Mostly," Calvin said. "Did you need for somethin', Daddy?"

"Yeah, well, sort of," Jimmy said. "You ever get into town?"

"Red Branch? Sometimes," Calvin said. "Whatta you need?"

"There's some business to take care of, thought you could do it yourself 'thout me to tag along." Jimmy looked away, embarrassed in spite of himself at this excuse for being once more the absent father. "Oughta be done soon, I hear tell."

"Whatta you want done?" Calvin asked.

"There's a bank account at the bank, first one you come to in the town, cain't 'member the name of it. I got the book for it, I'll give it to you." Jimmy looked as if he had delivered his message, but Calvin waited for more information. A bank? Whitmores didn't hold with banks.

"I hear you better get in there pretty quick and get that money out," Jimmy said. "Henry tells me banks is in a bad way. You stop by my house and get that bank book from me. Better make it soon."

Calvin paid a visit to his father to get the bank book, then went to his Uncle Henry's to see what he should do with it.

"You got a day off school comin' pretty soon," he said, "and you want to take that there book in and get the money out. All of it. Get your daddy to countersign in the book – nemmind, he already done it," he said, examining the book.

Calvin got a lift into Red Branch the day after Thanksgiving Day with Uncle Donnell, who left him off outside the bank and said he would be back about half past three when he was finished with the feed and seed people. Calvin wasn't sure he could use up that much time in the town, knowing no one and having nothing to buy. The line in front of the windows at the bank was long, and the sun was warm, so he walked around looking in the store windows for a while. Back at the bank the best he could do was sixth in line for one of the two tellers, and when he finally got his turn and said what he wanted, he was told that the person to see was the assistant manager, who was alone at his desk and had been all the time. Calvin felt a fool already.

"You Whitmores sure don't trust the bank," the assistant manager said after being told of Calvin's mission. "Your uncle pulled every penny out. This bank closing business is all a rumor, nothing but a rumor. Interest rates are low because business is bad, that's all. You can ruin a good business with bad rumors, you know. Especially in hard times like these."

Calvin insisted, and the papers were produced and filled in for him to sign. After he had signed everything, he said, "Whose money is this? Does it say here somewheres?"

The man looked more than a little surprised. "It's yours," he said, "if you're Calvin Whitmore. You said you were."

"That's me," Calvin said, "but how'd I get this money? Whitmores don't hold with banks, and none of 'em didn't have money, before the canal."

The man picked up the papers and riffled through them, looking for the record of transactions. "Here it is," he said. "There was just one deposit, into a savings account for your benefit, or your father if you died first. Deposit of one hundred and twenty-two dollars, made six years ago thereabouts, August 26, 1926. All the rest is interest payments. No further transactions."

"One hundred and twenty-two dollars?" Calvin sat back in his chair and whistled his breath out. "My daddy didn't have that kind of money."

"That's what it says," the man insisted. "Wait a minute. What's this say here? The initial deposit was by transfer from the account of Mr. Karl Whitmore. Looks like he transferred all the proceeds of his savings account to your name and closed out his own account. Yeah, that's what happened, you can see here."

"Yeah, that's okay," Calvin lied, "that's the way it happened."

"Do you want me to open a checking account for you, so you don't have to carry cash around? You're old enough to open an account on your own." The man desperately wanted the bank to save something from the transaction.

"No, thanks," Calvin said politely, "my Uncle Henry told me to bring it on home. I better do as he says."

Calvin felt rich and uncomfortable. He bought himself a Coke at the soda fountain, ordering it served in a glass with ice and a straw, not out of the bottle. The soda jerk told him that soda fountains didn't serve in bottles. Calvin enjoyed the drink despite his embarrassment. In the cigar store he bought some real cigarettes, getting them with no trouble about his age, probably because there was no one else in the store to see the illegal transaction. He looked in the hardware store for an ax handle but didn't buy one, bought a comb in the Kress five-and-ten, picked up a free railroad timetable at the Southern Pacific station and walked on down to the park to read it.

A concrete bench backed by evergreen shrubs, full in the sun, was made to order for him. He basked in the sun and studied the timetable until he had worked out how it made sense, idly thinking about what the places must be like that the trains went to. In his imagination they were exotic, colorful, full of people who laughed a lot and spent money without worrying about it – Placid City, Cloverleaf, Tipton, Chowchilla, Modesto, names to place in the list with the ones he learned at school, Rome, Athens, Paris, London. If you stayed on the train long enough one way, you ended up at Los Angeles, and the other direction you could go to Oakland and then somehow connect with places that made his head swim with thinking about them, Denver, Salt Lake City, Iowa City, Chicago. From there you could get to New York City. There was too much to be seen, more than he wanted to know about.

None of this speculation did any good. He felt the money in his pocket with a sense of dread. Unable to divert his mind from it any longer, he took out the cancelled bank book and looked at it closely. It held no clues. The deposit was shown, then every interest payment was carefully entered by hand, date stamped and initialled. Why Uncle Karl? What was it they were not telling him? Calvin could feel no gratitude for the money, only a deep, choked anxiety that surprised him by how close it was to a feeling of anger. He felt he was entitled to know something, anything, but he knew, as a Whitmore, he had no right to ask or demand.

He was hungry. He remembered the day long ago when he had come to Red Branch with Uncle Karl, and he decided to find the cafe where they had eaten. He searched through the park until he found the men's restroom and walked past it to the street beyond, which turned out to be the highway, then walked south along it, close beside the grinding roar and overcooked smell of the trucks. He paused on a bridge that carried the highway over a small irrigation ditch which seemed to be drawing a crescent around the heart of the town. He didn't recall any bridge, but he continued on. Shortly beyond the bridge he found the place, the Highway Cafe. Looking through the top half of the door he could see that it was busy, but there was room at the counter. As soon as he walked inside, he knew that he had made a mistake. The customers were all men, and everyone there seemed to know the others, and he was the outsider they all turned around to look at. Then he was all right; the same waitress who had served Uncle Karl and him all that time before put a menu and a glass of water down as soon as he sat on the revolving stool.

"You've been a long time coming back, handsome," she said. "Haven't seen you in a couple of months."

Calvin wanted to spin down off the stool and flee. He blushed harder than he ever remembered doing, hating himself for doing it as the red sweat broke out on his face and moistened the back of his neck.

"Hold on," she said, putting her palm over her mouth to stifle her giggle, "have I got the right guy?"

Calvin said quietly, "You're prob'ly thinkin' of my uncle."

"Oh my God!" she exclaimed. "Well, will you look at you. Mmm-mmm! I've never been a cradle robber before, but who's stopping me now, huh?" The men nearby laughed, and one shouted a warning about maneaters in the deep water.

Calvin couldn't answer her. Nothing in his experience had prepared him for the frontal assault of the rutting female.

"You having something to eat, honey?" she asked. "Or are you just gonna have a cup of coffee and look at me for your lunch?"

"I'll have an American cheese sandwich," he said. "With pickles."

"I'll put two pickles on the plate for you, loverboy," she said, "and I'll smear on the mayonnaise with my own lilywhite hands. How about that?"

"Thank you," he said.

"My name's Betty," she said. She waited for his reply. When it didn't come, she said, "You better tell me your name, honey. The nicknames I could give you would lift the hair on a bald man." The men roared with laughter, a good deal of it envious to a degree.

He told her his name and finally smiled. She smiled back and lifted the hair on the back of her neck with both hands, giving her a reason to lift her arms, which in turn lifted her breasts in doing so. Unable to help himself, Calvin stared at them as at some half concealed, enticingly wrapped presents in a store window. Betty held her pose, enjoying his admiration and knowing exactly how to proceed with her seduction.

"American cheese sandwich with lots of pickles and mayonnaise," she said. "And I think a glass of beer – 'specially for Calvin."

"I'll have milk, if you don't mind," he said. "Family don't hold with drinkin'."

"Suit yourself," Betty answered. She leaned forward on the counter, which pushed her breasts up to the limit of her blouse, and put an index finger on the tip of his nose. "I happen to know that's about the only thing your family don't hold with."

The man sitting next to Calvin clapped him behind the shoulder, laughing as if he had never enjoyed himself so much before. "You got her now, boy," he spluttered. "Hold 'er, Newton, she's aheaded for the pea patch!" He roared at his own wit and Calvin's mortification.

Calvin ate his sandwich and drank his milk without much more help from Betty, who was busy with her counterful of men. The story of her assault on Calvin passed from leaver to newcomer, so that Calvin was aware every minute that he was the lunchtime topic, today's comic routine. He had felt for a few moments aroused by Betty, old Adam between his legs had let his presence be known, but those moments had been replaced by a return of that suppressed anger that had surprised him in the park. He knew that it was his ignorance that was under attack. He was used to that, being a Whitmore. Something more than that was what had affected him. He felt cheapened by the conspiracy to keep him ignorant because he was easier to handle that way. Something like pride, some first, faint outline of individuality, was shaping itself. Betty and these men and the Whitmore hierarchy, all of them, they were doing something to make him less than himself, and for the first time he felt the need to resist.

When he paid his check and got ready to leave, Betty said, "You coming round to see me?" She simpered and added, for the benefit of the other men, "My house is out to Manzanita, real easy to find. And I got the afternoon off."

Calvin hunted for a polite answer to her jibe, to what he thought in his inexperience was her deliberate humiliation of him. He wanted to explain why he couldn't answer her in truth. What he came up with wasn't meant the way it sounded. "No thanks," he said, glancing at the counter lined with men who were ready to laugh him out of the cafe. "I can't handle an audience," he added. With the laugh turned against her, Betty could only glare furiously at Calvin's back as he went to the door.

“Nice goin’, sonny,” one man shouted, “but you better not come back!” Calvin had no intention of doing so. He pushed the door tight closed and walked back to the park. There he found another sunny bench, where the confusion of the day hit him. He didn’t feel angry now, only tired out, as if he had been stretching and straining all day. He went to sleep until it was time to meet Uncle Donnell.

When it came into view, the closed, tight, self contained, secure Whitmore compound looked good to him. He put the folding money and the bank book in the slit in his mattress where he kept his few treasures.

It was Calvin’s last year at Jurgens Elementary School. The three teachers had taught him all he was ever going to learn from a school, he felt, and he was sick of being the leader of the Whitmore young’uns. It was somebody else’s turn. It was time he took his full part in the farm. He was almost a grown man, and it was time the childish things were put behind him. He got his driving license in the spring as soon as he was sixteen, getting in under the age limit because Uncle Henry signed a letter saying he was no good to the farm if he couldn’t drive on the county roads. As a last treat to the kids, Calvin borrowed Uncle Karl’s new truck and loaded them into the back of it to take them to Red Branch.

The Depression had changed the town. It had been badly hit by the failure of the banks, and the smarter, snazzier, more modern people of the town, those who had looked down on the farmers as yokels, were on the grounded end of the seesaw now. It looked as if half the stores were closed down, and the ones that were left had only a few things in the windows. The Whitmores, untouched by bank failures and bankrolled by the water money, hardly knew about the Depression, and Uncle Karl’s new truck, the only new vehicle sold in the town so far that year, gave the game away. The few shoppers and the town merchants watched sourly as the Whitmore children, twenty-three strong now, the unlikeliest elite anyone could ever think of, climbed out of the truck and walked up the avenue to the shoestore.

What had drawn them to Red Branch was the advertising for *The Personal Appearance of Robert Wadlow, the WORLD'S TALLEST MAN*. No other topic had been in the minds of the children at Jurgens School for the past ten days. The posters said *Florsheim Shoes are proud to be able to bring the famous Robert Wadlow to Red Branch to open the new shoe fitting facilities in their store including an X-ray machine so you can see for yourself if your shoes are the right size*. That was the part that interested Calvin, not the world's tallest man; he was convinced that was a fake.

When they got to the shoestore, there was such a crowd waiting for the world's tallest man that the little ones couldn't see. Calvin led them across the avenue to the raised sidewalk in front of the hardware store. At exactly 10:30 a black LaSalle came down the avenue from the east, its white top down and folded behind the back seat. It moved very slowly, its white sidewall tires gleaming and the chrome spokes of its wheels sparkling in the sunshine. Two spare tires in their white canvas covers flanked the sides of the car like outriders. The body and hood of the car were so deeply polished that the sky splashed patches of blue in the black paint.

In the back seat was a big dummy. It towered a good three feet over the men in the car, bobbing its head slightly as the crowd came off the sidewalks to get a closer look, the laughter and catcalls growing in pitch as the joke became clear. The dummy was dressed in a brown suit, and a felt hat kept the sun off a spectacled face. The car drew up directly across from where the Whitmores were standing, and a clerk from the shoestore came around to open the door for the dummy. People laughed and pointed at their neighbors, doubling over at the hoax, clapping each other on the back and accusing each other of having fallen for it. Then the dummy turned sideways and looked down, concentrating on getting its huge feet out of the back of the car. Finally the feet were on the ground, and it stood upright and waved to the crowd, turning to all sides to accept the applause, then extending a monstrous hand to the shoestore manager to be shaken. Calvin felt the children push toward him in a mutually protective block, gaping at the creature before them. It really was a man after all, a giant of a man.

Robert Pershing Wadlow, born February 22, 1918.

Height and weight in 1935: 8 feet 7.4 inches, 420 pounds.

Shoe size: 37AA, feet 20 inches long.

The hat of a six-foot man just reaches the bottom of Mr. Wadlow's necktie. The eye of the same man is on a level with Mr. Wadlow's belt buckle. A six-year-old boy will come up only as high as Mr. Wadlow's kneecap.

The giant man had poor eyesight and dipped his head to peer down at his feet. He watched them as he walked, unsure of them in spite of his Florsheim shoes. He smiled steadily, a nice, friendly smile, as he walked slowly around the front of the car and turned to go into the shoestore. He steadied himself by putting his hand on the shoulder of one of his guardians as he stepped up the curb to the sidewalk, doing the same when he had to bend almost double to get in the door of the store. Calvin and the children hardly breathed, afraid every moment that this fragile monster was going to come apart as they looked.

A photographer spotted the collection of blond Whitmores and pushed his way across to ask if they would come over beside the car so that he could take a picture of them with the world's tallest man. The children teased to go, and Calvin agreed, taking the whole troop across the road. When Wadlow emerged from the store and returned to the car, the photographer pushed the smaller children up beside his legs and arranged Calvin on the other side of the man. Wadlow took off his hat for the photograph, revealing light brown hair, farm boy hair of the shade that bleaches out blond in the sun unless you use hair oil. A thick wave of hair fell down out of control over the right side of his forehead, but the rest of it had been trimmed by a barber to lie straight. His tweed jacket was a little too short, looking as if he had outgrown it and hadn't the money for another in these hard times, and his necktie ended halfway up his white shirt. The pants of the brown suit were belted high up on his stomach, the legs of them uncreased and unpleated so that they looked like two long tubes of cloth pulled carelessly over his legs. Calvin reflected that, if he hadn't been stretched and distorted, this monstrous boy could have been just an ordinary young man, like himself. He was instead somehow a figure of terror.

Wadlow's body was poorly assembled. Someone inspecting him like a machine would have said the parts for different models had got put together by mistake and would have sent half of them back for replacement. The difficulty would have been in deciding which half was the wrong half of the parts. His trunk and head seemed only a little larger than normal in size. His delicately shaped ears were set prominently on his head, looking like pretty, projecting shells. His long nose was nicely shaped, and his smiling lips framed a wide, pleasant mouth. But it was all too high up in the air, like some kind of display of a head rather than a head itself, the illusion that had led to the crowd thinking they were being fooled by a dummy. Below his trunk he was a different size. His underbelly puffed out and his buttocks were disproportionately heavy, bulging the jacket of his suit at the back. His arms, frightening in their length, matched his legs rather than his trunk, each one being longer than the height of a normal child. They ended in beefy hands, bigger than a face, bigger even than the heads of many of the people staring at him, with thick, deformed fingers twisting from them. His legs were out of all proportion to any other part of him, heavy and ungainly, just like tree trunks, pushing him up into the sky with a will of their own. All this was held up on feet that were like slabs of thick leather that he pushed along, overtaking one with the other with a slow, precarious inevitability.

Wadlow showed no sign of being saddened by his freakishness, returning the rudeness of the staring crowd with bland, undemanding smiles. He turned from side to side when not posed for the cameras, as if he knew his part of the contract was to make sure that all parts of the crowd were treated equally to his exhibition of himself, and the crowd responded now by pointing and laughing and making behind-the-hand jokes in full view and hearing of this creature who was and was not a man. Standing beside him, mystified by his indifference, Calvin watched his face carefully, peering up at him from below, watching the unstressed working of his jaw, the rise and fall of his adam's apple, noticing the odd absence of nostril hair that allowed Calvin to feel as if he was looking into Wadlow's head the way doctors and scientists would look into it when this unnatural man was dead. It came to him that the world's tallest man didn't care. He didn't give a damn. This man knew no attachment to the world of normally sized people. He was not one of them. Calvin wondered if this was something that went with being a giant, or maybe with being a freak. Would Siamese twins feel the same? Or that other freak the kids used as a tease for ugly children, JoJo the dogfaced boy? Was it safe to let freaks loose? Was it right to let freaks live?

The crowd was shifting now, pressing in closer, and the man beside Wadlow was answering their questions. Yes, he was Robert Wadlow's father. No, he didn't feel it was wrong to exhibit his son. Everything cost money, and everything had to be made to order, underwear, socks, everything. His glasses cost three times as much as any normal person's. Some people supplied things for the publicity, but that was only a help, not a solution. He thought his son except for his size was just like a normal person. His best friend was his younger brother. No, he didn't have any girlfriends. Wadlow heard this interchange and was as indifferent to it as he was to the crowd that pushed in and the hands that reached and the voices that cried out, "I touched him!"

When the pictures had been taken, Calvin waited to catch Wadlow's eye and thanked him as politely as the noise from the crowd would allow. In exchange the giant leaned down and stroked the blond head of first Francine and then Sweetheart, who had pushed their way to Calvin's side. When he touched their hair, his hand covered their heads like a grotesque, fleshy, hairless cap. He moved his hand to Francine's chin and tilted her face up so that he could see it better. The hand, bigger than her entire face, could have folded it up with one squeeze. It frightened Francine, and Sweetheart whimpered for her. Calvin reacted instinctively, taking Wadlow's arm just above the wrist to protect his sister. His fingers pushed into the malleable flesh where muscle should have been, and the great arm withdrew. The giant shifted his hand to Calvin's shoulder and, using the leverage, stood upright again. He was dough, Calvin thought, there was no strength in him, no muscle, only a repellent freakishness. It made his stomach lurch.

The police moved in, and the press of the crowd was released so that the Whitmores could move away from the LaSalle. Sickened by the monster's weakness, frightened by his own instinctive loathing, Calvin led the children back across the avenue to the safety of the raised sidewalk. He felt as well as heard the people in the crowd getting louder, rowdy, making dirty jokes about possible mates for the giant, the difficulties of finding a toilet for him, the size of the bed it would take to accommodate him and a girlfriend, the number of eggs he would eat for breakfast afterwards. They were excited in a primitive corner of their imaginations by an inoffensive, defenseless freak, while the freak, accustomed to the revelation of this normally concealed, atavistic, savage side of human nature, turned away from it into himself.

Calvin felt confused, shamed by the crowd and repelled by the giant, but more than that, appalled and scared because he had felt the atavism rise in him too. Faced with a shambling monster, he had felt also, "Kill him."

The men from the shoestore were joined by the Chief of Police and two of the men who had travelled with Wadlow, who pushed back the crowd from the giant so that the car door could be opened. He turned and sat down in the car seat, then slowly lifted first one immense foot and then the other, still smiling but once again tense and observant of what he did with his feet. The car door was slammed shut and the car moved sedately off, the crowd giving way, signalling his exit not with waves of goodbye but with a final bout of pointing, laughing, exclaiming.

As soon as the car left to take the world's tallest man to his next public appearance, Calvin led the way back to the truck and drove the children home. On the way the children were subdued, except for the older boys who had caught the crowd's fever and sat in one corner of the truck exchanging ribald speculation along the lines of "I wonder what he does when he wants to" and giggling uncontrollably at the scenes they painted in reply. Francine and Sweetheart had a little cry, because they felt sorry for the man they called Mister Wallow, but they were over it by the time the truck got them home. Calvin's only comment was made to Auntie Karl, who would have liked to have been able to go along: "I wouldn't be that guy for a million dollars, I mean it." Neither she nor the women to whom she repeated Calvin's remark believed that he really did mean it, but they were wrong, they hadn't been there.

7

Henry Whitmore stood beside his car holding up his hand for Calvin to pull his truck off the road and stop. He was chewing on something, a sure sign there was something on his mind.

"Calvin, I got a Mr. Lee Roy Stagg comin' to see me this afternoon. Never heard of him, and I don't know what the hell he wants. Tell you the truth, I can't be botherin' to talk to him. Would you do it for me?" Uncle Henry's questions often had a way of coming out sounding very much like orders.

Calvin nodded. "Sure," he said. "Want me to shortstop 'im?" When Uncle Henry in turn nodded, Calvin asked, "What time?"

"Four o'clock," he said. "Much obliged, Calvin."

Calvin put the truck into gear ready to drive on, but his uncle's hand stayed on the door handle. He switched off the noisy engine.

"You're comin' up nineteen this month, ain't you?" Uncle Henry asked.

"That's right," Calvin responded. He didn't bother to add the date. Another year, another leaf of the calendar.

"Time you had your own house," Uncle Henry said.

"I got my own room in the bunkhouse," Calvin said.

"Don't need me a house, 'less you got one needs somebody in it."

"You worked hard for it," Uncle Henry insisted, "time you had you a house. Come see me this Sattidy. Tell you what, you come along tonight. You can tell me what this here Stagg feller had to say."

Calvin waited at the bottom of their road for the visitor. He watched dust follow a car up the long, straight, county road, more out of interest that the road was so dusty so early in the year than very much interest in the visitor.

Stagg was a tall man, well built, with long lines curving down from the corners of his eyes that looked as if they should have met smile lines that curved up from beside his mouth. But this was not a man who smiled. Unusually for men in the valley he wore a thick moustache, what would be called behind his back a soup strainer, which almost but not quite disguised his habit of leaving his lips open about half an inch when he wasn't speaking. When he got out of his car and stood at ease, he held his hands one in the other with a thumb in his belt buckle to support them. He was a man who meant to dominate.

"Are you Henry Whitmore?" he asked, knowing this not to be the case.

"I'm his nephew, Calvin Whitmore. Uncle Henry asked me to talk to you instead of him. He's right busy today."

"Did he tell you why I wanted to talk to him?" Stagg asked.

"I don't think he knew," Calvin answered, "leastways he didn't let on."

Stagg tried a different tack. "You people out here heard about the trouble with the Okies the other night?"

"Nope," Calvin said. "What's Okies?"

"They're the people from Oklahoma, Dust Bowl people, coming out here to find work as migrant labor."

Stagg said it with a sneer that Calvin felt he had to respond to. "Ever'body out here come from somewheres else."

Remembering that an Indian family lived in Jurgens, he corrected himself. "Most ever'body, anyway."

"It's when you come and how you come that matters," Stagg said. "These people have got just about the clothes on their backs and nothing else, and they mean to do a little bit of work that qualifies them for welfare, and then sit and wait for you and me to support 'em. That don't appeal to me."

"That ain't a Whitmore way of goin' on," Calvin commented.

"I wouldn't of come if I thought it was," Stagg said. "I came to see your uncle because you got cotton. They'll want to pick it."

"Reckon he'd say let 'em," Calvin said. "One cottonpicker is as good as another one, long as they know their business and stay sober."

"But you'd want 'em to finish the picking and get on their way," Stagg said, "and they wouldn't do that. They'd take and live in one of your shacks like they were going to do what the pickers always do, work and move on, and they'd still be in that shack come Christmas time with twenty relations squeezed in there with 'em and more on the way." He paused, still suspicious and a little insulted that a boy had been sent to do a man's job. "I don't think your uncle would like that."

"No," Calvin agreed, "he sure as hell wouldn't." Stagg winced at this brush with mild profanity, tempting Calvin to repeat it. "They come an' pick, and then they get their ass' in gear and get out of here, or else we help 'em leave."

Stagg decided to shorten his interview. "We turned back a few Okie cars last week, at the county line. There's a whole camp of them down south, though, and not enough work. They'll try again, when there's cotton to pick." He brought a note of menace into his voice that Calvin thought was entertaining but not much more than that. He sounded a little bit like a preacher, and the Whitmores didn't hold with them.

"What did you want from Uncle Henry?" Calvin asked.

Stagg bristled. "I wanted to give him a friendly warning, for one," he said, "and I wanted to ask him if he'd help if they give us more trouble."

"Mr. Stagg," Calvin said, "he won't help you none, I can guarantee that. I might, if I knew in time, bein' one of the younger ones around here, but you won't get none of the old Whitmores joining up for anything. They don't do that." He said it as neighborly advice, and Stagg was pleasantly surprised by this tone.

Calvin continued, "You see this here road. Look back down the county road. I could see you comin' five miles off. When you get to that turn in the county road, if you don't turn with it and you keep straight on, you're on Whitmore land. We got us but one road up to the buildings, this one we're on, and there's a ditch either side. That wasn't no accident."

Stagg looked around him, aware now of his surroundings, the reputation of the Whitmores made concrete by the evidence before him. "It takes but one truck to block this road," Calvin said.

"I'm sorry I bothered you," Stagg said.

"Wasn't no bother, Mr. Stagg," Calvin insisted. "I'm not bein' unfriendly. Whitmores don't hold with strangers, th' old ones don't, but I ain't right sure that's goin' to be the way with us young'uns. Come back if you want my help. Don't ask for none from Uncle Henry, that's all I'm sayin'."

Stagg nodded, impressed by Calvin's frankness.

"Reckon we'll use the same pickers we always have, people who come up the valley from the south. They'll be along any day now to sign up," Calvin said. "Any others? One truck acrost this road, and that's it."

"Where you goin' all dolled up?" Auntie Karl asked Calvin.

"It's my birthday," Calvin answered. "I reckon I'll go into town and celebrate. Never done it before in my life, about time I did."

"You goin' on your own?" she asked.

"Yep," he replied. "Don't know no one else." He laughed.

"Don't even know what you're s'posed to do for a birthday party. Reckon I'll find out. Never had a birthday party in my life. Never had any kind of a party I can remember."

"Don't be too hard on 'em, Calvin," she said.

"Hard on who?" he said. "Whatta you mean?"

"Hard on your folks," she said. "It wasn't all your mamma's fault," she said.

Calvin was baffled. "I jist don't know what you mean," he said.

The girl, no longer fresh and pretty, plain now and preoccupied with other things, put her hand on Calvin's arm. "There's more to know," she said. "Bein' a Whitmore wife ain't always easy. Maybe your mamma had it hard, that's all I'm sayin'. That's all I'm gonna say."

Calvin was exasperated. "Woman talk! I don't know what in the hell you are talkin' about, do I?"

"No, you don't," she said. "You have yourself a good party."

As he drove into Red Branch, the evening sunshine flowed behind him like a golden river all the way up Greenfield Avenue. He turned north at the traffic lights and slowed down for a look at the new cocktail lounge near the bus station. Being on the shaded side of the highway, it was spooky dark except for neon beer signs in the windows. Over the door a cocktail glass with a cherry in it was drawn in blue and purple neon. It didn't look like a birthday party place.

He turned the truck around and returned to the traffic lights, turning east into the center of town. On the corner beyond the first block of stores was the Rex Hotel. A big front window had been slid up, so that he could see and hear men and a couple of women in the bar inside. He pulled up his truck and turned off the engine. The voices coming from the bar sounded friendly enough. When he went inside, they didn't stop talking to stare at him, either. A Spanish looking man behind the bar smiled and beckoned him to one of the revolving bar stools, away from an argument, friendly enough, that was going on near the juke box.

"What can I get you to drink?" he asked.

Calvin took off his hat and scratched his head. "I don't rightly know," he said.

"Beer? Bourbon and water?" the bartender asked. "John Collins?"

Calvin was lost. "Tell the truth," he said, "I don't drink and this here's my birthday. What do you suggest?"

"I be damn," he said, "first virgin I see in a long time." He smiled a bright smile that spread his red lips around even, very white teeth. "You have a Southern Comfort," he said. "On me." He poured a drink into a highball glass with chips of ice in it, starting the chrome pouring spout at the rim of the glass, lifting it to pour a long arc of the bronze liquor, then dipping back to the rim as the correct measure came in view in the glass. He gave the drink a single stir and smacked the glass down on the bar in front of Calvin, raising his half full beer glass to his honored guest and saying, "Happy Birthday! Many happy returns!"

Calvin felt warm and happy and welcome in among complete strangers in a town bar with a Spanish bartender. It was crazy and too hasty, but his face cracked into an open smile that he hadn't known he was capable of.

"Call me Gomez," the bartender said.

"My name's Calvin."

The stool beside him spun around. When it spun back into place, there was a blond girl on it. She smiled at him in the mirror, and he smiled back. "My name's Louella," she said. "Did I hear old Gomez say something about a virgin? I thought he was talking about me." She winked broadly at Calvin, trying for a wicked siren look, but she couldn't sustain it. She laughed and turned his stool far enough to allow her to take his hand. She shook hands, saying, "We're going to be friends. Happy birthday."

The conversation was difficult, and a girl with less

persistence than Louella would have given up. She told Calvin her name was Louella Parsons, like the famous Hollywood gossip queen, but he had never heard of her. When he asked her what she did, she said she worked as a waitress but her profession was barfly, and he didn't know what that meant. When she asked him where he lived, he said he was a Whitmore and blushed, and she didn't know damn from dishpan about that so they got no farther. When she asked him what birthday it was and he lied and said he was twenty-one, she replied that she was too, so that at least they were lying equally, if that passes for honest conversation.

If she had got up and left, he would have held her back by force. She was a pretty little girl with a bright, quick smile that left a trace of good humor on her face when it faded. She had a sweetheart face with a tilted nose and big blue eyes, and her mouth made a round, red O when she talked. She was a living magazine picture who had got up off a page and walked into the Rex Hotel, which was decorated in stars and had diamonds in the lights, where slick, tuxedoed customers and their velvet women paid their bills in gold dust before being bowed out into the night to drive off in their Pierce Arrow roadsters. Calvin felt as if he had lost any shape, that he was defined by what was coming at him from the lights, the mirrors, the drinks, this beautiful girl, the noise of the talk and the music. If there was such a thing as bliss, this was it, and when it was time for it to end, he wanted to die, right there on the splendid, polished floor of the bar of the Rex Hotel.

"You're getting drunk," Louella said. "How many of those things have you had? Gomez, what are you doing to this guy, anyway?"

Gomez smiled. "Only three," he said. "You make him drunk, not the Southern Comfort." He laughed, "Who's blushing now?"

"Let's take a walk," she said to Calvin.

It was dark now, and in depressed Red Branch there were

few lights showing, these being in hotel rooms and in apartments above the stores. The darkness felt friendly to Calvin; he walked the hard sidewalks on cushions, and the street lights might as well have been haloed instead of being strangely misted by whatever had happened to his eyesight. They walked for the sake of walking, saying little. Louella put her arm around Calvin's waist. Calvin thought it was a good idea, and he put his arm around her shoulders. She fitted perfectly the notch between his arm and his shoulder.

"You ever kissed a girl?" Louella asked.

"Nope," Calvin said.

They stopped in the doorway of the Sunlite Bakery and, with a little bit of tugging, Louella got her hands behind his head and bent it down to her level. She kissed him gently, then she kissed him again, parting his lips with her tongue and finding his own tongue with hers. Fire swept over Calvin, and the shock wave of an invisible explosion slammed through him. He was breathless, speechless. Louella took him by the hand and led him across the street to the professional building on the corner. Still holding her hand, he followed her up two flights of stairs to her room, content to let her conduct him into whatever mystery came next.

It didn't take long for the Whitmores to realize that Calvin had gone astray. He started work early, he worked hard, he kept at it until it was time to quit, and he never grumbled or shirked his part of the dirty work. The trouble was that he was happy. The closest thing to happy that a Whitmore was allowed was the way Karl used to be before he was married, an unconcerned floater who left the serious worrying to others. They didn't pry, and they didn't set a watch to see how often his truck returned at night and how often it returned at daybreak, but they knew.

Auntie Donnell was delegated to visit Calvin. He came back from giving himself a good wash in the ablutions block, in itself strange behavior for a Whitmore on a weeknight rather than a Saturday, to find her waiting in his house.

"Hey there," he said, "good thing I put my clothes back on already."

"Haven't seen much of you lately, Calvin," she said. "I just dropped by to see how you were goin' on these days." She pointed to something on the table with a clean dish towel over it. "Brought you a layer cake," she said. "You can have some with your supper."

"Thanks a lot, Auntie Donnell," he said. "I'll have some when I get home. I'm eatin' in town tonight."

"In Red Branch?" she queried. "What you doin' in there, Calvin, I didn't know you had friends there?"

"I'm makin' friends fast," he said.

"I hope they're the right kind of friends, boy," she said.

"They ain't Whitmores," he said. "Does that make 'em right or wrong?"

Auntie Donnell recognized the challenge and ducked it, saving herself some difficulty and storing up more for someone else another day. "You're a big boy now," she said, "you'll know the difference."

That wasn't what she had come to say or anything close to it. It had come out that way almost against her will. It wasn't only that she saw Calvin for the first time as a tall, handsome, vigorous man, not a "big boy" any longer, but also that she was bewildered by his good humor. Faced with someone who seemed, however momentarily, to have beaten life rather than experienced the reverse, she retreated.

Jimmy Whitmore brooded in his house. The darkness that had threatened for so long to close him in moved farther out from the corners of his living room every time he came home. The bedroom he left permanently dark, slinking into it late at night and out again early in the morning like some animal that must at all costs keep its lair hidden.

He had taken to avoiding the rest of the Whitmores. When he hadn't been able to keep himself apart, he had been on the receiving end of a few taunts, meant as inquiries, about

Calvin's secret life in Red Branch, thrown at him as if he would know what his stranger son was doing with his life, and begging the question why he didn't know exactly that. He consulted his companion, the darkness in his mind, and knew that he had been wounded again, by Calvin again. He skulked, when he wasn't forced by work to be with the other men, timing his movements around the farm so as to avoid any companions. He stopped using the privies, the place where people talked most openly from the privacy of their separate cells and therefore the place to be above all avoided. Instead, he took solitary walks to secret places in the orchards night and morning.

A remark meant to be heard by him let Jimmy know that Calvin was coming home most nights just before daylight. Jimmy got up early a few mornings and found that this was true. That led him to watch Calvin's leavings. He discovered that Calvin left as soon as he could get away, except on Tuesdays and Wednesdays when he delayed leaving until after nine o'clock. He guessed that whoever Calvin was meeting, and that seemed to be what was going on, was unavailable until late on those days.

This was in fact the case. As much involved as she was in her love affair with Calvin, Louella hadn't agreed to give up the movies. She couldn't, they were a part of her life. She could sooner give up her lunchtime work at Nick's Diner than she could overcome her need for the life she led as the companion of the movie stars. She and Calvin had agreed on a schedule. Movies being new to him and not something that ranked very high on the list of important things in his life, he would leave her free to see the program every Tuesday and Wednesday, which were the last night of the weekend program and the first night of the weekday program. If there was a special Sunday matinee, he probably would go to that with her. Sometimes, rarely, he would go during the week if it was a cowboy movie.

Jimmy picked a Monday night. He drove into Red Branch

after dark and began touring the sidestreets west of the highway. It was quickly clear to him that he had little chance of spotting Calvin's truck in that way. For a start the town was bigger than he had thought. He would have to look uptown. The idea of going to the center of town, to the stores and the businesses, made his soul shrivel to think of it. He hadn't been able to face Red Branch, ever since that night with his wife, when she went crazy under his hands and he had had to drag her away, he and Calvin, like a dead body, taking her out to the farm and turning his house into a living morgue.

He decided it would be easier on foot. He parked his car in the dusty, gray, waste ground beside the Southern Pacific tracks, near the grain storage silos so it wouldn't be seen. He walked across the four sets of tracks and around the deserted station. The moon of a clock on the station said nine and a few minutes. He walked past a well lighted place called the Mariposa Hotel, and then passed darkened, locked stores until he came to a cigar store. There was no one inside that he could see, but one light burned on the counter in a green-shaded lamp and a ring of light showed around a door at the back of the store. He had known enough about Texas towns to be able to recognize a gambling den when he saw one, but he didn't see Calvin as a gambler. He walked on, now following the sounds of music and voices coming from up the street.

At a cross street he saw Calvin's truck. It was parked diagonally to the curb with the back of it nearest the sidewalk. Jimmy snorted. It was a young buck's showoff way of parking, the sort of thing kids did so they could jump in their car or truck, full of shouting and beer, and roar away like they owned the world. His black loathing for the sort of people who shook life by the throat rose in him like bile in a sick man's stomach. The window and door to the Rex Hotel bar were open to the warm night. He looked inside and saw Calvin, sitting at the bar with a blond girl who, to Jimmy's eyes, was almost in his lap. Calvin was turned away from the door, and the girl was looking into his face, her arm loosely on his shoulder and her hand rubbing the crease at the back of his neck, while Calvin trapped her legs between both of his.

If Jimmy Whitmore had been a pressurized steam engine, you would have been hard put to it to decide if the gasket or the emergency valve blew first. He took four or five steps into the bar before planting his feet like the bad guy ready to deliver his challenge to a shootout. Even his hands signalled frontier justice, hanging tense but loose above the pockets of his old jeans.

"Calvin!" he shouted.

Louella looked past Calvin's head and saw a small, weatherbeaten, enraged man who seemed to have taken possession of the bar's floorspace.

"Good God!" she said. "Who's that?"

Calvin glanced to his right, looking in the mirror. "It's my daddy," he said. He swung around on his bar stool to face Jimmy, staying seated and leaving one hand on Louella's leg.

"You lookin' for me?" Calvin said. He seemed neither embarrassed nor angry, unaffected by the drama or the fury of Jimmy's confrontation. "Somethin' wrong?" he asked. He looked suddenly worried. "It ain't the girls, is it?" he asked.

Jimmy controlled the tide of his breathing long enough to reply. He shouted out, "You get your ass home!" The hatred flew not from his voice but from his entire body across the space at his son, then he turned and stalked out the door, his heels thumping the wooden floor, punctuation marks of his wrath.

Calvin watched him go. He turned back to the bar, picked up his drink and drank it down, rattling the ice flakes to get the last of it. He patted Louella's leg, saying, "See you later," and went out to his truck. He sat behind the wheel and thought about what he should do. He lit a cigarette and smoked it all the way down to a short butt. He flicked the glowing butt off his thumb with his middle finger, sending it in a fiery arc across the street to land in a splash of sparks and roll into the gutter.

Calvin reckoned that his father would have waited to see him follow dutifully out of the bar, and would be on his way back to the Whitmore farm by now. Whitmore sons obeyed; his father would expect Calvin to come home as ordered. He started his truck and pulled away into the avenue in a smooth turn. The traffic lights had been turned off for the night at the highway, blinking only their cautionary yellow at the empty streets. He drove slowly out Greenfield Avenue, past the black silhouettes of the giant trees of the park and the dark shapes of the civic buildings, over the canal, past the brightly lighted sanitarium, west on the broad avenue of diminishingly grand houses. At the end of the avenue, where the road he must take bore right through the vineyards and then due west as far as you could go until you came to the Whitmore road, Mrs. Rossi's Italian Grocery Store was open as usual.

Mrs. Rossi lived over and behind the store, with the one son who was still at home, and she didn't close the store until she lost interest in what was on the radio and went to bed. She was a motherly woman who had taken a shine to Calvin over the time that he had been stopping there for his housekeeping needs on his way into town. He pulled up in the bumpy parking lot in front of the store and went inside. She was in her back room drinking coffee and listening to "Fibber McGee and Molly".

"Calvin," she greeted him, waving him into her little sitting room. "What a you need? No eggs, I'm a out. Tomorrow night," she said.

"You still got a spare room?" he asked.

"Nobody rent it for a long time," she said. "You got a friend?"

"For me," he said.

She nodded and looked over at the radio as a gale of studio laughter swept out and over their conversation. She waited for it to die down, then looked back at him, looking at his face with interest but without any sign on her own face of curiosity.

She got up from her chair and held him by the upper arm, shaking it slightly. "Time a you leave a home?" she said. "Okay."

BOOK II

All the Livelong Morning

1

According to political philosophers, man has two kinds of rights, legal rights and natural rights. Legal rights are the ones he has and can go to court to protect. Natural rights are the ones he doesn't have except during an election. Chief among these natural rights for Americans are Life, Liberty and the Pursuit of Happiness, which have to rank with the words of *The Star-Spangled Banner* as expressions in a foreign language to all but about one percent of the population, so badly are they misunderstood or misinterpreted. They are, however, perfect for a populace that takes the attitude, Just give me the idea, don't bother me with details.

Calvin had been spared abstractions in his upbringing. Life was something you were born with but didn't either own or control. Liberty was a town in Kansas which had given its name to their longest-lived mule. As for the pursuit of happiness, unlike the older Whitmores he had heard of it when he went to school, but since he had experienced nothing which he could identify as this, the phrase remained meaningless.

At first, in their life together, Calvin answered Louella's repeated question, "Do I make you happy?" without a thought of what it meant beyond the deep satisfaction that they found in their lovemaking. Over the months a different idea began to evolve. He discovered that people thought it was possible to put together a lifetime that fitted a pattern called Happiness. Instead of a word, people actually had in mind something that lasted beyond a night or a weekend when no outsiders pierced the shell of their duality. Vaguely he accepted that you didn't stay a Whitmore and build a happy life. For other people, he also accepted, happiness was something real, but the content and shape of that happy life he could not nail down.

Except when he went to the movies with Louella. The Aragon Theater in Red Branch was on the outside distinguished only for the vertical sign written on sleek, flap-looking projections on its white facade, topped with the letter A arranged as something that looked similar to the little wings that ornamented the hoods of cars. A marquee hung over the sidewalk announcing the current movies and the coming attractions. Beyond the box office which stood under the marquee, the claustrophobic lobby was flocked and carpeted in plummy red, giving it the outline and attraction of the interior of Dracula's coffin. Twin ramps in an even darker red snaked right or left into the grand auditorium. With all that buildup, the revelation of the auditorium was a disappointment. A high ceiling was held up by flat, high walls, all of it minimally disguised by a few scoops and swirls of plaster, painted in a uniform silver blue. The only luxurious touch was the silver curtains which hummed and then retreated from the twinkling screen, with a faint clanking of the weights that held the skirts of the curtains to the stage, as the film image brightened into the only reality that was of any concern to the people in the place.

Once upon a time there were gods and goddesses who loved, tricked and fought in entertainments called Mythology, outdoors in the bright sun in the only show on earth. When the climate turned cold and the show had to be moved indoors, it all began to look pretty ludicrous, audiences had other things to do, and the backers pulled out. God came along and, like an old janitor with a broom, swept the trash out of the buildings and into the gutter and turned off the bright lights. He hired people to put on a new show called Religion which was very economical with illumination and paid off the backers handsomely with the longest run a show has ever had. When finally attendances began to fall, and people started running a slide rule over the real estate with an eye to realizing on the investment, along came the invention of the Freudian torch, which was a special light like a doctor's headlamp that was cheap to run but shone a penetrating beam into dark corners. Some of the gods and goddesses were called out of retirement by minority shareholders, given silvery moonlight to work under, and told to dust off the scripts where it all came out right in the end. To play safe, so that God couldn't see that the dirt and trash was getting out of hand again, the audience was left in darkness. In that way Movies were born and the pursuit of happiness finally became real: The reward for people who lived and behaved like movie stars, or hoped to when they had the chance.

That explanation may not be accurate or complete, but it would do for someone like Calvin who knew nothing of make believe. Louella insisted he had to see *Desire* when it returned for its third triumphant showing in Red Branch. He slept through seventy of its eighty-nine minutes and found the evening memorable for the fact that, for the whole of the nineteen minutes of the movie that he had stayed awake, the popcorn machine went wild and sent waves of smoke through the beam of the projector without interfering with the quality of the image on the screen. His exploration of fantasy was limited to the probable consequences of heavy rain or unbroken sunshine. For a young man who had not considered the question "Where will I be this time next year?" the leap from such poverty of the imagination to "Why couldn't I too smuggle pearls for Marlene Dietrich?" was an impossibility, even though he could see that it had clearly done wonders for Gary Cooper.

The same actor, Gary Cooper, as a cowboy was a different breed of cat for Calvin. The story was usually pretty foolish, and the scenery didn't stick to the Texas landscapes that he now dimly remembered, but he recognized the archetype as the cutout that the Whitmores stuck their heads through before they would consent to be seen. The morality, however, passed him by. He didn't recognize a west in which the bad man got his just desserts. There weren't just desserts, only success or failure, both relative to the needs of the characters. As a result he enjoyed the expertise of the staged violence without believing in it or the actors, who to his view functioned as appendages to guns rather than the other way around. His responses to the concoction of myth, idealism and violence known as westerns, if anyone had ever asked for his responses, would have been very depressing to the moviemakers.

Taken all together, the knowledge of the pursuit of happiness afforded by the Aragon Theater, and that seemed to be the only place where it was being demonstrated, led Calvin to conclude that there was something missing in other people's lives, not his, not because he had more but precisely because he had less. He, with his concept of a basic life that was meant to be lived on whatever terms were being offered by the lifegivers that controlled his existence, was incapable of a quest for happiness. He could see that the pursuit of happiness was such unrest and emulation and jealousy as that which animated the faces of the moviegoers, including Louella. He didn't scorn this quest any more than he envied it, because it was beyond him.

It was in many ways a strange life for Calvin. He lived in two places and worked at another one that was referred to as home. Sometimes at Mrs. Rossi's, sometimes at Louella's, he was always, as dependable as the sun, to be found during the working day at the Whitmore farm. The Whitmores needed him, and they wanted him back in the clan someday. No ultimatums were hinted at, and none was threatened. It would have been different if Jimmy had had his way. He didn't. Henry and Karl made it clear to Jimmy that he was blamed for the situation. Using the Whitmore creed of putting the clan above the individual, they told him to stay away from his son and leave things to work themselves out.

This suited Jimmy also. Increasingly he was a nocturnal creature. He did less than his fair share of work, but what he did was as much as his wasting frame would allow. He spent warm nights sitting in his doorway in a straight, hard chair, wide awake, listening and alert for nothing that anyone could discern. By day he worked as well and as long as he could, and then haunted the deeper groves of the fruit orchards where the gloom suited him, whatever the weather. The children avoided him, and he avoided the other grownups. Like the resident revenant, he became the stuff of scare stories among the children and cautions from the grownups. His eyes were things to avoid, and the path to the privies detoured behind his house on moonlit nights.

Pearl was the only Whitmore with enough curiosity and nerve to ask Calvin about Louella. He explained that she was a little bit older than him, with natural blond hair, as blond as a Whitmore's, that she didn't have any parents that he knew of, and she was a waitress at Nick's Diner, which was the first cafe you came to as you went south on the highway. The last was true, where she worked and where the diner was to be found, and the rest was, to put it nicely, misunderstandings.

Mary Parsons was not quite fifteen when she invented the girl known as Louella. She lived with her mother at the far end of Sixth Street in a house that was the last outpost of civilized Red Branch, where two fields tenanted by occasional cows separated the town from the non-white settlement known as Mexican Town. The line of a few low houses was all that could be seen of Mexican Town from Red Branch, and people who didn't live there didn't go there. Somewhere behind those houses a car with an air horn sounded out the four notes of "My dog has fleas" at strange hours of the day and night. People guessed it was delivering enchiladas.

Possibly the proximity of people with a secret life had an influence on Mary. More likely it was the combination of a long-vanished father and a mother who had never taken to parenthood that led Mary astray. In the spring of the year in which she would come of age – fifteen, that is – she peroxided her dirty blond hair, put on high-heeled shoes and stopped going to school. It took her mother eight days to notice a change in her daughter. By that time Mary had become Louella, her hair had become platinum blond, she had reshaped her clothes to show off the breasts and backside of a well developed woman, and as this new creation she had gone looking for her first man. In a fit of rectitude or jealousy her mother threw her out of the house, and Louella went to live in a one-room apartment above the dentist's office in the center of town.

Louella thought of herself as a good time girl as in the answer to the question, "You having a good time?" If you weren't, you needed her. She didn't exactly sleep around; those who knew her would admit that she was picky. Like the Wife of Bath, however, Louella was of the opinion that there was more selling of virginity going on than her kind of selling, and her product was quality tested. All of that stopped when she and Calvin met. He wasn't interested in her past and lacked any feelings of curiosity concerning her former men friends. The past existed only to shape the present; he liked the shape the present was in.

The future, that consequence of the present that has no existence, that no thing that is happy to be confused with the imagination, was what always threatened and eventually drove them apart. Louella was a creation of her future. Renaming herself after the gossip queen of Hollywood may have been a happy accident, with Parsons a convenient headstart. It was nice to roll Louella around in her mouth to one of her men, and to hint that her real future was with the stars of the silver screen. What was true was that having gone that far, she was certain that Red Branch was not going to contain her. As for Calvin, coming to Red Branch in the first instance, being conquered by Louella, breaking with the clan, these were events worthy of an entry in an annal. Beyond Red Branch lay dragons, kid stuff to Louella, not to be imagined by Calvin.

They were happy together for that spring and summer. It was a kinder summer than many, not so crushingly hot, thanks to a gentle, constant wind from the west that only occasionally had enough power behind it to raise the dust. There were days, however, when the evening wind failed, and the town burned long after sunset with a leftover heat like old anger. On one of these evenings they walked to the park to cool off, finding a bench that had benefitted from shade during the day but that was close enough to the open edge of the park to benefit now from what breeze there was. Calvin lay down on the bench with his head in Louella's lap and they talked about little or nothing as the light left and the dark advanced. A truck pulled up and stopped at the curb nearest them, and they heard the sound of doors opening and being slammed closed again. Then there was a pause and the sounds of voices in discussion, and the doors of the vehicle were opened and slammed shut. The starter ground and the truck belched the spiced stink of exhaust as the engine started and the truck pulled away.

Louella had pulled a branch aside to see what was going on. "Funny," she said, "did you see that guy? No, you're too slow, he's gone now."

Calvin roused himself sufficiently to say, "What guy?"

"There's a guy looks just like you, only he's older and thinner. I see him around the town every once in a while." Louella flicked him on the nose. "Don't be stupid, I wonder who he is, that's all."

"Looks just like me?" Calvin said. "Ain't no Whitmore. I'm the only one allowed out after dark, and they don't even allow that."

"I've seen him with Betty, from the Highway Cafe," Louella said. "Twice," she added, "here at the park. He just changed his mind and left. He and Betty, I think."

Calvin was interested. "Who?" he asked.

"This guy that looks like you," Louella said, "and Betty, the girl that's been at the Highway Cafe practically since they built the highway."

"I met her there once," he said. "Twice," he corrected himself. "Once with Uncle Karl and once on my own."

"She can't forget you," Louella teased. "She's had to go out and find somebody just like you."

"Sounds like it," he said, and he suspected who it was.

On a Thursday night in early October just before midnight, they heard from a distance the sound of a siren on a police car coming along the highway and turning up the avenue into town. It woke them both from their sleep. The car pulled around the corner and stopped outside the professional building. A door banged loudly and the siren growled its way to silence. There were steps on the stairs up to the dentist's lobby, then on up the stairs to Louella's apartment, followed by a light tap at the door. Louella got up to answer it, but Calvin pulled her back and went to the door himself.

"Who is it?" he said, speaking through the crack between the door and the frame. "Who do you want?"

"Calvin? That you?" The voice that questioned him was accustomed to giving orders and hearing answers.

"Yeah, it's me," Calvin said.

"Chief Thomas, Calvin, lemme talk to you."

Calvin pulled on the pair of jeans he had carried to the door with him and opened it. The night light in the hallway was dim and unhelpful. He recognized the bulk of Chief of Police Mort Thomas and went out to him, closing the door behind himself. He heard Louella come to the crack to listen.

"What's goin' on, Mort?" Calvin asked.

"I had a call from the highway patrol, describing a man that sounded like you," Mort said. "I came here first to see if it was you."

"Been here all evenin', Mort," Calvin said.

"It sure sounded like a Whitmore," Mort said.

Mort looked beyond Calvin where the door had been opened about two inches so that Louella could hear their conversation. Calvin followed his eyes, then looked back at Mort, who signalled a no with his lips and stayed silent.

"You want me to come with you?" Calvin asked. When Mort nodded, he said, "I'll get some clothes on."

Mort went back to his car, where Calvin joined him in a minute or two. Calvin lit a cigarette and waved to Louella, who was watching from the window, and Mort drove off in a hurry. He drove north on Bridge Street and crossed the river there before turning west for the highway, the car leaping and groaning as it met the camber of the streets at high speed. "Residential streets," Mort snorted, "never made for police work."

He turned north on the highway without saying anything to Calvin about their mission, adding nothing more until they saw flashing emergency lights in the distance. "It's bad, Calvin," he said. "I'm sorry to have to bring you." Calvin felt sick. The cigarette on top of the shortness of rest, now the tension – he fumbled in his pocket for a stick of chewing gum to take off the sourness in his mouth and stomach.

The night was filled now with the lights and noise of a bad accident. A patrolman's flashlight wagged at the car until Mort touched a button and the siren pronounced it official. There were ordinary cars pulled off the road onto the soft dirt of the shoulders. An ambulance waited, jammed in among police cars of various descriptions. A patrolman argued with the ambulance driver, telling him that the way had to be kept clear for the wrecker to come through, while the ambulance driver argued that the wrecker was going to come in from the north, not the south, and the patrolman ought to be worried about keeping a way clear on the other side of the wreck and let him get his ambulance where it was needed. People from cars blocked by the accident hung back, afraid of the action at the center but drawn to it at the same time, unwilling to leave or to press forward. The whale shaped bulk of a huge oil tanker truck, its headlights like theatrical lights for the people who crossed and re-crossed in them, the small lights that outlined its shape like festive lanterns at a celebration that had turned terribly wrong, defined the center of the accident. Above, beyond, and within the scene a woman's wail, like the keening of a savage, rose and fell without ceasing its terrible cry.

Mort took Calvin's arm and pulled him along when he felt Calvin begin to hang back. "Let's do it quick and get it over with, son," he said.

The patrolmen parted when they saw the Police Chief. Mort guided a way to the rear of the oil tanker where, illuminated by car headlights, a truck was smashed into it with the front axle and engine and part of the cab under the rear wheels and the rest of it a tangle of trash across the face of the oval tank. A woman knelt on the road, bending and swaying over the bodies of two children that she had recovered from the wreckage and arranged here as if for bed, blankets tucked around them and arms left free, the arms shattered and the heads awry and the blankets growing more red as she bent over them. Mort dragged Calvin past them as quickly as he could, to where police flashlights illuminated the upper part of the truck's cab where it embraced the oil tank. The body of the driver was trapped in the wood and metal, compressed along with the debris by the impact, pushed up into the upper corner of the cab as if he had been no more important than the road maps and chamois cloth and thermos bottle that the patrolmen were disentangling and removing while waiting for the wrecker.

Mort held Calvin's arm while Calvin looked at the body. He knew by the pull of the arm that identification was confirmed.

"Uncle Karl," Calvin said. He looked again at the woman, in her blood and grief still recognizable. "That there's not Auntie Karl," he said. "It's Betty, from the Highway Cafe. I don't know the kids."

"They're hers," Mort said.

"Let's go, please," Calvin said.

They had a thermos cup of black coffee from the emergency bottle in the ambulance, then got back into Mort's official car. Calvin directed Mort north to the truck stop at Manzanita, where a road turned west and, after some winding to avoid Las Cruces Slough, joined the county road that led to the Whitmore farm. There was a light burning in Karl's house, and a face looked out as the car drew up. The door opened before they had a chance to knock.

Pearl had a robe on over her day dress. She had been sitting up waiting. "I knew something had happened," she said. "He was so mad at me I knew he was goin' to do something silly. You got him in jail? Henry 'll go crazy."

She was clutching at straws. One hand held the door handle long after she had closed it, while the other pulled at her hair, tugging it back behind her ear.

She turned away from Mort after studying his face, looking at Calvin's to try to find something better. "What's he done?" she asked. "Where is he?"

Calvin opened his hands as if he could hold on to the right words, if he could only find them. "It's bad, Pearl," he said, in the extremity lapsing into her old name.

"He's dead," she stated.

"Killed in a car accident," Calvin said. He nodded foolishly, as if concurring with his own words. "North of Red Branch, on the highway," he added.

Pearl took it well. She stared at the men and gulped a few times, and her hand held hard to the door handle. "She lives at Manzanita," Pearl said.

*

After the funeral and the recriminations, the Whitmores accepted the truth of what had happened. It had been going on for a long time, Pearl said. Karl didn't seem to be able to do without more than one woman. There had been a whole string of showdowns, she said, but they never meant much. That last one wasn't any worse than the others. She didn't know where they had been, maybe just giving her children a treat, or taking them along while they went to a movie, she had no idea. He usually got back by midnight, so maybe this last one was worse than the others after all. There was something funny about it, because Karl's truck was going the wrong way, away from Manzanita, going south. Maybe this was the one where he was going to do like Calvin and not come back.

Jimmy Whitmore went to see Pearl the Sunday following the funeral. He took a bunch of flowers to her and asked if there was anything he could do. He looked better, and when she told him so, he said that he was sleeping better at nights now. There was nothing to watch for, he said, now that Karl was dead. Auntie Donnell, who was there also and was watching what was going on, told Jimmy he'd said enough and he could get out. Jimmy smiled, the first smile a Whitmore had indulged in since they got the news of Karl's death.

Oscar Krafft found his way to the Whitmore farm about two weeks after the accident. He said he'd come unofficially, to see how many of the children were coming back to school when the mourning was over. Since there was no Karl to take care of school matters now, a delegation of boys searched the farm until they found Calvin and brought him back to speak to Mr. Krafft. The janitor repeated the message, which seemed odd for a janitor, even one as independent as Krafft; and Calvin admitted that no one had put much thought into what was going to happen now, but the children would be back, he was sure of that.

Pearl joined them then, since they were outside her house.

She agreed that the children would return within the next few days.

Krafft said, "I'm sorry to hear about your father," his eyes taking their separate ways and his sneer showing no emotion beyond its own strange superiority. His overall bib bulged with his fists, as if it was having a hard time constraining them.

"My husband," Pearl said.

"I meant Calvin here," Krafft said.

"What's wrong with my daddy?" Calvin answered.

"I mean her husband, your father," Krafft said. "The man who died."

"What're you talkin' about?" Calvin asked.

"Mr. Jimmy Whitmore came to the school yesterday, and he got Miss Stoddard pretty upset. He got her to get out the school registration cards for you and your two sisters, Francine and Sweetheart." Krafft waited in a pause that gave him great enjoyment before he continued. "He scratched out his name where it says name of the father, and he wrote in Karl Whitmore."

Pearl turned to him enraged. "Shut up!" she shouted. "Get out of here!"

Krafft backed off, sneering, pleased at having done his dirty work effectively. "Sorry," he lied.

2

The split between Calvin and Louella wasn't a clean break. It wasn't a break at all, in some ways. Louella accepted that what had taken place had changed Calvin fundamentally, and he was no longer the same man who had fallen into her arms and shared her life for months that she now looked back on as a honeymoon of sorts. They remained best friends to each other, and they slept together from time to time. Louella entertained other men occasionally, with less enthusiasm than in the pre-Calvin past, her love life, no longer commercial, a hobby rather than a meal ticket. Her gusto for the chase returned, but she always remembered who Mr. Right was and had no illusions about finding a replacement for Calvin.

He in his turn began to pay more attention to the women, older than Louella but still young, who had been casting eyes on him ever since he came to live in Red Branch. It was good for Mrs. Rossi's business, the women coming in ostensibly to shop for spaghetti and olive oil and some of those good anchovies, and incidentally is Calvin here this evening? Like Louella's, none of his flings was serious.

There was in fact nothing serious in his life. He had known his mother as a lunatic, his father as an unloving disciplinarian, his real father as an uncle who from time to time could be a good companion, and his half-sister and sisters as his childish and uncomprehending sharers of a time of bitterness and pain and what he now recognized as hatred. He had found release with a girl who had accomplished her own rebirth, wiping out whatever she had been in deference to what she chose to be.

Calvin hadn't the imagination or nerve to try this feat. What was going to come would come in pieces, each one of them an individual novelty that, to his mind, added together did not make up a life. What a life was he didn't know, except that it was something indefinitely delayed. If he liked the look and feel of an experience as it came toward him, he would embrace it. If not, he would endure it, as the Whitmore existence had taught him so well to do. What was going to be different was, having been taught this much at least by Louella, he was able to embrace events and experiences and people even though he still knew nothing about giving back any of himself, that unknown quantity that he had been taught to loathe without pity. He was innocent, vulnerable and powerful, dangerously free of motives or tests for good or ill.

It was this pagan, amoral strength that began to attract to Calvin the attention of forces that were lining themselves up in the valley. The Whitmores, for all their internal catastrophes, had been created wealthy by the canal and were becoming rich as America began to come out of the Depression. Self-contained, sufficient unto themselves, the seismic change for them had come and gone, benefitting them enormously with no sign of an aftershock on the horizon. As for the others, however, the small, struggling farmer was about to become the swelling, rampant, successful rancher. The difficulty in this was that nothing in the life of the small farmer had prepared him to become his successor. He hadn't Louella's talent for rebirth any more than Calvin had.

Lee Roy Stagg had been the leader of these farmers four

years before, when he led their resistance and turned back the Okie convoys that streamed out of the Dust Bowl like army ants and threatened to overwhelm the valley farms and towns. He had organized a vigilante mob that beat and burned the Okies back to the Government camps down south, and the Okies had metamorphosed into migrant workers, tame farmhands, as a result. Power, however, lay dormant in those hands, belonging as they did to people who had grown desperate as they were denied the opportunity to use their labor to change their poverty-ridden lives. It was still there, even though they were now merely a miserable annual feature of Red Branch's harvests.

With only a token manipulation Lee Roy got himself made president of the cooperative that had been formed by the farmers to build cotton gins, oil pressing mills, feed plants and storage silos, fruit marketing combines, vegetable refrigeration plants, railroad sidings to all these, all the industrial panoply that spelled wealth as irrigation took effect and commodity brokers came to see the valley farms as their most convenient source of supplies. With the banks gambling on prosperity, and production expanding on the expectation of new markets, the farmers' dependence on cheap migrant labor increased. Lee Roy set to work to build secret defenses against the day that, in the name of fair pay for a day's work, some union man would try to organize the laborers so that they could get their hands on a part of this growing wealth. Almost alone among his farmers he recognized that the migrant laborers, poor, deprived, bitterly resentful, were going to have to be denied a share of the bounty and instead kept exploitable. In that state they were the key to the kind of success the farmers wanted for themselves.

He would not have said "Grind the bastards down!" because the other side of Lee Roy was his religiosity. Publicly he liked to be known and seen as a devout man. What he kept concealed was his fanaticism. His religion was his reason to live, and it could just as happily be his excuse to die. His four-square, tidy farm and his gaunt, forbidding wife were the backdrop to an inner life that was lived as a never-ending dialogue between Lee Roy and God, whose decisions were so similar as to be interchangeable. Lee Roy told himself that he existed only within the mind of the Almighty, that he was an insignificant speck of immortality. Somehow that speck had to be made to dominate other specks, so that the will of God could be made manifest in Red Branch. That his religious philosophy required specks of different size and greatly varying power didn't strike him as paradoxical. To this end – victory for the will of God through the good offices of Lee Roy Stagg – he worked and thought and prayed night and day.

"You ought to start coming to the movies with me, Calvin," Louella said. She turned sidesaddle on her bar stool and propped her head on her hand. "I'm tired," she added, "I don't want to do anything but go sit in that theater and watch a good movie."

"You make it sound real exciting," Calvin said.

Louella punched him lightly and took a sip of her lemon Coke. He continued, "You lost that argument about two years ago."

"No, it's this war business," she said. "The March of Time and the newsreels, you ought to come and see what's going on. All this Nazi stuff." When he looked at her questioningly, she added, "The Germans."

"For a war, there sure ain't much fighting," he said. "Don't look like it'll come to anything much."

"Maybe you're right," she said, losing interest.

"Somebody keeps pushin' this war at us like they're trying to sell it," Calvin said. "From the President on down."

"Whatta you mean, somebody?" Louella challenged. "President Roosevelt? Who else do you mean?"

"I don't know," he said, "you know I don't know nothin', all I'm sayin' is that we're five six thousand mile away, and except for the March of Time and the damn newsreels we'd never know it's goin' on." His speech on politics clearly embarrassed him. "That's all I'm sayin', I don't see why it matters to us."

She waved a hand in the air as if shooing off a fly. "All right, maybe it doesn't. Forget it."

He tried to say something more, but she snapped at him irritably, in a voice loud enough to turn two or three heads, "Drop it!"

Calvin leaned forward and put a hand on her mouth. "No need to get mad. What I'm tryin' to tell you is that I couldn't go anyways. Pearl wants to see me. Asked me to come by."

"Well why didn't you tell me?" she said. "You're driving all the way back out there tonight, and back in town to Mrs. Rossi's, and back out to the farm tomorrow?" Louella snorted in put-on indignation. "She might just have figured out it was better to see you when you were out there today."

Calvin shrugged. Women. He added nothing more and sat where he was.

Louella looked at her watch. "I'm going," she said. She kissed a finger and put it on his lips, waved to Old Gomez and walked out. Calvin watched her exit in the mirror, and when she had gone the half smile that had been on his face drained away.

He got to Pearl's house exactly at quarter to seven, as she had asked, and she came to the door as soon as his truck stopped. He parked it rear on to the curb, as he usually did, and in the reversing mirror watched her come out onto her porch. She was older by more than the eighteen months it had been since Karl's death, but she was prettier too. He didn't particularly enjoy noticing this. He didn't really like Pearl. She ran too scared for him.

"Come on in, quick," she said. "We only got a few minutes before the others get here."

Calvin knew nothing about any others, but he said no more than a greeting and went quickly into the house. She followed him in and looked for anyone approaching before closing the door.

"There's things I won't be able to tell you soon as they get here," she said, "and I want to." When Calvin looked baffled and showed his annoyance, she continued, "Let me tell it, and you'll understand later. I won't ever have another chance."

He nodded, still without speaking, and sat down.

Pearl had been preparing her speech at least all day, and it rushed out of her. "Karl – your father – wasn't natural in some ways. He wanted more than a woman ought to have to give in to. More than a wife ought to have to. I won't say more."

Calvin's stomach lurched, and his mind went white. He didn't want to hear this. Pearl kept her eyes away from Calvin's, pushing out her words. "By Whitmore ways Karl had a right to share your mamma with your daddy. No one's s'posed to know that until they have to. The women call it the Whitmore secret. I think you oughta know."

Calvin had put his hands defensively around the wooden arms of his chair when he sat down. Now he was hanging on to the chair as if he was on a wild horse. When he had been able to think about it, which was seldom, he accepted that his mother in her madness had deceived Jimmy, and that his daddy, cruel and cold as he was, had been made hateful by the deceit.

What was she saying now? Pearl glanced out of a window and rushed on with what she had to say. "What he wanted from your mamma was too much for her, but she couldn't deny him, that ain't Whitmore ways. What she did was deny your daddy instead of Karl. She couldn't have both. They was too much. Do you know what I'm sayin' to you, Calvin?"

He nodded, mute and stricken. He couldn't have spoken to save his own life.

"You're not to blame your mamma. It was a bargain, and she kept it, 'til she went out of her head. And you're not to blame your daddy. I think he's a good man, Calvin. And your father loved you, and he tried to show it." Thinking she heard someone, Pearl got up and opened the door.

"And my daddy beat on me the way he did to try to get back at his brother?" Calvin said. "Fine way to treat a kid, Pearl. Fine way to treat a wife, too." He made no attempt to hide the loathing for Jimmy that had surfaced since he had, in his own mind, got out from under having him for a father.

"They're comin'," Pearl said. "I didn't say nothin'."

They could both hear talking now, and Henry and Jimmy Whitmore came around the corner of the house. The talking stopped when they saw Calvin's truck. Henry led the way up to the doorway, and Pearl opened the screen door to them. Aware of the tension, Calvin said, by way of greeting, "Must be important. We only said goodbye to each other about two hours ago."

Henry took a chair. "Yeah, well, it is, Calvin."

There were few preliminaries to a meeting with Henry. As soon as Jimmy was seated, he began. "Ever'body knows that since Karl's accident, we'd have to change things around one of these days. We give it long enough now, so I think it's time. You all agree?"

His question was directed at Jimmy and Pearl, both of whom obviously had agreed ahead of this meeting. Calvin could only nod, aware that he had been bypassed in the important part of the process of change. He told himself it didn't matter. He was struggling to remain under his own control. Ever since Pearl had said what she did, he had wanted to laugh, and swear, and beat his fists on the walls, and kick shit out of something, anything.

"We got us an unusual situation," Henry said, "ain't no two ways about it. Actin' fair is always hard to do, but this time it's God damn criminal hard."

Jimmy looked out of the window at the evening sky and across the gilded orchards that sloped away from them.

"We have to give Pearl here a widow's share in the farm," Henry said. "And Calvin . . . ." Calvin tensed, ready to go ahead and burst into destruction if anyone referred to him as a son. "Calvin, you've got so important to us that we got to give you a share too, independent of your daddy."

Calvin let out his breath in a long sigh, and the worst of the rage inside him passed.

"About the time I got this all worked out, somethin' else come up. Calvin, I don't think you know about it." He looked at Pearl. "You tell him?" His question sounded like an accusation.

She shook her head. Henry was pleased at that and smiled at her. Then he shifted in his seat so that he faced Calvin alone. "Your daddy and Pearl," he said, "they're gonna get married."

Calvin was close to crying. He couldn't take it, all of it, it was too much. His head felt monstrously heavy, even when he rested it on his hand. The other hand he crammed down between his thighs to stop its shaking.

"So that means it's easier now," Henry continued. If there had been a hesitation while he made space for congratulations from Calvin, it had been so minimal as to be inconsequential. "I keep my share, a married man's share, and your daddy keeps his married man's share and takes care of Pearl, and you pick up a single brother's share like your Uncle Karl used to have before he was married. Karl's children and Sweetheart and Francine are all taken care of, like all Whitmore children." He didn't smile, keeping his hard, unlashed, unbrowed blue eyes on Calvin.

"How's that sound to you-all?" Henry concluded.

Calvin said, "Okay by me."

He fixed his eyes on the scene outside that Jimmy had employed for his detachment a few moments before. So this was all there was to be. There would be no explanations. It had been decided that the things that might matter did not after all matter. He felt a kind of outrage added to the anger that had become his comforter these past two years or more. Like a good Whitmore he pushed them back down, out of sight and out of mind. But not out of soul. Like a poor Whitmore, he guessed, like the odd Whitmore that rocked the boat so badly it sprang a leak from time to time, he had no intention of killing these feelings. He would allow them to have their full say, like friends.

"If it's okay with you-all, it's okay by me," he said. He returned his eyes to the group to find all three of them staring at him, waiting for a sign of his acceptance. He fixed a pleasant look on his face like hanging a curtain on a door window. The others relaxed and smiled, and the tension passed. Calvin didn't know which one he hated most, but he knew it wouldn't matter by tomorrow. It would matter someday, but not tomorrow.

To be a Whitmore, to have come in from the west side and taken up residence with a foreign grocer on the outskirts of town, to be the boyfriend of the town's most prominent good time girl – Calvin was Red Branch's most qualified outsider. He was by Texas parlance only riding shotgun to any upright citizen of conventional mold, possibly even he was the man with the rifle posted at the back end of the stagecoach to listen for the first zzzinnng of an arrow. There is, however, a power available to the individual on the periphery of a tight society which is bound in upon itself by the force of its own concentricity. He had no experience of this power, didn't in fact recognize that it was there. Louella on the other hand knew it very well, and would have nothing to do with it. She knew that this power worked in two stages. When it was invoked, it could accomplish things that no insider could achieve. When that was done, the same power would spin the outsider off into whatever limbo awaited him or her. When she left Red Branch, she intended to go on her own terms.

Children play a game, under many different names, that puts the strongest and bossiest person, usually the largest and least pretty girl, at the pole of a line of others, usually also girls, standing hand-to-hand to one side of her. On the far end of the line is a child who shortly will be a projectile, and by the rules of the playground jungle, this is usually a boy. The girl at the pole begins to whirl the girl next to her, moving her power down the entire line as the other girls feel this and imitate it. The line whirls faster and faster and the shrieks of the children build in volume until, barring the interference of a teacher or playground monitor, the force exerted at the end of the line becomes so great that the boy is flung away. He careens into space, dizzy drunk, knocking down any other child foolish or slow enough to be in his way, ending splayed out on the ground with cuts and bruises and damage to his clothing sufficiently major that his mother will that night refer it to his dad for discipline. The girls who were in the line hoot at the boy for his awkwardness and belittle him for being willing to be hurt for the sake of their amusement, and they congratulate each other, especially the one who started it, for humiliating their playmate.

It is essential that the boy shouldn't cry, no matter how he feels. No one admires a crybaby, least of all the crybaby himself. He must take the crowing and the screeching and smile, because the game isn't over, the best is yet to come. Back in the classroom, the girls write him love notes and pass them to him secretly from hand to hand, telling him they will be waiting outside school for him at three-fifteen, and maybe they will meet him at the bicycle shed and let him have one kiss if he returns a note saying he really loves them too. SWALK, and a heart with initials in it.

The next day he is forgotten, unless he can maneuver himself into the notice of a girl who will choose him for her next projectile.

Observers of this ritual game see the pain and humiliation and wonder at the willingness of that boy to subject himself to the whirligig of another's game, knowing what the outcome will be. Because it is the hidden part of the game, they fail to recognize that the love note is as important as any other part of it. They have forgotten what makes a game worth the candle.

A whirligig was just beginning its turn in Red Branch, and Lee Roy Stagg was playing the part of the powerful instigator in pole position. As he had expected and planned for, the barbarians were at the gates again. The fruit picking season had brought the annual rumblings of discontent and the threat of strikes by the migrant workers, instigated by radicals in their ranks. But, importantly, this time the threats came with a promise of assistance from a labor union organizer named Cappy Petrillo. He was a man with known and well publicized communist leanings, if not connections. With a communist tempting the migrants to organize for redress of their grievances, Lee Roy judged it was time for his second crusade, both against pickers who didn't know their place and, this time, against the atheistic communist who was leading them.

Without Stagg knowing it, standing behind him rather than next in line were the two men who represented law and order, County Sheriff Herb Atwater and Chief of Police Mort Thomas. The Red Menace meant little to them ideologically and nothing whatever in a religious sense. Their interest was to see the personal defeat of Petrillo and the consequent collapse of union organization of the migrant workers. Organized migrant labor meant only one thing to them, the threat of violence that accompanied it. If they could break this strike and defeat Petrillo, it would be an outcome which would earn them the thanks and votes of almost every citizen in the town and county.

The camouflage afforded by Lee Roy's activities suited the men of law perfectly. Thanks to Lee Roy, people in and around Red Branch were hopping mad, and they were frightened and outraged by the pickers' attempt to snatch from them the prosperity that had only just begun to return to the town and its district. But who were their opponents? Pickers, the lowest form of agricultural worker, ignorant, unwashed, half-starved. There was nothing to be afraid of. Lee Roy believed this, and he assured Calvin and the rest of the farmers it was a just cause that called for an honest fight, with the outcome a foregone conclusion. If the farmers and their supporters showed strength, organization and unity, they would win. They held the trump cards, work and the money that went with it. The strike would collapse.

That wasn't the way the policemen looked at it. They had both witnessed the terrible ways in which desperation arms the underdog, and from the time of the Okies the migrants had been no laggards when violence was offered to them. The outcome, as Chief Thomas said to his colleague, would not be a nice little two-step of a fight and a victory parade of trucks blowing their horns up and down Mariposa Avenue. It suited the policemen's purposes to let the town believe in this fantasy and get on with its fun – some excitement, a few bruises, nothing that would matter very much. They knew, however, that for their purposes the pickers had to be taught a lesson that would not be forgotten, and to that end they were preparing a response to the strike that was intended to be memorable and violent, beyond the imaginings of Lee Roy and indeed the town. To set that response in motion, they only needed someone to provoke it.

Since Lee Roy already had his eye on the young man he wanted for the end of his line, it was ironic that it was Louella who involved Calvin. She took pity one hot July Saturday on the farmer who first was threatened with a strike of his pickers, and who in pride and ignorance was attempting to deal with this on his own. After he confessed his troubles to her over a cup of coffee at the diner, she persuaded Calvin to let Lee Roy know that the first shot in the war, so to speak, had been fired. Calvin agreed, thinking that he made no commitment by putting in a telephone call.

The following night it was the turn of fate. After a picnic beside the river that lasted until after dark, Calvin and Louella followed a mysterious, unlighted truck into the wheat land on the east side, guessing it was a kid up to some kind of tricks that might end in a laugh. It was instead an agitator working for Petrillo, who burnt down a shanty town that harbored potential strikebreakers. Calvin once more did his duty, this time as a witness, and reported to the sheriff what they had seen.

In these ways, both forces turning the whirligig were reassured they had the right man for their projectile. It remained only to place him where they needed him. It was not evidence of this but merely a premonition that made Louella suspect that by their two well-meaning actions they were being drawn into a fight that was not theirs, that Calvin with his untargeted strength and uncommitted status was likely to be wanted for a struggle that he could still as an outsider avoid. He made promises to her, of course, that he would steer clear. It was, he was convinced, only a short, summer storm of a fight after all, nothing to get worried about. As arrogantly confident and lighthearted about the conflict as any man in Red Branch, he was certain he could be both in and out; it was a men's party, something to enjoy, no more than that to him, and Louella's fears were the rustlings of dead leaves.

Stagg, however, knew his man. A young man is most vulnerable when a test of his manhood is offered to him in terms that suggest no one else could possibly fit the requirements of the task – something an older man knows is a lie. More than twelve hours had gone by since Calvin and Louella witnessed the burning of the shanty town when there was a skirmish at the Court House, which Calvin missed. It had begun to feel to him, the outsider, like someone else's party when Lee Roy asked him to be his eyes and ears in the town, to be in effect his lieutenant, a position he could trust to no one else. Stagg said he needed for his good right arm someone who knew the mind and pulse of the town. Calvin was clearly not that man, but he didn't see the fallacy, inevitably preferring in his mind to alter his reality to fit what was being offered to him. It was a role, a powerful one, a man's place in a man's affair. It wasn't in him to refuse, any more than he could assess what his apparent disloyalty would do to Louella's feelings for him.

She came to the Rex Hotel bar late in the afternoon for her sundowner with Calvin. Before she entered she could see and feel and hear the buildup to a righteous, man's war. As soon as she saw them together, she saw it in their demeanor and behavior: Lee Roy had his lieutenant and Calvin was a key player in this, to her, indefensible game. Seeing she was not wanted, well aware of her status in Lee Roy's opinion, knowing any doubts she gave voice to would be erased by Stagg's confidence, Louella went to the movies, her solution to all problems.

Calvin had been drinking steadily but sparingly all day. Louella's walkout had sobered him down, as had the shadow of loneliness that comes to the bachelor when other men go home to a wife and home and supper. By evening the bar was empty of those good old boys who had been his companions in each fantasy confrontation they had fought that afternoon. There was only a sorry-for-himself young man who came in worn out and stooped from bucking sacks on a McCormick reaper, too tired even to make a play for two girls who eyed him and giggled from time to time. Calvin scratched his head and decided to try to make it up with Louella, readjusted his hat, and set off to find her at the movies.

The woman in the box office had herself confused with the gypsy in the carnival booth who tells your fortunes for a quarter. When Calvin slid his two-bits across the zinc counter for a ticket of admission, she said the main feature was about to begin but he had missed the good one, the B movie, "About gangsters trying to steal gold from a valley full of lepers in Tibet and the monsoon has softened the snow pack and an avalanche will hit the place if they fire a gun. One of the gangsters forgets and fires his, and everybody dies in the avalanche except the good guy and the girl, who turns beautiful when she gets cured of her leprosy as soon as she comes up out of the valley. Good movie," she said.

He went inside and crept up the sloping gangway, unable to see anything in the deep darkness, rubbing his knuckles along the flocked, corrugated wall to make sure he didn't lose his way. He stood at the back until he could see, finally spotting Louella slumped down in her seat and engrossed in a travelogue about Pago Pago, which is what it said on the screen even though, confusingly, the Pete Smith voice said Pango Pango. He slid into the seat beside her as soon as the ad came on the screen for drinks, popcorn and candy available in the lobby.

Louella shifted in her seat until there was space between them and whispered, "Does Lee Roy know you left him to come and find me? Naughty, naughty."

Calvin put his hand on her thigh, as much to calm her as to enjoy the touch of her. "He's gone home for a while," he said.

"Maybe he's got the same thing in mind that you have," she said, removing his hand. "With that skinny wife of his who'd bleed to death if she cracked a smile. Good luck to him."

"Don't be like that, Louella," Calvin said. "Let's talk about this." As he said this, Leo the Lion roared his invitation and the title card for the main feature rippled into focus on the screen.

"There's nothing to talk about, Calvin," she said. "You know how I feel. I'm beginning to get a pretty good idea how you feel about me, now."

"Aw, come on," he said. He suddenly felt that he wanted to be argued out of his involvement, all of it, but he wasn't going to beg.

"No," she said, "you either make yourself available to Mr. Big Boy Stagg, or you listen to me and keep your distance from him." She turned to look at him in the blue gloom. "That's the big difference between us. I know when people are trying to make use of me. I guess you don't."

The people sitting behind grumbled together, and then

moved seats until they were a non-hearing distance away. Since the rows of seats at the theater were set too close together for a man with Calvin's legs, he sat with his knees pushed against the seat in front, until the woman sitting in it chose that moment to turn around and glare at him. He apologized and pulled himself upright. A man's voice two rows behind said, "Can you skootch down so my kid can see? Thanks." Sometimes, he thought, everything was against you.

He asked Louella, "What's this movie?"

"Keep your voice down," she answered. "It's about Edison, with Spencer Tracy. You know, Thomas Alva Edison."

"Jesus Christ," he said. "Two hours, and when you get to the end, you've got a light bulb." In spite of her anger with him, she had to push the sleeve of her dress into her mouth to stifle her giggles.

"See you later," he said as he left.

"What's wrong?" the gypsy called from the box office as he passed.

"Your air conditionin's too cold," he answered. "Prob'ly it's that avalanche."

It would be two hours before they could talk. By that time, he felt, he would have forgotten what to say. A favorite saying of Karl's came back to him. "All dolled up and no place to go dancin'," except in Karl's case he'd had someplace to go to all along, and he'd gone to it. That phrase said it all right, though. Back at the Rex Hotel, the sack bucker was still there, very drunk by now and every inch the comedian, telling the largely empty bar in a loud voice that he was a back sucker, while Gomez hovered in preparation for throwing him out. Red Branch had had its fun for that day, and the only thing left was the radio until it was time for lights out. Propped up behind the bar was a handbill for a new restaurant that called itself a chop house, south of town on the highway. Calvin decided to try it out.

The chop house was a square building that gave the impression of having gathered itself in while the space around was blacktopped for a parking lot. A tall steel pole held a neon outline of a steak over a fire, with wiggly lines for steam or smoke rising around it. Inside, a middle-aged waitress brought Calvin a glass of water so cold it numbed his teeth, and the air conditioning was going at such a blast that he had to raise his voice to order his steak and turn up his shirt collar to protect himself against the arctic breeze. The peach and grapefruit juice that started his meal was equally cold. He was a little bit worried about prospects for the steak, but when it came it was only just off the sizzle, tender, thick and very good. He took his time, fending off the hoverings of the waitress. When he had finished, already the last customer in the place, he ordered hot apple pie a la mode and coffee. He was sitting over his coffee refill and a cigarette when the air conditioning was cut off for the night.

At almost the same moment Police Chief Mort Thomas and Sheriff Herb Atwater came in together. They said hello to him and sat down at a table as far as possible from Calvin, where they talked together over cups of coffee. He was surprised that they could come into a restaurant at closing time and order only coffee. Maybe that was one of those special privileges of the police that people made jokes about, he thought. He finished his coffee and cigarette and got up to pay the bill at the cash register. When he went back to his table to leave a tip for the waitress, the sheriff called out, "Here, Calvin!" and stood up and held out his arm as if he was ready to clap it around a nearby shoulder and it was Calvin's shoulder he preferred.

"You got half an hour for two working officers of the law?" he said. It wasn't really a question.

Calvin went over to their table. At a gesture to the waitress from the sheriff, another cup of coffee appeared. The restaurant lights were turned off except for those that shone through from the kitchen, leaving the three men in conspiratorial half light.

"Thought you'd never finish your God damn dinner," Mort said.

"You're waitin' for me?" asked Calvin.

"Look around you," Mort said, "there's no floorshow."

Calvin saw a door open onto a secret world, a man's world, bigger than the door that Lee Roy Stagg had opened, and he went through it with a silent shout of utter happiness.

The policemen left the sheriff's car in the parking lot and rode in Calvin's truck, directing him to drive south to the Placid River. Just over the river bridge was a two-room agricultural inspection station consisting of a weighbridge, a glassed observation room, and an office. They pulled behind it and slipped in through a rear door into the windowless, office section of the building.

A desk light was on, showing some maps and pieces of paper that the occupant of the room, a policeman fatter than Mort Thomas, had been studying. He got up to greet them and shook hands with Calvin before anyone could introduce him by name. After he had locked the outside door, he went to a second door connecting with the observation room of the station and called in a tall, heavily built man who had been sitting there in the dark. He walked toward them deliberately, making every footstep thump like a cowboy boot on a barroom floor. The gun on his hip was in a non-regulation holster, and in everything but his uniform, which was that of the State Highway Patrol, he looked like Randolph Scott just before the shooting started.

The tall man nodded to the sheriff without greeting the others. "Nobody followed you," he told Herb.

The sheriff gestured toward Calvin. "This is the man who's gonna coordinate things for you," he said. "Calvin, this is . . ."

The man held up his hand and Sheriff Atwater stopped his introduction. "This is the head of a riot squad I'm, you might say, borrowing from the State Highway Patrol," he said. "This is the man who's going to help you to break up that meeting tomorrow."

"He doesn't know about the meeting, Herb," Mort Thomas said. He looked out of patience with his colleague.

"Of course he don't, Chief, I know that," the sheriff said. "He's about to find out, now, isn't he? Y'all just go right ahead."

Chief Thomas started. "Cappy Petrillo is calling every migrant worker in the Red Branch area out on strike tomorrow morning. They're going to barricade every farm on the west side. I've had a tipoff. Sometime, my guess is in the afternoon, Petrillo's going to pull his strikers off their barricades and bring them to Garfield Park for a mass meeting. The strikers don't even know that yet, but the police do."

The sheriff added, "The idea is to intimidate you farmers with a show of labor solidarity, before you get their demands. A show of strength, you could call it."

"Farmers don't scare easy," Calvin said.

"Speak for yourself and leave a few of your buddies out," Mort said. "They'll cave in if he makes this strike go on for even a few days, and you'll have yourselves a union to deal with from now to kingdom come."

The fat policeman spoke up. He had a peculiarly high, precise voice that should have come from a thin man in glasses instead of this brute with hands like cuts of beef. "The strike technically is illegal," he said, "Petrillo doesn't have enough members yet to get a legal strike ballot, but that's not the problem." He nodded his head at the sheriff and permitted himself a thin grin.

"Mr. Stagg is trying to get Mr. Petrillo legally, but he's a good long step behind, and he's going to stay that way, I'm very much afraid. Mr. Petrillo is an old hand at this sort of thing." Sheriff Atwater spoke like a very kind man who had sized up his available assistance and found it regrettably wanting. "The best interests of this community will be served if the police forces assist in breaking this strike, because I'm just afraid Mr. Stagg's efforts are not going to succeed, not in the short term, anyway. So far, we can't do anything, however."

He leaned over the desk, jabbing a forefinger into a green blotter to make his points. "The way for us to help is to separate Mr. Cappy Petrillo from his supporters, take him right away from them. You see, Calvin, if the migrants saw that all they were going to get was a whole lot hungrier, they'd give in and go back to work as meek as could be. The only way to get them to do that is to take Mr. Petrillo out of circulation for a while. Now, that's a police job, and Chief Thomas and I are, you could say, rarin' to go. But most unfortunately, our hands are tied. Someone has to untie them."

He shifted forward so that his face was close to Calvin's, a look of grave concern on his face, and he touched him on the shoulder as if he was conferring the sixty-sixth degree of Masonic honors upon him. "You're going to do that for us, Calvin." He sat back, nodding his head wisely, saying, "Yes, sir, that's just what you're going to do for us, you're going to untie our hands."

Calvin's head was whirling. "I don't understand," he said. "Why don't you just arrest him, or something like that?"

"What's he done?" Mort asked. "Tell me that, and I'll throw the son of a bitch in a cell quicker'n you can swat flies." He held up his hands in supplication, expressing the policeman's frustration that the Petrillos of this world had to be criminals first and prisoners afterwards.

"It's not a police matter yet," the sheriff said. "Not . . . yet." He emphasized and prolonged the two short words ponderously. "You understand?" he added.

Calvin looked at the big, silent man sitting beside him, and looked back at the fat policeman. He began to understand. The fat policeman smiled encouragingly as he saw the light dawning in Calvin's eyes, and the tall patrolman reached over and took Calvin's shoulder in the grip of his huge paw, shaking him slowly, smiling at him like a real comrade.

The sheriff's long face widened in an open, toothy smile.

"That's right, Calvin, you're going to get Mr. Petrillo to give us a violation of the law, and we're going to do the rest. It's a little bit dangerous, but I assure you, son, it's got to be done. Thank the good Lord you agreed to help us."

Mort, impatient as always, said, "You go to that mass meeting tomorrow, and you make sure things get out of hand. Simple as that."

"You mean I start trouble, so you can get Petrillo," Calvin said.

"No, huh-uh," the fat policeman broke in. "Trouble starts while you're there, and the police intervene to protect you from Mr. Petrillo. That's what happens."

The sheriff nodded encouragement to Calvin. "We'll give you the details tomorrow, Calvin, we got it all worked out. All we need is you to say yes." He turned to Mort. "I think he can do it, don't you, Chief? Whatta you think he'll say?"

When Calvin didn't answer immediately, Chief Thomas said, "It's gettin' late, son. Just give us the word."

Calvin took a deep breath. "Yeah," he said, "okay."

The sheriff cleared his throat. "Now's as good a time as any, Calvin, I think, to explain a little something that I'm certain sure you already understand, but we need to be positive about it." He smiled warmly. "No word about this breaking up the mass meeting and taking Mr. Petrillo into custody, about it being set up by the police in advance, is ever, ever to be mentioned. You understand, son? You say we set it up, and we'll say you're lying. You understand?" He smiled even more warmly and reached a paternal hand across to touch Calvin's forearm in reassurance. "There's times that the needs of the people are above the law. We take an oath to protect the law, and the law is the people. Sometimes we have to interpret things in our own way, to make it all come out right in the end. You got any problem with that?" Calvin shook his head.

Mort added, "We're going to be there to protect the people, and you're the people, son."

Sheriff Atwater nodded, content that Calvin understood perfectly. "You're okay about this, now, aren't you, son?" the sheriff asked.

"Have I got any choice?" Calvin asked.

Sheriff Atwater slapped his knee and laughed heartily, and after a few seconds the others joined in, Mort shaking his belly in a kind of rumble, the fat policeman delivering a treble wheeze, and the big patrolman laughing from deep in his throat like a diesel engine on a very slow idling speed.

"I agree, Calvin, I agree," the sheriff said when he could find the breath to speak, "you don't have much choice, do you. That's a good one."

It was long after midnight when Calvin returned to Mrs. Rossi's from the meeting with the police, too late for talking with Louella even if he had still wanted to. He stopped short of going in, wanting to think, knowing that if he left it until he got into bed he wouldn't stay awake. He took out a cigarette and lit it, using the snap of the Zippo like a starting gun to his thoughts.

It was dangerous work, they had said, but it had to be done, and he was the right man to do it. He was in it now, not at the outside but at the very center of events, and it pleased him that he was. Here was what he had longed for, a chance to be someone who wasn't himself. This was a Calvin chance, not a Whitmore one. No more of this hanging back with the rest of the Whitmores while the world went by on its business. He wouldn't listen to Louella. That was woman talk. He wouldn't listen to the hollowness inside himself, either. This was his chance. Whatever he was going to be would come from the approval in men's eyes. That was where the person he wanted to be could begin his life. That was reason enough to be doing whatever it was he would be called upon to do.

3

She had noticed the difference as soon as she got up that morning. The town sounded different, it even smelled different. From her window on the side street she could see what seemed to be a choreographed succession of cars going somewhere only to return immediately, drawn back by the excitement that she didn't want to know about. She crossed the hall to the dentist's waiting room in order to look out of the window at the front of the building. Below and to her right was the center of the turmoil, Tom Potter's store. She heard the voices that were strange to the usual crowd, and smelled the reek of their cigarettes, and felt underneath these the male exultation that greeted a good fight. She retreated to her tiny apartment, not wanting to know if Calvin was one of that crowd. She dressed to go to work at the diner and, walking across the avenue and down the side street before turning toward the highway, closed her eyes and ears to the possibility that he might be there.

Ears are, however, made to hear, and it was only minutes before someone came into the diner for a cup of coffee and referred to Calvin's part in preparations for resisting the strike. Lee Roy Stagg calling Calvin his right hand man? She didn't want to believe it, but then again she had seen last evening the fever in his face, even though she had heard the doubt in his voice in the dark of the theater.

All morning the counter was crowded with men she had never before seen in the diner who ordered bacon and eggs, or a sandwich, or just a cup of coffee, and swallowed it down without a hope of tasting it, speculating on what the next few hours would bring, hardly able to suppress their delight at the spate of rumors that indicated what was coming was a once-and-for-all fight with the pickers. The pickers. They had become not people, the same people who had worked the crops year after year, but some kind of an awkward, mean animal that had gone loco and forgotten where its meals came from and had to be beaten back into its proper state of obedience. And the farmers, they too had changed, into an undisciplined, confident army whose secret strength remained a secret even to its recruits, invincible by wish and belief and unaware of where its weapons were to come from, but certain of their superiority in this fight.

The early lunch crowd, Louella's responsibility, melded into the noon lunch crowd, Hazel Klinghofer's shift, with far too many customers to allow Louella to go off duty. At a few minutes past twelve-thirty a man with floppy overalls and a Mexican straw hat burst through the door of the diner, shouting "Listen up! Listen up now, all of you!"

There was instant silence. "The strikers are leaving their barricades," he said, speaking loudly and clearly like an ancient herald, "our farm roads are clear. Hear tell they're coming into town, for a big strike meeting at the park. Chief Thomas says we're to stay away. Don't go getting into trouble, just stay away. Everybody hear that?"

"Couldn't help it," one man called at him, but his attempt at humor fell flat.

"What're we supposed to do?" another asked.

The herald said, "I'm going out to my place and see if they done any damage. Maybe I'll be the one to put up the barricades and keep out the God damn pickers. Suit yourselves."

In five minutes the diner was empty. Hazel told her to go home, she wouldn't get overtime anyway, but Louella was reluctant to go. The atmosphere was too strange. She was not a girl who was easily cowed, but now she was frightened. She gave Hazel a hand in washing the steel surfaces with disinfectant, and she steel wooled the stains around the grill. By half past two there were no further obvious excuses. She hung up her apron, then changed her mind and rinsed it out and hung it out behind the back door to dry in the sun. Ten minutes to three. She went into the ladies' room and fixed her face, trying to powder away the sweat that persisted under her eyes, and then fiddled with her hairdo, attempting repeatedly without hope to lift it into a cooler position off the back of her neck, until she could delay no longer and, like someone trying the temperature of the water of a swimming pool, stepped tentatively out of the diner one cautious foot at a time. Three-fifteen. The only disturbance to the profound quiet of the town on a sweltering afternoon was the faint, distorted boom of a PA system coming from the direction of the park.

She didn't like the idea of walking along the highway. She didn't want to walk beside the park, and she didn't want to be approached by anyone in a car, feeling a sudden, irrational fear of someone driving up from behind and surprising her. She took the alternative route, a roundabout set of detours and shortcuts that eventually brought her into First Street. The sound of someone speaking over the PA was loud now, and she could tell it was coming from the bandstand in the park. She turned at the Presbyterian Church to walk the block to the highway and cross to the safe, eastern half of town. On the shady side of the church, she knew, was a drinking fountain that had a flow of water strong enough to wash out the taste of rust when you ran off the warmer, surface water in the pipes. She could do with a nice drink of cool water, and she felt more confident now. She went to the fountain and let the splash of the runoff water help calm her tight but relaxing nerves.

Out of the fierce sun, in the blinding contrast of the building's shade, she bent to take a drink, when out of the corner of her eye she saw movement. She screamed and backed away, kicking off one high heel shoe and seizing the other in her hand, ready to use the heel of it on her attacker. In response she heard a scream so like her own that she thought for a moment it was an echo. Between the back steps to the choir robing room and the east wall of the church, in the space usually sanctified by thrownout flowers, a picker's child – straight hair held back by a barette, faded cotton dress, arms and legs as brown as a Mexican's – had folded herself into a knot, her face hidden in her hands, her screams now coming regularly, like the squawk of a damaged wheel as it turns.

Without approaching her, Louella called to her, trying to calm her. "Honey," she called. "Little girl." Remembering a name once used in the diner by a picker woman to soothe her child, "Sweet thing," she said. The screams stopped, replaced by sobs, then by silence. The hands loosened until the girl was looking at Louella through her fingers.

"Do I look like I'd hurt you, honey?" Louella asked. "Come on out. You can't cram yourself in that corner. Come on, now. You're making a terrible mess of your dress, honey, you better think what your mother is going to say."

The girl stood up, looking with more alarm at her dress than at Louella.

"That's better," Louella encouraged her. "Come on out now."

The child took several steps away from her hiding place and waited. Louella approached her quickly but gently and put an arm around her bony shoulders. The girl didn't respond with any warmth, but she also didn't shrink away.

"That's better," Louella said. "What are you doing here, honey?"

"I got the cramps," the girl said. "Somebody said they was toilets over here, but I cain't find none. I was stayin' in the cool hopin' they'd go off."

"How do you feel now?" Louella asked.

The girl stood up straight and let her body tell her the answer. She smiled shyly. "Reckon you done scared 'em off," she said.

"Yeah, well they might come back," Louella said, "I've had my experience with them, I can tell you. It's best to sit here in the cool for a while longer." She led the way to the shaded concrete steps while she was saying this, and the two of them sat down.

"What's your name, honey?" Louella asked. "So I can stop calling you honey."

They giggled together, and the child's voice whispered something that Louella didn't catch. When Louella cupped a hand behind her ear, the girl said, "Rae Sue Parkerson, ma'am."

"Rae Sue!" Louella exclaimed. "It's amazing when you think of it, isn't it, that there's so many pretty names in the world and you hear a new one all the time. Rae Sue," she repeated, "that's really beautiful."

"My mamma give it to me 'fore she died," Rae Sue said, "last thing she done."

"Is that what your daddy tells you?" Louella asked.

"No 'm, I remember it, I was there," Rae Sue answered. "They called me Sister for seven years, takin' their time thinkin' up a name they liked for me. Folks like the sound of Rae Sue, guess it was worth the waitin'."

"Well, Rae Sue, I like it, for sure. And my name's Louella."

"Louella," Rae Sue repeated, "we got us a Louella out to the camp, but she don't look a bit like you. She ain't pretty."

"Thank you!" Louella said. "Girls need a compliment like that every once in a while, don't we."

"I don't know," Rae Sue said, "ain't nobody ever told me I was pretty, because I ain't. If they did, I'd know I was talkin' to a liar."

"Whoever told you you weren't pretty?" Louella demanded.

"My daddy," Rae Sue answered.

"I'd like to meet him and give him a piece of my mind," Louella said.

"No you wouldn't," the girl said. "He ain't nice and I ain't pretty. We make us a good fam'ly, I reckon."

"Won't he wonder where you are now?" Louella asked.

"I 'spect he don't even miss me," Rae Sue said. "Hope he don't, leastways. He'll whup me when I get back if he knows I'm gone."

"Even for feeling sick? For cramps?" Louella asked. She had no patience with stern fathers and her voice showed her scorn.

"Female troubles," the child said, "he don't wanta know about 'em, says it's what killed my mamma and he don't wanta worry twicet in his lifetime."

Louella sucked in her breath in outrage and stood up, her quick anger showing in her clenched fists. In the next moment she was sitting again, holding the girl in a protective grip and glaring out at the man-ridden world. She could find no words that would reassure Rae Sue as she felt the girl deserved, as all girls deserved.

"Let's see if we can find him," Louella said. "If he tries to do anything to you, I'll tell him some of the facts of life. Rae Sue, you're my friend, I'll stick up for you."

"You can come he'p me look," Rae Sue said, "but when I find 'im, if you're my friend really, you'll just go 'way afore he sees you. He won't be nice to you. My mamma said he don't know how to behave to a lady, that's his trouble. It's got him in jail oncet."

Louella took the girl by the hand as they walked the few steps to the corner of the church. Thinking about what Rae Sue had said, she glanced to their left and across the street toward the jail. With a wash of cold horror, she saw a file of men in uniform coming out of its tall, studded door, armed with what looked like stubby shotguns and wearing gas masks. She dragged the girl back behind the wall of the church, crouching down and pulling Rae Sue down beside her. All the dread she had felt that day centered now on what she had seen. She felt sick to her stomach, and nerve and words failed her. She had seen riot police in newsreels often enough to recognize them. And she had seen, too, the pictures of what riot police left in their wake.

"What's wrong?" Rae Sue asked. "What's goin' on, Louella? What're them policemen doin'? Is my daddy gonna be all right?"

She scrambled to her feet and struggled to break free while Louella held her back. "I gotta go find 'im," she said, pulling herself away from Louella's protecting hands.

The girl ran across Park Street into the gloom of the trees behind the band shell. Louella ran after her, carrying her shoes in her hands, but the child was much too fast for her. Rae Sue had disappeared by the time Louella got to the band shell. She skirted the crowd, watching the shrubs and bushes for any movement that might indicate Rae Sue's presence. When she got to the last rows of seated people, she turned to cross the open lawn with the intention of making a circuit of the pickers' meeting, but she found that the crowd was so large that her way was blocked by people standing on the grass at the rear to listen. She decided to work her way through them, thinking she might glimpse Rae Sue making her own way through the seats to her father.

As she was squeezing through gaps in the standing crowd, something happened at the front to cause a heave of people toward the rear, and then a counter-wave of movement back toward the front. The disturbance spread quickly through the crowd, and she could see over the heads in front of her men and women jumping up to stand on benches, shouting incoherently and waving their arms. The feel of panic like a wave of heat swept back through the crowd. Women shouted names, answering the shrieks of lost and separated children, and a torrent of them both began to beat against the people in the rear, making for the open lawn of the park. Men running as if into battle tried to push and beat their way forward against this disordered flow of women and children. A woman fell near Louella, her eyes staring wildly, panting like a wild animal, her panic preventing her from regaining her feet so that she fled on all fours until another woman jerked her to her feet and she could begin running to the safety of open ground.

Convinced that her new friend was in terrible danger, Louella followed some men moving forward so that she could try to catch sight of Rae Sue. She glanced at the stage to see what was happening. She could not believe the evidence of her sight. Calvin was up there, and as she watched, astonished by his presence, a small man smashed a wooden chair over his head and shoulder. Lacking any understanding of what was happening, emptied of sense and emotion by what she was witnessing, Louella stood transfixed as Calvin fell. In her vulnerability she found herself pushed aside and then to the ground by the swirl of people coming at her.

As she fought her way to her feet, she saw a riot policeman appear on the opposite side of the benches. He lifted a stubby gun and fired in her direction, and a gush of gray vapor spread between her and Calvin. A scream rose from the entire crowd, and the men turned back from trying to press toward the stage. One of them ran into Louella, knocking her back into a laurel bush, out of the way of what was now a stampede. Women, children and men alike battled each other to get away into the open park. The gas became a solid cloud, thickening and growing behind them. She could feel the scorch of it in her nose and throat. She scrambled through the bushes in the direction of the town, separating herself from the fleeing pickers, before she remembered Calvin lying on the stage. Would he still be there? Should she go back to him?

It hit her then with the force of a blow that he had fought, that he had been at the heart of the fighting, that it was Calvin's tear gas they were trying to escape from. Her eyes streaming tears, she ran through the park to the highway, up the two blocks of the avenue to her apartment, leaving behind but still pursued by the screams of women, the shouts of the men, the terrified cries of the children, and over and under it all the smell of the gas.

He had not known what to expect. It had been his first serious fight, something he had kept from Lee Roy and the sheriff and the police chief. He remembered in slices of vision the children trampling each other to get out of the fighting, and the screaming mothers trampling others' children as they fought to find their own. There had been a painting in a book at school, full of pink women and bronze men, with the men taking away all the babies. It was called "The Slaughter of the Innocents" and Miss Thompson had pointed out how kind the artist had been to record the action before the terrible consequences that were coming, that what he had recorded was the anguish of the women, in its way worse than the blood because it was not going to end until they themselves died, but nevertheless easier to look at. Everything had its price, she said, even innocence. The women in the painting, some of them, looked like Louella. He steered his mind away from her.

Calvin had been hurt in the riot, his riot, when Cappy Petrillo smashed a folding chair over him. This was, however, Petrillo's one effort at defense, and he and his strikers had been defeated. Late that same night in darkness and confusion, when the strikers tried to storm the jail and release Petrillo, Calvin's shoulder had been re-injured, and he had stumbled half-conscious across town to the hospital. He had been sedated and taken to the operating theater, where a bone surgeon wired his separated shoulder back together.

When he could consider such things, twenty-four hours later, Calvin became conscious of an air of infinite sadness, a silence of respect, that cloaked the faces and voices of everyone he saw in the hospital. He insisted on being told why this was, and his nurse explained that, after he had left, the strikers set fire to the jail and had to be dispersed by the shotguns of the riot police. Richie Thomas, Chief Thomas's boy, wanting to see the excitement at the jail, had been in the line of fire when the riot police shot over the heads of the rioters.

"He might just as well have been in front of a firing squad," she said. "I haven't seen Chief Thomas, some of the other girls have, but I don't really know how he's coping with it. All right, I guess, after all, he's a policeman."

While Richie Thomas's death deeply shocked the whole town, Louella and Calvin were cut adrift from their old lives by the tragedy. She sided instinctively with the underdogs, the migrants, without any reason beyond the rightness and honesty of her own rebellion against her constricted, directionless life. Even though she couldn't stomach their filth and ignorance and the places they consented to live, their bad manners and their dirty ankles as she labelled it, they fought in the same army – even though she didn't fight. Her engagement in their cause, whatever it was, was total if only spiritual. Calvin's emergence as the leader of the farmers against her underdogs was to Louella nothing less than a personal betrayal. What they had shared together, in effect her old life, was over, finished, gone.

Calvin had suffered in another way altogether. He had been through his blooding, his baptism of fire, in pursuit, he thought, of a conventional place in Red Branch life, maybe a place of distinction in the eyes of the town. He had entered the conflict as an unknown force, to the town still identifiably one of the secretive, suspect, questionable Whitmores, and to himself a young man convinced that he should never have breathed in a breath of life. He had carried himself before Red Branch as a man of substance and importance when it came to beneficial violence, a hero when one was needed. It had not been something to be enjoyed, but something that had to be done. Having done it, he found he still, like any borrowed hero, had no place in the town. The gulf between celebrity and acceptance yawned as wide as the one that divided a Whitmore from respectability.

Louella put her life in her mother's hands, since she and Calvin between them had destroyed the old one. Her mother, that shadow figure she seldom saw and never listened to, told her to "come to her senses" and get out of Red Branch to a place where she could make a clean start. It wasn't a solution that recommended itself to Louella, but she would have to look for a better idea. Meantime, she voluntarily imprisoned herself at home.

Similarly Calvin, aside from being unable to work because of his disabled arm, found himself cut off from the Whitmores, both the farm and the people, for reasons that he could not explain. He could not articulate what had happened to him. He knew only that he now realized he had been driven out from the Whitmores a long time ago, that he wasn't one of them, that it would be more painful to go back to them than he could tolerate. His attempt to be someone had at least gone that far: He had ceased to be the Whitmores' Calvin.

The mangled, discarded body of Karl, guilty though it made him feel to admit it, had bought Calvin his liberation. That picture of Karl, Uncle Karl, his father Karl, pushed like refuse into a corner of a cluttered, dirty, bloody wreck of a truck, the picture that was one of his hauntings, was to him like the picture of the three people that was on the cover of the *Saturday Evening Post* or *Collier's*, one of them, on the Fourth of July. The man in the middle was carrying the Stars and Stripes, and the man beside him played a little fife, and a boy marched with them beating a drum for their cadence. Or maybe the man was playing the drum and the boy was playing the fife, it didn't matter which, except that Calvin thought of himself as the boy and couldn't conceive of mastering the fife. And yet, there was a gun in the picture somewhere, and someone was bandaged. Never mind. The picture to him was about the boy, who was free. Where he had come from, what place and home and people he had come from didn't matter. He had joined up. He had found his independence. The inbuilt contradiction did not occur to him.

They avoided the subject of the riot the first couple of times Calvin came to see Louella, then they approached it gently but directly, finally after the time for sparring had gone by they argued and shouted at each other. Calvin admitted that he wished it had never happened, that he had been left alone, but he defended his actions, saying that what he had done had been done because he was trying to protect others, like the farmers and their families and even the Whitmores. Her accusation that he had been showing off that day in the park, playing the tin-star hero was the way she put it, sent Calvin into a spasm of anger that was slow to subside, because it was too close to the truth that he could not acknowledge to himself. He didn't himself claim that it was heroic, he insisted, even though other people said it had been and he was proud of that, but it wasn't the way she said, that he was swaggering or showing off.

To make peace, Louella backed down and condemned instead the people who had maneuvered him into his role. But she blamed Calvin for making his strength and his courage available, and on this she would not compromise. She, the movie addict, said he was behaving like one of those cowboy heroes, the man who won the west and all that crap, and everyone knew that was playacting. And what had he thought about her, and his promises to her, when he came riding into Dodge City, helping the police gas those people and frighten them out of their wits? And what about Richie Thomas at the end of it all?

Her charge upset Calvin deeply, more than her previous accusation, mainly because he was not free to show that she had hit on part of the truth. Despite the guilt he felt at being involved in the boy's death, a guilt that raided his dreams like an avenging devil, his promise to the police still bound his tongue. In his heart he knew that this, the tall cowboy in the white hat, the peacemaker whom he scoffed at when he saw it at the Aragon Theater, was the model for his behavior. How could he defend himself against that, and why should he have to? Wasn't that the definition of a hero that Red Branch would recognize? Why was this not good enough for Louella, and why was it not good enough for himself? What was it that made the two of them so different from other people in Red Branch that they lived by, and judged themselves by, another set of rules? He had no answers.

What brought their arguments to an end was the admission that blame was less important than the knowledge that they had been equally damaged, that they had suffered through an experience that would either part them or unite them. They had to decide which it was to be. Calvin drew the obvious lesson. "Do you want to marry me or not?" he began to ask her every day. At issue for him was whether they should go back to their old ways, and grow apart, or whether they should be married and live together in a way that he understood husbands and wives did – though neither had any experience of that in the lives of the people around them.

Louella couldn't answer the question. She longed for the answer to come the way it did in the movies. He would take off her glasses, which was something of a problem since she didn't wear them, and notice that behind her glasses she was beautiful, faithful, loving, and waiting for him to wake up. He would kiss her, and that would be that. Or he would come up on his horse while she was walking away from him, pouting, tired of his ignorance of her love for him, and he would suddenly see that they were meant for each other and lift her up to sit in front of him while they rode off to the nearest justice of the peace. For either script to work, she had to be in love with him. She thought she must be in love with him. The trouble was that she didn't know the answer to the question, "Why do people marry?"

"I read somewhere in a magazine," Louella said, "that before you get married, you ought to sit down with your fiancée and answer a question, and she ought to do the same. Which fiancée is the man? The one with two e's or one?"

"That's a pretty dumb question to make such a big deal about," Calvin said.

"You don't know the question yet," she said.

"You just asked it," he insisted.

"Not that one, you lunk head," she said.

"Why'd you ask me then?" he said.

"Oh dear God," Louella moaned. "Calvin, who cares how many e's there are in fiancée?"

"You do," he said, "or that magazine you read it in. But I'll be damned if I can see why. What's it supposed to tell you if I know the difference? I don't, anyhow."

She threw a pillow at him, then reclaimed it and tried to smother him with it. "You're doing this on purpose, you big, stupid . . . Why don't you be serious?"

"Ask me a serious question," he said.

"Okay," she said, arranging herself on the studio couch for a serious conversation. "The question is this: Why do you want to get married?"

Calvin was taken aback by the question. "You really mean this, don't you?" he said. "Lemme think for a minute."

Louella picked up the pillow again, ready to lob it at him. "You have to think about it? Don't you know why?"

"Well, because I love you, of course," he said, "but I did – love you, I mean – even when we weren't going to get married. I guess I want to get married to you because I want you as my family," he said. "Somebody that belongs to me, and me to her. And all that goes along with that." The answer appeared to please her, and he was relieved.

"I guess I'd say the same," she said.

"I thought you was all for your independence," he teased.

"Not from you," she replied. "No, not any more."

"What's changed, then?" he asked.

She studied his face carefully. "You don't know, do you.

Not even my mother, and she thinks she knows everything about me. Old Gomez is the only person who ever guessed. I could never figure out how he knew."

"What's the mystery?" he asked.

"That I'm scared of being alone," she said. "I've got only one nightmare in this world, and it's that I'll turn around from doing something or looking at something, and there won't be anyone there for me. It's pretty strange. I've read about people who think they're invisible, that something happens to them and no one can see them, and they get passed by, just ignored, by everyone. But with me it's the other way around. I'm here, but no one else is."

"Kind of spooky," he said.

"I don't want to be in with a crowd," she said. "I'm not like other people. There's something different about me. I don't want to make the same mistakes they did. Or the ones they're going to make."

"No one's ever going to think you're one of a crowd, Louella," he said.

She smiled at his gentle joke, but she was not going to be deflected from what she wanted to tell Calvin. "I worked out a long time ago that there was only one way to beat it. You know you're real, and alive, and here, you know what I mean, when someone else is looking at you. Loving you. I used to think that meant anyone who found you attractive, who wanted you. You know what I mean. But it didn't work out. The only way I'll stay alive is if you're there to look at me."

"Hey!" he said. "You're puttin' a whole hell of a lot on me, there."

"That's right," she agreed. "Can you take it?"

"Reckon I can," he said. "People depended on me before, but ain't nobody ever loved me for it up to now."

"Why do you talk Texas when you try to get serious about how you feel?" she asked. "Did you know you do?"

"I suppose it's another part of me that's gotta be taken out and polished up," he said. "We make us quite a pair, Louella," he added.

"Does it worry you?" she asked.

He shook his head. "Everything's new," he said, "and I don't know enough about it to get worried. Leastways not yet."

"Newlyweds," she declared. "We're supposed to feel that way. C'mere, handsome, and give me a great big kiss. Ain't love grand?"

Marriage with Louella was the end of the line for Calvin as a Whitmore. He went to the farm on several false errands, until late in September he found Henry alone, unattended by Jimmy or any of the young men who were vying to take Calvin's place. As simply as he could, Calvin explained that he found it was going to be impossible to come back into the clan. There was going to be, he foresaw, too much of a pull, first one direction and then the other, between what was right for him and what was good for the Whitmores. He was leaving for good.

Henry was not surprised. Unworldly as he was, he had seen it coming. He offered to put together a deal to buy out Calvin's share in the farm, and to present it to the other senior partner, Jimmy, when he had got it worked out. "That way, there won't have to be no meetin'," he said. Calvin was genuinely touched by his considerate thought. When Henry had done his figures, the sum he offered for Calvin's share was big, large enough for Calvin to set himself and Louella up in a small farm of their own.

Calvin didn't return to the Whitmores to say goodbye. It was as though the injury which had taken him away from a working role on the farm had become, while no one was aware of it, terminal.

At ten-thirty sharp, as arranged with Calvin, Lee Roy walked into Nick's Diner. He had given up wearing work clothes.

Now he was dressed in a dark business suit, but as a compromise he wore brown shoes and a Western hat. With his heavy moustache the outfit looked like a disguise. Calvin could see that he was halfway to an evangelist already – the half that was costumed for the part.

Lee Roy had been caught out in the investigation of the riots. It emerged that he had been pushing all along for a confrontation with the strikers that would bring in Cappy Petrillo, to him the notorious proponent of atheistic communism disguising himself as a union leader. He saw it as his Christian duty to entice Petrillo to Red Branch in order to stir up the migrant workers with his communism so that it could be revealed for what it was, an anti-God conspiracy, and so that it could be seen to be defeated in full public view. He had been one step ahead of everybody, so he thought. And he was indeed ahead of everybody except the two policemen who, as Calvin was one of a very few to know, had given Lee Roy full rein to get his confrontation so that they could finish off the threat of organized agricultural labor.

Branded a provoker by the investigating judge, Lee Roy had turned the label to what he considered an advantage, proposing to continue in the guise of an evangelist his crusade against the forces arrayed against God. He was going Back East to train for his ministry, he announced, and he would be back one day. Maybe by then, he thought, the death of Richie Thomas would no longer be held against him by people who didn't understand that there was a price to pay for anything worthwhile.

Now he was trying to sell his farm, and Calvin was looking for one. Calvin had all the time in the world, and Lee Roy wanted to get going on his new life. The result was that the price was right. He brought with him to Nick's a letter that set out the details of the deal, so that Calvin could get his lawyer to draw up the papers.

"There's just this one thing, Lee Roy," Calvin said, "about the house."

Lee Roy nodded and hmm'd, and Calvin looked down the counter and winked at Louella.

"You were tellin' me that Mrs. Stagg was gettin' a man to go through the house with a paint brush so it would be all ready for Louella to get to keepin' house." Lee Roy repeated the nod and hmm. "I don't think you ought to bother with that. Louella wants to do things like the paint and curtains herself. She don't feel she wants to move in and put on another woman's shoes. It's her first home, you know how it is."

What Louella had said was that following a Bible-belter like Mrs. Stagg into that house would be like moving into a funeral home. She would go on condition she could do what she wished with the color scheme, and what she would wish would be anything that Mrs. Stagg would hate.

"Just knock off a few dollars, and I'll give it to Louella to spend. Make her feel better, you know how women are," Calvin said.

The discussion moved to things like crops and records of production, suppliers and contracts and buyers, things and business arrangements that had worked well, and some that hadn't – the unnecessary, polite fussiness of the outgoing and the incoming owners. Calvin suggested he take Lee Roy's letter uptown to his lawyer right away. They got up from the counter stools, slid their coffee money across the counter and were walking to the door before Louella came out of the kitchen and called goodbye. Lee Roy smiled and bobbed his head, but the words of goodbye stayed at his lips.

They stood beside Calvin's truck for a last few words, then shook hands on the deal. Calvin climbed into his truck, and Lee Roy turned as if to go to his sober black Chrysler. He turned back, coming to the passenger side of the truck and climbing in to sit beside Calvin. "There's just one bit of unfinished business, Calvin," he said. He was nervous now, wiping his hand across his moustache and looking beyond Calvin as if the words were printed out there and he could read them off as he said them. "All that strike business," he said.

The subject had not been opened between them unless in a group. Calvin wondered, nevertheless, what more there was to say.

"I appreciated your support, Calvin, you know that. And also, you had the chance to make me look like a fool and you never did. I appreciated that, I want you to know that." Lee Roy's sincerity was making him sweat.

Calvin said, "When was that? When could I make a fool of you?"

"Meeting you and the rest of the boys in that bar," Lee Roy said, "and the cigar store. A man of God, a man of peace, in places of sin and at those riots. Things I shouldn't do, according to my religion."

As always when Lee Roy became holy, Calvin felt the temptation to shock the man. "Hell fire, Lee Roy, that's your business. It don't make me no never-mind."

Lee Roy made a quick stab at the logic of the Texas lingo and gave it up. "No," he insisted, "you could have laughed at me, to my face or behind my back, but you didn't. You were very loyal. You're a sincere friend, and I wanted you to know that I realize that."

"That's all right, Lee Roy," Calvin said. "Don't mention it. I'll get up town now, I think."

"I just wanted to tell you so you knew I appreciated it," Lee Roy said.

"That's okay," Calvin said, "I know now. You could tell me that 'thout puttin' your hand on my leg, now couldn't you, Lee Roy." He tried to say this like a hard man, but it came out gentle and puzzled.

Lee Roy opened the door and got out, all of a businesslike bustle, waved a hand in farewell, and went to his car. Calvin discovered he needed cigarettes and went back inside the diner for some.

His hand was shaking when he took out his change. Louella

noticed it and said, "What's wrong? Has something gone wrong?" She teased him, hanging across the top of the cash register and raising her hand to her round O of a mouth in mock horror. "Has God's good right hand man told you all about me? Are you going to tell me our wedding was all a terrible mistake?"

"No, it's nothin'," Calvin answered, "the deal's going through on the farm and the house. Just a nicotine fit, I guess. Almost run out of cigarettes."

"That's enough to make your hand shake," she said.

"Yeah," he agreed, "mighty close call."

BOOK III

Meridian

The red sun was pasted in the sky like a wafer.

1

First Photo

Louella is sitting in a room of their house, which is new to her and Calvin. The photographer, Calvin, has retreated into another room to take the picture. There is a wide, wooden, decorative arch around the entrance to the room, very handsome, with built in shelves at the sides of it down to the level of wainscoting that continues from the arch all around the inside of the room. A flood of light coming from the right and behind the photographer indicates that the room is contained within the house, intended as a dining room perhaps, communicating to the outside only through another room. It has very little furniture in it, three chairs and a love seat, with a folding screen that can be pulled across the arch to give the room its privacy. A log cabin quilt of glossy squares is thrown over the love seat, and Louella is sitting on it, one hand extended along the back of it and her bare feet drawn up behind her. The room is a boudoir in the old sense of the word, a sulkery, a place where she can be alone. Although the black and white photograph can't show it, the room is painted bright red. Louella reasoned that a red room which functioned as her retreat from the world was the last thing that would ever have won the approval of Mrs. Stagg. The room made the house into her own. She looks confident and happy, though the smile is strained as she attempts to hold her expression for the time exposure.

Second Photo

Calvin and Louella are smoking cigarettes and drinking tea at their table after a dinner at the new Chinese restaurant in Red Branch. Since it is a professional photo, there is a photographically printed label on the bottom of it saying "Forbidden Garden Restaurant, May 14, 1941. Aragon Studios, Red Branch."

The table is in a booth that is decorated on its back wall with dragons and lion dogs snarling from the top of a carved and painted oriental arch. Beneath the arch is a photograph of the great palace of the Forbidden City in Peking. Around this the wall is papered in long strings of lotus flowers, and a Chinese lantern with tassels dangling from it to within a foot of the table hangs overhead. The tassels are so low that it looks as if you would have to peer around them to see the person opposite.

Louella is looking stricken. The occasion for the dinner is to try the new restaurant, and also to celebrate Louella taking over as manager of Nick's Diner. Nick decided that, since his marriage broke up, he wanted to join the Army and help keep the country out of war. He had telephoned that day from the Presidio in San Francisco and told Louella he had passed the physical and would have two or three weeks to take care of things like going to Reno and filing for divorce. The authorities in Nevada will waive the six weeks' residence requirement, he has been told, for men going into the Army. It is definite that she is now in charge of the diner.

Calvin decided they had to celebrate. He took a change of clothes to Louella at the diner, and she arranged for the short order cook to close up at eight sharp. Calvin picked her up at seven, all dolled up and ready to go dancing. She left a float of change in the drawer of the cash register and took the day's takings with her in a brown paper lunch sack. They went to the Rex Hotel for old times' sake and had two drinks, the first one on Old Gomez, who was pleased to see them since they don't get into his bar all that much now that they live twelve miles away.

They left the new Plymouth sedan where it was parked and walked the two blocks to the Forbidden Garden, where they had the special meal for two plus extra duck breast slices in sweet and sour sauce and a slimy green chop suey that neither of them liked. After lychees in syrup so sweet it puckered their mouths, and fortune cookies that prophesied long life, wisdom and praise from their descendants for Louella, and warned Calvin against false philosophers, they had a fresh pot of tea to slake the thirst that had come upon them. Taking advantage of a special attraction for the first week of the new restaurant, they had a picture of themselves taken for only a dollar. At almost the exact moment that the photographer flashed his bulb at them, Louella remembered that she had left the paper sack with between three and four hundred dollars in it lying on the floor beside her bar stool at the Rex Hotel.

What happened next was a shout of "CALVINNNN!!" that brought every head out of the other booths and produced a crash from the kitchen as a plate of bean sprouts hit the floor. The dash back to the Rex Hotel from the restaurant was good for them, Calvin said as they ran, it settled their meal. When they got there, the sack was gone, and Gomez knew nothing about it for at least a minute, when he couldn't keep up the pretence any longer and got the sack out of his cubbyhole and placed it beside Louella on the bar like the gift of the magi. She lay on the bar on her chest and stomach and ordered Calvin to push her on her bottom so that she could slide across, grab Gomez, and give him a kiss. Sliding back, her dress failed to slide with her so that she had to sit on the bar and step off onto a stool while Calvin held it to keep it from revolving. It was like a scene from a sophisticated party in a movie comedy, she thought, and she was wearing some new lacy panties that she wasn't ashamed of so what the hell. It was a memorable occasion.

The look on Calvin's face in the photograph reflects none of Louella's panic, since he didn't know about it until seconds afterwards. What is in his face is something more complex. He is envious of Nick, not for the divorce but for joining the Army.

Third Photo

This is a picture cut out of the *Red Branch Herald* of December 9, 1941. It shows Isao Nakagawa and his family being loaded into a commandeered school bus by Sheriff Atwater. He has the help of a deputy in civilian clothes, who is wearing a plaid lumberjack jacket with a star pinned to it looking shiny and out of place.

It had been a bright day on Sunday the seventh. There was no wind, hardly even a breeze, and the sun showed that it still had power in it by warming the land as if spring was only just around the corner. Calvin walked through the orchards before lunch to satisfy himself that the pruning had been done thoroughly. When he got back to the house, Louella was sitting on the porch in the sun, bundled up in a coat that she normally wore only for shopping trips. She had been frightened by what she heard on the radio and had come outside to wait for him. The program of hymns and sacred melodies that she listened to late on Sunday mornings had been interrupted several times to announce the news of a Japanese sneak attack on Pearl Harbor. When Calvin took her inside to listen to the news, the announcers followed each other with worse and worse accounts of what had happened. The Pacific fleet was lost, Army defenses had been bombed out of commission, casualties would be very high.

They had a sandwich and some alphabet soup while they waited for the broadcast from back east that had been announced. When it came, even though it was a call to war, it was confusing. It was the surprise of the attack, or the time of day, or the bright, inviting day itself, or the fact that it was a Sunday. In spite of the grave voices and repeated statements about how shocked people were, the evidence of their senses and intuitions told them it was a weekend, when serious things like the start of wars didn't happen. People were away, for one thing. It wasn't clear if President Roosevelt was in Hyde Park or Washington. He said things that should have been shouted, but his voice had as much worry as outrage in it, as if he couldn't offer a definitive way to respond beyond this temporary ritual of words.

Calvin and Louella got out the car and drove into Red Branch to be near other people and try to calm their confused thoughts. Mrs. Rossi was in tears, because she was afraid the Japanese attack would be used to declare war on her family in Italy – fears which came true the following day. Between Fifth and Sixth Streets a gang of boys on bicycles had gathered on Greenfield Avenue in order to imitate aerial dogfights and ra-ta-tat the Japs out of the sky. War as they understood it was already real to them, and they liked it very much. Tom Potter had opened the cigar store and brought a radio from home, and the place was packed with smoking, swearing, furious men who couldn't wait to get their hands on dirty, sneaking little yellow Jap bastards, and who knew, to their frustration, that they were too old to be enlisted in anyone's army. "If only I was young enough I'd show them" rose from the men and hung over them like a malediction. The Rex Hotel bar was crowded also but comparatively subdued. The mix of men and women included more young people than Tom Potter's customers, those who would logically be drafted into a branch of service, and the wives and girlfriends they would leave. Their mood was somber, befitting their newly clouded future. They talked in quiet voices, their attention, even their eyes, directed to the little black bakelite radio on its shelf above the Wurlitzer.

Gomez said, shaking his head slowly, "A few hours and we got war. We lose peace" – he snapped his fingers after drying them on the bar towel – "just like that. Where is the leaders?"

Mike at the barber shop, Nick's brother, had a telephone call at lunch the following day, around the time that President Roosevelt was asking Congress to declare war. The call was from Nick's wife, whom Nick had been unable to divorce in under six weeks after all. She had received a telegram that Nick had been killed in the bombing of Scofield Barracks in Honolulu. She also phoned Louella at the diner, asking her to let the regular customers know and to keep the place going because she and Nick's children would need the money now. He was the first casualty of the war in Red Branch.

The next casualties came the following day. Sheriff Atwater had instructions during the night to round up all Japanese and take them to Placid City, where buses or trains would take them to a reception center. They were going to be interned as enemy aliens. By morning he had organized a school bus to pick up the Watanabe family from their fresh fruit and vegetable market south of town, and then the Nakagawa family from their truck farm west of town, next to Calvin's farm. A photographer and reporter went along to record the event. The sheriff refused to answer the question "Why?" put to him by the Japanese families, but the reporter was able to tell them that they were suspected of preparing to support Japanese submarine crews that were going to land saboteurs on the coast any day. People were saying, he told them, that all the Japanese had short wave radios that could reach enemy U-boat commanders, and things like direction beacons were installed in their chimneys to guide aircraft to targets. The Government was calling them Nisei, which meant they were Japanese who had been born in the United States, not really Americans.

Patsy Watanabe and Joe Nakagawa, both of whom had been born and raised in Red Branch, protested that they couldn't read Japanese and were American citizens, not aliens. Joe pointed out that they didn't have either a short wave radio or a chimney. They were told to be quiet and go along with their parents. In Placid City the families were put on Greyhound buses and driven down south to Santa Anita Racetrack, which had been turned into a temporary concentration camp. In a few weeks the Watanabes were sent to a reopened, deserted Army camp on the edge of the desert east of Los Angeles, and the Nakagawas were sent to a similar camp on the cold, arid plain in the center of the State of Washington.

Calvin had a visit the same day from an official of an agency of the Government that was so new it still hadn't a name. Its business was to make sure there was no interruption to agricultural production while the armed forces buildup got underway. The official said that the Nakagawa truck farm was going to be put in Calvin's management and control, as if he had leased it. The entire property was his. He implied that Calvin would not be allowed to join the armed forces, even if he wanted to. His wartime job was farming.

Fourth Photo

This is a head and shoulders picture of Calvin taken when he was told he had permission to see the Nakagawas at their internment camp. He had the picture taken at the Aragon Studios in the morning and in the afternoon handed a print of it to the sheriff to be verified and made into an identity document, just in case there was any trouble in being allowed into the camp. It was the best he could do, because he didn't have a birth certificate or any other personal document, except his driver's license.

He drove north, taking two days to make the unfamiliar journey, growing used to mountains and forests and stretches of coastline until he almost stopped feeling hemmed in by scenery and overwhelmed by variations of greenness. He grumbled to himself that he'd seen enough God damn trees to last a lifetime and he still had the return trip to do. He found the internment camp, a collection of long, wooden buildings with a high, wire fence around it. The buildings were nothing but bunk houses, they might have been copies of the one from his childhood on the old farm. The old attitude of Whitmore submission came upon him so strongly at the sight of them that he could hardly bring himself to request to see Mr. Nakagawa, and when the Army commandant said he would have to come back tomorrow, he turned and went without question or protest.

It was Joe Nakagawa who came to the reception hut to see Calvin. They shook hands awkwardly. Isao Nakagawa couldn't see anyone. He sat in silence throughout the day, Joe said, talking only to his wife, who washed him and rubbed his legs and treated him like the child he had become. He was to die later that year, for no other reason except that he had given up living. Calvin told Joe what had taken place with regard to the farm. Joe wasn't interested, giving some advice and coming to an agreement on a lease.

The reception room was cold and depressing, with yellowish wooden chairs and a few old magazines on a brown, steel table. The curtains were tan monk's cloth, so skimpy that they barely covered the window glass. Calvin got permission for the two of them to walk together on the recreation field, a bare piece of ground with a baseball diamond and a set of speedball goalposts. Joe was short and thin with a contrastingly large, round head. His light frame seemed to be made of tight elastic. He had the bandy legs of the Japanese worker, seeming to trot instead of walk everywhere. His tight arms barely swung as he moved. Calvin looked across his head from his height, noticing with surprise that this man, two years younger than himself, was balding at the crown and going gray before his time.

Joe was interested only in hearing what the people of Red Branch said about his family. Did they protest to the Government? Did they try to get the family released from the camp and brought back? Did the children at Jurgens School miss his younger brother and two sisters enough to write the Governor or the President to have their schoolmates released? With each of his questions he implied that he knew the answer, and that it was as if the Nakagawas had no longer a place there in what had been their home. When Calvin had to leave they shook hands like stoical men do, and Joe's eyes vanished into the slits of his eyes as he screwed them up to smile, but his mouth refused to turn up and remained a thin, tight, compressed line of grief.

The drive back south gave Calvin time to sort out the Nakagawas' quandary in his mind. Isao and Joe were casualties of the new war as much as Nick was, he reasoned. It was the Japanese warlords who were responsible, he could see that, starting the war in such a way that the Nakagawas were interned . But what little he knew about history taught him that we don't trace responsibility back to the real criminals very often. Instead of the man who pays him, we hang the hired man for accepting the money. The Nakagawas were fenced off from the rest of Americans in a cold and forbidding concentration camp, not quite like criminals, condemned to a bleak future that looked to be stretching out for years in front of them, for the reason that they couldn't be trusted to refuse the money like good Americans. Where once they had been neighbors, they were now enemies.

He had known the Nakagawas for several years, or at least he had seen them from time to time, but now that they were Japs, little yellow men who looked more brown or tan than yellow, he looked at them differently. Their black eyes and their straight black hair, their stature, their ability to be still and loud at the same time – they were different. They were not to be understood without hard study. You wouldn't deal with them casually, or make a bargain without long thought.

According to the normal rules, they could not be trusted. They would look at things in a different way, through a special set of eyes with special references to past experiences that could not be shared. They had secrets, too, and people with secrets were possibly dangerous, you couldn't really tell. They had all the disadvantages of Whitmores, in addition to looking and behaving like foreigners. And knowing what he did about Whitmores, it wasn't difficult for Calvin to distrust and even detest Japs.

On the other hand, he found it difficult to feel that way about Joe Nakagawa, impossible even. Joe was an identifiable individual, a known quantity. Or he had been, when he was in school. Now that he was removed from there, he was something or someone different, but it was hard to say what. The little man was a victim, a casualty. Such persons were sent to places to recuperate, to be restored. That wasn't the function of a concentration camp. Therefore, the stain or taint of which he was a victim, for which he was being isolated, was acquired from the camp, from his new identification as a Jap. Joe Nakagawa, Calvin realized, was lost now, and he would not recover.

The day after his return from Washington, he went to the Nakagawa truck farm. Because of the time of year, very little was in the ground. The small squares and oblongs, hemmed together by a bordering ditch and path that ran around each small unit, looked like a playground awaiting its influx of children. The ones with blue shirts would play there, and the yellows here, and the reds over beyond them. Then he realized that the pattern was not a playground, it was an oriental rice field divided into paddies. The pictures that he had seen in books, of stooped figures under conical straw hats wading through muddy, green water, were so easily transferred to this scene before his eyes that he could almost see the figures in their shorts and gathered up skirts making their way from the house. It would all have to change. Not even Mexicans would do that kind of work.

He walked back to the packing shed. It was a long, rickety shed open along one side. Down its center from end to end a concrete sluice carried a clear, cold stream of water for washing the vegetables before grading them, then washing them again when they were sorted, then again when they were bundled and ready to be packed into crates. He remembered his one or two visits here, the half dozen people busy and unwilling to stop to greet a visitor, smiling and courteous but with something else on their minds. Like the Jap ambassadors on December the seventh, courteous, polite, diplomatically correct, while the bombs fell on Pearl Harbor. He found the pipe that carried the artesian well water to the sluice and pulled it aside so that the water flowed directly to the outfall. He would have the shed torn down, he decided.

Fifth Photo

At the Fourth of July picnic, 1942, with all the farmhands. The tables are set up in the orchard nearest the house, the coolest place they could think of, and close enough to the house that the food could stay in there out of the heat until it was wanted. Mrs. Rossi is sitting next to Louella as their special guest. Her son is in the Army now, having enlisted to show that he and his mother were good, patriotic Americans. He would be killed early in 1945 in the Italian campaign.

Sixth Photo

At the Fourth of July picnic, 1943. The couple sitting next to Calvin and Louella are Herman Sanger and his girlfriend, Barbara Ferguson. The four of them have become best friends. It is a new experience for Calvin and Louella, being two people who did not have the kind of youth that allowed for close friends. Herman has a heart murmur that keeps him from being drafted. He is classified 4F and, with the exception of a physical every six months, is no longer of interest to the Selective Service Board. His disability is so slight that he can work, as he puts it, like a Jap. He is helping Calvin run the Nakagawa land; later on in the year he will take over the management of that altogether, leaving Calvin to concentrate on his own farm and the new land he is bringing into production west of Stagg's original farm.

Barbara, like Louella, is a businesswoman in Red Branch. She took over a car and truck tire distribution agency when her father went to Richmond to work in the Kaiser Shipyards. With tires rationed, people put their name on a list and got a ration priority, and when a tire came in that was the size they wanted, if they had a high enough priority, they got it. It was an uncomplicated job, she had thought, her only problem being to recover customers who had been lost because of her father's alcoholic tantrums. He took against people when he had had too much to drink and picked fights with them for no reason. What she learned as she made sense of the books and accounts was that he had been funding his drinking by illegal dealing in rationed truck tires. When she confronted them, she was told by the men who had been benefitting from this that they had no intention of letting it stop. As they put it, they had the goods on her dad, and if she put them out of business, her father would do his war work in jail. She considered giving up the whole tire business, and talked to Louella about doing that. Lately, however, she had gone quiet about it, and Louella and Calvin assumed that she was now as deeply involved in the racket as her father had been, and they were trying hard to ask no questions and invite no confidences.

Herman is about Calvin's height and build, possibly a little bit heavier, but has coal black hair. He is a pleasant, assured, but modest man, who likes to flash a toothpaste smile that looks as if it has been practiced while he is shaving. Barbara is more than his match. She is very tall, almost as tall as Calvin and Herman, with large, haughty, blue eyes. She has long, wavy, brown hair and dresses in men's clothes, usually blue workshirts and jeans. She strides about like a man, too, and when she stands quietly smoking a cigarette, she puts one hand in a front pocket of her jeans like one of the boys. But she is no boy. Her body and her eyes declare that she can have any man she wants in the whole wide world.

In this photograph Louella has not changed in any way. Having looked as if she was twenty when she was fifteen, her age has now caught up to her appearance without altering her. Calvin, on the other hand, looks older, more than the year if you compare the two pictures of the Fourth of July picnics. He is older in the face by virtue of a few lines; other men would no longer call him a boy, or address him as son. It is however more than that. He looks restless, and he looks baffled by his disquiet.

2

October 1942

Fall in the valley is not a unique season in terms of weather. The warmth gradually turns itself down as if on an exaggeratedly gentle temperature control, and the approach to winter in consequence lacks the traditional melancholy of the dying of the sun's light. Melancholy is the last adjective that might be applied to the light. The shortening days end in a succession of theatrical sunsets, each one more technicolored than the previous one, saturating the huge evening sky. A pedant would explain that this is because of the buildup of dust particles in the air as the prevailing wind weakens with the decline in the sun's heat. A fantasist would say that it is a competition among celestial designers of light and color displays. A resident would say that everything being colored orange, or magenta, or red, or bright pink can be unsettling, prompting thoughts of earthquake weather and the day the world ended. There is something too fierce about these sunsets, and they can be frightening and depressing.

"It's scary," Louella said. "Calvin, tell it to stop."

He laughed and pulled down the window shades on a view

of the peach orchard colored vivid purple and shadowed in violet.

Louella had been pacing between the kitchen and the living room, putting a supper together as if she hadn't left the diner at four o'clock, carrying things from one place to the other only partially to be carrying, as much to be checking on her customer's welfare. Calvin had some folders of letters and bills open on the floor. He leaned forward from his easy chair and read them from afar, expecting them to make more sense that way than close up. She stood behind him now.

"You'll have to give up and get somebody to help you," she said.

"I'd get somebody if I could find him," Calvin said.

"You're not looking for anyone very hard," she replied.

"You don't know the kind of people there is to pick from," he said.

He slid the papers together and put them back into their folders. "I just can't get the Nakagawa place to pay for itself," he said. "We've had it almost a year, and it's still not workin' out. It don't fit in with the rest of the land."

"It's not meant to," she said. "It's theirs, not ours."

"Jesus, Louella, don't start that argument again," he groaned, "I'm not strong enough tonight." He picked up the folders and put them on an end table, then peeked around one of the drawn window shades to see what progress the sunset had made. "The argument's bad enough. Makin' up afterwards is enough to kill a man."

She didn't like their lovemaking being disparaged. "We're getting on each other's nerves," she declared. The fruit dish she was at that moment placing in the center of the dining table went down with an unnecessary thump, and Calvin looked at her to see if something more was coming. She turned back to the kitchen, however, and closed the door after herself. He heard the clang of a frying pan and shortly afterwards smelled meat cooking.

A radio program of dance music by Artie Shaw from an

Army camp somewhere killed conversation during the meal. Afterwards, when a simulated broadcast of a football game came on, they switched the radio off.

"How's the new girl workin' out for you?" he asked. "You think she'll be okay?" He snorted, "You think this one 'll stay for a while?"

"She's expecting," Louella said. "She'll do a good job for about six months. She's scared. Husband's in the Navy and it's her first baby. She needs the money."

"Could she run things for a few days?" he asked.

"I guess so," she replied. "Maybe she could."

"We need a week off, Louella," Calvin said. "They tell me down at the town that there's next to no deer hunting this year, and there's plenty of cabins for rent up in the mountains."

"I won't go near any deer hunters, you know that," she said. "How about the snow?" she asked.

"None to speak of yet," he said. "One thing to say for the war, the weather forecasters are one hell of a lot better than they used to be. We'd know a long time ahead if there was a storm coming, in plenty of time to get back down to the valley."

The idea didn't please or displease her, in keeping with her mood.

Calvin read the situation and said, "I'll find out about a good place. You see what you think about it."

He switched the radio back on and found a music program. They read for a while. Louella put her magazine down and said, "You ever been up in the mountains? The high ones?"

"Nope," he answered. "Not very high."

The subject of the place with the carved angel was a closed one. He had never told her about it. Besides, that hadn't really been the high mountains. The new road carried cars past a sign marking three thousand feet in altitude in one long, straight grade, in a single effort going above the range of mountains that Jimmy Whitmore had tried to make into an eldorado.

"Me neither," she said. She opened the magazine again. "What do you wear in the mountains?" she said, leafing to the fashion pages. He knew they were going.

He took the old pickup truck for the trip, being unsure about the roads. They drove east through the stubbled wheat fields on a straight, undulating road until they met the highway into the mountains that came up from the south. The valley dropped away from them in shades of tan as they climbed the grade. After an hour or more the highway turned toward the genuine mountains at last and bent its way into deep clefts between ridges of forested land. Their route took them off the highway then, across a small river bridge, and they began a long climb along a narrow, twisting, gravel road. They lost the oak trees of the lower mountains and entered stands of pine of different kinds, with red barked cedars growing among them on the more open slopes and black firs in the depths of the thicker woods. Chokecherry bushes, almost nude of leaves, crowded the edges of the road where springs leaked out. A dog coyote stared at them from a thicket of red berried gooseberry bushes, a skunk stopped their progress as it claimed the roadway at one point, and gentle deer walked nervously on their impossibly delicate legs to safety in the dense forests. With every mile Louella came alive with wonder, and Calvin warmed with pleasure at her quickening interest.

She was a strange being. A creature of the car culture, she had never lived in a family that possessed a car. Her chosen Hollywood ethos prescribed a car, especially for someone who had gone further and chosen for herself, to adopt whenever it suited her, the role of the starlet with the heart of gold. She had perfected the gestures of the sort of blond who lived for the moment she could wrap a chiffon scarf around her neck, get in the convertible and, as the tall, dark man drove her at maniac speed along a Riviera coastline, throw back her head and laugh while the wind whipped orgiastically through her hair. (In the next shot, perfectly coiffed, she sips champagne on the terrace of the casino.) And yet Louella had created herself in a universe that was roughly circular and a mile in diameter, walking distance from the high school to the Aragon Theater in one direction, and the length of the walk from the library to Nick's Diner in the other. The odd trip to Placid City to shop for clothes at Gottschalk's only proved that Greyhound buses actually went to the places printed on the front of them. Cars, vehicles that moved a person to another setting, weren't to the young Louella imaginative devices. Now suddenly Mrs. Louella Whitmore, she was the star of her own movie, and her imagination was trailing in the wake of reality.

For Calvin Louella's wonder at the beauty around her was cathartic. He had no memory of his time in the mountains. All his memory of those summer days narrowed down to Annie Evelyn. He worked hard to keep them green in his mind. She was, until Louella, the only person who had ever loved him. His devotion to her was not dented by knowing that she shared only half his blood with him. And the mountains had been the place where he had left her.

The road came out of the forest to string itself along the flank of a mountain. Nothing but trees and a few boulders lay between it and the bottom of a canyon well over a thousand feet below. Louella shrank from her seat toward Calvin's side at first, then gradually eased back so that she could look down into the gorge. As they climbed, the ridge opposite became topped with successive domes of granite, and the floor of the canyon could be seen in glimpses through treetops to be steps of waterfalls carrying a river down from a high valley ahead of them. When they got to it, where the mountain and the ridge squeezed almost together to produce this dished valley, the river ran tamely through glittering sand and silver rocks and stands of white trunked aspen trees with golden leaves. A mile on, the valley narrowed and twisted before opening out to reveal a small settlement of wooden cabins. The first of the high mountains rose like a monarch above them, and the tall, symmetrical pine trees of what remained of a virgin forest spread their lace branches among them.

"I never want to leave here," Louella said.

Their cabin was simple and clean. Once they had built a fire in the huge, black, iron stove, it was warm and comfortable. The sunlight was close, tangled in the tops of the giant trees, and the breeze whispered in a lisping, smoky treble as it lifted and swung the long pine limbs. Through the trees the mountain top, serene and without favor, Buddha among its neighbors, signalled the state of the day like a massive weathervane, clouds streaming away from it to show the wind's direction and speed, the granite slabs near its summit shining and coloring as the sun passed through the sky. A single patch of snow, bordered with stunted trees at its lower edge, lay over part of the mountain's top like a scarf that was in danger of blowing off. As evening came on it changed to pale yellow, then gold, then pink, finally lavender, and then scarf and mountain disappeared.

Into their black, untroubled sleep a mountain lion's scream intruded from somewhere above them, waking Calvin and causing Louella to stir. He got up and looked out on a scene scribed in black lines on polished steel. The moonlight seemed not to have a single source but instead streamed down from above as if a floodgate of light had been opened. He walked out onto the porch and looked through the trees at the mountain. Moonlight had restored the whiteness of its scarf of snow. He woke Louella, and they sat on the front steps wrapped in thick comforters off the spare bed, taking in the beauty of the night.

In the morning after breakfast they walked through the silent, untenanted cabins to the settlement's single store. It sat in the open, high up on wooden steps with a boarded skirt around it. Behind the boards the winter's dry wood was stacked against the day, which would come in a month or so, when snow would close the valley. A note on the door at the top of the steps said that fall opening hours were lunchtime and late afternoon only. It wasn't yet ten o'clock. They walked on toward the river, as long as they had come that far, and had gone about a hundred yards when a voice called from behind them. They turned to see a dark haired young man standing on the store's porch calling and waving to them.

When they had returned to within talking distance, the man said, "That sign's for the deer hunters. I never lock the door on people from camp, if I'm around someplace." They joined him on the porch steps. "You're the people staying up at Skytrees, aren't you? I'm Herman Sanger," he said. "I'm holding the fort for the Tolsons. They've gone down the hill already." He laughed at their expressions of confusion. "Clive and Dolly Tolson own this store, and some of the cabins in the camp, and they've gone down to the valley for the winter. Most years there's already snow by now."

"What about you?" Calvin asked. "You don't try to stay up here for the winter do you? I heard tell the road's blocked for four months or more."

"I'll get out as soon as it threatens to start snowing," he answered. "I'm a mountain man. I'll stay 'til the last dog is hung."

"That's Texas talk," Calvin said. "Where'd you learn to say that?"

Herman shrugged. "It's Indian talk, too. I'm a quarter breed."

Louella asked, "From these mountains?"

"Yeah," he said, "not far away. I was born in Bear Flats, little one-horse town you came through on the highway. We owned these mountains once."

"Do you ever get mad because they were stolen from you?" she asked.

He laughed and smiled a white man's toothy smile. "Naw," he said, "my granddad would have given them away, if anybody had asked. Maybe he did and he just forgot."

"He couldn't have!" She laughed. "You're making it up."

Herman was ready to talk. He picked up his cue with another smile. "He could, though, he really could. For the last twenty years of his life he did nothing but sit on the porch of the general store in Bear Flats with one of those Indian hats flat on his head and a blanket from Sears and Roebuck wrapped around him. People would stop and take his picture, and he'd pull out a card and sign it for them and charge them fifty cents a snapshot. He made his beer money that way. Old Benjamin Sanger, he's still somebody they talk about there. He would've sold anybody anything, not meaning it, of course, any more than any Indian does."

He invited them in, and they walked through the large store to an equally large kitchen that ran along the whole width of the building. They got acquainted over mugs of very strong, bitter coffee from a granite colored enamel pot kept permanently hot on the back of the big kitchen range.

"Funny thing about my grandfather," Herman said. "Half the time he was sitting there on that porch, he was making up dumb Indian names to write on those little cards. Two Ponies, and Red Arrow, and Bear Tracker and all that stuff. I think he even called himself Straight Arrow, but that was a little too phony to be true and he dropped it. He used to get books out of the schoolteacher to give him ideas for more. Old cowboys and Indians books."

He told them the history of the camp. These mountains were discovered early, he said, but when no gold was found this high up, it meant they were left alone until the valley towns were built out of Sierra timber. The cabins were all that was left of a lumber company that boomed and busted in cycle with California real estate. Sugarpine Camp had turned into a nice, small, family resort, until now the war made it a question if it would be able to keep going.

"People haven't got the gas rations to run up and down like they used to," Herman said.

Replying to the unasked question, Calvin said, "I farm on

the west side of Red Branch. Reckon the Government owes me the gas for a little vacation. I work hard for 'em."

Herman said, "I go to Red Branch every once in a while. You wouldn't see me though, I go in and out as quick as I can. I have to report for a physical for the draft board. I'm 4F. Got a heart murmur. Never knew it until I took my physical for the draft. I've been healthy all my life."

Calvin said, "People think I'm 4F too, because I'm not in the service. They say some pretty bad things, behind your back but so's you can hear. Until I tell 'em. Do they do that to you?"

"I don't have much to do with people," Herman said. "It's the Indian in me," he added, and the men laughed.

Louella was not used to keeping silent while men talked across her. That wasn't the way Calvin treated her. She felt deliberately ignored by this man with his black shirt and black hair and flashy smile, somehow she was in his way.

"How about showing us your mountains, Chief?" she said. "Did we bring any wampum with us, Calvin? I know we brought firewater."

Calvin had not known Louella tease so close to the bone before. Maybe it was the diner, he thought. Maybe that was the way she had learned to deal with the men there. Or maybe it was something to do with Herman that he hadn't seen.

Herman looked at her very hard before answering. "If you can take it," he said, "sure, I'll show you. I don't have to hang around here waiting for customers."

The river was named Sand Creek, a strange name for it, Calvin said, since it ran over rock most of the time. The three of them hiked up it – walking Indian file as Herman observed, making Louella frown and look away – along a narrow trail that clung to the edge of the stream or took them over smooth rock faces, before looping back to Sugarpine Camp. Another hike took them west to where the ridge peaked and a succession of deep canyons made steps of the mountains down to the gray haze of the foothills miles and miles away. One day they walked along an abandoned railroad line that had been part of the logging operations – the rails were ripped up and sold to the Japs for scrap before the war, Herman told them – until they got to the foot of a high stone ridge, where Herman showed them caves that the hibernating animals would soon be using. A fault in its rock cap made a narrow passage, allowing them to climb up to a wide, long plateau of granite that rose gently to a blunt peak.

On its bleak summit, beside a pocked outcrop of rock, Herman scraped around in a pit carved by the wind and filled with the sand of the decomposing stone, to show them fragments of flint left by the Indians. "They came up to places like this, where they would have to carry everything with them, to chip arrowheads. I don't understand it," he said. "You see, look at the stone, there's no burn mark, there's no evidence they built a fire and pitched camp here, and they couldn't have had a camp up here anyway because there's no water. I wonder about it a lot. I find places like this and I think to myself, there's something to all this stuff about magic after all. You know, what they called medicine. I can understand it. You had to have good medicine on an arrowhead if it was going to kill an animal. You know the sort of thing I mean, animals have spirits, and places where animals were hunted have spirits, all that sort of stuff, and it would take magic to defeat the spirits. I can believe that. They came up here, places like this, for their magic. And for us it's all gone. That's what I don't understand. Not the need for magic. The fact that it's gone, that's the mystery." Embarrassed by his speech, he giggled and said, "Well, for me, anyway."

Herman came to their cabin to have a cup of coffee with them that first night, and after that he came every night to eat supper with them.

"Don't you get lonely up here?" Louella asked. "I sure would."

"Yeah," Herman answered, "I do, no doubt about it. A lot of the people who used to come up every summer didn't come up this year. I didn't have much to do."

Calvin thought possibly Herman had misunderstood the question, but he chose not to rephrase it. Instead he asked, "What do you usually do, then?"

"Everything," Herman replied. "I'm kind of the camp handyman. Chop wood, fix the plumbing, lay water pipes, work in the store. Whatever needs doing. Mainly I fix up cabins after the winter and open them up for people before they come for the summer."

"You been doing that year after year? Is that interesting?" Louella asked.

"Not very," he admitted. "It keeps me here in the mountains though."

"Do you love the mountains that much?" she persisted.

He hesitated before answering. "Yeah. And I need them," he said.

When they had been there for five days, they decided to stay more than the week that had been arranged, if it could be done. They drove down the road they had taken to get to Sugarpine Camp until they found a turn for a Forest Service station a few miles to the north. There, the ranger let them use the Service telephone to call collect to the diner. The new girl, Florence Biles, said things were going fine and they could stay as long as they liked, and she would phone Calvin's foreman to tell him about the change in plans. The ranger said the weather forecast was still clear, with no snow in sight. They drove back to the camp and stopped at the store. Herman was loading some boxes into his covered pickup as they got there.

"Just when we decide to stay, you decide to pull out," Calvin said.

Herman laughed and flashed his smile. "No, nothing like that, Calvin," he said. "You're going to stay a few days more, huh? I have to make the last run to the wholesaler's, to take back goods that we can't keep and lay in a few things just in case I got caught by the snow. I'll get supplies for you too. I need some things, as long as I'm still here." He looked at the clear, bright sky, as if doubting that snow could ever fall from it.

"Still waiting for that last dog to be hung," Calvin said.

Louella chimed in, "Don't say that, you guys. It's awful."

"It's only Indian talk, Louella," Herman said. She stuck out her tongue at him. She had apologized once, she wasn't going to do it again.

"Where do you go?" Calvin asked. "Where's the wholesaler?"

"Place called Gold Creek," Herman said. "It's the only one around this part of the mountains. I'll stay overnight, be back tomorrow."

Something about Gold Creek pinged in Calvin's memory and he frowned.

"I'll leave you the key to the store," Herman said, "don't worry, you won't go hungry while I'm gone."

"We can manage 'til you get back," Louella said. "Bring some fresh meat and bacon if you can, and milk. We're okay for butter. Oh, and bread, too, please."

"That's on my list," Herman said. He looked at Calvin, who was still frowning. "I was going to leave you the key up at your cabin."

"I didn't figure you were runnin' out on us, Herman," Calvin said, "don't worry about it. I just thought of something, that's all. Everything's fine. We'll see you tomorrow. Come for supper?"

"Yeah," Louella added, "we'll put a plate on the table for you."

Herman looked embarrassed. "Don't count on me," he said.

Shortly after noon the following day, while they were hiking south out of the valley along Sand Creek, Louella heard a car engine on the road that led to camp. It was enough of a novelty that she called to Calvin and the two of them stopped to look at the place where they would see the vehicle, where the road came nearest the creek. A dark green Forest Service truck came slowly into their view. It pulled to a stop after it had passed from their sight, and they could hear the whine of its gears as the driver reversed. He stopped and waved to them, then got out and clambered down the rocks that edged the roadbed to come to them. It was the same ranger they had met when they made their telephone call.

"I didn't think I'd be seeing you again, Mrs. Whitmore, Mr. Whitmore," he said. He had taken off his ranger's hat as he approached, and now he bobbed his head in a show of courtesy.

"We're on a little hike," Louella said.

"I mean, I was looking for you," the ranger said. "Had a message for you."

"I knew this was too good to last. Was it from a woman named Florence Biles?" Louella asked. "Does she need me to come back?"

"No, it's for Mr. Whitmore," he said, "from the deputy sheriff at Gold Creek. Herman Sanger's had an accident, and he told the deputy that he thought you could help him out. I wrote it all down. His truck's off the road eleven miles back down the road. He needs you to meet him there at three o'clock. He'll be back to his truck by then. I'm supposed to phone Gold Creek if you can't make it."

He handed Calvin the message on a piece of official memo paper. Calvin glanced at it and looked at Louella. "Guess we better go," he said.

"Sure," she answered.

"I don't know what I can do," Calvin said. "We'll go along and see."

The ranger smiled and put his hat back on, then touched it at the front as he bobbed his head to Louella. "Still no sign of snow," he said as he moved away.

They were ten minutes late getting to the scene of the accident. A small stack of boxes and packages was sitting on the side of the road, the only things to be seen against the backdrop of Sand Creek Canyon that plunged away beneath them. Calvin pulled up and stopped just past them. He held Louella's arm as they stood on the roadside and looked down into the canyon, which was so deep and its slope so steep that even Calvin felt dizzy. Herman's truck was on its side about forty feet below the road, all its wheels in view, apparently held by a fortuitous rock. Herman himself was struggling up the incline with a cloth bag.

"Herman!" Louella shouted. She put her hand to her mouth in horror. "Are you all right?"

"What the hell happened?" Calvin called. His voice echoed through the silent miles of canyon.

"Ran off the road," Herman answered. He advanced several feet before saying any more. "It was my own fault." He was puffing from the effort of scrambling up the canyon side. "This is the last of it," he called. "There's nothing that'll break. I'll throw it to you."

He scraped with his feet until he had a firm foothold, then whirled the bag around his head and let it go. It sailed through the air, just making it to safety at the edge of the road. Louella retrieved it as if pulling something precious away from a terrible trap.

"You want me to come and give you a hand?" Calvin shouted, and the echo again taunted him with his own voice.

"No," Herman answered, "I'm finished now." He advanced a few more feet through the dry bear brush. "I need you to carry this stuff to the camp, that's all."

"Sure, we can do that," Calvin said.

Herman didn't waste any more breath on conversation. He dug his feet and hands into the soil and undergrowth and worked his way up to the road. Once there, he sat down on the edge of it, facing down over the abyss, puffing and getting his breath back. When he felt able to talk, he turned to them and said, "Ran off the road. My own fault. Must have been looking at the view, or something."

The whites of his eyes were yellowish and disfigured by red veins like scratches. His breath came heavily, stinking of whisky and vomit. He saw that Calvin understood, and he put his face in his hands and rubbed it violently.

Stacked on the side of the road and directly above the truck, a pile of rocks had been heaped up by a road crew during the summer, clearing a slide that had come down the bank onto the road. The crew hadn't come back to take the rock pile away. Herman had missed it by a few yards when he had gone over the bank. Now he sat beside it and rested an arm on the rocks, looking down at his wrecked truck below.

Calvin turned away. He didn't know Herman well enough to make any useful comment, and it wasn't his place to chide him about driving drunk on mountain roads that seemed made more for goats than cars. He tugged Louella by the sleeve, and the two of them began to move the boxes for the store to the back of Calvin's truck. When they had finished this, and Calvin had climbed into the back of the truck to tie down the load, they heard a scraping sound. Herman was pushing against the pile of rocks. The ones on top loosened, and as they slid he pushed on the rocks lower down, and then others, so that in a matter of seconds he had a rockslide moving. The first of them slid slowly, the ones behind more quickly, and these struck the slower ones and bounded into the air as if they were suddenly on springs. The mass of them picked up speed, sliding as if they were on a sheet or platform, moving as a single but diffused projectile. A few loose, bounding stones hit the truck first, then the bulk of the slide struck. The truck lurched, swivelling around the rock outcrop that was holding it, before nosing down the steep mountain side and turning on its top. The cab roof made a smooth runner, and the truck, shaking its wheels at the sky, slid away, going faster by the second. It struck another outcrop but this time took to the air, turning and bouncing again and again, down and down the hundreds of feet into the depths. A violent swinging of pine boughs marked where it plunged into the forest in the canyon bottom, nothing more except for the train of stones and sand that followed and the echoes that died away.

Calvin threw the chop bones out for the wild animals and came back to the dining table. He winked at Louella, and she got up to make another pot of coffee. He opened a fresh pack of cigarettes and put them in neutral territory, in the center of the table next to the baking dish they were using as an ashtray. Herman needed to talk. He felt sorry for himself, Calvin judged, now that the drink and the excitement were played out, and there were people to listen.

"It's something to do with being an Indian, or part of one," Herman said. "I don't believe that old firewater story, though." He looked at Louella, and she blushed.

"No," he said, "I mean it, it's not the Indian coming out in me, I just have a drink problem. It's there all the time, and it just gets out of control. So sometimes I'm a drunk, like I was last night and this morning. When I'm drunk, like in Gold Creek, I'm just an Indian on the firewater. That's what everyone thinks."

Louella flared up. "God help me, Herman, I didn't mean that," she said. "I've apologized a dozen times!"

"No, I know you didn't," he said. "What I mean is that when they see me drunk, that's what they say, and they don't think any more about it. They see it start to happen and they just let me go ahead, get it out of my system."

"The longer you stay up here, the longer you keep away from trouble," Calvin said. "Is that it?"

"Yeah," Herman grunted.

"And you're sayin' you drink like you do partly because people think that's what an Indian would do anyway? Is that what you're trying to tell us?" Calvin stared at Herman as if to divine if he was being told the truth.

"The Tolsons think they help me by keeping me up here," Herman said. "I guess they do. I don't know."

Calvin was aware that, by telling part of the truth or answering only part of the question, Herman had once again slipped out of an answer that was important. He let it go, but the tactic annoyed him.

"What happens in the winter?" Louella asked.

"I usually don't get any further than Gold Creek," Herman admitted. "They know what to expect there. I work a few days, in the gas station or the garage, and then I go on a binge. When I'm over it, I go back to work. In March I come back up here. As soon as the snow will let me."

"That makes for a lousy kind of life," Calvin said. "Enough to drive a man to drink."

"What do you mean by that?" Herman demanded.

"Well, goin' on like that," Calvin said, "it's a sure way not to get cured."

"You don't think much of me, do you," Herman said.

"I probably wouldn't look twice at you if you was drunk," Calvin said, "unless you got in my way."

The frank comment was more than Herman had bargained for. He turned his head away and stared at the back of a chair.

Louella said, "In my diner I see a lot of drunks. They come in to get some coffee and try to keep a meal down, trying to sober up. They're usually a lot older than you." He didn't answer but continued staring. "What kind of a drunk are you?" she asked. "Are you one of the mean ones or one of the sloppy nice ones?"

Her tease earned a grin from Herman. "What do you think?" he replied.

"Sloppy nice," she said. The two of them laughed at this.

Calvin's voice was pitched at a tone that was friendly but serious. "What do you want from us, Herman?" he asked. The other two looked at him in surprise, and he looked back at them as if to say that he was only being helpful.

"I mean," he persisted, "you sound like you want

something, or you'd like something, from one of us anyway. You don't sound like you just want us to listen to you." He paused. "Maybe I got that wrong," he said, "but I don't think so."

"You're sure ruining a beautiful friendship," Louella said to Calvin.

He shrugged and turned his eyes away from Herman, waiting for him to speak. Louella took the loaded ashtray to the range and, opening one of its circular ports, tipped the debris into the fire.

"I needed somebody to kick my ass," Herman finally said. He fell silent again, and the others waited, also in silence. "It's winter coming, I guess, and you two came up here when there was nobody else around. It seemed like it was meant to be this way. I didn't plan it, not really. I kind of thought, would it work out if you were around to talk to me, if you knew the kind of person I was. It might help."

"It didn't help yesterday," Louella reminded him.

"That was habit," Herman said, "the end of the season blowout. It was going to happen no matter what. It happens every year."

"Shit, man," Calvin said, "how many trucks 've you rolled down that God damn canyon?"

"Only one," Herman replied. "That's what probably started me thinking, the truck. I'm going to have to leave when you do. I was going to beg a lift down the hill with you, and close the place up for the winter."

Louella talked late into the night after Herman had gone, Calvin listening and occasionally thinking about what she was saying. She had a need for Herman, he decided. The man was weak, but he was also amusing. He, Calvin, was neither of those, he felt, in Louella's life. Not lately, anyhow. Here was a lame duck, a wounded deer, any of the cute little Walt Disney creatures you wanted to name that she had seen at the movies. She could mother him, watch over him in her spare time. They would take Herman to the valley with them.

*

They took him to Mrs. Rossi's, and she rented her room to him without question. He found a job immediately as a tire fitter at Commercial Tire Company, working for Barbara Ferguson, who was managing the business while her father went up north to work in the shipyards. Calvin staked Herman to a down payment on a used car, to be paid back in installments. Every Saturday he was to bring his payment to Calvin at the farm, and he was to stay there for the night so that he wouldn't be tempted to drink up his week's pay.

Knowing Barbara well enough to speak to, Louella phoned and arranged a date with her for late lunch at the diner. She told her over the phone that she wanted to talk about Herman. Their date was a few days after Herman had started work. When she arrived, Barbara was ready and willing to talk about her new employee.

"We met him at Sugarpine Camp," Louella explained, "and we found out he wanted to come down to Red Branch for the winter, so we brought him, and we're kind of looking after him."

"Does he need a nurse?" Barbara asked. Her sarcasm had a sexy edge to it.

"Sometimes," Louella said, "but not the way you mean."

"Sorry to hear that," Barbara replied.

"What do you mean?" Louella asked.

Barbara backed away from the direction she had taken. "He's 4F, so I know he's got some kind of a problem, but I didn't know it needed treatment."

"He's 4F because of his heart," Louella said.

"Oh, well, okay," Barbara said. "If it's his heart, I can help. I'd already thought I would anyway. He's a good looking guy."

Her frankness won Louella over, and they laughed conspiratorially.

"It's his other problem, then," Louella said, "since the heart's taken care of. He hits the bottle."

"Damn!" Barbara said. "Dammit to hell!" She was angry and upset. "I thought when my dad left I got rid of all that."

"I used to see your father in here," Louella said. "Herman hasn't got the same kind of trouble. He doesn't need it all the time. He's a binge drinker. He saves it up for a big blowout, and then he regrets it afterwards."

"If he does it at the tire shop, he'll regret it right away," Barbara said. "Huh-uh," she shook her head, "no go."

"I don't think he will," Louella said. "When you pay him on Saturday, he brings his money to Calvin, he owes him some, and he stays overnight. Herman thinks that will keep him on the straight and narrow. You'd know during the week if he had fallen off the wagon."

"Louella," Barbara said, "I grew up reading the signs. You don't need to tell me anything about it."

"What do you think?" Louella asked.

"You mean will I keep him on?" Barbara countered. "I will for now." She paused before adding with a wink, "I'll give him more than one chance."

Louella reported to Calvin that Barbara would be good for Herman.

Three Saturdays after he came to Red Branch, he telephoned at six o'clock to speak to Calvin to say he wouldn't be coming out to the farm that night but that the money was safe and he would come out on Sunday to pay it.

"Are you drinkin'?" Calvin asked him bluntly.

"No, Calvin, I swear I'm not," Herman answered. "I won't touch a drop, I swear it. Don't think I'm doing this so I can tie one on. I won't, believe me."

"Then what the shit are you doin', buddy?" Calvin asked.

There was a rattling of the telephone at Herman's end and the sound of a laugh, before Barbara came on the phone.

"He's spending the night with me," she said. "Sweet dreams," she added, and hung up.

Everything was fine, except that it wasn't. Barbara and

Herman were in love, and happy as lovers. He hadn't touched a drop of liquor in the weeks since he had come to Red Branch. He had paid off the car loan and settled into life in the town as if he had always had it in mind to leave the mountains and come to the valley.

It was a cold day. The short warm spell that comes sometime around Thanksgiving had not materialized yet, and the earth gave off a damp chill that the wan sun was powerless to counteract. Herman and Calvin were walking through the orchard that lay between the house and the new land that Calvin had bought to the south. It was a good, sound orchard, and Calvin explained to an inattentive Herman that he hated to see it go, but he couldn't manage it and the new land as different kinds of crops. The orchard would have to be dug out, except for about a half acre to the south of the house to protect it from the heat from the new, open fields. The Government wanted potatoes. What the Government wanted, it got.

A glance at Herman showed him that he hadn't a very good audience. He cut short his explanation. "Well," he said, "that's a boss's problem, not very interesting to anybody else."

Herman had heard that remark, at least. "That's what Barbara says to me about the tire business, says it all the time, puts me right in my place. Then she turns around and treats me like I'm the boss's husband." He had stopped, surprised by the accuracy of his own summing up of his disquiet. "That's just exactly the trouble."

Calvin felt a milestone being reached which required a serious conversation, and he steered their way to a pump shed and the concrete standpipe beside it that flooded the orchard in spring and summer. They sat on the edge of the pipe, ignoring the cold and discomfort.

"The trouble's with your workin' life, not your lovelife, from the sound of it," Calvin said. "At least that's different, you gotta admit that."

Herman smiled and nodded, choosing to say no more.

Calvin understood this clue. "You mean it's causin' trouble with your lovelife too," he said. "We ain't gonna talk about that, buddy," he said. "That's not somethin' we can discuss. Let's stick to the business side of things."

Herman expressed his thanks by stretching his hand to Calvin's shoulder and touching it in friendship.

"You think you're going to have to move to another job, if you're going to stick with Barbara?" Calvin said. "Is that it?"

Herman nodded. "They want me at the Highway Garage to work in the shop. The partners have both been to see me. Barbara went crazy. Threw me out of bed, accused me of fixing to leave her. Then she turned around the next day and started ordering me around like I was employed to take out the garbage."

"You are," Calvin said, "if that's what she wants."

"Yeah," Herman admitted, "I am. But not after six o'clock, not at night."

"Yeah, well, that's where the ice gets thin, and I ain't no skater," Calvin said. "So what do you reckon is going to happen?"

"I really don't know, Calvin," Herman said, "I wish I had an idea how it could work out. I'll change tires for as long as I have to, if Barbara 'll just get off my back. She makes sure I know she's the boss, so I treat her that way, then that makes her mad. She doesn't like her man working for her any more than I do, but she won't let me go either. Jealousy, I guess."

"Maybe. Or maybe it's the booze," Calvin said.

"Jesus," Herman said, "I hadn't thought of that."

"Maybe it's not your prick she doesn't trust," Calvin said, "maybe it's your appetite."

Herman rubbed his face with both hands without replying.

"You think she might be right?" Calvin asked. "Now that you think about it?"

Herman nodded and remained mute.

"You think she'd listen to a proposition?" Calvin said. "Or is she going to keep you on her apron strings come hell or high water?"

"That's where I belong," Herman said. "Trouble is, that's the way it looks, too. Like I can't get away."

"Now you said it, buddy," Calvin said, "it's the way it looks that's rubbin' you the wrong way, that's the trouble." His voice was deadly serious, grim, and the force of Calvin's conviction in what he was saying struck home to Herman. "The way things look to other people counts for a hell of a lot to a man. Women forget that. They've got their clothes and their lipstick. A man's trouble is the way he looks when another man sees him with a woman, draggin' along behind her. The rest of the time, hell, every man can do the rest, he can show what he's made of, we all know that."

"I'll have to think about that," Herman said. He was smiling again now. "It depends where she's dragging me to. To go back to what you were asking, about Barbara, I think she'd listen, but I don't think she'd buy."

Calvin ignored his doubts. "I've been thinkin'," he said. "You don't know shit from Shinola when it comes to farmin', but you know how to make things run. The trouble with my farm right now isn't my farm, it's Nakagawa's, the one I got stuck with by the Government. The one that's keeping me from where I'd like to be. I could run things here, even with the labor shortage, if I could get the God damn Nakagawa place off my neck. It's only about half turned around from truck farming. You know what I'm thinkin', I can tell. You could run it for me. You could take the sucker off my back for me, and we'd be here to keep you dry, just down the road, whenever you needed us to help. You'd have to see a lot of me, because I'd have to teach you and check on the work. You wouldn't be able to cheat on the quiet and get your bottle out. O' course, nights with Barbara would be a little bit shorter, at least for a while. Do you think she'd go for it? Well, shit, would you go for it, first?"

"God damn, Calvin, you sure know how to make a man come close to crying," Herman said.

It was fixed between them in only a few minutes, and it was agreed that Barbara would be persuaded, if necessary by Louella. They walked back to the house, both of them still considering the consequences of the partnership.

"You'd have to give up the mountains," Calvin said. "You could get away in the fall, like we did, but that's all."

"I'd thought of that," Herman said. "The Tolsons could find somebody else." He gave no indication of his own feelings, once more retaining his private counsel, and Calvin didn't press him.

They were again silent, Calvin thinking with relief of leaving the peach orchard as it was, and being free to develop the new land, maybe to try some new ideas. And then he thought of another year of work. He was suddenly aware that he was stale, and that an irritation at the farm and all that went with it, even Louella, was building up in him, and the partnership with Herman would only alleviate it, not remove it.

"Calvin," Herman asked, "what did you mean back there about something keeping you from where you wanted to be?"

The question matched so precisely Calvin's awareness of his mood toward his life that he felt irrationally that his thoughts had been overheard, and he snapped his head up as if he had seen something ahead of him, in among the peach trees, that had shocked him with its appearance.

"I didn't mean nothin' by that," he said. "I was just saying that things were piling up, making me wonder if I was getting anything out of all the hard work." He considered his reply and added, "That's all it was."

Late that night, sitting up after Louella had gone to bed, he thought about the events of the day. It was settled. He had a partner who could take some of the sweat out of his days and nights. He could try to regain his zest for the farm and the life he and Louella had together. Barbara would go along with it. He and Louella had two good friends.

He realized that he was going to start off this new relationship with a lie. What he was being kept from, what he wanted more than the life he had, was to go into the Marine Corps. What he had said about the way men saw other men wasn't true for others, but he didn't know that. What he had said had always been true for himself. He existed in others' assessment of him. Louella had her doubts about him, and always had; but she was a woman and his wife, he didn't have to worry about it if only Louella saw the truth. It was other men's eyes which mattered to him. To Red Branch men he had once been a hero. Now? In their eyes, he was convinced, he was dodging the war. He wasn't a draft dodger, no one could accuse him of that. He wasn't 4F either, he hadn't that excuse. He was doing a vital job for his country in wartime, he could go along with all that patriotic stuff, and now with Herman's help he could do it even better. But it wasn't a hero's job. Someone else would hold the gun, and face death, and deliver death, and, dead or alive, live a hero in other men's eyes.

3

Seventh Photo

At the Fourth of July picnic, 1944. The group in the center of the picture is now down to only three. Barbara is living with Chuck Bolger in his big white stucco house on Lake Street, opposite Tom Potter's. The whole story is pretty complicated. Her father came back from the shipyards less and less often, even though he appeared to have his drinking under control and could not blame his absences on lost weekends. Her mother, a dark, plump woman who gave Barbara her challenging eyes, became suspicious and had Herman drive the three of them to Richmond one Wednesday afternoon. She inquired at the shipyard for her husband and got from the man at the gate the time he would be coming off shift. The three of them waited in the car until he came out. They then followed his car to a tiny house in El Cerrito that perversely turned its back on a bay view, looking instead at a bare hill crowned by gaunt eucalyptus trees and some oil storage tanks. They waited in Herman's car until shortly before six, when a light skinned negro woman, in her twenties and very beautiful, drove up to the house and let herself in with a key. A few minutes later Mrs. Ferguson took advantage of the fog and dark to creep up and spy through the gap left by the venetian blinds. The two of them were in their underwear but getting rid of it pretty quickly, lying on the couch in the front room making love. A card above the doorbell read Norm and Gay Ferguson.

Barbara's mother was dry-eyed about the whole business, taking everything her husband had got, knowing that he couldn't face up to the scandal of living with a negro woman if it ever came to court. Barbara took advantage of the situation to sell the tire company, fraudulent deals and all, to Al O'Driscoll, who owned the cocktail lounge on the highway. His lungs were riddled with TB, in an arrested state but dangerous nevertheless, and the smoky, stagnant air of his bar, and the temptation to drink away his pain and worries, were killing him. He was going to have to be a silent partner in the cocktail lounge while he did something else for the rest of his living. Most of the liquor he bought for his bar was smuggled in tax free from Canada by the same people who dealt in unrationed tires from Ferguson's Tire Shop. That made it easy. They put up the money for the sale and everybody was happy, especially Barbara and her mother, who made a killing.

Loaded with money and with time on her hands, Barbara joined the country club that had been created out of the golf club to try to keep it afloat while most of its playing members went off to the war. One of its prominent members was a man named Chuck Bolger who had a huge spread of wheat land to the east of Red Branch. He and his wife lived in a modern design house with round windows and wrought iron balconies, making it look like a ship without a hull becalmed on Lake Street. Mrs. Bolger was a successful past president of every guild and improvement association the women of the town had ever been encouraged to organize. In 1943, after each branch of the service had got its women's auxiliary, she applied to the Navy and was commissioned an officer in the WAVES. There were pictures in the paper regularly as she went up the promotion ladder like there was no one else in the women's service who knew one end of a boat from another. People in Red Branch said it was that house that did the trick. Very soon she was, in her way, more successful than her husband.

He spent less and less time with his acreage and more time than was good for him at the country club. He and Barbara became good friends, no more than that. One day in the raw early months of 1944, Chuck was celebrating his wife's latest promotion too enthusiastically at the country club. He had a drink too many and slipped on the steps between the cocktail bar and the dining room, hitting his head on one of the steps as he fell. He was hospitalized with concussion and a blood clot in an eye socket. He was kept in the hospital for only a few days, and then was ordered to go home and stay in bed and allow himself to be waited on. When it came to finding a trained nurse, however, there wasn't one to be had, the demands of the war had seen to that. Barbara volunteered, moving into the guest bedroom so as to be there night and day to do the nursing. Sometime during his recuperation she moved into the master bedroom, and when Chuck was well and could see visitors, it was discovered that Barbara was the mistress of the house.

Herman stayed out on the old Nakagawa place, moving into the house and setting up a bachelor residence for himself. He avoided Red Branch and worked himself silly. He drew closer to Calvin and Louella as his friends and neighbors. The three became as interdependent as a family. The closeness appeared to please and suit them all.

There is a ghost in the picture that you can see only in Calvin's eyes. A month before, at five in the morning, Calvin had been restless and unable to sleep any longer. He got up and dressed, then turned on the kitchen radio low so as not to wake Louella while he made some coffee. Instead of the weather forecast and swing music, announcers were reading bulletins about D-Day, about infantrymen landing on the

Normandy coast of France from the sea and behind the German lines by glider. In that way Calvin learned that another great event had passed him by.

Shortly before the previous Christmas he had been in Red Branch and run into Eddie Slattery. Eddie had his son Eldon with him, and they were on their way to the Rex Hotel for a drink to celebrate. Eldon had finished high school a semester early in order to take a job with the electric company. The draft board had changed his plans for him, however, and he was leaving the next day for basic training as an infantryman. His dad was very proud of Eldon. In the army he was taught how to say "Yes, sir" and given a gun and sent to England, where he joined a battalion assigned to the second seaborne wave of the invasion. On the seventh of June he had taken about fifty steps into France when he was killed.

Calvin had become obsessed with the idea that Eldon had gone to France instead of himself. He had become two people, the second one being a dead boy that he barely knew, the first one a man who hid his shame in his orchards and fields while something great and exciting and worthwhile and noble passed him by.

The approach to the Nakagawa place, if it had been designed, could not have done a better job of making the last piece, the house, look good by contrast with what came before. A wooden barn that leaned where the wind had pushed it was succeeded by a tractor shed that substituted decaying tarpaulins for a door, the pitted road then turning past a group of sheds with no known use, some shacks that had once held ancient relatives of the Nakagawas, and the sluices and pipes of the former packing shed that Calvin had torn down. The house itself was one of the older style for the area, two storied, every window balanced by another, every detail in its place, aiming for serenity and finding rigidity instead.

With Barbara's defection, Herman needed a project badly, something more personal than the farming, which was going very well. The day the papers came through from Joe Nakagawa giving Calvin a free hand with everything, land, buildings, development, Herman rejoiced. He loosened one cornerpost of the barn until he could put a long chain on it and pull it out with the tractor. The building settled slowly as the post came free, then swivelled around its lost member and collapsed in a single piece like a matchwood House of Usher. With its supporting neighbor removed, the tractor shed leaned to a forty-five degree angle, considered the situation, and expired into a neat stack of scrap wood. The chain, looped around each shed and shack in turn, dragged the smaller buildings to join the fate of the barn. In the end all that impeded the view of the house was a pile of ash to be spread over the fields and a smaller pile of scrap metal and porcelain waiting for the next trip to the dump.

The wreckage yielded enough good timber to allow for gingerbreading along the eaves and the porch, and the severe house began to smile, if only slightly. Except for the bathroom at the top of the stairs, Herman left the upper floor alone and set himself up in some comfort on the ground floor. Neither he nor Calvin had ever enjoyed an independent bachelor life in their earlier years, and now the setting up of Herman became as important to Calvin as to the occupant. The building of a breakfast bar in the kitchen, modelled on one pictured in *Family Circle Magazine* from the Safeway store, allowed them to make the old dining room into a living room. What had been a living room became a den and office where every aspect of the running of what they now called the Jurgens Land was analyzed. In a short time it became the office for all of Calvin's land, and he began to spend long evenings working over plans, invoices, costings, Government reports, tax returns. Quickly this became a two-man job with Herman essential to the work done and the decisions taken. The partnership took on solid shape as Herman welcomed his full share of the work and the decisions. Out of gratitude or enthusiasm or something more complex than that, Herman took on whatever work was, so to speak, in the pending file. Increasingly Calvin found himself examining the evidence of tasks already completed and decisions executed, while he was still weighing consequences. He was pleased, but the pace was not his. In a few months Calvin to his great surprise discovered he had time on his hands. With Louella spending long hours at the diner, he was as free as a bachelor, as free as the real bachelor.

Following the path indicated by the junction of friendship and business, they should have become men about town, which in Red Branch meant companions at the bar of the Rex Hotel, or the Regency Hotel, or the Highway Cocktail Lounge, except for the nights that they faced each other over the poker table in the back room of the cigar store. That was ruled out by Herman's weakness for whisky and Calvin's failure to appreciate poker, which to him remained a primitive and longwinded way to lose money. On the evenings when Louella wasn't closing up the diner, they ate together at what was now called Whitmores Ranch and afterwards talked and listened to the radio, before Herman went back to his farmhouse for some late office work and early bed. On other nights they ate together at the diner at a table squeezed into the corner near the cash register.

"Why don't you go uptown?" Herman suddenly asked Calvin one night. "No point you waiting here. I'll hang on until Louella's ready to close up. I'll run her out home, to the ranch, you suit yourself when you want to come on back out."

It was the first time the proposal, which had hung in the air above the three of them, had been put into words. Calvin looked at Louella, but she looked away and pulled on her cigarette, unwilling to give him any unspoken advice.

Calvin said, "I'd kind of like to see what's news at the Rex." He waited again for Louella's comment, but she remained aloof. "Thanks," he said. "I won't be late." The arrangement became standard with them.

When one evening this arrangement broke down, it was

Calvin who suggested that it was time Louella learned to drive, so that she could be independent and have her own car. She laughed at the idea but remembered it, coming back to it when the days lengthened and it was no longer a matter of learning in the dark. Calvin's attempt at a lesson with her was a disaster, partly because he resented having to try to argue her into understanding what she was supposed to be doing while all the time he was wishing he was at the Rex Hotel.

He complained to Herman, "Louella always expects too much out of anything with a motor. She wants to tell it to go, and leave it to do the rest for her. I swear she don't begin to understand what a gear is for."

"Sounds pretty normal for a woman," Herman replied, choking Louella with indignation and inhaled cigarette smoke.

When she could speak, she complained in her turn. "He doesn't have any patience," she said. "He can sit and watch his crops grow and say it all takes time, but if it's me, it's got to be right now, right the first time, or else he pops his cork." She dismissed her driving prospects. "I'll never learn how to do it, not with him."

Herman accepted the challenge, or the invitation, whichever it was, and the pattern of their evenings changed again. When they ate at the diner, Calvin was released to go uptown while Herman stayed behind to give Louella a lesson by letting her drive back out to the ranch. He waited there with her until Calvin came home, and then took himself off to his house. When Louella got her license and bought a car, Herman went to the diner as Calvin's passenger, waited for Louella, then rode with her to his house. Sometimes she left him off there and drove home immediately, and at other times she stayed there talking with him until she thought Calvin would be due to come home. Once in a while he would join them there for a coffee nightcap.

The three of them were aware that their shared life could have been the subject of gossip. There were, however, no eyes to see and therefore no mouths to gossip. Their lives were private, protected by the isolation of the Jurgens house and the ranch house, as well as the suspicion each of them harbored as facets of their personalities and backgrounds. Themselves outsiders by nature, they regarded the conjoined world that lay beyond their acres as something to be avoided. If they had had drawbridges to pull up to insure their isolation, these would have been in regular use.

"Give me a little more to do, Calvin," Herman said. "Give me more to do for you on the ranch. I've got plenty of time. Jurgens practically runs itself. It just goes by the calendar. We stick the stuff in the ground, and the sun and the water do the rest. I've got all the time in the world. You let me run the orchards for you, and you take it easier. What do you have in mind for the potato crop this year? The Government still want those extra acres planted in potatoes?"

They were standing outside the Jurgens house when he said it, Calvin could remember it clearly later on, when he found it necessary to think about it. Herman was leaning against the porch railing with his foot up on the step, trying to light his cigarette with a match struck on his jeans. It should have been a cowboy trick that looked as good as it did in the movies, with that flash of a Herman smile at the end of it, but the wind got to each match when it was somewhere between his backside and his cigarette and in the end he'd had to accept the offer of Calvin's lighter.

Maybe it was the pose he was striking that made Calvin aware afterwards of something artificial in the scene. Maybe it was the ease with which Herman dispensed with Calvin's contribution to the running of the ranch. It was the first time Calvin had been able to put a finger on what had always made him hesitate about Herman. He recognized now that Herman held back something, a little something that was part of the truth, in order to, as the saying went, keep his powder dry. Something under the mattress, a little extra in the bank, a rainy day insurance policy – call it what you like, what Herman was doing was making sure things would work to his advantage in the long run.

Well, Calvin said to himself, maybe that wasn't such a bad thing, as long as it worked to the advantage of the three of them, not merely the one of him.

Even though he didn't drink on the job, Mort Thomas had taken to spending more time at the Rex Hotel now that his son was dead and his wife had gone away to forget about being Mrs. Thomas. He listened, with the fat of his belly lifted up onto the bar to give him a little ease, and occasionally he chimed in on the talk, but generally he spread a newspaper out on the bar and idled through it, grunting once in a while when something struck him as worth his attention. It was natural, therefore, that he and Calvin shared an interest in the war in the Pacific, after he had told Calvin:

"I tell you, Calvin, if I could turn back the clock I'd be a Marine. They know what they're doing. Even their asses are tough as old leather. They get their orders, they do it. Just like that. Animals. The right kind of animals. No need to think about it, no need to think about anything. Just do it. Just like that."

Whether he was thinking out loud when he said it, or whether he said it for Calvin's benefit, divining somehow that it was this which was torturing Calvin at his most secret place, it was impossible to say. Mort's business was reading men, their motives and their thoughts. Something that Mort saw or found or intuited in Calvin, before he said this or after this time, bound the two men together in their acknowledgment that unthinking brutality in a just cause was a need and a desire that they could not dismiss. It was this comradeship that allowed Mort to be the only person, aside from Herman, who knew what agony the war had become to Calvin.

When Herman came into the office, he found Calvin wearing

the expression of Jove the Thunderer surrounded by a splay of all the books they possessed. The bookcase, which was supposed to be attached to the wall, lay among them.

Herman smiled his smile, in the circumstances the wrong thing to do. "Lookin' for something?" he asked.

"No!" Calvin shouted, "I'm playin' tic-tac-toe, you stupid son of a bitch! What the hell do you think I'm doin'!"

Herman turned and went back out the door, followed in a moment by Calvin. "Shit, man, I'm sorry, I didn't mean that," he said.

"I know you didn't," Herman said, trying his smile again, more appropriately.

"I went lookin' for a dictionary, just a plain little ol' dictionary, and I couldn't find none, so I looked in the God damn bookcase and it come off the wall, and now I got this mess." Calvin gave a kick to a large, dark, important looking book which slid to the other side of the room and thumped into the wall.

Herman laughed, but Calvin didn't join in. "You're losing your sense of humor, Calvin," he said. "Come on, laugh at it."

"All I want is a God damn dictionary," Calvin said, and he returned to rummaging through the heap of books on the floor.

"Last I saw of it was in the kitchen, on top of that pile of newspapers you keep looking at," Herman said.

Calvin went into the kitchen. In the corner behind the dining table was a stack of newspapers, with the red bound dictionary on top of them. The chair nearby was still pulled away from the table where he had left it last night, as was the empty coffee cup that he had drunk from.

"Damn," he said, "I guess I read so late I forgot all about it." He tried a wry grin. "I'll clean up the mess in there."

"Don't worry," Herman said. "I'll put everything back. I wanted to change everything around anyway. You don't mind, do you?"

Calvin looked at him to see if there might be any other message forthcoming. "No, I don't mind," he said, "long as I can find what I need." When he turned to go back to the office, Herman reminded him, "Don't forget the dictionary." Calvin stooped to pick it up. Herman added, "What did you want to look up?"

Calvin said, "Just a word that's been a bee buzzin' around in my head all night. I read it last night, and I thought I knew what it meant, but I didn't. Here it is."

He put his finger on the dictionary entry for Atoll and read aloud, "A coral island or islands, consisting of a reef surrounding a lagoon." Beside it was a poor quality line drawing of what looked like an oval track for racing palm trees. "Jesus, that's a big help," Calvin said.

"What did you want it for?" Herman asked. "Atoll, I mean. How do you say it anyway?" He turned to the pronouncing key and tried the various possibilities until they decided on the pronunciation.

Calvin led the way back to the dining table and, sitting down where he had been the night before, lifted the top newspaper from the stack and spread it on the table. He pointed to an article on an inside page.

"This here," he said. "About the role of the Marines in the war in the Pacific," he said, paraphrasing the headline. "It says here that a lot of the campaign will consist of atoll hopping."

Herman giggled. "If you don't know what atoll means, that can give you some pretty funny ideas of what the Marines are doing," he said.

Calvin was not amused. "Let's look at that dictionary again," he said.

Between them they worked out what it all meant, the special hazards of attacking an island over a razor sharp coral breakwater and a shallow lagoon, the task of regrouping for attack on the next one, the distances and logistics involved. The burden of the article that Calvin had puzzled over was that casualties would be high.

Herman looked down at the stack of papers. "You think a lot about this, don't you, these days. How come?"

Calvin didn't answer, contenting himself with looking again at the paper on the table. "Elite corps," he read from somewhere in the article.

"Where do you get all these papers?" Herman asked.

"Old Gomez gets 'em for me, keeps 'em for me at the Rex," Calvin answered. "I pick 'em up when I get in there. Bus depot's never open by the time we get there."

"Every day?" he asked.

Calvin nodded. "Takes some reading to keep up with them," he said. "That's what's keeping me up late these nights."

Herman teased, "That's part of it." He got two bottles of pop out of the refrigerator and opened them on a gadget screwed to the wall. "That God damn radio, Calvin, it's your business and I'm not complaining, understand, but I'm going to move my bedroom upstairs. That's if you don't mind."

Calvin's response was uncompromising. Herman was always changing something, it seemed, and he had got used to it. "I don't mind a bit. I'll help you with the moving. Just don't ask me to stop listening to the radio, that's all. I can't listen to it at home 'thout Louella whining at me. Don't you start."

"I guess I need more sleep than you," Herman said. "What do you listen to? I could hear it going at three o'clock the other morning."

"War reports," Calvin answered. "Speeches, from Washington, sometimes from England. Communiques. Statements from high commands one place or another. Stuff that people don't like to listen to in the daytime. It don't make for easy listening." He pulled a hand over his stubbly cheek. "Stuck out here, it makes me feel like I'm alive, anyhow, even if I can't fight." He thumped the table with a fist. "God damn it!" he shouted. He pushed away from the table and slammed out the door.

"For Christ's sake, don't keep asking me, 'What's got into

you?' " Calvin shouted. "The answer is 'Nothin'!' I keep tellin' you, 'Nothin'!' "

"Okay, okay!" Louella shouted back. "You say it, master, so it has to be true. I hope it is. If I've done something, I want to know it, that's all."

Another day, another argument, Calvin thought. As regular as God damn orange juice with breakfast. There were times when he knew another set-to was coming and he wanted to run away, like a little kid, before he did something wrong. There were other times when he could feel it coming and he wanted to plead with Louella, Stop me, please stop me, because I don't mean it and I don't know what to do about it.

He didn't plead with her, however, because he knew that would be the opposite of what he wanted, which was to feel the separation growing between them, until the day came when he could run away.

Tom Potter, at his cigar store, finally said out loud what a number of Calvin's friends had been too shy to say to his face. "You're looking what my dear old mamma would say 'Right peakid,' Calvin." He said the dialect in an exaggerated drawl, with the humor of it almost covering his message. "You got something wrong with you?" he asked. "Been to the doctor?"

Calvin came back at Tom with his strongest Texas talk. "Ain't no doctorin' needed ner wanted, Mister, don't hold with it nohow."

They laughed, but Tom wasn't finished. "Okay, pal, okay. But you look kind of used up lately. Not the old Calvin, for sure."

The comment struck a raw spot. "Ain't no such thing as the old Calvin, Tom, he's gone. Finished." Calvin said it ferociously.

"I don't get it," Tom said. "You're still a young man."

"Wrong man in the wrong place at the wrong time," Calvin said. "Gimme some of those Chesterfields for a change. Lucky Strikes taste like stable scrapin's."

He directed his attention to the money he offered, took the cigarettes, and left the cigar store without again looking at Tom.

D-Day. On the afternoon of the sixth of June, when he telephoned the diner, Calvin had to leave a message with Florence Biles because Louella had gone uptown to the bank. "I'm at the office, for now," he said, "but I'm going out. Tell her I'm trying to get all the chores done so I can get back and listen to the news. I won't be coming in for supper tonight. Tell her I'll open a can of something here. Herman 'll be there as usual, I expect."

Florence was a scrawny woman with medium blond hair that she pulled over her face in imitation of Veronica Lake. She had large, pale blue, watery eyes so prominent and mournful that anyone knew at a glance that her life was miserable. In consequence she attracted few people willing to listen to her life story, substituting for that deprivation as keen an ear for gossip as there was in the town, and a subtle, practiced tongue for passing it on.

Calvin hardly emerged from the Jurgens house for the best part of a week. He spent most of the days rushing to do necessary tasks on the ranch and farm, between news broadcasts. All night he sat up with the radio and the maps that the city papers printed. As Calvin's obsession took its toll of his strength, Herman filled in for him, his smile more triumphant than reassuring. For the first time he took on some of the work of the ranch, not only the Jurgens land. Since it was just the two of them, he and Louella ate every night at the diner, economizing on gasoline by travelling in one car when they could. They made a handsome couple.

Florence Biles overheard comments from them about Calvin's isolation. Accustomed to Louella's hardedged humor, she nevertheless misread it, either by accident or intent, when Louella complained about losing a husband. She counted up the nights Herman, not Calvin, had been the male in the dinner party. She overheard them planning for things that had to be accomplished at the ranch, for all the world as if they had inherited the full responsibility and had formed a new partnership. Before the end of the month the story was tickling ears in Red Branch that the Whitmore marriage was in trouble, that Herman hadn't been thrown out, that Calvin had withdrawn himself from wife and home.

There was little sympathy for Louella; as Florence said to Ethel Wooley, her cashier friend at the drug store, "She's got two men to choose from, and ours are gone to the war. What's she got to complain about?"

To which Ethel added, with malice, "Yeah, I forget now, which one of them is the one that's 4F?"

It was not in Louella's nature to have either a confessor or an adviser. She was and always had been a partner to her men. How Herman had taken on this role in her life she would have been unable to say. He did not insinuate himself into it, nothing so indirect as that. He seemed to take it on as a right, as an asexual third person in this close triangle. She found herself speaking to him almost as if she was writing an entry in a personal diary, especially on the nights after they had eaten together in town when they drove back out to the ranch in isolating darkness.

She had been quiet for some miles. She sighed and put out her cigarette. "I don't know what to do," she said, only that, and Herman knew what she meant.

"Now the invasion is going good, I think he'll let down a little bit. You know how he feels about the war. He's got all excited about it," Herman said to Louella. "I'm running the ranch and the farm okay. He's got nothing to worry about there. Let him know he can count on me."

That too was a new note that Herman had introduced without preamble or modesty. He was now the mainstay of the business, not Calvin. Louella was still not sure how it had happened. She saw it like one of those stagecoach scenes. Calvin had looked away for a minute to see what the Indians were up to, and when he looked back the driving reins were no longer in his hands. As a passenger she had to admit the right person seemed to be telling the horses what to do.

"Do you think that's a good idea?" Louella asked. "Maybe he ought to think we depend on him more. He's kind of forgotten that I do. He's gone so much." She didn't have to explain that she meant Calvin was gone from her bed so many nights.

"I think he ought to feel free to come back into the work when he feels like it. He can't deal with it right now, that's all." Herman's voice was gently reassuring, but there was also a slightly galling, new note of superiority.

"I guess you're right," Louella said.

"You can count on me," Herman said. "You both can."

Calvin came in late one night on the edge of being drunk. Louella had been reading and waiting for him. "Where you been?" she asked him. "I was worried."

He said nothing. He sat on the side of the bed after he had taken off his clothes, but he made no further move toward her.

"What's wrong?" she said.

"Nothing," he said. "Except it's all over town that you and me has split up, and Herman's the big chief now."

Louella sat up in bed and switched on the light. "What!?" she shouted. "Where did you hear that garbage? Who said it?"

"You won't believe this," he said. "Tom Potter said Mort Thomas was in asking questions about us, so I phoned up Mort and asked him what the hell did he think he was saying, and he said he was only asking because the sheriff had been on to him about it. Seems like they still keep an eye on Herman, because of his reputation. Once a bad Injun, always a bad Injun, I guess. Or maybe they know something we don't."

"What a crust!" she exploded. "What the hell has Herman got to do with it, anyway?"

"Your trouble is you ain't got no imagination," Calvin said.

"Other people think you have, that's for sure." When she didn't take the hint, he was angry. "What the hell do you think Herman might have to do with it, for Christ's sake? What do you think they're thinkin'?"

The realization, when it came, made Louella shudder from head to foot. "Oh, my sweet Jesus," she moaned. She began to cry.

"It ain't worth cryin' about," Calvin said. "Get mad, that'll make you feel better if anything will."

Between her sobs, she said, "It's not fair. I've got nobody in my bed, either you or Herman. It's not fair."

"Calvin," Louella said, "Listen to me, just listen to me for once in your life. What is so all fired important about this war? What is it?"

He laughed in disbelief. "Important?" he echoed, "about the biggest thing that's going to happen in our lives? You want to know what's important about it?"

"You said in our lives," she responded. "That's the part I don't understand. What's it got to do with our lives? There's two kinds of life, Calvin. One of 'em is maybe about wars, and politics, and things that find their way into history books. That's not my idea of what's important in my life, and you know it. The other kind of life is what our lives are all about. Are we going to have a family?"

"What?" he stammered.

"Kids!" she said. "Are we going to have kids?"

"What are you talkin' about?" he said.

"That's what's important, that's what I'm talking about," she said. "What does a war matter, really, to us? If you were to be killed, then it would matter, to me, Calvin, not to a history book, and to a baby of ours if we had one. Can't you figure it out for yourself? A war? A Hitler and all that? Who does that affect?"

"Are you tryin' to tell me that none of it means anything?" he asked. He was outraged at her selfishness.

"I'm saying it only means anything to me, or to you, or to the person like us. I'm saying the history book is worthless, it's useless, it's probably lying. The only way a war happens is when it happens to a person. No one joins big causes, Calvin, no one who has a brain, unless that cause is some part of themselves." He tried to turn away in disgust, but she held his chin. "No, you look at me, Calvin, and you tell me what part of this war hits you. You're one of the few people in this whole county, this whole valley, who has a reason to stay here. You're growing things, crops, and you're married to a woman who can't think of what to do if you're not around her. You talk about the war effort. You're killing yourself for the war effort, and it's hard on me, too. But Calvin, let it stay there at that, please, for both our sakes. Do our part, and then let it go. Please."

"You can't see past the end of your nose," he accused her. He sneered, "Where would anybody be if everybody was like you?"

"Exactly where they are now," she said, "no better and no worse. People are like me, Calvin, not like you. The world is made up of people!"

"It's made up of cowards, if they're all like you," he said.

"And wars are fought by cowards," she answered. "You're such a fool, Calvin, to think that wars are fought by heroes!"

"They're won by heroes," he said.

"They're won by whoever is left alive," she said. "They're fought by whoever has to, and that's not the same as winning."

"Jesus!" he exploded, "if you was in the Army you'd be in front of a firing squad in about two shakes of a cow's tail."

"No I wouldn't, buster," she said, "they'd never get that satisfaction."

"So there'd never be an Army if people like you was drafted," he scoffed.

"Oh, yes," she mocked, "there'll always be armies. There's always people who think like you do."

"Then what the hell are you talking about?" he demanded.

"Other people don't have the reasons you have to stay here where you're needed," she said.

"I forget my reasons," he said, "tell me again."

"You're one of the precious people able to grow things and feed other people. That's more important than – I don't know, maybe more important than a hundred tanks."

"And what else?" he said.

"And then there's me," she said. "I need you."

Something in her voice, possibly the truth of it, caught at him and calmed him. "I'll think about it," he said quietly.

Calvin had looked for Louella in the orchard and called her name several times. When he came into the house, there was still no sign of her, but the screen was pulled shut across the red room. He looked over the top of it to find Louella reading a magazine in a circle of light from the standing lamp. She was wearing the same housecoat she had put on in the morning.

"Damn!" Calvin said, "look at the pile of cigarette butts. You been in here all day?"

"What if I have?" Louella snapped.

"Nothing, nothing, forget it," he answered.

"I will," she growled back.

He pulled the screen aside. "It's a nice day," he said, "come outside. I'll fix you a drink. You been in this room all day."

"It's my room," she answered. "It's the one part of this house that belongs to me. And you always know where to find me. That's assuming you ever want me."

"Louella," he said, "don't be like this. It's my fault, I know it, I don't know what's wrong with me. I'm not turning against you. It's me."

"You have turned against me, Calvin." She said it without rancor, with great sadness. "I don't know why. You did it before, but then we both knew why. I don't want to be just your best friend, Calvin. We're married, you're my husband. Have I gone ugly or something?"

"Nothing like that," he said, "don't talk crazy. It's just me."

She blazed up. "Well I'm just me! Get out of my room!"

Herman found Calvin at the desk in the office, looking through some old tax returns which he had picked up in order to look busy. When I look up, Calvin thought, he'll give me that God damn smile, and I don't think I can take it one more time. He kept his head down, trying to signal to Herman to leave him alone.

"We've got to make some decisions, Calvin, and I can't get you to talk about your plans. What do I do? Just take over? What do you want to do about it?" Herman asked. He struggled to find just the right sound of sincerity for his voice.

Calvin rubbed the back of his neck. He smiled wryly. "You're askin' me? Seems like you already know the answer. You're running the show, you keep on the way you've got it set up," he said. "I'll get back into things one of these days. I'll make it worth your while." He wondered what he would find to do when he decided to get back into the running of his land, if there would be room for two of them when that happened, but he said nothing.

"You sure you don't mind me sort of taking over, Calvin?" Herman said. "I'm only doing it 'cause things need to be done. If you don't like it, all you gotta do is say so, you know that."

"No, that's okay, just keep it going," Calvin answered. "I'm here in the office if you need me. Are you happy about the money? You satisfied you're getting a fair shake on the deal? Something's wrong. Is it the money?"

"That doesn't bother me," Herman responded. He looked shy as a boy, smiling up from under a wave of black hair. "It's you and Louella I'm worried about."

"Did she tell you to talk to me?" Calvin asked.

"Not in so many words. No, not really," Herman said.

"Then don't ask me," Calvin said. Why couldn't he bring

himself to call Herman's bluff and tell him it was none of his God damn business?

Herman tried another tack. "A lot of the time lately," he said, "you seem like you're mad at me. Am I doing something you don't like, Calvin?"

"No," Calvin said, "sorry, forget it." How can I tell him I know what he's up to, replacing me in my own life, when I need him to do that?

"There's something," Herman persisted.

"No, it's nothin' really," Calvin said. "Just that we seem to get in each other's way sometimes. Sometimes I feel like I'm in your way. I guess I am. I get the feeling that you kind of fixed it up that way." He could bring himself only to deliver this mild reminder that Herman's tactics weren't unobserved.

Herman sat down and leaned across to Calvin, putting his hand on Calvin's forearm and shaking it. His grip was hard, even though he was smiling his widest smile. "Come on now, Calvin," Herman said, "don't look at it like that. Maybe I do things without asking you too much. Maybe I ought to back off."

"No, no, it's gotta be done," Calvin said. "I can't get used to the idea of bein' sort of surplus. Guess I ought to." Guess I'll have to, he added to himself.

For part of his wakeful night, he thought about Herman's role in his misery. It was his own state of mind, he decided, that made him suspicious of Herman. It wasn't really suspicion, either, it couldn't be, since Herman's tactics were so blatant. He was taking over. Anytime Calvin wanted to, he could stop it. All he had to do was to come back to life. Coming back from the dead, however, was beyond his ability, and like a drunken gambler watching a cardsharp, he watched Herman deal the cards to his advantage. Well, let him. Whatever the game was, Calvin had lost interest in it.

*

"I guess if I want to know what's going on, I have to ask Herman," she said.

"Same goes for me," he answered. They were both sullen, sharpening their claws on each other.

"You getting jealous?" she teased.

"If I was, I'd do something about it."

"Oh, I'm impressed. Big stuff."

"Don't push me too hard. I ain't no gentleman."

She laughed at him. "You think I don't know that?"

"I guess you'd be the one to know."

"That's right. I would. I look at Herman and I see a gentleman. I look at you and I see good old Calvin Whitmore." She mocked him in his Texas dialect, "And he sure as shit ain't no gen'l'man, lemme tell ya! He ain't even no man!"

Calvin stood as if struck. "I told you," he said, "I don't know what's wrong." He stood silent, and she stared back at him, aware of finally having gone too far, of having wounded them both, deeply. She was unable to go to him, even though to herself she was unable to keep up the pretence of loathing him.

"I'm goin'," he said.

He moved to the farm house, taking over the downstairs bedroom that had been Herman's. In place of the punishment of the past few months, he set himself a strict but healthy regime. He woke up early, had a good breakfast, consulted with Herman on what had to be done, and then did chores that as much as possible involved physical effort. He had lunch in Red Branch most days, at the Rex Hotel, where he picked up the papers. He called in at the cigar store to see if there was anything for him, since he had begun to use it as a convenience address for personal mail. He went back to Jurgens for whatever business needed to be seen to, then at about three o'clock tuned in to the first of the news broadcasts that were being aired at what was night back east, in

Washington and New York. Soon after six he had a supper that he cooked himself, and by eight o'clock, when it was past midnight back east, he switched off the radio and did more chores on the farm or the ranch until it was too dark to see to do them. Then he had a shower and turned in for a few hours sleep. About two or two-thirty in the morning, he regularly woke and listened to news from Europe, then switched off and slept again.

His body responded and he became restored to the lean, strong man he had been. He was however not the same man, as he had told Louella. His mind was entirely on the war and on his lack of involvement in it. Despair, like an old sheet dividing the bunkhouse of his childhood, took the light from his eyes and left only shadows. He loathed Louella for, as he saw it, helping to keep him out of the war, for needing him so much he felt stuck to these acres like February mud, and for thinking her need was enough to keep him here. He thought he had no feelings any longer about Herman, certainly, paradoxically, he felt no thanks for the fact that he, Calvin, was free of obligations on the two farms. He felt for himself an upwelling of the old hatred and disgust at his ability to tolerate the meaningless, bleak, empty despair within him. This time he would do something about it, he determined.

4

The Marine lieutenant announced to the five of them, "That's it. You're Marines." He looked at his round wrist watch. "You've got two hours to take care of personal business. I want you back downstairs in the military reception area at four o'clock on the button. You'll be travelling all night on the bus. We've got sandwiches and coffee. I recommend you go out somewhere and find a nice place and enjoy the last civilian meal you're going to have for a while, for about six weeks as a matter of fact. If you come back drunk, you're out of the Corps before you started. If you don't come back by four, the Shore Patrol will be after you and the first thing you'll know about the Marine Corps is the inside of the brig. You're recruits now, and don't forget it."

He smiled a lopsided smile that had very little of humor in it. "Life is earnest, life is real," he quoted sententiously. Calvin felt antagonized by his showing off and was tempted to challenge him by asking where those words came from. Then he remembered that he was no longer Calvin. He was what he had longed to be, a Marine recruit, the lowest of the low, as the recruiting sergeant had promised.

They got to boot camp soon after three in the morning. Someone led them to a shower room and told them to stay there. They sprawled on benches to keep off the cold concrete floor, dozing and smoking, beyond conversation in a half-world of weariness and anticipation. About five a man came in with towels and soap.

"Take off your clothes, pile them up to go into your lockers, when you get a locker, take a shower and wait for me to come back for you."

About six he came back. "No food until you've had your physicals."

He came back in half an hour. "Okay, leave your towels, carry your clothes, follow me."

Naked as specimens, the recruits filed behind him to a waiting room, and in another half hour their physical examination began. After two hours of it, it dawned on Calvin that this wasn't entirely a physical. They had been through that less than twenty-four hours before. He became aware that he was no longer a man as he had known and used the term. He was an animal, and the examination was designed to determine if he was a useful animal. He was filled with a delight that threatened to become hysteria. It was exactly what he wanted, what he needed. Animal. Useful animal. Someone else deciding what use. He wanted to laugh out loud. The doctor put the naked men in a line facing away from him and told them to bend over.

"Now spread your cheeks," he said. "Nice and wide. Spread your asshole until it hurts. Good."

He looked at each of them in turn. "God how I hate this job," he mumbled.

Calvin burst out laughing and continued until the corpsman slapped him on the buttocks with the flat of his clipboard. "Officers make jokes," he said without a trace of humor, "recruits keep a straight face. You speak when you're spoken to, otherwise we don't want to know you've got a voice. Got it?"

Calvin nodded and submerged the hilarity. He felt that he had never been so happy in his entire life.

*

They were told to make a file. Someone passed the word that this meant to get in line. Some Marines in fatigues came in and slid up a wide hatch at the side of the room. The file of men passed in front of the open hatch and shouted their clothing sizes while the people behind stacked up the clothing for them. At the end of the line they were given a needle, a spool of white thread and another spool of olive green thread. "Now make 'em fit," the platoon sergeant ordered.

At mail call Calvin's name was called. He ignored it. The same thing happened several times, and each time he ignored his mail. The corporal in charge called him out of ranks. He addressed him in front of the rest of the platoon.

"Your name Whitmore," he asked, "or have you changed it without fuckin' telling us?"

"Yes, sir."

"Well, which the fuck is it? Is it Whitmore, or did you change it?"

"Whitmore, sir."

"You don't want your mail," he said.

"No, sir," Calvin answered.

"Afraid it's bad news?" he asked.

"No, sir," Calvin answered.

"Did you come into the Corps to get away from your wife, Whitmore, like half of this fuckin' platoon?" he asked.

"No, sir," Calvin answered.

"Do you mind if I throw your fuckin' letters in the garbage?" he asked.

"No, sir," Calvin answered.

"Okay, I'll do that, and I've got witnesses." He started to order Calvin back to ranks, then thrust another question at him. "Do you still deny that you came into the Corps to get away from your wife?"

"No, sir," Calvin said.

*

He learned how to do a spit shine.

He learned how to relieve himself even though there were no walls between the stools in the latrines.

He learned that it was possible to stay awake all night on guard duty, take a two-hour break, and turn out for PT.

He learned that a uniform was a casing which had to be kept in perfect condition so that the anonymity, the inhumanity of the individual who wore it was preserved and enhanced.

He learned how to tuck in his chin and lock his shoulders back, while keeping his knees flexed so he didn't feel faint when standing at attention on parade, so that he could appear to be a man without flaw or fault, a paragon among animals.

He learned how to forget he had learned anything, reacting instead of thinking, putting aside his mind and all that was rational in it. He learned how to be thankful for the gift of unthinking, and welcome the gift of insensitivity, and narrow feelings down to the few things that mattered among dehumanized men.

At the end of six weeks he was told he had made it over the first hurdle. He would be retained in the Corps. He waited in line for a telephone and finally got through to Louella.

They had little to say to each other. "Would I know you?" she said.

"I ain't got no hair, if that's what you mean," he said.

"That wasn't what I meant," she answered.

"Reckon you wouldn't," he said. "I've stopped makin' decisions, just doin' what people tell me to do. It's good that way." He had dropped into his old Texas way of speaking, as if years had evaporated from his life.

"Oh, sweet Jesus," she said, almost singing the sad words.

"Make yourself a life, Louella," he said. "I love you, but that don't do you no good at all." He was crying now. "Say goodbye."

"I love you too," she said, and clicked the phone dead on him.

*

His Drill Instructor was slight and wiry. He had no normal voice below a shout. Even when he was six inches away from his quarry, face to face, he shouted. Calvin looked straight ahead as demanded when he was spoken to, or shouted at. The lower level of his vision took in the DI's mouth. He studied the working of the human lower lip, dividing its functions into three parts, one dominated by the jawbone, another by the upper lip, and the third by the requirements of speech. He also examined the dental work on the man's lower molars, dividing it between what was done by a civilian dentist and that done by the horse doctors used by the Corps. It amused him to do this, but it had a purpose too. He was dehumanizing the DI. He would never know him as a man, even if the man were to want that. Calvin wished to know no one as a man or woman. He was being reduced by the military system to a number attached to an animal. He wanted to return what he regarded as a favor.

The PT instructor was a huge man, tall, and muscled where no one else had been in Calvin's experience. The recruits said his strongest muscle was the one between the ears. As if to prove it, he had large, flat, leathery ears with thick, rounded lobes hanging from them, the only bits of soft flesh on his body. Among the men his name slipped from Jumbo to Dumbo in one easy sidestep.

Calvin had already discovered that discipline functioned through the selection of scapegoats. But Dumbo's behavior exceeded this from the moment he set his large, dark eyes on Calvin. He hated Calvin irrationally and invented occasions to show it. There had been no incident or provocation that Calvin could recall. When he asked the other men in the platoon what he had done, the most sensible answer he got was that Dumbo looked half Indian and Calvin had blond hair, what there was of it.

"Keep your hair short, Whit," the man said. "He couldn't get a handful of it no matter how bad he wants to scalp you."

One of the sports they had to play was touch football. Calvin groaned whenever he saw the ball booted up high into the air in his direction. Dumbo always arranged to be on the opposing team, and when he saw the ball come anywhere in Calvin's direction he set off like Johnny Weissmuller with a crocodile in his sights. The instant Calvin put a finger on the ball, Dumbo "touched" him with two straight arms backed with two hundred and eighty pounds. Calvin had grown used to the bulk of the man interposing itself between him, from his position on the ground, and the sun, leaning over him with hands on hips, saying, "Still can't fuckin' take it, huh Whitmore? You'll never fuckin' make a Marine."

Dumbo gigged Calvin on things like allowing his canvas tennis shoes to have grass stains on the soles, and wearing an athletic shirt with a mud stain which was the result of one of Dumbo's own touch tackles. Eventually there were enough gigs to assign Calvin to a seven-mile solo run in full field gear, the standard punishment that most of the recruits drew at some time. He was assigned the last starting time of the offending men who had to do the run. It was a very hot October day. They were in the midst of a heat wave, with temperatures as high as in the summer and a hot wind ceaselessly nagging away like sandpaper on glass. At the last minute Dumbo set the starting time for the first man at nine-thirty instead of seven-thirty, forcing Calvin to set off at eleven in the morning when he should have been away at nine. Dumbo had rigged the punishment so that it was a showdown, with Calvin either running through the heat of the day or putting failure on his record.

Calvin accepted the showdown. He started well, setting his pace and getting his second wind early. After about a half hour the sun began to annoy him. It seemed to be caught in his head somewhere after the three mile marker, and he tried to shake it away from his brain, but it wouldn't leave him. He felt he couldn't lift his head to get his breath properly without losing his sight in the fierce brilliance exploding in his head. He kept running, slowly but steadily.

He had been running without any thought of time, so he had no way of knowing when it was that he began to feel afraid. The sun was going to attack him, he was convinced. The first attack came in the arroyo, when the sun took his sight away and he could not get out. He was unable to discern colors, only shapes in a tan landscape. In a panic he doubled back to the mouth of the arroyo and climbed up the slope, still running, in order to stay on the higher ground. From up there he might be able to see where he should go. He couldn't find what looked like a trail, but he thought he would strike it if he kept to a straight run toward the hills. At the hills, he thought he had come too far, and he turned to his left, still searching for the trail.

The second attack came a short time later, when he was running along the flank of the hills beyond the tank training ground. His mental compass unaccountably spun around. The ocean, he felt, was beyond the eastern hills, and the hazy gray mass to the west was a mirage designed to trick him. He turned back toward the hills. When he was unable to find a way through the hills, he turned back again and ran in the opposite direction until he found some half demolished gun emplacements. He gave up on finding a trail. He knew he was completely lost, and he would have to find a way out for himself. No one would find him, the sun would mislead them. He would have to wait, harbor his strength, and try again when the sun relented. He burrowed down in a sandy pit, convinced that the burning heat was lessening while at the same time shouting at it to let him alone.

Between three and four an officer with binoculars reported buzzards circling the firing range. A search party using the safe corridor through the range made its way there and found Calvin alive but raving, scratching at nonexistent ticks that were in reality sun blisters. When he was brought out his body was bloated and red, and his eyes stared at an alien world that no one else could see.

When he returned to the platoon after three weeks in sick

bay, Calvin learned that the commander had given Dumbo the lowest level of punishment allowed under military law and taken him off PT duty, making him gunnery instructor instead. He was still the instructor several weeks later when Calvin's gun crew of four men marched to the range to begin training with field guns. In a classroom in a hut they learned disassembly and assembly, the theory and calculation of shell trajectories, use of a plotting board to calculate the effect of side winds and head winds and following winds. They practiced safety drill, learning the primed and safe positions for each of the mechanisms in a gun, and what to do in an emergency. When they were ready, they abandoned the training gun in the classroom and went outside, where a howitzer was assigned to them for total disassembly, cleaning, oiling and reassembly. When it was in perfect condition, they trained with dummy shells and battlefield simulations, then with blank shells.

Dumbo through all of this was circumspectly faultless. He showed no favor or ill favor to Calvin. The other men in the crew felt he was possibly not helpful enough, but they were satisfied that they were not being picked on.

The final day of training was live ammunition firing. It was a bleak day. The false summer of the fall had turned to wet fog under overcast skies with a foretaste of winter. The crew drilled several times and went through a dummy run with a shell casing until they were perfect in their procedure. At eight o'clock the flag went up at firing range control, red for danger. A jeep flying a red pennant escorted a small armored truck behind the line of gun emplacements, and each crew off-loaded one shell into the bunker.

Calvin's crew was fourth in firing order. Dumbo went along the line of the other three as they prepared, loaded, readied and fired their first shells. Each satisfying blast brought a roar of approval from all the crews, and Dumbo smiled. He came behind Calvin's crew and watched them go through the now familiar routine. Calvin felt no particular thrill at the idea of live firing, only absorption as he went through the habitual movements that had been smoothed by practice into something that was almost a dance. Move to the left, come back to the right, bend forward and push, come back on release, kneel on the right knee. He watched the shell casing drop into its slot and saw it picked up by the ramming mechanism. Something made him glance back. A piece of metal on the shell casing was curling up like a thick wire hair as it moved toward the breach. A damaged shell would breach fire, Calvin's mind told him, printing the words behind his eyes as the shell slid inside now, the firing mechanism swinging into place, the pin on its way toward a shell not seated in the firing chamber.

"Breach fire!" Calvin shouted.

The other three men dived over the sandbags beside the gun. Calvin threw himself at the revetment behind the gun to get over it, clawing at the sandbags, as Dumbo jumped past him into the emplacement, his face the color of wine, veins distended like knotted cords under his skin.

He grabbed Calvin's leg and pulled him back into the emplacement. Holding him by the back of the shirt, he shouted at him, "You fucking coward! You son of a bitching . . ."

Calvin felt himself taken up and overwhelmed by the rolling blast that filled the sand and air and all of space around him.

He was becoming a philosopher, he guessed. He had discovered that something that could be measured and tested, the air and what was in it, could be replaced by something very different, something that was not an element at all. He saw clearly, brilliantly, realizing for the first time in his life that he was highly intelligent, capable of observations and assumptions and conclusions that were worthy of men he had never tried to emulate. The air, a composition of elements, could be replaced by something which was only a sensation.

He had seen an old movie once which was toned in sepia. This was an accurate comparison. The elements in which he normally existed had been replaced. He searched for the name of what had replaced them. He went through fear, panic, happiness, exaltation, sadness. He decided that it was pain. It was everywhere for him, and he was not sure where he was located in it. There was no reason to open his eyes, because he would see nothing but pain. He kept them closed. Pain and sound. He could hear part of the time, when the rushing, sucking sound of the pain slackened.

There were men around him. They were doing things that rocked him. It didn't matter what they did, because the pain wrapped around him and rocked with him as if he was wearing it. There was a scraping sound of metal on metal. He thought of can openers and the noise when the lid has to be peeled back. He opened an eye that he thought was his and saw the inside of a tin box, a very large one. Doors on it banged shut behind him. An ambulance. The field ambulances they called meat wagons. Someone was dead. There were people around to take care of it. He went to sleep.

When he opened his eyes, he found that he was lying almost flat on his back, tilted up slightly on one side near his hips. He tried to settle himself flat, but there were soft obstructions to prevent that. Over his head was a grid of shining metal pipes. Through the haze of the pain, which he now remembered had replaced air, he saw bottles of blood and clear liquids and cloudy plasma hanging from the pipes, and then he saw other tubes snaking through the pipes. It was a workshop, he concluded. Machines swished rhythmically, one of them beside him. He was on a bed, or maybe he was above it. From one of the blood bottles a tube came down to him, and from the machine beside him another tube came toward him. That must be attached to what covers my nose, he thought. He made his skin become sensitive. It could feel a movement as if a light breeze was blowing over him, nothing else. He caught sight of a white shape moving through the pain in his direction. He wanted it to be only himself here, so he closed his eyes and disappeared from sight.

"Shit!" the voice said. "He's pissed hisself."

"Jesus, you are stupid," the other voice said. "He's going to, ain't he. He's incontinent. You know how to spell it? You know what it means? Do you?"

"Well, sure."

"No, stupid, I mean what it means for you."

"I don't get you."

"Did you put a waterproof sheet on?"

"No."

"Then you can change the whole God damn thing, right down to the pad."

"Shit." There was a long pause, filled with movements as Calvin felt himself pushed and rocked gently from side to side while things were taken out and replaced under him. "When are they gonna have the God damn bed ready?"

"Soon as they can. We just gotta wait."

"Can I have a cigarette?"

"Ain't s'posed to around patients. He ain't going to complain. Guess you can. Yeah, go ahead."

Calvin couldn't smell the smoke. He tried but he couldn't find it. He couldn't find the strength to open his eyes, or to smell. He could hear, but that was all. He heard a noise from a distance.

"That's it. They're ready for us. Get rid of that cigarette. Don't let the nurse see you with it."

"I ain't that stupid." Calvin felt the capsule or bubble or whatever he was in begin to move.

"What's that noise?"

"It's that wheel. Started squeaking again."

"Didn't I tell you to oil it? Didn't I tell you to oil the cocksucker? Huh?"

"I thought I did."

"I can't make up my mind. I just can't decide if you're a wise guy or a stupid son of a bitch that oughta be taken out and shot."

"I thought I did it."

"Jesus! Okay, Mister Stupid Wiseguy, you wheel this cocksucker in by yourself. You go right ahead and grab the glory. I don't even want to be around when the ward nurse hears you coming with this thing. You just go ahead and have yourself a good old time."

Calvin tried again to open his eyes. He thought if he could do that, he might be able to thank them. He gave up the effort and disappeared again.

He started from far back, like taking a jump over a waterhole in boot camp. When he got to where he was going, he grunted and pushed and his eyes opened. A man in a white suit came out of the darkness and bent over him.

"You awake?" he said.

"Who? Who?" Calvin mumbled.

"I'm an orderly. You're in a ward. Hospital. You know?"

"Uh-uh," Calvin grunted. He tried to say something more, but what it was kept getting away from him when he tried to speak.

"You want something?" the orderly asked.

Calvin tried to nod his head, and felt something hard and breathtaking hit his body. "Jesus Christ, buddyboy, don't do that," the orderly said, pushing Calvin's shoulders back and holding his head steady. "Don't try to move. You're not ready for it."

Calvin tried again to speak. "Hurt," he whispered.

"You bet you're hurt," the orderly said. "Just take it easy now. By Jesus you are well and truly hurt. But everything's gonna be all right."

Calvin repeated, "Hurt."

"You mean you want something for the pain?" the orderly said. "Buddyboy, you're shot so full of stuff I couldn't get any more in. With the morphine in you, why, you're worth more to the Marine Corps dead than alive. Just goes to show you that Uncle Sam looks after the least deserving of us, don't it. Change Uncle Sam to God and you could make a Sunday School lesson out of that, now couldn't you. Hey, buddyboy, now don't cry, you're all right, Robbie's here, we'll take care of you. Tell you what, I'll get you something to help you get to sleep. Just a second, now."

The orderly reached up and pushed a button over the bed. He moved around the bed smoothing the sheets until the nurse came.

"He's awake," he told her, "trying to talk."

"Huh-uh," she said, "not yet. Put him back under."

"Okay," Robbie said.

Much the same sort of thing had happened to him when he was about twelve, Calvin remembered. He had flu, he thought, or maybe it was the time he had mumps. In broad daylight these same shapes had started to appear, whether he kept his eyes open or closed didn't make any difference. They appeared to be made of brown smoke. They took place in the center of his vision, wherever he looked. There was an invisible line drawn down the middle dividing the shape into identical halves. All the changes that occurred on one side also occurred on the other. He tried to stare at the shapes, which was almost impossible because they changed so rapidly they wouldn't be still to be stared at. He wanted to decide if one side was the original and the other was the mirror image, if one began a movement and the other picked it up. It was impossible to tell. Hell, he thought, don't worry about it, it's a free show. The brown smoke when it was dense was the brown of his old dress shoes, and then it thinned to a pale, smoky tan, even sometimes going wispy like only a film of smoke, the way everything looked on days when the pain was bad – no, that wasn't true, the film of smoke that came with pain was a mixture of red and gray. What the hell, let it dance for me, he thought.

*

They brought in a boy from boot camp. He had been hit by a jeep. Head injuries. He was put in a bed next to Calvin because it was the only floor space in the ward. The bed was like a play pen for a large child, made of metal pipes. He fought when they tried to put any clothing or bedding on him. If they covered him with a sheet, he wet it as soon as he could or soiled it if he had to. So his unmarked body, hairless except under his arms and at his crotch, lay spread out like some kind of background waiting to be made into an advertisement. He was tied to the four posts of the bed by the wrists and ankles. He smiled and laughed the whole time. His eyes were bright and seemed to react to everything said to him. He looked like a nice, humorous kid, the sort you would want to know, except that he was naked and he talked non-stop, cussing out someone who was not in the ward in language that Calvin had never heard before, filthy, crude obscenities that he was unaware had been invented. He was there for four days in that condition, until suddenly he went silent and sleepy and he was taken to another ward to be prepared for brain surgery.

The space was taken by wheeling in another bed, a standard one this time with sides fitted to it, as Calvin's bed had. The orderlies brought in another boy. His head was wrapped in bandages, with only the right eye and ear showing. When he was fed, the bandaging was pulled down so that the right side of his mouth was revealed. Below his mouth a tight, stiff bandage strapped his jaw firmly and immovably. The boy made no attempt to speak or establish contact with his one eye. He lay on his right side or, after a day or two, sat up in the bed wide awake and immobile. He was there a week, when some officers came to see him and he was taken into the orderly's cubicle for a conference. In another few days his mother came to take him away. He had signed himself out of active duty in the Corps. Treatment would be continued in a veteran's hospital near his home. Robbie told Calvin the night the boy left that he had tried to blow his brains out but had missed and shot away about half his face. Calvin's mind for the first time touched on Dumbo. But he turned away the thought, not yet ready to pursue his last memories of the gunnery instructor.

He was tired of the bed and the pain. As a concession to Calvin, the side restraints had been taken off his bed, to make him feel less hemmed in. Tonight the concession did no good at all. He felt stifled, cooped up. Robbie had given him what they called his goodnight kiss, a shot of morphine before he went to sleep. Tonight he couldn't sleep. He was angry with Robbie for denying him another shot, and bored with the games and tricks he played on himself to overcome sleeplessness. He lay awake listening to the sounds of the men in the other beds. The old sergeant back in the corner finally smoked his last cigarette and began to snore. Robbie was in his cubicle with a radio playing softly, cigarette smoke clouding the light that leaked out around the door. Calvin might just as well have been alone in the night in an otherwise empty hospital.

He moved his legs in the exercises the physio had taught him. He swung them slowly up and over, letting the weight of them lift his rigid upper body off the bed. He did this several times, getting the feel of the lift and planning the timing of the movements. He gave his legs a good swing, right over the side of the bed, letting them lift his upper body from the shoulders, fixing them so that the rigidity carried down all the way to his hips. At the last moment he used his hands and arms to push himself the last few inches until he was sitting upright. He held his weight then on his arms, letting his feet take their time to find the floor, gradually easing the weight off his arms and transferring it to his feet and legs. The pain lunged up through his body from the wound in his back, but he was ready for it. You could live with pain, he had learned, as long as you housebroke it.

He moved one foot about six inches and shifted his weight. It was all right, he could walk. He wondered why he had been so confident that he could do it. Holding on to the frame of the bed, he walked around it in the dark and silence, wanting no one to witness his triumph, his bare feet silent on the lukewarm floor. He repeated the circuit. To the left of his bed was another wing of the hospital. Lights were burning there on the ground floor, as they did every night. To get to the window, to see what was over there, suggested itself as the one thing in the world he most wanted to do. It meant crossing open space, maybe ten feet, with nothing to hang on to. Calvin remembered how he had swung on ropes across mud pits. You never looked down. You kept your eyes on where you wanted to go, and your mind and body did the rest. He lifted his eyes from his feet and legs and fastened them on the light coming in through the window. His bare feet measured out the distance in a solemn march, and he was there.

When he looked down he thought at first it was incomprehensible. A line of windows ran the length of the building, all of them giving on to the one ward. Glittering metal tubes ran in a complex grid between the ceiling and the beds of the large room. Looking in through every window he could see the same. From this grid hung ropes and slings that held some of the naked men up off the beds beneath them. Other men lay unmoving on beds. Through the grid passed pipes and tubes that were connected to the men. Bottles hung above every bed, feeding down to them. In among the beds and slings and paraphernalia strolled men and women in white uniforms, looking and feeling and prodding at the devices. Calvin remembered it, and the recollection made him shudder with horror. The place was a cold hell, glistening with white and polished steel. His stomach turned over in a dry heave, and his legs shook.

Robbie had come up silently behind him. "Hey, buddyboy, you want to go back now? You had enough, huh?" He spoke just above a whisper, soothing and settling Calvin, taking his arms from behind and supporting him as he turned away from the window. "That's it, take it slow, one step at a time, we can do it without calling the nurse, don't worry about that. Hey, yeah, that's fine. You're doing good." They crossed the gulf of floor to the bed. Calvin sat down on the edge of it while Robbie lifted his legs, and between the two of them, they turned him so that he could lie down. "Hey, buddyboy, we're gonna have to get you a longer bed, you're just about touching the bottom here. Yeah, you're getting there, the old spasm must be loosening up. You oughta tell the doc tomorrow. Oh, I guess it's today now, isn't it?"

Calvin settled down flat on his back, exhausted and riddled with pain. Robbie got a chair and pulled it up beside the bed. "Couldn't sleep, huh? Decided to do some exploring?" He pulled out a pack of cigarettes and gave one to Calvin, taking one himself, and found his Zippo and lit them. "I guess you didn't like what you saw, huh."

Calvin took a while to answer. "I guess I'm ready to know all about it. I remember being in there, down there."

Robbie helped him out. "We call it the meat market. There's not many that comes out of there, buddyboy. Not still alive. You almost didn't, I guess you know."

Calvin said, "I don't know nothing. I didn't want to hear, and people stopped telling me. You want to tell me about it?"

In the anonymous dark Robbie told Calvin what had happened to him. Dumbo had been killed, and Calvin had had part of the bone structure of his lower spine sliced away by pieces of the exploding gun. When he was brought in he was classified as a terminal casualty. When his vital signs recovered, however, a young doctor thought it would be a good idea to see what kind of a repair job could be done. The experiment might be useful for the casualties coming in from the Pacific Islands campaigns.

Calvin thought again of useful animals, but said nothing.

The doctor found that his spinal cord was not badly damaged and the paralysis was likely to be only temporary, most of it at any rate, so they worked on him, and sure enough, it turned out that he was paralyzed more with shock than real wounding. If he had been left in a sling in the meat market, he would have died. The surgeons performed some operations, and then he came on this ward.

Robbie said, "And you just answered the big question, buddyboy, because to tell you the God's truth, nobody, but nobody knew if when you got down off your bed you could walk. It's gonna hurt like shit for a long time, I'll tell you that for no money at all, buddyboy."

"I'm gettin' out of here some day?" Calvin asked.

"It sure looks that way," Robbie answered. "Well, you wouldn't stay here in this hospital, anyhow, but it looks now like you're going to make it all the way back into, well, life. How about that, huh?" He pulled on his cigarette so hard the tip glowed from red to yellow. "Maybe you'd have some good news to tell your wife. Maybe now you got good news you'd like to tell her about it."

"She might not think it was good news," Calvin said, the lie almost blistering his tongue as he said it. "Jesus Christ, why did I say that?"

"Never mind," Robbie said, "it's just something to think about, something we been wondering about. Go to sleep, buddyboy. Give me your cigarette, I'll put it out for you."

Robbie walked to the window and flicked the cigarette in a long arc, yellow against the black of the night, into the space between the two buildings. He looked down at the meat market and then came back to Calvin's bed. "You got out of there, buddyboy, one of the lucky ones. Guess you were meant to live, huh? Go to sleep."

In the rehabilitation hospital they held up mirrors so that he could see his scars. They told him he had to get to know them, just as he had had to get to know the pain. Okay, he thought, they're like a lot of people I know, you can know them as much as you need to but that doesn't mean you're going to like them. Dumbo's action in pulling him back into the emplacement, which enraged him whenever he thought about it, had given Calvin a leverage of sorts. The head of the board that evaluated men's prospects once they were released from treatment told Calvin that, given the circumstances, he was going to bend the rules if necessary to see that Calvin had a chance to return to duty, since he wanted so badly to do that. It wouldn't be full duty, of course, only light duty, but a genuine assignment. There was still a war to fight and Japs to beat.

When Calvin tuned back into calendar time, it was early fall, almost a year since he had run Dumbo's cross country. It occurred to him for the first time that life might be made up of little incidents that were sequential in a random way that was unimportant, because eventually however the incidents arranged themselves it turned out to be a sequence of destruction. Was that the story of his life? That run that could have killed him led to Dumbo's move to gunnery instructor, which led to the accident that should have killed Calvin. Somewhere in school he had heard about Nemesis. He reckoned that he could draw a picture of Nemesis that would come out looking remarkably like Dumbo. What had dead Dumbo looked like? Had he been taken to the meat market or straight to the morgue? Did he have a wife and kids? Poor little bastards if they looked like him. Think well of the dead, he thought. He dismissed that idea as horseshit. Don't think of the dead. That's enough.

He was finally well enough to leave hospital care. The personnel director had a job for him at a training school for cadet naval officers. Security at the school was handled by Marines, who also trained the cadets in drill and ceremonies. Would Calvin do it? He smiled, expecting immediate, enthusiastic agreement. Calvin surprised him, however, with his caution. He would have to speak to the hospital commander, he said. The personnel officer agreed, reluctantly.

The three of them met the following morning in a sunny dayroom overlooking the serene ocean.

The commander said, "This is pretty unusual, Whitmore. What's the problem? If there is one."

"I'm afraid there's a problem, all right," Calvin said. "I don't think I can do without my goodnight kiss, three times a day."

The personnel officer looked amazed. The hospital commander steadied him with a gesture.

"Hmmm. Yes. I didn't know that."

"Nobody else does, sir," Calvin said.

"Somebody should have picked it up before now," the commander said. "We won't keep you here to be treated for that. You'll have to be assigned where there's a hospital unit, or at least a sick bay that's manned by an officer." He turned to the personnel officer. "Do they have one there, at this school?"

"Yes," he answered, "they do. But I thought Whitmore was going to be discharged from treatment."

The commander turned to Calvin, forcing him to say it. "It's the morphine, sir," Calvin said. "I can't do without it."

5

The naval training school was a small college that had been taken over for the duration of the war. It sat in a bowl of the hills behind San Francisco Bay, the buildings white and low with similar porticos on all of them, in an architect's uneasy cross between a mission style and a classical yearning. The cadets were the only students there, with the exception of some scientists and their staff who were working on something that was so high security and cosmically secret that they were excused from the ultimate seal of loyalty to the republic, a name tag.

Calvin arrived there wearing corporal's stripes and was put in charge of training, manning and maintaining a secure watch. What it meant was that the cadets were on a watch rota doing six-hour duty, and Calvin's major jobs were keeping the night watch awake and introducing the trainees to the nation's secret weapon, paperwork. He also had a problem keeping the cadets on watch from taking bribes to let other cadets out or their whores and girlfriends in. In his disinterest he had forgotten that the need for sex, or the need to show off about it, was so demanding among the very young, and something which would have amused him at another time became his biggest problem in an undemanding job.

He established a routine for himself. He had his meals early, breakfast at six-thirty, lunch at eleven, supper at five. He set the watch at six in the morning, twelve noon, six in the evening, and twelve midnight. Between breakfast and eight-thirty he did his administrative work, mainly checking, correcting and filing watch reports. He taught military ceremonies, drilled or conducted inspections from then until his lunch time. In the early afternoon he went to the gym for his prescribed set of exercises and a workout or a swim. After supper he read or listened to the radio in his quarters behind the security office. Just before midnight he locked the safe and signed off on it, and after he had set the midnight watch, he went to bed, leaving an order for the cadet on watch at the duty desk to wake him at five-thirty.

The sick bay was located in the main building, adjacent and connected to the residence hall which was the cadet dormitory. The cadets had to leave the building and report to the sick bay by way of an outside door. Calvin persuaded the medical corpsman to unblock connecting internal doors and give him the keys. He reported for his first injection at a quarter to six. The buzz flattened out in ten minutes, in time for him to set the morning watch. He went again after he had finished lunch, just before setting the noon watch. Once he had eaten supper and set the evening watch, he went to his quarters, which consisted of three rooms behind the duty desk, and put up the Do Not Disturb sign. He took off his tie, shirt and pants and hung them up carefully. He found his book, usually something on current history, pulled back the wool blankets on his bed, switched on the radio, and waited.

The cramps invariably began by seven. If only his legs cramped, he pummelled them with his fists to relieve the worst of the spasms. If they were in his stomach as well, he couldn't lean over to massage his legs and had to lie prone on his bed, flat on the cool sheet, concentrating on relaxing the muscles just under his rib cage. If he tightened up and communicated the cramps to the scar and the area of the wound, he had to strip off his T-shirt and struggle onto the tile floor, letting the cool of it take off the worst of the surface pain. The cool floor also helped when the sweats started, if they were bad. The sweats were on the other hand a good sign, because they indicated that the spasms were past their worst and would gradually recede. The important thing he had to keep in mind was to let the spasms have their way, not to become tense in response or even in anticipation, because this sent the pain down his left leg, and when this happened it could be hours before it receded. It was important not to think about them, not to clench his jaws or fists, not to arch his neck in sympathy with the involuntary arch of his back. He had made a map out of the fine cracks of the ceiling, giving the countries and continents names, looking for evidence of major cities and waterways, the climate and vegetation and indigenous people. He concentrated on this imaginary world, the only creation of his imagination that he could recall, inventing details to prolong its diversions while the attack went on. When it was over, he would drift off to sleep for as much as an hour.

At about eleven he showered off the sweat, changed his underwear and put his uniform back on, and went to the sick bay for his goodnight kiss. After the injection he had a cigarette with the corpsman, who liked Calvin to sit and shoot the bull for a while. This was almost the hardest part of the day, when the lift of the morphine made him want to laugh out loud, and the tide of refreshment, like a cool, scented breeze after a hot day, swept through his entire body, while he was forced to sit and gossip about a confining existence that could not contain the elation he felt. Then it was time to come back and set the watch. He was usually asleep by twelve-thirty.

He had been aware of a recurrent dream for some time. He couldn't put a date on when it had begun, any more than he could remember the details of the dream as he first dreamt it.

It became fixed as an event of a certain part of his sleep pattern, impressing itself upon the time shortly before he was called by the watch in the morning. He began to recall details of the dream, putting them together piece by piece until he had a picture of it, a script for it, and began to welcome it as part of his routine. It wasn't pleasant, but it was diverting, since he didn't believe that there was truth in dreams. There was about it an unsettling sense of regret and of dread that was not focused. It was both comforting and frightening, like a familiar mystery.

The location was one that Calvin remembered from a picture in a book about an English general who had been given a castle for being a hero, presumably for killing more English soldiers than any other Englishman had yet done. There was a big wrought iron gate, all spears and curls and decorations, hung between massively ugly stone pillars. Beside one of the gateposts, attached to it by more of the wrought iron, was a small house. It was one story, made of stone of the same color as the pillars of the gate. It had small windows, and he could imagine it was very dark inside day and night because the window glass was cut into diamond shapes with wide glazing strips separating them. The roof had a wide overhang at the eaves, and it rose in four symmetrical planes on the four equally sized sides of the house, rising not to a chimney but to a point, where it was crowned with an iron spike which looked as if it had been poked through the roof by a giant, splintering some other iron in the process into strips that drooped beneath the spike.

The house was shaded by a mass of overhanging trees, and large shrubs crowded all the ground around it. The narrow road it stood beside bent away into shrubs and trees and disappeared. There was no path to the front door of the house, only a strip of grass between the road and the doorstep. A stone path led from the front door, however, to the left and around the corner of the house, separating the house from the dense shrubs. The path stayed close to the house until, at its rear, it met a stream, where it stopped. Beyond the stream there were glimpses through green leaves and branches of a sunny space. In his dream Calvin peered through the greenery as often as he had the opportunity, but he had never yet seen anyone on that road or out in the open grassland beyond.

No one seemed to live in the house. It was used only as a setting. Calvin came through the gates and up to the house in his dream, passing over the grass and finding himself on the path without having walked to get there. He was standing in front of one of the windows. It was open, and Annie Evelyn leaned on the sill talking to him. She was a girl still, but Calvin was a grown man in his Marine dress uniform. They talked again as if they were children, happy in what they had to say, keeping threatening things about their mamma and daddy out of the conversation. As they talked, people they didn't know appeared at the front door. To all of these people, because one group would disappear and be replaced by another, Calvin with Annie Evelyn's agreement explained that it was kind of them but he was aware of the problem and he knew he would have to take care of it in his own way. The talk was gentle, murmurous, like the sound of the stream that ran behind the house. Everyone in turn became convinced without much effort on Calvin's part that he was right about it, and once they were satisfied that he was protecting Annie Evelyn, they disappeared.

After several of these conversations it became clear that the problem centered on a dog. It looked like a sheep dog that Calvin remembered from Texas, but this one was coal black and longer in the leg than theirs had been, he thought, and Annie Evelyn agreed. The dog seemed friendly. It stayed several feet from Calvin near the corner of the house, occupying its ground, which was the path. It teased at him as if it wanted to start a game. When he moved to go to it, it wagged its flag tail and ducked around the corner, inviting him to follow.

When it became clear that no other visitors were coming, Annie Evelyn retreated into the house and closed the window, and Calvin was free to walk along the path toward the dog. It trotted ahead of him until it was caught between the stream and the man, so that it had to sit and wait for Calvin's approach. He knew then what he had to do. He walked to the dog and extended his hand, always his left hand, and the dog took it with a sense of canine duty, clamping its teeth on the wrist and the heel of his hand. There was no pain and no blood, but the grip was like steel. Neither Calvin nor the dog felt any anger or hurry. He knew that the next part of the ritual was to try to break its grip. Moving deliberately, almost languidly, he tried to throttle it with his right hand, then he picked up a stick which was always lying in the same place and tried with this to lever the dog's jaws apart. This was of no avail and the dog hung on, shaking its head to invite more trials of strength and wagging its tail.

He found himself beside the stream with the dog in the water. He pushed his hand down into the clear water until the dog's head was under it. The water was very cold, biting immediately at his fingers. From underwater the dog looked back at him, friendly and trusting, its dark eyes blinking but otherwise showing no awareness of a struggle, much less a death struggle, even as bubbles came from its mouth to indicate it was drowning.

At this point in the dream the shrubs would become less dense and the light beyond them would penetrate to where he crouched. This somehow gave him power over the dog. In the brightening light he watched as the dog vanished, knowing he was now going to get free of it, but also knowing that it was not really dead and their business, his problem, was unfinished. At the last moment of the dream he realized that he had intended to get to that open, sunny ground beyond the stream, but the cold of his hand told him that even ridding himself of the dog, drowning it once and for all, would not be enough to let him cross the stream.

He could not tell how long it was after the dream finished before there was a knock on the door, which was the watch waking him up as per standing orders.

The bad times, as Calvin thought of them, the hours spent cramping and sweating and waiting for that goodnight kiss, were getting longer and harder to bear. The pain was affecting him again, coming without warning at times when he had done nothing to revive it. The corpsman refused to increase the dose of morphine any more than he already had. Calvin was afraid to ask the medical officer; he would say he ought to have another look at it, which meant referral back to the Corps. That had happened once, and the reviewing doctor was unhappy with having to let things go on as they were, even though in the end he did. Things went wrong one morning. The watch knocked on his door, and Calvin called "Okay" and threw the blanket off and sat on the edge of the bed. Fifteen minutes later, when Calvin had not relieved the night watch, the cadet came back and, following orders, came into his room and found him still sitting there. He had been unable to get out of the dream about the dog, Calvin realized when he thought about it. He had to throw on his clothes and set the morning watch without his shot from the sick bay, and he made mistakes, not bad ones, but ones that made the cadets look at each other. He turned it into their fault and told them off, saying they were pretty damned worthless if they couldn't set a watch without him.

He changed the routine, then, to have the orders of the day written up by the night watch on the duty desk, so that they would be ready and waiting in case there had to be a quick turnaround again. He was convinced it was his medication; it wasn't the strength it used to be, and the dosage ought to be increased to compensate for this. When he complained to the corpsman that he wasn't helping him, the two of them got into a cussing match and after that there was no more shooting the bull to go with his goodnight kiss. That was no pain to Calvin, but it didn't help matters. With the medical officer and the corpsman both grown wary of him, he knew he had to watch his step. He kept more to himself than before, shortening the time he spent over meals with others in the mess hall, taking his coffee breaks on his own.

The medical people had warned him that the efficacy, as they called it, of the morphine would come and go. He hadn't understood, because they hadn't told him his tolerance to it would increase. He thought therefore it was poor supplies that was the trouble, something that would put itself right, if he could ride the problem for the time being. They had also warned that he shouldn't try to "bump it up" in any way. At the time he didn't know what they meant, any of them, only that the warning was given so often and so insistently that it must be important. He considered, now, what they meant. He was aware that he could prolong a buzz by black coffee and chain smoking. He supposed they meant extra pills of some kind, things like that. It was a temptation, even the thought of it.

One night the watch disturbed someone trying to sneak back in after lights out. The watch didn't catch the man, but in the chase a paper bag with a half bottle of bourbon in it was dropped on the stairs and turned in unbroken with the incident report. Calvin stowed it in his personal locker for a few days, as evidence. On an evening when the cramps were more than he could stand, he took the bottle out and had a swig from it. It ran through him in a hot shiver, and some of the turmoil inside him subsided, in a mild way releasing him as it did when he had his shot, like a partial shot of morphine. If this was bumping it up, he was all for it. He replaced the evidence with another half bottle and laid in a stock for himself.

People, he felt, were different to him. They were more like light switches, either on or off. If they were on, he could deal with them, unless they caught him at a bad moment. If they were off, he hadn't time for them and told them so. The people he couldn't stand were the ones who condescended, especially if it was a snotnosed cadet. If he thought one of them was looking down his nose at him, he found a way to put him on report. He knew that he was building a roster of enemies when he needed people to be on his side, but he had to put them in their place. There were people against him, he had to build his defenses.

Maybe, he thought, that was the identity of the black dog, the people who were against him. He had thought at one time it was the morphine, but that didn't make good sense. The dream began to worry him. Some part of every day he spent thinking about it, what it could mean and what it might foretell. He had begun to believe it might have some power. He was suspicious about it, like walking under ladders. He told himself he wasn't superstitious, but it was as well to keep an open mind about strange things like a recurring dream.

In his preoccupation with his constricting life, Calvin had lost his passion for the war news. The Battle of the Bulge had passed almost unnoticed. Patton's race across Germany had only gradually impressed itself upon his thought. It was different now. Classes had come to a stop. The cadets crowded into any room with a radio in it as the news from Berlin came in. Despite the confusion, when the tanks held back so the Russians could go in first, that part of the war was coming to a close. There was an end in sight, within days rather than weeks.

In that way V-E Day when it came was well prepared for. The school commandant gave a forty-eight hour pass to everyone except a skeleton crew of personnel. Calvin volunteered to remain on duty, while the cadets piled into chartered buses and made their way to San Francisco, where the celebrating had already started. The first of the casualties was brought back by a Shore Patrol less than twenty-four hours later, dead drunk and rolled for every penny he had. Telephone calls brought news of more, some of them stowed for safekeeping in the brig at Treasure Island. Calvin was up almost all night taking calls from there and from San Francisco, then from Alameda as well. The offenders were returned in batches all through the night and the following day. It was good humored. There had been a few fights and some incidents involving women who, unlike most of those in the crowds downtown, objected to screwing a stranger in a taxi or behind an advertising sign just because he was in uniform. Most of it was simple drunkenness, with the cadets being picked up for their own safety, and the order from the commandant was to go easy.

Calvin wrote up a report for each and sent the cadet to his room under restriction, no more than that. But it took time, and there was no one else to do it. He had to keep going. There was no one to help him, and the loss of sleep and the extra responsibility seemed to use up the effect of the morphine too quickly. He had to go to his store of whisky all day and all night and then the next day as well, each time downing a shot of it and rinsing his mouth with Listerine to kill the smell. The morphine and whisky and lack of sleep built up in him a lightheaded assurance. Then his mood swung the other way, he was angry, he would take care of everything on his own, the last thing he needed was interference. He constructed a wall of self pity around himself, and beyond that lay the enemy. He took refuge behind his office desk and refused to come up to the duty desk, shouting orders at the cadet on duty with him and finally retreating to his quarters. By the second night he was unable to take an emergency call which reported that one of the cadets had been pulled down off a lamp post in Market Street by one of his fellow celebrators and had punctured a lung in the fall. The duty cadet did his best with the emergency, then gave up and called the officer of the day, who found Calvin insensible, lying on his bed on his stomach with his shirt and his T-shirt pulled up to give his fiery scar some relief.

Corporal Whitmore was relieved of duty while a medical

report was prepared. It wasn't that he had done anything that couldn't be forgiven. The image that he presented to the officer of the day, of a man suffering beyond endurance from that wound, convinced the commandant that a medical evaluation was needed. A sensible person would have agreed, but Calvin was beyond that and took it badly. He added the officers to his list of people who were ranging themselves against him. When he met the evaluation board, what was really a reserve brought upon him by his suspicions of everyone around him was misread, so that he presented himself to the commandant as a man trying his damnedest to make up for a slip committed under severe provocation. He commended his dedication and restored Calvin to duty, verbally reprimanding the officers responsible for failing to provide relief for him during that forty-eight hours of duty.

The officers had no way of knowing that the black dog of Calvin's morning dream now wore the face of almost everyone he came into contact with. There had been an alteration in the dream, also; when he thrust his hand into the water to drown his persecutor, Calvin did it with venom and held it there as long as the cold would let him. In his dream he was convinced that he would one day be able to tolerate the cold longer than the dog could be deprived of air, and he would kill it for good and all.

A cadet came into the locker room of the gym with a message. Corporal Whitmore had a visitor. The duty officer had taken her to his quarters.

Calvin tried to sound lighthearted. "Blond?" he asked.

"Brunette, sir," the cadet replied.

"Well," Calvin drawled, "I'll come anyway." He took off the swimming trunks and put on his uniform and walked up the hill the short distance to the headquarters building.

His visitor was Barbara Ferguson. She had lost some weight, which emphasized the planes of her face, and she had put on a dress for the visit, which allowed her long legs to show to good advantage. There was a time when Calvin would have welcomed her, since the trouble was between her and Herman and nothing to do with Calvin, but he was unaccountably upset by her being there, as if she was an intruder who should have known better.

They fenced with small talk, and Calvin had some coffee brought for them. There was a reason for her visit, he knew, which he instinctively feared. He didn't want to know it. He wanted to leave her, and hear nothing.

Barbara said, "It looks like the war's going to be over soon, doesn't it."

He answered, "Yeah, we've got the Japs to take care of, but it's comin'."

"People are coming back already," she said. "Guys who were in the army, coming back to Red Branch, getting a real old hero's welcome." She paused, and he knew something was coming. "What do you think you'll do when it's over?" she asked. "Are you going to stay in the Marines?"

"They wouldn't have me," Calvin said. "I'm on light duty, that's the best I can do. Anybody who can't go into combat 'll be out."

"That doesn't make sense," she said. "The war will be over."

"Combat duty is just another way of saying one hundred percent," he explained. "I'm not that, won't ever be, I expect. They'll discharge me."

"You're going to come back, then," she said.

"I haven't really thought much about it," he said. "It's not something I think a lot about. I expect I'll have to one of these days. I don't even know what it's like there any more. It's a long time since I thought about it." He looked at her. "Is that why you came?"

She nodded. "This thing between Norm and me, Norm Bolger," she said, "I guess you know about it." When he nodded, she continued. "It's just about over. He won't say so, but I can tell. He's getting ready for his wife to come back."

She laughed when she saw the surprised look on Calvin's face. "He's no different from all the rest of the war wives in the town. They've had their fun, now it's time to get back to their own beds."

He tried to laugh with her but made no other comment.

"That's why I came to see you," she said. "About Herman. I think we can start over again. We're grown up now. We know more about ourselves."

"He was pretty tore up when you left him," Calvin said.

She tossed her hair and made a face. "Yeah, I guess he was. I was kind of surprised myself, the way things worked out." She thought a moment, put a cigarette in her mouth and pushed her face forward for Calvin to light it. She looked at him, sizing him up while her cigarette was lighting. He remembered that sort of look, that calculating face over a cigarette, from the movies Louella used to drag him to see. "I want him back now, anyway, and I think he'd come back all right, if Louella would let him go."

He had not wanted to think about it. He had refused to let himself know what he already knew. He had cut her free because he had to have his own freedom, freedom to unman himself, take himself right down to rock bottom so that he could come back up from there, like a man, and he had meant it when he told her to make a life for herself. But he had known the truth of his actions, and now it came at him as clear as a painted message on a fence wall. All the time he had not wanted her to do any such thing. He had wanted her to want him so badly that somehow, by some kind of magnetic pull that would bring him back from wherever he had wandered to, maybe even from death itself, he would come back. He had thought that, as in one of her movies, the ones that he had always said he couldn't watch, a woman's love, Louella's love, could bring that happy ending. That's why he couldn't watch those movies. They threatened to make him cry with longing.

Barbara had been talking about Herman and Louella, but

he hadn't heard her above the sound of his own thoughts. "They're living together at a little house where the Atwater mansion used to be. I guess it was a housekeeper's place a long time ago. The mansion burned down, did you know that? It burned down last year. Herb Atwater collected one hell of a lot of insurance, I'll tell you. Almost set fire to Mrs. Rossi's too, the burning stuff floating around. There's a family living in Nakagawa's house, the Jurgens place. Your old house is empty, closed up. The farm's going good, though, Herman's done a good job for you. The war's been good for you guys. Everybody's gone bigtime. It's all rich ranchers now. You hardly hear of a poor farmer anymore. Not in Red Branch, anyhow."

Calvin made a discovery that night. He found that you can wait in your sleep for a dream to come to you. Sometime near dawn the gates appeared before him and he passed through them, across the grass and along the house to where Annie Evelyn waited for him at the open window. They held their conversations with the inquisitive strangers until they left, satisfied. Then Annie Evelyn smiled at Calvin and went inside, closing the diamond paned window after her, and he was free to turn his attention to the dog. They drifted to the stream's edge, where the dog turned and gripped the hand and wrist that Calvin extended in friendship. The ritual of the throttling and levering over, the dog appeared in the water. Now something changed. The face of the dog was replaced by Herman Sanger's, the black body miraculously containing Herman's, floating on purest water. Calvin pushed his arm deep into the stream, watching the fixed smile on Herman's face as the bubbles began to rise from his nose and mouth. The light from the summer meadow flooded in as he did so, making patterns from lines of bronze and yellow and blue that played on the white bed of the stream. The cold was intense, but Calvin kept his hand pushed down to the full depth of the water. He felt he couldn't stand any more, but he pushed at his own left arm with his right one, forcing himself to keep it there. At the last moment of his endurance he saw a flicker of fear in Herman's eyes, an acceptance that there was an end in sight. That satisfied Calvin and he lifted his hand, knowing that he could kill to escape this creature.

There wasn't one single, definitive statement. It was a rolling awareness, like gossip magnified to an art of the gods, beginning in the middle of the afternoon and overwhelming them in minutes, like the mushroom cloud itself. The tales of a bomb, one bomb, that had wiped out Hiroshima began modestly, as if to repeat the statements made in the news broadcasts defied credibility and made the teller idiotic. The cooks and orderlies in the galley opened the coffee line early, long before the chow line itself would begin to operate, and the cadets gathered in the mess hall. CBS radio was switched into the speaker system. They listened with awe, elation, joy. It was deliverance for these young men. They would not go to war.

Nagasaki, and then it was over. As V-J Day celebrations began, Calvin reported to the officer of the day and asked if he could go on leave. Remembering the experience of V-E Day, the officer agreed, thinking it was another example of Whitmore's accurate appraisal of the requirements of the situation, very much to be commended. Calvin got a seventy-two hour pass, and, using the commandant's signature on the leave paper, drew morphine and syringes from the corpsman in sick bay, promising not to exceed the dosage.

After a lot of phoning, he found a taxi company that could be bribed to send a cab. The driver, for an additional tip, got him to the Southern Pacific station in time for the train south through the valley. There were few other travellers; most of those were men accompanied by other men, drinking and talking loudly, their feet cocked up on the seat in front of them, swigging steadily from half bottles of whisky. Relief at the end of the war, more than a sense of victory, ran in their conversation, with over that the wild, incredible stories of the bombs that had wiped out the Japs. Calvin avoided them and pretended to sleep in a corner of the day coach. In Red Branch another taxi drove him to the Regency Hotel, where he took a room at the back, away from a view of Greenfield Avenue. He was satisfied that he had not been recognized by anyone in the crowd of people packing into the bars, or in the cars driving in a chain up and down the avenue blowing their horns with kids shouting out the car windows, exactly as he remembered it when Red Branch had won the high school football game against Placid City.

When the cramps started, and the shaking and sweating, and now a yellow film that came down over everything, he lay on the bed. It was too soft. He got himself off the bed onto the floor, first putting a sheet from the bed over the scratchy carpet. He stared at the strange ceiling and thought about anything other than the assault upon his body. The war was all over now. Soon the men in training would be discharged, and there would be no job for him. He would get a disability discharge, and he would come home a wounded hero who had never fired a shot in anger or patriotism. He had Dumbo to thank for the fact that he would never know if, deep down, he was the kind of animal who could have killed an enemy face to face. He knew it wasn't courage that was at issue. It was to do with who or what he was. A man who existed could pull a trigger and erase a life. If he, Calvin Whitmore, could do that, he would be alive, he would prove that he had lived in spite of no father and no mother, in spite of Annie Evelyn being taken away from him, in spite of having no future because he had no past. He would be Calvin the way Louella was Louella in place of Mary. Someone, something, would have to move aside and make a space for him.

Holy shit, he moaned, the pain was the worst ever. He rolled on his side to try to ease the fire in his wound, but the spasms drove him onto his back. He tried to get up, to walk or sit or get under the shower, but his legs were so knotted they could not carry him. He rocked from side to side, panting and trying not to moan, and when he thought it was going to kill him this time, he broke into a sweat that washed his skin from the roots of his hair down to the spaces between his toes. As soon as his legs would let him, he stumbled his way to the bathroom and got out his morphine supply. It was four hours early, but he couldn't take any more.

He went down to the bar of the hotel at nine. The crowd had thinned out, and the people who were left had had a lot to drink and were coasting now. He found a stool at the bar next to an elderly man who was nursing a bourbon highball. Calvin had a bourbon and water and smiled to himself as the liquor bounced somewhere inside him and opened a channel that let in some brightness. The man said his name was Fred Prout, and he was a high school teacher. He was out celebrating for all the young men and women who had passed through his hands and had gone to fight for their country. It had been the making of them, he said. He knew all their sins and shortcomings, and they were all absolved, every one of them, by their service to their country.

Then he started to tell Calvin about the sins and shortcomings of the men and women who had not been able to achieve absolution because they had been denied the opportunity of going into service. He talked about the cheating on rations and profiteering and underhand property grabbing that had gone on while the war diverted people's attention and the opportunities multiplied. He mentioned by name the war widows who had miraculously given birth when they hadn't seen their husbands in as much as two years. He ran through a list of town worthies who had found other partners for the duration and were now busy putting that behind them in order to be in the front rank when the grateful people turned out for the victory parade, welcoming back the Red Branch heroes. Calvin listened hungrily. He fed on it like a pelican, putting it all inside somewhere so that he could use it piecemeal to keep him going.

At ten o'clock he said goodnight and went up to his room. He cleaned himself up and put on a fresh shirt. He had another shot of morphine, waiting for the buzz and enjoying it, letting it stretch itself out for as long as it pleased. Afterwards he washed out the syringe carefully and propped it above the wash basin draining onto some toilet paper. He took a small bag out of his canvas overnight bag. In the Corps it was called a dittybag, a name he always thought imbecilic but had to use to make himself understood. He put some money in his pocket and, taking the dittybag with him, took the elevator to the lobby.

The second feature was still on at the Aragon Theater across the street. Judging from the name on the marquee it was a cowboy movie, and he doubted Louella would be there. He crossed the avenue to where he knew the taxis waited for the end of the movies in order to pick up fares. A dark red Ford with a silver stripe painted badly along its sides was waiting, its driver smoking and listening to the radio.

"You free?" Calvin asked.

"No, but I'm not very expensive," the driver said. He rattled it off, giving away the secret that his wit was all patter.

"You know the old Atwater mansion?" Calvin asked. "West, far end of the avenue?"

"Burned down," the cabbie said.

"I heard that," Calvin said, "but I still want to go there."

"Sure," the cabbie replied. "Hop in, as all of us say in the movies."

In the car and moving, Calvin felt that it was indeed like the movies. The whole thing was a movie. It was a script of some kind that he was following. When he stopped the cab and told it to wait for him just short of the Atwater mansion's grounds, he recognized it as the movie of his dream.

The place must have been let go long before it burned down. A street light near the far corner of the property gave a dim, creamy glow over everything. Trees towered over a ruined garden. Shrubs fought with other shrubs, struggling away from long, rank grass, now dry and rasping. Everything in nature seemed in a conspiracy to fill the void left by a vanished, stately mansion in its green enclave, making it into a sanctuary for snakes and scorpions. Inside a rickety fence, reached by an even more rickety gate that had defied attempts to patch it together, a small house stood to one side of the mansion's grounds. It was almost lost in the rampant growth of decayed grandeur. When Calvin saw it, he drew in his breath as if he had seen a ghost. It was the cottage of his dream twisted and corrupted and turned to evil.

He got around the gate and went up to the door. It was unlocked, as he knew it would be. Louella had given up locking doors after once locking herself inside her apartment. The screen door had no retaining spring, and he silently propped it open. The front door grunted a bit but opened easily. He waited in the living room for his eyes to grow accustomed to the dark. To his left he could see the open door to what he took to be the kitchen. To his right a closed door was edged in faint light. He crossed to the door and listened at it but could hear nothing. He opened it a crack and looked in. Louella and Herman were lying on their backs naked and asleep. The sheet had been pushed to the floor in their lovemaking. Louella's nipples and the flesh around them were still crimson and bruised, and Herman's cock was stretched and red and twisted like something discarded.

The zipping sound of the dittybag being opened woke Herman. As he roused in the bed, Louella woke also. They stared at Calvin with their mouths open, pushing themselves into sitting positions, Louella reaching for the sheet to protect herself with. She turned on her side in order to grope on the floor beside the bed to retrieve the sheet. Calvin took advantage of the separation between the two bodies to take a gun from the dittybag and point it at Herman. He let the dittybag drop to the floor so that he could hold his right hand, the gun hand, with his left, because the hand holding the gun had turned so cold that Calvin felt he might not be able to go ahead with what he had to do. The first two shots threw Herman's body against the wall behind the bed. Then he began to collapse, so that he looked as if he had glanced down to examine his chest to see what had hit him. Calvin heard four more shots being fired without realizing he was still pulling the trigger.

He left the house to the sound of Louella's screaming and walked, in no hurry, to the taxi. He directed the cabbie to take him back to the Regency Hotel. Once in his room, he packed his overnight bag and waited for the police to come for him. There was a vacant space in the bag that he couldn't account for, until he remembered that it had been taken up by the dittybag when he came. He wondered how long it would take the police to arrive. He assumed it would be Mort Thomas, and he wondered vaguely how the years might have altered him. He picked up the telephone beside the bed and waited. A soft click was followed by the dry, disinterested voice of the desk clerk.

"Yes, sir? Can I help you?"

"I'm expecting Mort Thomas, the Chief of Police," Calvin said. "Tell him I'll leave the door open and he can come right in."

BOOK IV

The Sun Going Over

1

The immediate problem was what to do with himself. The jail would have been more convenient in some ways. It smelled like that soap they had had to use on the kids, he remembered, when one of them had come back to the Whitmore farm from school with head lice, but you could get used to it. The doctor could have come in regularly to give him the shots. When Mort said no, however, he didn't argue. The court bailed him in the care of the police, and Mort said "Go home," and that was it. That was it. Some door had shut behind him. But where should he go? Where was home?

"Don't go to Mrs. Rossi's," Mort said. "It wouldn't look right. It's too close to the Atwater place."

Auntie Donnell had come to see him in jail. She said she had Pearl outside wanting to see him as well. Calvin wanted to throw them out with his own hands. The refuge they offered to him, the chance to be re-absorbed by the Whitmore clan, made him sick to his stomach just to think of it. Whatever the Whitmore farm had been, it was never home.

Gomez could probably find him a room in the Rex Hotel. That would mean walking through the bar, though, past all the people he had known and the others who would come in to have a look at him. He couldn't face that.

It would have to be the ranch house. He borrowed a car from the Highway Garage, for twenty dollars deposit and the promise that he would be buying a used one from them as soon as he got himself fixed up with a place to live. He drove to the sign that read Whitmores Ranch and left the car beyond it on the side of the county road. He walked up the dirt road to the house, avoiding the blacktop road that led to the farm buildings. The house looked empty and closed, the shades and curtains pulled tightly over every window. He tried the door cautiously. It was locked. He breathed a deep sigh, relieved that Louella was not there. He unscrewed the black smoke hood from the imitation carriage lamp that lighted the porch and found the spare key still in its place.

Cranky from lack of use, the lock grated and the door hinges squeaked. He left the door open in a hope that the flat air would find its way out without his having to open windows. It was as static and gloomy as a museum. Nothing had changed, he thought, before seeing that everything had changed. Louella had carefully replaced everything as it had been when they first lived together here. Things that they had later moved around had been put back in their original places. Things that had been bought later, when it started to go wrong between them, had been removed. It was the house as it had been when they replaced the Staggs with themselves. He went to the arch that led to the red room. The folding screen was pulled across it. When he pushed it back, Calvin found that the room was empty. The chairs and the love seat, and the small wicker table that Louella had bought later, were all gone. He understood then that Louella had given the house back to him. This was her response to his rejection. She had given him the only thing that she could think that he wanted, which was a life without her. Her generosity, not her rejection, had made her do it, he understood that.

Mrs. Rossi gave Calvin a hug and a kiss and said almost nothing while she got his groceries together. He took them back to the house and carried them inside without being seen;

later, when the light of day had left the curtains and he knew the hands would all have gone to their homes, he hid the car in the tractor barn. He left the curtains closed and the lights out. He brought a chair and a small table into the red room, and got a mattress and blankets to make up a bed in the corner of the room. Lights in there wouldn't be seen by anyone outside. He could get to the kitchen and bathroom at night using a flashlight. Otherwise he would live in the womb of the house. Mort Thomas would know, and no one else.

The cramps and pain and sweats began almost as soon as he had installed himself in the red room, and they went on for several hours. At the end of them he didn't bother to shower, knowing they would come again soon. He crept to the kitchen and fixed a sandwich for himself and ate it in his room, and afterwards settled down to try to sleep. He counted up the time and found that it had now been fourteen hours since his last injection, a longer interval than he could remember. In that time something had become reversed in his body or mind, or possibly both. He lay in the dark and dropped off to sleep, only to be wakened by dreams that seemed more real than waking life. It happened each time he fell asleep, so that he lost track of what was sleep and what was a dream and what was conscious reality.

Sometime during his dreams or his wakings the room lengthened. When he turned on the flashlight he found that the screen had retreated several yards from where it had been before. When he switched off the flashlight, it switched itself on, so that he must have been looking at the lengthened room in his sleep, and yet now the room was as he had seen it when he had seen it in his sleep. He got off his bed and crawled around the walls of the room. He counted the number of times he moved his arms as he crawled first along the right side wall, then along the screen, then down the left side wall, then along the back wall. It had been a square room, but now it was twice as long as it was wide. He crawled back to the left side and toward the screen, getting to his feet when he reached the screen and fumbling along the wall for the light switch. It was retreating up the wall, making him reach up to at least his own height for it, and sliding up the wall as he pushed the button to switch on. Nothing happened. He thought the electricity must have gone off. He had tried it before and the light had come on, he was certain of that. Suddenly the light came on of its own accord, then went off, then came on again. He took advantage of a moment when it was on and tried to walk quickly to his bed, but the bed went away from him as he walked to it. He found he could not approach it directly and had to follow along the wall again until he came to it. Once back there he resolved not to leave it again, even though he could feel it withdrawing from the walls of the room. The room had begun to widen, he realized, marooning the bed in its center. He could feel the wall next to him, at the end of his arm, and yet he knew that it was moving away, beginning its movement slowly and accelerating as the moments passed.

When the bed was afloat somewhere in the middle of the room, and he was adrift on it like a survivor on a life raft, his bad leg began to swell. He knew he was too far from anywhere to swim through the black water beneath him for help. His leg became stiff, locked from hip to toes. He ripped his shorts off while there was still time, before the swelling made the leg of his shorts into a sort of tourniquet. He rubbed the leg, trying to keep the circulation going, but it had happened too quickly. All the feeling drained from his leg, as if it had a leak somewhere. It grew stretched and stiff as a tree trunk. He scratched at it with his fingernails and could feel nothing. The skin was not his, it was the bark of the tree that had taken his leg for its own. Now something gnawed at it, boring from inside out, something trapped and innocent that had to be released. He located where it had to come out and lacerated the skin with his nails, trying to free it. It broke free, he could feel it coming through his skin, and with that the feeling began to trickle back into his swollen leg. The light came back on for a few moments, allowing him to see that where the creature had come out there was a bloody wound. He was relieved to see it, things would be all right now. He lay back and lost consciousness, dropping into the dark pool underneath him as he rolled off his floating bed.

When he surfaced from the black lake, he found himself beached in the far corner of the room. His leg had recovered, but he could feel that it was bloody. At the other end of the room something tried to get through the screen. It was an animal that responded to the scent of blood. He knew that because a voice, that of one of the lecturers at the cadet training school, explained it to him. It was, the voice said, similar to his black dog, not identical, of course, since he had killed that. There was a way to get rid of it. This was to exchange the wound in the leg for the wound in the back. The scar and the mangled flesh that it covered would not attract the beast. He must strip off his T-shirt to begin with. Calvin pulled at the seam around his waist until he broke it and ripped the shirt to the neck. Now, the voice instructed coolly, turn to face the wall. Calvin protested that this would mean he was lying on his leg, his bad leg, which was hurting him already. Never mind, the voice said, if you want to get rid of the beast you have to make the leg hurt worse. Calvin turned to face the wall, lying on his side, and as he knew it would, the pain from his leg moved up through his hip into the wound. He shouted to the voice that he had it all wrong, that his instructions were wrong, they had to be, but the voice insisted. Calvin lay facing the wall, howling with pain, doing to his body exactly what he had avoided doing for over a year, while the voice told him that it could see the beast sniffing around and having doubts, now pacing back and forth behind the screen, now retreating and then advancing for another sniff, finally disappearing. The voice said that whatever he did, Calvin must remain in that position. He was panting with pain, trying to force it out of his brain by holding his breath for as long as he could, until finally he could fight it no longer; he gave up and fell into unconsciousness again.

He woke to gray light. He was sprawled on the floor as if caught in the act of searching for his bed. He crawled to it in its corner where he had left it a long time ago and fell onto it, feeling it was at least a place of safety. He looked down at his left leg, which was smeared with dried blood, and could not remember how it had happened. He lay flat and waited for the cramps to begin, and the pain, and the sweats. He could no longer remember how many times he had done this.

The telephone rang in the kitchen. Calvin switched on his flashlight and got to his feet. He found that the extra light was unnecessary, that it must be daylight outside. The voice on the telephone was Mort Thomas's.

"Just checking, Calvin," he said. "Didn't hear from you, so I thought I'd better see what was up."

"I'm staying here at the house," Calvin said, "hiding out. Don't know what else to do."

"No, that's about all you can do," Mort said, " 'til you get yourself a lawyer."

Calvin did not respond to that. Mort waited for a reply, then accepted that there would be none forthcoming.

"You okay?" he asked. "Physically, you know what I mean."

"Yeah, I guess so," Calvin said.

"Doc was asking about you," Mort persisted. "Wanted to know what was up, same as me." He paused, then added, "You got some of your medicine out there with you, Calvin, that you didn't tell me about?"

"I'm all right," Calvin said.

"Did you cheat, Calvin, did you have some hidden on you all the time or stashed away someplace?" Mort asked. "It's all right, you can tell me, people do that when they have your problem. I know that, I'm used to it." He waited for Calvin's reply. When none came, he said, "You've got an excuse,

Calvin, you don't have to be ashamed of it. Did you hide some away?"

"No," Calvin said.

"Then what the shit's going on, Calvin?" Mort said. He was getting mad.

"What day is it, Mort?" Calvin asked.

"Jesus Christ almighty," Mort said. "Calvin, what the shit are you doing?"

"I'll handle it!" Calvin said, angry in his turn.

"This is Thursday," Mort said.

"When did I come here?" Calvin asked.

"Jesus Christ," Mort moaned. "You hang on, Calvin, I'll be there in about twenty minutes."

"No!" Calvin shouted. "When did I come here? How long have I been?"

"I released you Monday," Mort said. "I better come out there."

"You'll have to break the door down to get in, Mort," Calvin warned. "Leave me be. Just leave me be, y' hear?"

"You're supposed to have help when you do that, Calvin," Mort pleaded. "You're not supposed to do it without a doctor. That cold turkeyin' is dangerous."

"Leave me be, Mort. I won't have no doctorin', you understand?"

"It affects your heart, God damn it, and your head," Mort said.

"You mean I might end up dead?" Calvin asked. He laughed and laughed and hung up the telephone receiver.

The first indication that he was better was when Calvin could distinguish day from night when he came out of sleep. Sleep was so full of demons, so packed with violent events that took him to the edge of his death, and waking was so full of the pain and torment that had produced the violence of his sleep, that he didn't care if it was day or night, or last week or next week. Reality in the form of the most basic observation that it was either day or night was therefore significant. He thought that it was like beginning to read. Out of the confusion and the meaninglessness and the threats were coming the first letters of an alphabet that would separate his mind from the chaos that had overtaken it.

He came to the conclusion that he didn't understand pain. He had thought it was a sensory reaction, that it was literally something to be felt. He knew now it was a great deal more than that. Where was pain coming from when there was no source for it? How could it travel in the snap of the fingers from one place to another? How could it at one location obliterate his ability to think, and at another clarify his mind until what he had done and what was to come supplied more torment than the pain?

He did not understand what the tormenting visions were telling him over and over again about what had taken place concerning Louella. In his waking and sleeping dreams she became confused with Richie Thomas, and she was killed by the tall man who led the riot police, who pointed his riot gun at her and shot her. She vanished, holding her hands in front of her face and crying, and the tall man disassembled his gun and revealed to Calvin that the riot gun camouflaged Calvin's own target pistol, which he showed to him, smiling, for Calvin's approval. Louella became confused with Dumbo, also, standing over Calvin on the revetment behind the field gun, ordering him to run until his heart swelled and beat so that he thought it was going to explode, then stopping him in the nick of time and making him lie in the sun where he felt his skin frying like bacon on the open fire at the gold camp in the mountains, letting him fry and fry until there was an explosion and his back blew open. Louella replaced Annie Evelyn at the little English house and came outdoors to stand behind him, just behind his shoulder, at the stream while he drowned the black dog that turned into Herman Sanger, but when he lifted the body out of the cold water it was Louella herself who had been drowned. Worst of all was when he observed himself from a distance walking into the bedroom at the Atwater house, unzipping the dittybag and taking out the target pistol. The observing Calvin told the other Calvin that he knew that he had taken the pistol from the firing range back at the cadet school, shaking his head at this violation of regulations that was sure to get him into trouble. The observing Calvin watched the assassin Calvin take aim as Herman woke up, watched him pull the trigger twice, then watched as it became Louella who bent her head to look at the wounds in her chest, watched the killer Calvin fire four more times, watched Louella shudder as the unnecessary bullets found her body.

He thought it must be a sign that he was getting better, reclaiming these terrible dreams from the fragments of horror that flickered in front of and behind his vision day and night. He was better. But he would have used a syringe if there had been one there, and he would have got himself raving drunk if he had had any liquor, he knew that. He took cold showers, and began to try to live by the clock by forcing himself to eat a sandwich made from the remains of what was in the ice box at something like a meal time. There was a small, fenced yard at the back of the house containing garbage cans and an unused dog house. He opened the window shade onto this private place and let the sunlight into the kitchen, but then he heard sounds from the farm buildings and closed it tightly again.

Very late one afternoon someone knocked on the front door and followed this by rattling the door knob. Calvin hid in the corner of the red room and listened. He heard his name being called and then shouted. It was Mort Thomas's voice. Calvin could tell that Mort was standing with his mouth close to the door frame, trying to get a reply. He said he wanted to talk to Calvin. Walking silently to the door, Calvin stood to one side and opened it for Mort, flattening himself against the wall as if a sniper was outside waiting for the merest glimpse of him.

Mort came in and punched the light switch. He saw Calvin against the wall and involuntarily put his hand on his gun.

"Jesus H. Christ!" Mort said.

Calvin was wearing a Marine Corps T-shirt and a pair of work jeans that he had found in the house. His feet were bare except for a pair of straw Japanese sandals that had been left in their house by the Nakagawas. He had not shaved since leaving jail, and his hair was mashed flat in patches from the sweats.

"You look like shit, Calvin," Mort said.

Calvin could find no reply.

"You looked at yourself in the mirror lately?" Mort asked. "It's time you did."

"I'm clean," Calvin said, "that's enough."

"You don't smell it," Mort said.

"I'm still sweatin'," Calvin said.

Mort sat down and, taking over, gestured to Calvin to sit opposite him. "You look like you've lost about thirty pounds," he said. "How's the rest of your health coming?"

Calvin said, "Better every day. I'm getting there."

"Still bad?" Mort asked.

"Getting better," Calvin answered.

"Let's see your arms," Mort said. "Come on, hold 'em out. Let me have a look at them. That's right."

He crossed to Calvin and examined them, looking for fresh needle marks.

"Addicts don't tell the truth, Calvin. I've got to be satisfied we're talking to each other in the same language. Not that I don't trust you, I just don't trust you." He was satisfied. "Okay. Good. You think you can stick to it? No back-sliding?"

"I'm over it," Calvin said, "the worst of it. I have to get well, that's all. I'm getting there. By the trial, I'll be clean of it. It only hits me once a day now, about five o'clock. Out here I know there's no way I can get ahold of what I need, and there's nobody to hear me crying, and I roll around and sweat it out. I put on a good old show, Mort, it wouldn't be fittin' for your jail. I'm sleeping better, too. I haven't got through a whole night yet, but I'm getting there. I'm going to win, Mort."

The arrogance and assurance of the reformed addict played on his face, and Mort saw it with satisfaction. He smiled, chuckling with approval, and slapped his cap on his knee. Calvin misread the gesture. In his invalid's sensitivity, he saw in it not confidence in him but doubt that he would win out over his addiction, even mockery of his promises. He stood up, pushing the top of his head at the sky and tucking his chin into his chest, demonstrating that, if only for a few seconds, he could pull himself ramrod straight into a Marine brace. There was a hint of a pull on his arm that would end in a snappy salute again, one day soon.

"I'll know what they're doing to me when I go to that gas chamber. That's for sure," Calvin said.

2

Headline in the *Los Angeles Times*:

RETURNING VETERAN KILLS WIFE'S 4F LOVER

The newspaper editors from San Francisco and Los Angeles sent reporters not from the top flight but very close to it. It was the state's first big story of its kind.

Together with the more and less local journalists, they took up two rows on both sides of the center aisle of the courtroom. Spectators had been lined up outside the courthouse since dawn, and now they packed every seat in the place even though it promised to be a serene, beguiling and glorious October day. There was a lot to look forward to. It was the first appearance of the new district attorney, Dick Friedland, in a murder trial, and the first time Walter Halbkeller, deacon of the Presbyterian Church and one of God's own people, had served as foreman of a murder jury. Red Branch was full of the rumor that there was some sort of trouble over the defense, and everyone waited for the first appearance of Calvin's attorney.

And that was the source of the first big surprise of the trial. Judge Dix had barely warmed up his gavel and delivered his customary warning to the spectators, whom he loathed and detested but had to admit to his courtroom, when he asked for submission of the plea of the defendant. He asked, "How does the accused plead?" and heard silence in response to his question. He repeated the question and stared hard at Calvin, sitting significantly alone at a table in the well of the court. He turned to the clerk of the court. "Mr. Clerk, what's going on here?"

The clerk got up and walked toward Calvin. "You going to change your mind, Calvin?" All he got for his trouble was a slight shift in Calvin's hunched shoulders.

He turned back to the bench. "Your honor, the defendant refuses to plead, because he says everybody knows he did it. And he told me he won't waste your time with a defense attorney."

The judge banged his gavel a few times, more to give himself something to do than to restore order. He took the hammer end of it in his hand and pointed the handle at Calvin.

"Young man," he said, "no one commits suicide in my courtroom. You understand that? Do I make myself clear?"

He tried to make it sound mean and cantankerous, but it came out sad and despairing. He held the gavel in both hands, studying the top of Calvin's head and what little he could see of his face.

"Mr. Whitmore," he said, "Corporal Whitmore," he corrected himself, "you'd do me a big favor if you could look at me and let me see if we're getting anywhere with you. Justice isn't easily arrived at. Don't make it worse for me than it already is. All right?"

Calvin looked up at him and nodded. He took his hands from between his legs and crossed them in his lap, resting his elbows on the arms of the chair. When he straightened up, he looked again like Corporal Whitmore, and the whole courtroom sat up and adjusted garments and posture.

"The defendant isn't entering a plea, which in law is a plea of Not Guilty," the judge said. "Court is adjourned while we try to figure out what to do about an attorney for him." He looked at the spectators. "Give your names to the man at the door and come back in two hours. Go get some lunch or some peanuts or something. Maybe the circus will be ready for you by then." He smirked his contempt at the ghouls, stood up and pulled his gown around him like a dress extra who knew what to do with a toga, and swept from the bench as well as a man of five feet six inches with an attack of sciatica could do.

Tullio Contini was sulking in his tent. There it was, the biggest trial in the history of Red Branch, the sort of trial in which a young attorney like himself could make his name, and he couldn't find a way into involving himself in it. He had pestered, he had lurked, he had fetched and carried, all to no purpose. Whitmore wouldn't let Tully represent him, in spite of the outline of the defense case that he had prepared, and that was that. He sat behind his desk in his office over the First National Bank straightening a paper clip before bending it into an oblong and attaching spit wads near its four corners to look like the tires of a skeletal trailer. The public spirited citizens who had tentatively briefed him to take the case for the defense, who for the most part wanted to paste a black eye on Dick Friedland more than they wanted to see Calvin Whitmore acquitted, had blended in with the wallpaper when it was time to commit their names and their money to a defense fund. He was young in the ways of the law, but it was already clear to Tully that public spirit gave way to private penury when the starting pistol was raised.

His telephone rang. He reached for the receiver with his left hand while his right scribbled the time, 10:20, on a note pad, as he had been taught to do in law school. "Tullio Contini, attorney-at-law," he said.

"Judge Dix," was the reply. Tully sat up straighter as if in the physical presence of the judge, who ate casual attorneys like Hershey bars.

"Yes, sir, Judge," Tully said, "how can I help you?" He did a double take in the privacy of his office, the object of it being the telephone receiver. "Judge Dix? Really? I thought you were in court."

"Just be quiet and listen to me," said the judge. "I'm told by my less than reliable spies that you prepared a case for the defense in the Whitmore trial. Is that right?"

"I laid it out, that's right," Tully answered.

"You still got it?" the judge asked.

"Sure," Tully said. "Has he changed his mind? Is he going to plead?"

"No," the judge said. "I entered a plea for him and adjourned."

"Oh," Tully said. The conversation seemed over before it had begun.

"I'd like you to work for nothing," the judge said. "No point in beating about the bush. It's a son of a bitch of a case, Mr. Contini. Your client will be an unfriendly witness, if he'll testify at all. He's ready to say it was premeditated, all the rest, doing everything but walk on his hands to get to the gas chamber. It's a loser."

"What would I do, then?" Tully asked.

"Find the motive, the one that matters," the judge said. "I won't accommodate Whitmore's death wish without knowing why he did it. If then."

Tully was inexperienced but not stupid. He knew the sound of doubt when he heard it. "No fee," he said without expecting an answer. "Expenses?" he asked.

"Up to a point," the judge said. "I think I can get a gentleman or two to cover that for you. Reasonable expenses."

"How do you plan to proceed?" Tully asked.

"Opening submission, identification of exhibits, maybe a couple of witnesses to identify the defendant, that sort of thing." Judge Dix waited. "Well? What do you say, Contini?"

"I don't want to be known as the guy who works for nothing," Tully said.

"Nobody will know, young man, I think you know you can rely on me for that," the judge said. "I'll see you in my chambers in ten minutes, and we'll resume at eleven forty-five. We'll sit through lunch and adjourn early." He sounded neither pleased nor satisfied when he hung up the phone.

"Mr. Friedland," the judge said, "you're going to have to cooperate with me on this, now, or we'll all come out looking like God damned fools." He jabbed the damp, smelly, chewed end of his cigar at the two men while scratching at his shins with his free hand. He had pulled up his gown into his lap, where it lay bunched up collecting cigar ash, making him look like a disreputable old widow who smoked cigars and liked showing her underpants and didn't give a damn who knew it. The windows were closed tightly, and the tan curtains, yellowing in their ancient folds, defeated any beam of light that was attempting to make inroads into Judge Dix's version of stygian gloom.

"I'll put it to you this way," he said. "You're not going to get your conviction if you challenge counsel for the defense on the grounds that he's not speaking for the defendant. I warn you. I won't give it to you on that. You're going to have to give Mr. Contini a free hand in presenting a defense that is contrary to the defendant's wishes but in his best interests. Now is that clear?" he asked the prosecutor.

"The prosecution and the defense are going to argue this thing out as if the defendant isn't there?" Friedland said.

"That's right," said the judge. "Which he very well may not be. If Whitmore can't behave himself, he'll leave the court and we'll proceed without him."

"That wouldn't look very good on appeal," Contini said.

The judge swivelled his chair in Contini's direction, doing it deliberately, moving the chair first and following afterwards with his head and finally with his eyes, like an ice skater doing a twirl in slow motion.

"Jesus!" he snorted. "I thought you were smart,

counselor." He stuck the cigar in his mouth and just as quickly took it out again, leaving a brown smear on his lower lip that began a hairline trickle down to his chin. His voice was loud with contempt and ridicule. "This bozo will never appeal in a million years, a billion years. We, the three of us – this band of brothers, may I call us? – we have to achieve justice in this court. Do you understand? I don't want a verdict, you peckerhead, I want justice. Can I get it out of you? Huh? Can I?"

So this was a sample of the famous spit roasting that he'd heard about. He had been Dix'ed and he knew it. He longed to be able to mop out his armpits, and his tongue and brain seemed unable to team up to deliver an answer.

"Corporal Calvin Whitmore, gentlemen," the judge said, "don't you forget him for a minute. Anytime I want to throw you off the case, Contini, he's my excuse. Any time I want to declare a mistrial, Friedland, the same goes for you. Now let's invite the trained apes back and get this God damn show on the road!"

He looked at the mess of tobacco wilting in his fist and registered disgust, then tossed it into an evil, stinking spittoon beside the American flag which slumped from a spiked stick behind his desk. He wiped his mouth with the back of his hand and examined the brown smear of evidence before he growled, "Jesus Christ! I hope now this God damn war is over, Tom Potter can get hold of some decent God damn cigars!"

JEAN CRAVITCH, MAID, REGENCY HOTEL: I went back upstairs just before leaving for the night to make sure his room was all right. There was a complaint about the air conditioning from the man who had that room the night before. While I was there I decided to check the supply of towels and things. There was a hypodermic syringe washed out and drying on the shelf under the mirror, the one in the door of the cabinet, over the wash basin. I noticed it because those things give me the creeps. I can't stand the thought of having needles stuck in me, especially the idea of sticking them in myself. Ugh! I opened the door of the cabinet, that's over the wash basin, to see if there was extra soap for him, and I knocked off this medicine bottle, but it fell onto the floor and didn't break because it landed on the bath mat. So naturally when I picked it up I looked at the label, and it said morphine. I thought, cripes! this guy is a dope fiend, and I got out of there, fast.

No, I didn't see a gun. Yes, I saw a little zipped up bag, like all the guys in the service get. Usually it holds toilet articles, when I've seen them in the hotel. This one didn't, because his toilet articles were all rolled up in a white washcloth sitting on top of the toilet tank. I remember, because when I saw it I hoped the toothbrush didn't decide to roll into the toilet. Ugh!

CINCINNATUS TRASK, TAXI DRIVER, SILVER STRIPE CABS: I wasn't really looking for a fare, being V-J night and all that, I thought I'd be lucky to get a fare after the show was over at the Aragon Theater, because I thought everybody would go to a bar or down to the dance at the Memorial Hall. I figured I'd be busy later, but not then. To tell you the truth, he kind of scared me when he came up beside the cab. He startled me. There was just something about the way he did it. He was kind of excited, but you could tell he wasn't drunk. I just had the feeling, I don't know exactly why, but you know, the feeling that something big was coming up for him. Well, shoot, what I'm trying to say is I've seen guys look and act like that when they've got a Yes over the telephone and they're on their way over to the girl-friend's. What they want out of you is to drive the cab, shut your mouth, get 'em there in a hurry and afterwards forget you ever saw them. Only, this one was very different, because he told me to wait for him. I figured it was going to be a quickie, but Wow!

Sorry, your honor, my mouth kind of runs away with me.

MORTIMER THOMAS, CHIEF OF POLICE, CITY OF RED BRANCH: Yes, sir, I've known Corporal Whitmore for a long time. I knew that he'd split up with his wife, but I didn't know how much he knew about what happened after he left his ranch. They'd split up before he left, he told me, I saw him here in town when he had already quit farming, and he was just waiting around for the date of his induction physical in San Francisco. That was the last time I saw him until I arrested him. He's a fine young man. I never had any reason to doubt his integrity, no sir, or his good judgment. Maybe some of us were a little surprised when he up and married Louella Parsons. Yes, sir, that's Mary Parsons. When they were going together, they were kind of off again, on again. After her husband left, I used to see Mrs. Whitmore pretty regularly here in town. She and Mr. Sanger seemed happy enough. I think most of us who knew them thought it was a good thing that the three of them had got it settled. We thought there would be a divorce when Calvin got back, and that would be that. The last weeks that Calvin was here, before he went into the Marine Corps, he and his wife were pretty unhappy, it didn't take much to see that.

Well, Mrs. Whitmore telephoned, you have that report from the police blotter, it says it was eleven-twenty. I was off duty, but I was uptown, just in case there was anything that needed my attention. People were pretty excited, a lot of parties, lots of cars out on the streets. The call came to the jail, and the sheriff's deputy on duty phoned around until he found me. I guess it was eleven-thirty. I went out there to Mrs. Whitmore's house. She was in the kitchen in her bathrobe. Kept trying to throw up and couldn't do it, so she couldn't talk. I found the body of Herman Sanger in the bed, the only bed in the house. It was unclothed. He had five bullets in him, and there was a sixth one in the wall. They came from the gun over there, a target pistol, GI. Well, as soon as I saw it was Government issue, it doesn't take a genius to figure that one out, I went into town as soon as the forensic crew got there. He wasn't at the Mariposa Hotel or the Rex, but there he was in the Regency Hotel sitting in his room waiting for me. He said right away, I didn't even have to ask, "I killed Herman. Arrest me."

Yes, your honor, I have some experience of murders. There's always a good motive, a strong reason. There always was, up until now. If you look at it one way, it's obvious that he killed Herman for taking his wife away from him while he was away in the Marines. If you look at it another way, that doesn't make sense, because he and his wife had split up, and there's no evidence that he had made an attempt to get together with her again. No, sir, I can't verify anything, he refuses to talk about it. Then there's the drugs. He was addicted to morphine, as a result of his injuries in the Marines, and people will do strange things under the influence of drugs. But you see, he knew about his addiction and what it was doing to him, and what he told me under questioning was that it was driving him away from people. He wouldn't have a reason to be trying to come back to his wife. It isn't the sort of thing they would do, either the defendant or drug addicts in general, to do what he did. If I can say so, I'm no expert but in my experience with the Mexicans around here and their dope, a man in Calvin's situation would be more likely to kill his wife than her boyfriend. Calvin being Calvin, he'd be more likely to kill himself in the first place.

Yes, sir, I'm aware of Mrs. Whitmore's background. I object to that comment, it's not accurate to say that I'm protecting her. She was a little bit wild when she was young, people said she was man crazy. Okay, the men called her jail bait, I'll agree. But that's all past. From the time after my boy was killed in the riots, I've never known her to be anything but a good wife to Calvin, until they split up. She didn't do like a lot of the war wives in this town, that's for sure, and that's one thing to be said for her. She's behaved a hell of a lot better than women of a lot better reputation in this town.

I'm sorry, your honor, I apologize. I know that two decent people are getting dragged through the mud, and I don't want to add to it, that's all. Yes, sir, I'll shut up.

Mumbled through his teeth as he passed counsel's tables to resume his seat: And I don't give a doodly squat if you two hangmen want to call me a hostile witness.

"I call Mrs. Mary Whitmore to the witness stand."

Louella had remained out of sight ever since the murder. As she came in now from the room where she had been waiting, the spectators were as silent as in church. She was dressed in white, emphasizing the platinum blond of her hair, and highlighting even more than that the extraordinary whiteness of her skin. She looked as if blood had been withdrawn from her body, and some chalky, floury substance had been substituted. She didn't look at Calvin, though she must have been able to feel his eyes on her face, reading in its tense serenity the appalling misery that she was still going through.

Dick Friedland was not looking forward to this. He had questioned her at the time of bringing the charge against her husband, and he had interviewed her since that time. Mrs. Louella Whitmore, fifteen years his junior, made him realize he didn't understand the ABC's of life. He had a wife and two children, the boy older than the girl, and they had a dog named Skipper, and they all lived happily in a large house on Bridge Street that was in a large yard shaded by big trees, of which one, out in the back yard, had a swing hanging from a branch and when you swung very high, trying very hard, you flew out over the fence around their lives and saw tumbledown houses among the eucalyptus trees across the bridge. He had beavered away all his life, starting with a paper route, a job after school, honor society in high school so he could get a college scholarship, Phi Beta Kappa, law school and a pass of the bar exams on the first try, two years private practise, election to city attorney, election to district attorney. He had lived as if he did things because it was understood that a person was meant to do them and they existed for you to do, taking them in order and doing them well, with the doing the only motive or justification that was necessary. He had never asked Why? of his father, and there was still no Why? in his life.

This young woman represented something else, which he didn't or didn't want to recognize, doing things because they came from a force that he had never felt. He was frightened by her, and attracted to her, immensely. His job now was to destroy her.

They established who she was, her age, all the rest of the preliminaries.

FRIEDLAND: Can we go back to this change of name? You were born Mary, but you say that when you were fifteen you changed your name to Louella. Why was that? You didn't like being called Mary?

LOUELLA: I changed my name when I left home.

FRIEDLAND: You left home when you were fifteen. Does that mean you stopped going to high school?

LOUELLA: Yes. I was too old. I wasn't a kid, like the rest.

FRIEDLAND: But you were only fifteen. What did your mother think?

LOUELLA: She didn't like it at first, but it didn't really matter to her.

FRIEDLAND: Where did you live? Did you stay in Red Branch?

LOUELLA: I rented a one-room apartment from the dentist, in the professional building. I had a job, I could pay for it myself.

FRIEDLAND: And you lived there on your own?

LOUELLA: Yes.

FRIEDLAND: But you weren't always alone.

LOUELLA: No.

FRIEDLAND: Who stayed with you there?

LOUELLA: It isn't a big secret. You don't need to play it up for the newspaper reporters. You've won your election, you don't need to do this to me.

[*Judge Dix intervenes and admonishes the witness*]

I liked men. I still do. I left school because I wanted to live my own life, and that included meeting men. I met them at the diner, where I worked, and I met them socially, and when I liked them, they came back and visited me at my apartment. If this was Hollywood, you'd call me a good time girl. In Red Branch, before the war, they called me a slut, but I didn't look at it that way.

FRIEDLAND: So you had different men friends, and you entertained them at your apartment. What changed that?

LOUELLA: I met Calvin.

FRIEDLAND: The defendant.

LOUELLA: I met Calvin. We fell in love, well, I fell in love with him, and I stopped going out with anyone else.

FRIEDLAND: You stopped seeing any other men after you met the defendant, until you were married in, let's see, 1940, November of 1940.

LOUELLA: Well . . . you'll probably drag somebody up here to say I'm lying. Calvin went through a bad time before that, I think it was early in that year, it was about six or eight months after we'd been together. He didn't know any more if he wanted to stay with only me. He wasn't sure any more what he wanted. We were still very close, but he wanted us to. . . . I don't know, I didn't really ever know. I think he wanted more time and more elbow room, that's the way I thought about it. We both tried to go back to living something like we had before we met. I went with a few men then. He went out with a few women who were after him.

FRIEDLAND: You would say he was always attractive to other women, then? Even when he devoted all his attention to you?

LOUELLA: Oh, yeah, sure.

FRIEDLAND: And was he still attractive to women after you were married?

LOUELLA: They looked at him a lot.

FRIEDLAND: That's interesting.

LOUELLA: Why? That's life.

FRIEDLAND: What is interesting is that after you parted, and after your husband went into the Marine Corps, and after you lived with Herman Sanger, your husband seems to have continued to behave like a loyal husband by not having any other women friends.

CONTINI: Objection.

JUDGE: Sustained. Establish your facts before you refer to them, Mr. Friedland.

FRIEDLAND: Now, you had a very close friendship with the defendant, and then there was some kind of a cooling off. What brought you together again?

LOUELLA: The riots. I wanted him to stay out of the whole thing. It wasn't his fight, any more than it was mine. He got dragged into it. He was in the middle of it when the women and children were stampeded out of Garfield Park, and I hated him for it.

FRIEDLAND: You were on the side of the strikers and the communists? Are you involved in that kind of politics, Mrs. Whitmore?

LOUELLA: I'm on the side of people who can't speak up for themselves, like me. Like my husband. There's an expression I don't like that says it, I'm for the person who is being taken for a sucker.

FRIEDLAND: You think somebody made a sucker out of your husband in the Garfield Park riot?

LOUELLA: I know they did. When it all ended in Chief Thomas's boy being killed, I thought I could never forgive Calvin, until what he said let me know how he had been used. When I could forgive him, we decided we would get married.

FRIEDLAND: I don't entirely understand, Mrs. Whitmore. What do you mean, your husband was used?

LOUELLA: It's hard to say. It's very hard to explain. There's something about him, whatever he does, whatever reason he seems to do it for, he's innocent. People see him do something wrong – terribly wrong, awful – and they look at him, and they know he's innocent. Look at him now.

[*She breaks down, and Judge Dix recesses the trial for fifteen minutes*]

FRIEDLAND: So you were married, and you went to live on your new ranch. Was everything all right between you and your husband?

LOUELLA: It was fine. It was very happy, that time of ours.

FRIEDLAND: Did you ever think there was a problem anywhere, any dark clouds on the horizon?

LOUELLA: Not really. [*She pauses*] I think if I'd been looking for one, I would have seen something when Pearl Harbor happened. My husband was unhappy when he saw men his own age being drafted and joining the service. It seemed natural to me, that he would feel like that, but now I wonder if it was more.

FRIEDLAND: What else could it be?

LOUELLA: I think he began to resent me then, without meaning to, I mean. I think he began to feel that I was keeping him at home when he ought to be at war. I think he partly wanted this, too.

FRIEDLAND: That's too complicated for me, Mrs. Whitmore. You think he began to feel you were keeping him from doing what he wanted to do, which was to go off to fight in the war? But you also think that he wanted you to keep him away from the war. That doesn't make sense, Mrs. Whitmore. He joined the Marine Corps, nobody drafted him into it.

LOUELLA: It makes sense to a woman.

FRIEDLAND: Try me again.

LOUELLA: He knew I didn't want him to go to the war. I needed him. I'm not as strong a person as you and most other people think I am, that's something only he and one other person knew. That bothered him, made him feel like he was tied to my apron strings. But also I think, he wouldn't admit it, another part of him didn't want to go to anybody's war. People look at him and they say, Hey, here's Randolph Scott, we're okay now. They've got it all wrong. He didn't really want to get involved in the riots, and when they ended the way they did, he took it personally, and he needed me. That's why we got married. After Pearl Harbor, you see, I kept him from doing what he thought he ought to be doing, in two ways. He had two ways to grow to hate me, and it started then, I think. I don't blame him.

FRIEDLAND: You say to grow to hate you. Do you really believe that?

LOUELLA: Yes. Of course I do. He came there to the house, and he ended up doing it the man's way. But he came there to kill me, not Herman. I was the one he wanted to shoot.

[*Judge Dix bangs for order and threatens to clear the court if the rubberneckers can't restrain themselves, and recesses for lunch. The newspaper reporters compare their quote of Louella's comment to make sure they get it verbatim. She is left alone on the witness stand, sharing a first long glance with Calvin, until the clerk tells her she can leave. Tully Contini scribbles notes like a demented schoolboy*]

FRIEDLAND: How did your relationship with Herman Sanger develop?

LOUELLA: We met Barbara Ferguson and Herman Sanger in 1942, I think. A long time ago, anyway. Calvin and Herman had this sort of shyness in common about wanting to be in the war but not talking about it. Herman was 4F because of a heart murmur. The four of us went out a lot together. Later, after Barbara sold her business, we didn't see them so much socially, but Herman was like Calvin's foreman. After Barbara left Herman, he moved out to a house near us, and we saw him every day. He was a best friend to both of us. That's all. He never touched me, I'll save you the trouble of asking.

FRIEDLAND: What happened to change things? We know they changed. How did it come to happen?

LOUELLA: Calvin was changing. Time was going by, and other people were fighting the war. He used to say they were fighting his war for him. He gave more and more of the running of the ranch to Herman to do. He didn't do anything else with his time. He started to sit up all night trying to pick up news on the shortwave radio. He made himself a den, and he went in there and spent his time, day and night. I didn't please him any more.

FRIEDLAND: Are you saying he stopped being your lover?

LOUELLA: That's right. I didn't know why. I don't to this day. After D-Day the names of the boys who were killed came out, and that was it. I knew I couldn't keep him any longer. He hated himself and he hated me. So I let him go. Herman was the only person who knew about it, the only person I could talk to. I talked to him because he was Calvin's best friend. When Calvin went into the Marines, he made it seem as if he had died, he wanted it that way. I felt like a widow. I turned to Herman. It took us a while to feel we weren't cheating on Calvin, but finally we did, and we didn't make any secret of it. We moved out of Calvin's house, and Herman ran things for him just as if he was only a paid ranch foreman. I thought the next time I would see Calvin would be in a divorce court.

FRIEDLAND: What happened the night of the murder?

LOUELLA: Well, we didn't feel like celebrating in town. We had a steak dinner, Herman had got some steaks from a neighbor who killed a beef. I had a couple of drinks and we went to bed. We must have dropped off to sleep, because the night light was on when I woke up. Herman woke me when he sat up in bed. Calvin had opened the bedroom door and was standing looking at us. He had a little bag in his hands, that one over there on the table. I didn't like the way he was staring at me, and I sort of instinctively reached for the sheet to cover up with, and it was on the floor. I leaned over to pick it up and wrap it around me, and when I looked back Calvin had the gun in his hand. Then he steadied his hand with the other one, and he started shooting. I screamed, I think, and in that little room I was deaf from the gunshots, and I closed my eyes and waited to feel what it would be like, dying. But he left me alive.

FRIEDLAND: No further questions.

CONTINI: No questions at this time, your honor. I'll be calling this witness in defense of my client.

[*When she leaves the witness stand she has to pass the jury box. The foreman of the jury, Walter Halbkeller, has seated himself at the end of the row of seats closest to her. Being of an older generation, he finds a famous gesture from the past, from a women's final at the Wimbledon tennis championships. He mimics Helen Wills Moody's demonstration of contempt for her opponent by turning away his head as she passes and putting a handkerchief to his nose*]

Headline on the front page of the *San Francisco Chronicle*:

SENTIMENTAL WIFE
TIGHTENS NOOSE ON
MARINE KILLER'S NECK

3

Gomez had kept his mouth shut for as long as he could stand it. He knew the men in his bar thought he didn't possess the equivalent of a white, American brain, and that his opinion was of less value than the air it was exhaled upon, but he had been silent as long as he could stand it. In his passion, his Mexican voice returned.

"You guys eess crazy," he said, "you don't know nothing about people. All you talk about eess a man will do thees, an' a man will do that, an' you don' know nothing about what you talking about. Look, you know Calvin, I know Calvin. One time he deed sometheeng becauss people wanted heem to do it. The riot. What happen? A boy wass keelled and Calvin wass hurt. What happen? He marry Louella. Don' say all thees stuff about how he hate Herman or else he hate Louella or he hate both of them together. That eess not Calvin. You making heem eento one of you guys. He eess not. Dreenk an' shut up!"

Tom Potter had told Mort Thomas a long time before the shooting, letting it drop in idle conversation after Calvin had gone into the Marine Corps, that there was an arrangement for private mail between them. It was the sort of information that Mort received and tucked away in the untidy drawer at the back of his mind. Now he went to see Tom, just to cover his ass. He didn't want anyone digging it up after the verdict was in and saying that the police hadn't done their job. Whatever he found now, he could keep it to himself.

"Those letters for Calvin, Tom," he said, "the ones you mentioned a long time ago. You still got 'em?"

Tom let the surprise show on his face. "Why now?" his expression said, but his mouth said only, "Sure, you want 'em? Calvin walked away and never came back for any of them. Wouldn't let me forward them to him." He nodded in the direction of the back room and disappeared into his office. Mort led the way to the big poker table. Tom followed with eleven envelopes, unopened, that he placed on the table in front of Mort and turned to go.

"You gonna stay?" Mort asked. "Leave the door open so you can see if you got a customer."

The letters came from several valley towns, postmarked late in 1944. "These've been hanging around a while," Mort said.

Tom explained, "He got all the others. Then they stopped coming."

Mort grunted and put the letters in a line in front of him. He got out a pocket knife and, using the small blade, slit each of the envelopes in turn, leaving the letters inside them.

"Help me a little bit here, Tom," Mort said. "What am I gonna find?"

"Can't help you," Tom said, "so help me God. They don't look like the ones that usually come here. Ones about women. For people with problems with women. Those are the ones they usually want to have sent here."

Mort spread his large hands and started extracting the letters, taking the envelopes in order from left to right. When they were all unfolded and lying in the light, he looked at each of them in turn, reading what was on the front page without touching it, turning it by holding it carefully by the lower right corner, turning it back face up when he had read the reverse side. When he had finished he made no comment beyond gesturing with a sweep of his hand, inviting Tom to read them.

Tom picked up the first and read it, then the second. "Are they all like this?" he asked.

"All the same," Mort said. "Same God damn thing. He must 've got their addresses out of the papers, when their sons were confirmed killed. People he didn't know. I wonder what the hell they thought when they got a sympathy letter from a stranger. Generally, when you lose someone, people shun you, can't cope with it or else they think you cope best on your own. We coulda done with sympathy letters from strangers when we lost Richie." He shook his head at the letters. "I'll be damned," he said, "there's still surprises in store for us, Tom."

"Why do you think he did it?" Tom asked.

Mort shrugged. "Same reason he ever did anything," he said. "Because he felt like he had to." He looked around the hard light to face Tom. "That doesn't answer your question," he said, "but it's as much of an answer as you'll ever get out of Calvin."

"What do I do with them?" Tom asked.

"Put 'em back," Mort answered. "I'll write a note to go with them, saying I opened 'em. He might want these some day. Or he might not."

The Jefferson Grammar School Parents' and Teachers' Association met after school was out, with special pay for two teachers to supervise the playground so as to make it possible for more mothers to attend. The meeting was crowded, and the two supervisors felt overwhelmed with children.

The business of the meeting was to help with giving answers to inquisitive children about the current court case. In other words, how do you explain adult sexual behavior to children without explaining sex? Fathers in Red Branch didn't talk about sex to their children, boys or girls. Most of the mothers weren't ready for that hurdle either, the exceptions being women who had been nurses for a while. It was the school nurse who addressed the problem when, one by one, the girls came to her with their worries. For the boys the years until a high school biology teacher would do a similar task for them yawned emptily ahead.

The answers provided delicately by the panel of wives of local ministers of religion left no mother in doubt that the right way to proceed was to pray that her child didn't ask the more embarrassing questions. The only discussion of concrete value was one which differentiated between execution in an electric chair and execution by gas chamber. Mrs. Sanders used the opportunity to obtain the backing of the PTA for her resolution to press the state legislature to resist demands to experiment with other methods of execution and stick to the use of the gas chamber on the grounds of humanitarianism.

When the meeting ended and the ladies filed past a table for cups of sweet tea with slices of lemon floating in them, their talk revealed attitudes that might have been useful to the competing attorneys. On Herman Sanger, little was said. Scorned and almost forgotten, he was the subject of only one question of significance, which was Mrs. Fowler's inquiry, "Does anyone know where his family buried him? Did he have any family left?" On Calvin's crime, there were two lines of thought. On one hand the comment travelled from mouth to mouth that the Whitmores were the kind of people who held to the old ways of doing things, where a man's wife had to be protected no matter what, but of course they were a very strange group of people. On the other hand the comment travelled from mouth to mouth in the opposite direction that it was a waste of a fine young man to defend a wife like that, and the guessing was that she had pulled him down to her level. What this made of the conviction in Red Branch that a gun in a husband's hand was the best protection for his family remained an undebated question.

On Louella, there was only one point of view.

Tullio Contini had studied carefully the manly art of someone else's defense. There were, he knew, only two ways to inflict the kind of punishment necessary to defend a client in a court of law: One was to punch hard, the other was to find a patsy to lay the blame on. Friedland had done the punching for him already. He had demonstrated to the court that Louella was no respectable American's idea of a loyal wife. She had refused to show any sign of belief in Calvin's right to dominate their marriage. It was his, in law and in tradition, to do with as he chose. She had also, disastrously for her, refused to show any sign of regret for her loose morals before the marriage or for her decision to count the marriage as a lost cause simply because her husband lost interest. She had not waited.

Tully knew how Friedland would use this. He would use it to show the kind of provocation that any red blooded American would be unable to let rest, provocation that would drive Calvin Whitmore to kill his wife's lover in cold blood, and pay with his life for doing it. The premeditation had been proved by the theft of the gun, the murder had been witnessed, the motive was easy to demonstrate. What Friedland didn't have was an admission from Calvin that this was actually his motive. That was what Tully had to work on. In Louella he had his patsy.

"Your honor," Contini said, "unless my learned friend has strong objections, I don't propose to call the defendant to the witness stand."

There was a buzz of disappointment from the ranks of the merely interested. Judge Dix hammered his gavel as if the wood block he hammered on was their collected heads. "Mr. Friedland?" he asked, when there was suitable silence.

"I have no objections, your honor," Friedland said. "The defendant's confession has been admitted into evidence. If counsel for the defense proposes to leave that unchallenged, I have no objection." He said it as if he questioned the tactics and sanity of Contini, viewed as a matter of course from his superior position.

Tully Contini was busy shuffling his papers when this shaft was aimed at him, and it flew over his head as a clean miss. "Call Mrs. Mary Louella Whitmore to the witness stand," he said.

CONTINI: You have already told this court you decided to leave home at the age of fifteen and live a life of immoral conduct.

LOUELLA: People like you would call it that.

[*Judge Dix bangs his gavel and points at Mr. Contini without saying a word*]

CONTINI: You have described yourself as a person who made decisions with regard to your conduct that some people might regard as immoral.

LOUELLA: I don't care what other people think.

CONTINI: That's what I am saying, that your disregard for convention extends to conduct that may be regarded as immoral.

LOUELLA: Yes.

CONTINI: And later, when you married him, your husband accepted that.

LOUELLA: Yes.

CONTINI: He never objected?

LOUELLA: No. He told me he had no right to object.

CONTINI: You mean that he had done worse things himself?

LOUELLA: No. He meant that he couldn't be anybody's judge. He doesn't have a very high opinion of himself. Not high enough.

CONTINI: That's interesting. Other people seem to think he has every reason to have a high opinion of himself. I wonder if you understand him as well as you think.

LOUELLA: I was the one who was married to him.

CONTINI: We'll come back to that later. Now, you also told this court that about the time of Pearl Harbor, your husband showed signs of being unhappy with the kind of life the two of you had decided on.

LOUELLA: He got restless. Yes. He seemed to be divided between the feeling that he ought to be a part of the war and the need to be here farming.

CONTINI: And looking after you. You made a point of saying you needed him.

LOUELLA: That's right.

CONTINI: In what way are you an invalid, Mrs. Whitmore?

LOUELLA: What do you mean?

CONTINI: In what way are you different from other war wives, or I should say from other wives who became war wives? They fended for themselves. Why couldn't you?

LOUELLA: It wasn't just me. I tried to explain, my husband and I needed each other. We're not like every other couple.

CONTINI: So you say. Did your husband ever say that?

LOUELLA: He didn't have to. We both knew it.

CONTINI: If it wasn't true, Mrs. Whitmore, do you think your husband is the sort of person who would let you go on believing that, out of his regard for you?

LOUELLA: Yes, he would, and that's what I'm talking about. Other men wouldn't. Calvin would. But that wasn't what happened.

CONTINI: How do you know, if he didn't say so?

LOUELLA: I knew. That's all, I knew.

CONTINI: Now for the next three years, Mrs. Whitmore, according to your testimony, your husband grew away from you little by little. For the same reason, that he wanted to be a part of the war.

LOUELLA: That's right, and I explained why he couldn't leave.

CONTINI: You've said it again. He couldn't leave.

LOUELLA: That's right.

CONTINI: But I have to put it to you, Mrs. Whitmore, that is not true.

LOUELLA: What isn't?

CONTINI: That he couldn't leave. He could have left any time he wanted to. Do you agree that there is nothing in the marriage vow that says a man's wife is more important than his country?

LOUELLA: That's up to the two of them, man and wife.

CONTINI: No, with respect, Mrs. Whitmore, that isn't true. That is seditious, and if you put it into practise, it is treasonous. A married man's first loyalty is to his country, and his wife is expected to do her patriotic duty and support him. On the evidence, your husband seems to have known that. It's different to a certain extent if a man has children. He might have wanted to stay if he had had a family. Why didn't you have a family, Mrs. Whitmore, if you wanted so desperately to keep him at home with you?

LOUELLA: That's my business!

[*She waits for intervention from the judge, but it doesn't come. She realizes she is alone, and is being set upon, and there is nothing she can do*]

I decided. We decided. We weren't ready for kids.

CONTINI: There's a lot of deciding going on, Mrs. Whitmore, and it sounds like you're the one doing most of it.

LOUELLA: That's a woman's prerogative.

CONTINI: Umm, now, I don't think that's strictly true. I agree it is probably true to you in your own mind, judging from some of the things you have said. However . . . So your husband is drifting away from you. What did you do?

LOUELLA: Knowing my husband, I did the only thing I could do, give him time to come back to me.

CONTINI: Nothing else? Special vacations? New hobbies, or friends?

LOUELLA: No. It wasn't that sort of thing that would keep him.

CONTINI: But I thought I heard you say you did encourage new friends.

LOUELLA: Yes, in a way. When we got friendly with Barbara and Herman, I encouraged that.

CONTINI: It was good for both of you.

LOUELLA: Yes. Herman took a lot of the work off Calvin's shoulders, a lot of the worry. They were good working together, and we all four got along well together.

CONTINI: And for about two years, that is about all that you did to try to bring your husband around.

LOUELLA: I suppose so.

CONTINI: And then in early 1944, Barbara Ferguson dropped out of your group of special friends.

LOUELLA: I think it was then, yes.

CONTINI: It was. I have her statement, if you wish me to introduce it into evidence.

LOUELLA: No, that's okay.

CONTINI: And the result of her breakup with Herman Sanger was to bring Herman closer to you and your husband, in order to help him.

LOUELLA: That's right.

CONTINI: And your husband had no objection? None that you could see, without him having to tell you?

LOUELLA: No. None at all.

CONTINI: None at all. If I heard your testimony correctly, you told the prosecuting counsel in direct evidence that your husband began to stay away from your bed.

LOUELLA: Yes.

CONTINI: Now you've told this court that you and your husband didn't talk about a lot of things, you just knew them.

LOUELLA: Some things.

CONTINI: And it didn't occur to you that your husband was telling you something special by not sleeping with you?

[*He waits for a reply, but none is forthcoming*]

It didn't occur to you that it was only a short step from your husband's bed to Herman Sanger's bed? Are you saying that your husband didn't think of that?

Are you saying that he didn't know exactly what would happen after he left, given your appetite for men and the way you had turned away from him for three whole years?

LOUELLA: This isn't fair, what you're doing to me.

CONTINI: I'm trying to get at the truth, Mrs. Whitmore. But all right, we'll leave that. Let's go ahead a few months. In October 1944, one year ago, your husband was almost killed in the course of duty. How many times did you visit him?

LOUELLA: I didn't, and before you start in on me again, I'll tell you why. It was because I know my husband, which you can't get through your thick skull, and I knew he wouldn't want me there. He had told me to make another life. He wanted me out of his way, so he was free to do whatever he felt he had to do. How could I help him by showing up at his bedside for a big reconciliation scene? That would be the very last thing he would want. I know him.

CONTINI: You might have tried a reconciliation, Mrs. Whitmore. But of course, you couldn't, because by that time you were Mr. Herman Sanger's mistress. Is that right?

LOUELLA: I don't know. It might have been by then. I wasn't Herman's mistress, as you put it, until we moved into the Atwater house. You've done all the prying, when was that?

CONTINI: It was the same week as your husband's near fatal injury. That accident was almost very convenient for you, wasn't it?

[*His comment jolts her physically, and she flinches*]

And did you keep up with his progress? Were you aware of where he was when he left the hospital? Specifically, Mrs. Whitmore, did you know about the morphine treatment and its effect?

LOUELLA: No. He had dropped me. I gave up. Maybe I shouldn't have, but I did.

CONTINI: On the night of the murder, Mrs. Whitmore, when you woke up and looked at your husband, of course we realize everything was strange for you, but did you feel that your husband was the same person that you had known as Calvin Whitmore?

[*She covers her face with her hands while he waits*]

Take your time.

LOUELLA: No. He wasn't the same. I haven't wanted to think about it.

[*She sighs deeply and stares above the heads of everyone in the courtroom*]

When I woke up and looked at him, what I did was to reach down for the sheet and cover myself up. Only it wasn't there, it had slipped to the floor. I leaned over to pick it up. It wasn't easy to do that, and I can remember feeling something hurting when I had to bend that far down. I wouldn't have done that for Calvin. But I did it to hide myself from the person who was in the room. I didn't know he had a gun. I didn't care about being caught in bed with Herman, I didn't even think of it. It was just that I looked at him, and I thought I wanted to hide my nakedness from him. And that's something I would never have done, hide from Calvin.

[*She looks at Contini, as if he can explain her discovery*]

CONTINI: You were looking at the man your husband had become, Mrs. Whitmore, thanks to the demands made on him by trying to live with you, and the injury that you ignored, and the effect of the morphine. You might just as well have been the one pulling that trigger, Mrs. Whitmore. No further questions.

Headline on the front page of the *Placid Citizen*:

DEFENSE BLAMES ERRANT WIFE FOR MURDER

Dick Friedland had taken Judge Dix seriously. He wanted his conviction, but he was just as determined that the conviction should be seen to be an act of justice. He was confident he had the right jury foreman for his purposes. Walter Halbkeller was one of the quiet Bible-bashers. He liked it to be known that he was a servant of God in whatever he did, while at the same time he would turn his face away in disgust if he saw one of the Pentecostals on a street corner shouting a "Come to Jesus" message and banging on a banjo. Halbkeller knew a sin when he saw one and was quick to punish it with his contempt. However, it wasn't contempt that Friedland wanted from the foreman, but judgment. That was what he must work on in his summing up to the jury, and Halbkeller was the channel by which he would get that to the jury as a whole.

Friedland's difficulty was that he had too much to work on, too much time as much as anything. The time that it had taken Whitmore to get into the Marines, the time it had taken previously to see that he had married the wrong woman – there was something wrong. He wasn't some big, dumb ox. He wasn't even an emotional, big, dumb ox. Words like love and hate didn't come to mind when Friedland looked at this murderer. A word like murderer didn't come to mind either. Whitmore's wife had been right about one thing, almost the only thing she had been right about: Whitmore carried with him a strange innocence that was impervious to what he had actually done. That had to be overcome.

Tully Contini liked papers. When he wrote a note, he put it down on its own on one piece of paper. He liked to think of himself as an organized man, imagining himself writing books like those 'Inside' books of John Gunther's, which read like a compilation of notes that had been assembled according to the author's outline by an anonymous assistant and polished into shape by the master. Here he was now like some anonymous assistant, at his desk in the bank building, arranging and rearranging his sheets of paper. Tonight, however, he no longer liked his papers. They didn't fit together.

It was Whitmore's fault. He couldn't be put on the stand, because he couldn't be relied on to say anything that was in any way useful for his defense. The one thing that needed to be said was the answer to the question, "What about Herman Sanger?" Tully thought he must be the only person involved in the trial who was aware of the forgotten victim. And Whitmore was the only person who could answer the question. If they knew how Whitmore felt about Sanger, they might know enough about Whitmore to get to the truth of this whole affair. But they didn't. So be it. He would have to go for the jugular of Mrs. Whitmore. He settled down to write his notes into a form that he could speak from tomorrow.

Walter Halbkeller sat on his own in the little office at the back of the Presbyterian Church. As deacon he had things to do to prepare for next Sunday, not knowing how long the jury would be out once they had been charged and retired. Tonight, however, his mind didn't extend to next Sunday.

He opened a drawer of the small desk where he sat and found a nail buffer. In a corner of a tray that held odds and ends – paper clips, screws that might come in handy, buttons off so-far-unidentified shirts – a small bottle of nail varnish was wedged into an upright position. When he unscrewed the top of the bottle, a pungent smell more at home in a furniture workshop than a church vestry filled the small room. Leaving the bottle wedged where it was, he carefully drew the brush out and examined it for loose hairs before dipping it and wiping it to get just the right amount of lacquer on the brush. He spread his left hand on a blotter, separating the little finger from the others. Its three-inch nail curved delicately, pampered and coaxed to a parchment yellow that shaded to pink over the flesh of the fingertip, with a discreet white moon almost concealed at its base.

He put the brush back into the bottle as he spotted a minute imperfection on the nail, using the buffer to remove it before returning to the ritual of preparing the brush to apply the lacquer. He propped the heel of his right hand on the desk to keep it steady and stroked the lacquer onto the nail. Then he held up his hand, turning it so that the back of the nail was shown, and painted that side also. That done, he put his left elbow on the desk and returned the lacquer and buffer to their places with his free hand. From the top drawer he drew out a Bible. He opened it to the front and turned pages until he came to some passages about Moses, leader and lawgiver, his favorite character in the whole of the Bible. Having read these, he turned more pages until he came to the Ten Commandments and read them intently, forcing himself to examine the familiar laws in word by word detail. After that he turned to the Beatitudes, reading them just as intently, then back once more to the Ten Commandments. The laws of God, leavened with mercy – when it was deserved.

The lacquer was dry by now. He studied the nail carefully, intently. God's fingernail, a living symbol of his devotion to the almighty, an intentional impediment to the unhindered use of his left hand, a constant reminder that he was placed on earth to do God's work in whatever guise it presented itself. He put his left hand on the Bible, feeling its morocco cover with the protected, sensitive flesh of the mound of his little finger. He tapped the book with the tip of God's fingernail and felt the push at the base of the nail go through his whole body. He smiled and put the Bible away, closing the drawer and rising at the same time. He knew what his verdict would be, and he determined to take the jury along with him.

Judge Dix was moved to be sarcastic. "You haven't been treated to Thomas E. Dewey for the prosecution, nor Clarence Darrow for the defense, I guess you know that by now," he said to the jury members. "Let me see if I can sum their arguments up for you." He made a scrabbling motion with his hands and leaned forward. The two attorneys approached the bench. "Let me have your notes," the judge said, "maybe I can do a better job than you did."

He spent a few minutes looking over the short, neat summary of Friedland and the sheaf of pages that represented Contini's notes, while everyone in court fidgeted. "All right," he said when he was satisfied, "here it is." He looked up and glared at the two attorneys, signalling a correct-me-if-you-dare warning that everyone in court could interpret.

"The prosecutor's case is, he says, based on the need to enforce the letter of the law. The defendant has come back from a war that was fought, if it was fought for anything, to uphold the legal right of people to live in peace. That's politics, and it's beyond me to explain how war means peace, but what it comes down to is that this man here had no right to take the law into his own hands, in the opinion of the prosecutor. He claims he has established intent, which is premeditation, and that's necessary for a conviction on the charge of first degree murder. The defendant stole a gun from the pistol range and went to a lot of trouble to keep it hidden until he wanted to use it. The prosecutor produced a confession, and he established the truth of the defendant's confession, because he produced an eye witness to the crime. His only problem was motive, which he was not quite honest enough to admit. His argument is that the defendant is a typical man of a type we all recognize. This man debated with himself and his wife about going to war, and when he finally did, his wife took that as the end of their marriage. After he was in the Marines, she took a lover. Once he was able to, he came home and killed the man who had taken his place. That case, if you accept it, is a case of murder in the first degree.

"What the prosecutor didn't say, because that's not his job, is that the defendant's wife doesn't agree with this motivation. Now, you might say, she wouldn't, would she? However, if you think you go along with what she said about her husband, about the marriage being over for other reasons and about her, his wife, making the decision to take another husband without first going through the divorce courts, if she could get a decree, then you have what's known as mitigating circumstances and you don't have a charge of first degree murder. Even though he's still guilty. The difference is that in this state first degree murder is a capital offense, and I don't need to explain what that means. Everybody clear on that?"

Judge Dix looked at every juror in turn, ending with Halbkeller. Each of them nodded with the exception of the foreman, who was preoccupied with looking at his fingernail, to the judge's annoyance.

"Now for the defense," the judge said. "The defense attorney's case is one that comes from an old French saying, 'Cherchez la femme'." He looked around the court, pleased with himself because it was nowhere in Contini's notes. He repeated the phrase, making it into four words and laying equal stress on each, "Share shay lah fem," and following with a translation, "It means keep your eye peeled when there's a woman in the case. And there is a woman in this case, gentlemen, very much so." Halbkeller looked up with a face of stone.

"Mr. Contini's case, gentlemen, is that the defendant married a woman at a time of great difficulty for him, of weakness. She was not of a good character, which he chose to ignore at the time, and he learned to his cost that leopards don't change their spots. She used her power over him to get him to marry her in the first place, and he says she has a lot of power, you only have to look at her reputation to know that. She went on using the power she had, to get him to stay away from other people and pull away from Red Branch, then to stay away from the war. Mr. Contini says that she broke her husband's spirit, until she went one step too far and introduced another man into her life. He said some pretty harsh things about Mrs. Whitmore which probably ought to be challenged. In particular, however, I'll remind you that he said she introduced Herman Sanger into their little family out there on the ranch in order to make her husband jealous, to put some life back into their marriage. It didn't quite work that way, he says. Mr. Sanger took over the running of things. This stirred up enough of the manliness in the defendant that he went off to join the Marines, but it also started him brooding over what his wife had done to him. He had a terrible accident, and he had just as terrible a time getting over it, and then the last straw got dropped on his back. He found out his wife and her lover were living together as man and wife. As a result of his injury and his problems with morphine, he got it in his mind that he had a right to do something about this. So he killed the lover.

"Now gentlemen, that makes a pretty spicy story, and it's your job to decide if this constitutes a defense in law. All I can add without prejudicing your decision is to point out that if the defense counsel is correct, the wrong person is on trial here. Since the defendant admits he pulled the trigger, that's pretty hard to believe.

"Anyway, there you've got it. The defendant killed a man, that's not in doubt. Did he do it because he figured he was above the law and had a right to take a human life in a private war? Or did he only pull the trigger because he had been made to do it by his wife?

"Any questions? No? Let's have a decision. Don't be too long about it." He banged his gavel and pointed with its handle to the door to the jury room.

The little room where Calvin waited was no bigger than a good sized clothes closet. He dragged the only chair to the side of the room that formed a party wall with the corridor, and pushed it behind the door. He was hidden there even from people who slipped past the single guard in order to poke through the rooms of the building in an attempt to see the killer face to face. Sitting there he looked due west, able to watch the October mist begin to thicken as the afternoon dragged on, with the creamy haze of it turning gradually more yellow, giving way to pink and then, suddenly, gray.

He had no thoughts, no curiosity, no articulated needs or desires. He concentrated on one thing only, to get through the trial so that he could get all those eyes off him. In all his experiences, throughout the whole episode, that was what he found he could not cope with – the looking itself, yes, but also what was behind it, curiosity, horror, amusement, bafflement, lust, contempt, hatred, sorrow, revulsion, everything but the one characteristic that he longed to see, disinterest. It was the blurred line, the lack of distinction between fame and notoriety, that he saw in the eyes beholding him that he found most disturbing, leaving him undecided if he was only a criminal or also a freak.

It was dark when Tully Contini came to get him. The lights in the corridor were on, and the courtroom blazed with illumination from the suspended white balls that had previously seemed merely an obtrusively globular decorative touch. They went back to sit for the last time at the long table, now so well known to Calvin, who had sat through the entire trial with his eyes on the table top, studying the grain of the wood, letting it lead him anywhere it wished so long as it was not in the direction of a pair of eyes. They stood for the entry of the judge, who immediately called for the jury to be brought into court. The twelve men filed in looking embarrassed by their prominence, except for Walter Halbkeller, who swept the courtroom with defiant eyes and set jaw.

"Have you reached a verdict?" the judge said.

"We have, your honor," Halbkeller intoned.

"Is it unanimous?" the judge asked.

"It is," the foreman answered. When the judge nodded for him to read it, Halbkeller cleared his throat and momentarily closed his eyes.

"Vengeance is mine, saith the Lord," he pronounced in a loud, preachery voice. "We find the defendant Not Guilty."

*

When his phone rang, he shoved his papers away and grabbed for his notepad, writing 7:20 pm while saying "Tullio Contini, Attorney . . ."

The voice of Judge Dix, tongue sharpened with bourbon, cut him off. "I know, I know," the judge said, "and I wish to Christ I didn't."

Contini didn't expect compliments from anyone for his work, certainly not from the judge, and he knew he was in for it. He kept his mouth shut and waited.

"Well, Counselor," the judge said, "you won it, thanks to that Holy Joe, and from my viewpoint, which is a superior one, you got the right verdict, but I wanted to make sure you don't have a good night's sleep on your success."

"What do you mean, Judge?" Contini asked.

"I mean your asinine summing up worked," the judge said, warming to his oratory, "you laid it up so that horse's ass of a Halbkeller couldn't miss it. Your motive, however, is completely and utterly wrong, as you know. I asked you for justice, and I got bull crap. Serves me right. Next time I'll know better and save my breath. When you're older, assuming you gain some horse sense over the years, you may learn a little bit about people. For the time being, stick to defending parking tickets."

"Judge," Contini blustered, "I believed what I was doing was right and correct."

"You disappoint me even more," the judge snarled. "And you can take a running jump on the blunt end of my gavel for your expenses. Goodnight."

The caretaker said the only place big enough to hold the press conference was the courtroom itself. The reporters, having left only a short time before, crowded back in, bringing with them the previously excluded photographers. The caretaker set a chair in the well of the court, in front of the judge's bench, and shooed the gentlemen of the press behind the barrier of the long tables that had served the needs of the attorneys and the defendant. Once he was satisfied, he went to the door that communicated to the witness room and opened it. The flash bulbs popped as the celebrity made his entrance and seated himself. Walter Halbkeller was ready for questions.

When he telephoned the story to his paper an hour later, Chappy Sims said it was the God damnedest press conference he'd ever seen. It was as if Halbkeller had taken over for the judge.

The *Sacramento Bee*, October 17, 1945:

FOREMAN DEFENDS ACQUITTAL OF GI KILLER

by Chapman Sims

"When you set out to punish, make sure you find the source of the evil," Mr. Walter Halbkeller said last night in explanation of the sensational acquittal of Corporal Calvin Whitmore (See story this page - Ed.). Claiming credit for leading the jury to its verdict of not guilty, Halbkeller, assistant editor of the *Red Branch Herald*, said, "Whitmore has suffered enough for a crime that was forced on him. Out of mistaken loyalty, he did what by his code any husband has a right to do."

The foreman denied that the decision is a charter for GI husbands to take the law into their own hands. He accepted that some GI wives have strayed from their marital vows during their husbands' absence. But he said the unusual circumstances of this case aren't likely to be repeated. "Most wives," he said, "are not deliberately immoral." When asked if he meant that Mrs. Whitmore was such a wife, he added, "You must make up your own minds. We made up ours."

Halbkeller stated that the jury had not acquitted

Whitmore because he had taken a husband's revenge on his wife's seducer. He said the jury had discussed that thoroughly. The pattern presented by the prosecution, of the western tradition of the husband as a guardian of his wife's innocence, would have led them to convict the accused, if they had believed that was why Whitmore killed Herman Sanger.

Instead, they believed Whitmore had been driven to the murder by his wife's behavior over a long period of time. They were not totally convinced by the defense, but that part of it had made the deepest impression.

"On the witness stand," Halbkeller said, "a great deal became clear. Mrs. Whitmore branded herself a loose woman." He added, "From that kind of immorality great tragedy must flow, as it did in this instance. Corporal Whitmore is as much a victim as Herman Sanger, the man he shot."

Mr. Halbkeller, deacon of the Red Branch Presbyterian Church, was asked about newspaper speculation that he was maneuvered onto the jury in order to represent local feelings against the wife of the defendant. He stated that he knew feelings were running high against her, but that didn't interfere with his judgment. "I am capable of doing God's work wherever I see it," he said, adding that he thought the verdict would satisfy all sections of opinion.

BOOK V

Sunset and Evening Star

1

Calvin sat up all the way to Oakland on the night train, unwilling to trust himself to sleep. He slumped against a window, huddled into his greatcoat, fearful of being recognized. Some men going back to their shipyard jobs in Richmond were drinking all the way, steadily pushing themselves into insensibility. When it was time for them to get off, they were beyond knowing where they were. The police had to be called, and the men were carried and rolled out of the train, leaving behind them a sour smell that caught in Calvin's nostrils, reeking of gutters and degradation. The train was late into the Oakland Mole, and the train crew called for everyone to hurry. Instead, he sat on a bench in the terminal and let the ferry to San Francisco go without him, so that he could walk out onto the dock in the night air and let the thin wind from the west cleanse him while he waited for the next boat. It was a clear, black night. Up beyond the effect of the city lights, the stars spattered the darkness. He told himself that it was over, finished, and at the same time he knew that it would never be completed.

At the Ferry Building he reported to the duty officer in the cramped, smoky U.S. Naval Authority office. He was arrested and given a cup of coffee, and an hour later a van took him and the night's trawl of drunks to the brig at Treasure Island. A few hours later, when the business of the day began, a car came from the cadet training school for him, and he was driven to the commandant in his office. It had been the Office of the Dean of Men in peacetime, its wide, stone mullioned windows turned away from the busy campus to contemplate a small glade of lawn surrounded by a collection of subtropical trees and shrubs. In this otherworldly atmosphere they talked like two men who shared knowledge of a dark secret that had climaxed in tragedy. The commandant flattered himself that he understood everything, and Calvin let him have his illusion. In the evening another car took Calvin, now a civilian, back along the bay, through the squalor and muddle of the waterfront, back to the Mole, where he took the night train south back to Red Branch.

It was still dark there when he got off the train. A switch engine was making up a train of freight cars, blocking traffic between the east and west sides of town. Calvin walked south a block to Park Street and waited for an opening that allowed him to cross the tracks. He stayed on Park Street walking west, all the way west, where the street ended at the end of the grounds of the Atwater mansion. He circled the grounds until he came to where the little house should have been. Part of it was left, the foundations and some exposed utility pipes. Everything else had gone, torn down and carried away, the rickety fence, the mailbox, the bloodstains, everything gone. He walked on, then, until he came to the back gate to Mrs. Rossi's. The summer lawn chairs had not yet been put away. He pulled two of them together, wrapped himself in his greatcoat, and lay down to sleep. Mrs. Rossi, wakened by the sound of the gate, watched from her bedroom window upstairs and decided to leave him alone. He knew where the key was when he wanted to come in to his room.

By mid-morning the wind had risen and brought in a weather front from the west. The clouds squeezed the color out of the autumn trees and shrubs, and a cold rain began to fall. Calvin disguised himself in a raincoat and Tino Rossi's grape picking hat, grateful for the need of them, and walked by back streets to Louella's old house. Knowing that if he hesitated he would indeed be lost, he went directly to the front door. Once he had knocked, he opened the screen door and listened with his ear to the wooden door for any sound of life inside. He knocked again and continued listening, but the silence was complete.

The porch roof leaked where shingles had been blown off in a storm some years before. He pushed back into a dry corner and lit a cigarette. A boy was making his way across the pasture land from Mexican Town. He squeezed under the barbed wire that was supposed to protect Red Branch from the undesirables and came along the sidewalk. He stopped outside Louella's house and looked at Calvin.

"You lookin' for the famous lady?" he asked.

"Yeah," Calvin answered. "You come along here many times?" He unconsciously dropped into pidgin lingo to talk to the Mexican boy. "You know where she is?"

"Yeah," the boy said. "How much?"

"Two bits," Calvin offered.

The boy spit on the sidewalk. "Nah. Four bits."

"Come and get it," Calvin said. He fished a fifty-cent piece out of his pocket and held it out to the boy as he approached the porch. "Where is she?"

"She wass livin' in Messican Town while the murder trial," the boy said. "Lass night she don' come. But she leave all her stuff in her house. She be back." He shrugged. "Don' know when." He smiled, his even teeth splashing their whiteness across his dark brown face. "They tell you at the store which house she in. Thass all. Enough for four bits?" He laughed, hugely enjoying the joke, and ran away down the street toward town.

Calvin retraced his way to Mrs. Rossi's. He used the telephone to rent another car from the Highway Garage. Mrs. Rossi got some food together from her delicatessen counter, putting it and a half loaf of bread in a paper bag, and Calvin took it with him when a boy with red blotches on his face brought the car. He returned the boy to the used car lot, then turned back toward the town. He turned the wiper down to slow speed, leaving the windshield smeary and hard to see through, as hard for anyone outside to see in as for him to see out. He turned west on Greenfield Avenue without being spotted, he was sure, and drove out of town.

The ranch house looked shut and untenanted. She would still have her key, he was certain, since he hadn't found it when he came back before. He stepped lightly up onto the porch and got the spare key from its hiding place. He let himself in and closed the door behind himself, taking off his coat and hat and laying them on the chair by the door. He waited there, facing the screen to the red room. She took her time about it. He heard small noises, and waited. Finally she pushed back the screen and came out. She was wearing her old pink and black kimono that he hadn't seen since the days of her apartment over the dentist's office. She had chopped at her hair with scissors, so that instead of being wavy and smooth it was frizzy and alive with whiteness. She wore no lipstick, and her eyes were shadowed with their own darkness so that her smoky blue eyes burned out of a hiding place.

"Hi," she said.

"Hi," he answered.

They stood awkwardly, looking at each other the way people do in waiting rooms or offices.

Louella broke the silence. "I've been eating your stuff, the food you left," she said. "Hope you don't mind."

"No, no," he mumbled. "Is there any coffee left?"

"It's stale," she said. "I'll make some more, shall I?"

"Yeah," he said, "yeah, that'd be good. I've brought some lunch, Mrs. Rossi made me bring it. It's in the car, I'll get it." He waited to see if this was acceptable. When she nodded and went to the kitchen to make the coffee, he took this as assent and ran through the rain to the car to retrieve the paper bag.

Back in the house, he spead the contents on plates on the table in the corner of the living room and sat down to wait for her and the coffee.

They said very little as they ate. They were both hungry, and both were surprised that they could feel hunger again. When they were finished they had a cigarette. Calvin remarked that the rain looked like it meant business, and Louella picked at the leftovers.

They were silent then, until Calvin said, "When I understand it, I mean when I can make some kind of sense out of it, I'll tell you." He paused, astonished that he had broached the unspeakable subject. It had simply come out of him, as something that he had to say, without his controlling it in any way. "I promise to do that, if you'll let me."

Louella pinched her nose and pushed the tears back to where they came from, determined not to give way.

"Yeah, I'll let you do that," she said.

"There's just this, for now," Calvin insisted, "let me tell you."

"Okay," she said.

"You got me wrong," he said. "They all got me wrong." He looked at her, but she wouldn't return his gaze. He touched her wrist and shook it slightly until she looked him in the eyes. "That wasn't meant for you. I wouldn't have hurt you. Never. Never in a million years. Believe me."

She stared at him intently. She seemed to be trying to replace someone or something, or to replace a memory with this reality facing her now. "I guess I'll have to believe you," she said. Some of the old Louella surfaced from the wreckage and she flared up. "I believe you because I want to believe you, Calvin, and you know it, and you could tell me any damn thing you wanted to, and you know it!"

"I do now," he said, defending himself.

"Don't take advantage of me, Calvin," she said.

"I've never done it before," he said. "I won't be startin' now."

They had both put out their cigarettes. He offered her another one. She took it and put it down on the table.

"This coffee's gone cold. I'll heat it up," she said.

He followed her to the kitchen and offered her the cigarette again. She took it, and he lit it for her, then lit his own. They had always had a way of sizing each other up through cigarette smoke, an act Louella had picked up from bad movies. It had been something they laughed about, but they had made it into their own charade with their own meanings. Louella said, "Let's see, how does the line go? What's a nice boy like you doin' in a place like this? Or maybe, Aren't you afraid to be seen with a woman with a reputation like mine? Something like that."

He picked up the banter as well as the hard reality underneath. "Don't forget, Ma'am, I'm a man with a past," he said. He pulled on his cigarette deeply and exhaled a thick cloud that filled the space between them.

She put on a face like Claudette Colbert being tragic, which came out as a woman not looking forward to telling her husband about the total on the grocery bill. "At least you have a future. All I have," she gestured extravagantly, "is this."

Calvin caught the mood and returned the gesture. "I never thought I'd have a chance to say it," he said in an aside. Then he squared his shoulders and raised his head theatrically. "Let me take you away from all this," he pleaded.

Louella had to laugh. "God, you're a terrible actor," she said.

He said, "Okay, then, I won't try to act. I mean it. Let's get away from all this." She stared at him, emotions clambering over each other. "Coffee's boiling," he said. He took the pot off the stove and put it to one side, then led the way back to the living room.

"How can we?" she said, "Get away from it, I mean."

"Maybe we can't," he answered. "We got to try," he added, "got no choice, either together or on our own. We're alive. Something's got to happen."

She struggled to suppress the wild pleasure that had flooded her, trying to keep it out of her face. "But – what about – ?" she said, and was unable to continue.

"We won't never forget it," Calvin said. "Don't suppose we're meant to. Like I said, we're alive, and we gotta do something." He paused before adding, "Even if it's only kill ourselves."

Louella didn't like the reference to killing. She took in her breath, and seized Calvin's hand, digging her nails into the palm of his hand. He shook his head and stroked the back of her hands, and she relaxed.

"Let's start over," he said. "We're two different people now, we can do that." His head dropped, but he kept her hands in his. "What you said in court there, some of it was wrong but most of it was right."

"I don't remember any more what I said, I don't want to remember any of it, ever," she said.

"What you said that was most right was how we changed," he said, "and how we didn't rightly see what it was doing to us."

"Did I say that?" she asked.

"We're changed, that's all, we're not strangers," he said. "What I did was me, Calvin, but there's more to me than that, you know that. I don't know yet what to do about it, about everything, but I want you with me. What do you say?"

"Oh my sweet Jesus," she said. The tears came in rivers down her face, and she buried it in the palm of his hand. He stroked the back of her head with his other hand, pulling at the short hair and trying to force it back into its place.

"Sure made a mess of your hair," he said.

She snuffled and said, "It'll grow out. I was getting ready to dye it red."

"Jesus Christ," he said, "I only just got here in time."

He left her to pack her belongings at the house in Mexican Town. After leaving a check for the car with the blotched boy at the Highway Garage, Calvin went back to Mrs. Rossi's for his few belongings, and back out to Mexican Town to pick up Louella. She was almost disguised in a sou'wester hat and slicker. They avoided the town and drove to the house to pack the rest of Calvin's things. Louella went inside to assemble a basic housekeeping kit that would keep them going for a few days. He was loading everything into the car when Chappy Sims from the *Sacramento Bee* found him.

The reporter identified himself and said, "You look like you're leaving."

"That's right," Calvin said. "I need a change of scene, I guess you could say."

"You have time to give me an interview?" the man asked.

"No, I told you guys you'd have to get my news from Tully Contini," Calvin said. "He's such a wise guy, he knows more about me than I do. Talk to him."

"I just wanted an interview to wrap up the story," the man insisted.

"Nope," Calvin said.

"Can you tell me where you're going?" he asked.

"I don't know myself," Calvin said, "can't tell you when I don't know, now can I." He glanced over the reporter's shoulder and saw Louella standing still. She had been approaching the front door with a load for the car, and she had stopped when she saw the stranger.

"I can follow you," the man said. "But I'll settle for an interview, and then I'll leave you alone."

Calvin considered this, and came to a decision. He gestured to Louella to come out of the house. In her hat and raincoat she was unrecognizable to the reporter. "We're goin' away together," he said. "That's enough of a story to get you off my ass, ain't it?" He lapsed back into the Texas good-old-boy language, mocking the reporter who was too green to understand the mockery. He shook his head and shrugged his shoulders, unimpressed by the offer.

Calvin laughed at him. "I'm offering you a scoop, mister. Don't you get it?"

"You and this woman are going away," the man said. "So what?"

"Well, shit, honey, guess we gotta spell it out for him," Calvin said. "Take off your hat."

Louella put down the boxes she was carrying in her arms and posed on the top step. She cocked a knee, just like a starlet who has used a silver shovel to plant an oak tree in the garden of everlasting memory of our departed four-legged friends. Putting one hand on a hip, she used the other to push the brim of her sou'wester back provocatively, before lifting it off in the gesture usually accompanied with a Ta-Ta!

The reporter goggled at her. He turned to Calvin. "You and her?" he stammered. "Christ almighty!" he shouted as he ran for his car.

The story cost the newspapers a fortune. Their reporters had returned, the verdict was old news, there was no further mileage in Red Branch stories. Until they were scooped, and they all had to go back there.

Walter Halbkeller met the assembled press the following morning. He stood on the top step of the *Herald* building and glared at the cameras and the reporters.

"I'll say this once, and once only, and then you can get out of here because you're not getting another word out of me.

"I didn't know anything about this until I read the papers this morning, the same as you. If I had known about this, things would have been different. We would never have acquitted him if we'd known he would go back to that woman."

Those were the last words he ever said on the subject.

The telephone at the Regency Hotel had been ringing all morning with men trying to get a plate at the Lions Club luncheon meeting. The manager had squeezed every table he could into the dining room, and as a consequence some of the irregulars like Tully Contini had to be content with a view of a corner and no elbow room. The placement actually suited him; in his present mood, facing the world was not his first option, but he couldn't be seen to be running away either. He was studying a pink and purple print of a particularly agile dancer, one who seemed able to disengage her leg from her hip when her art required it, when he felt a tap on his shoulder. Before turning to see who it was, he adjusted his face to a suitable Lions Club model, professional and optimistic, banishing the gloomy fury that was in his heart.

It was a beaming Judge Dix. "Didn't know you were a Lion," he said.

"Only when they let me out of my cage," Tully replied. His accompanying laugh was forced and silly even to his own ears.

"I don't get here very often myself," the judge said, "but I couldn't miss it today. An unrivalled opportunity to learn about my own case, wouldn't you say? Yes sir, I can pick up all kinds of tips on how to handle my next murder case and save myself a phone call to boot."

"Phone call?" Contini queried.

"Yeah," the judge said, "I intended to phone you, wanted to make sure you heard the news. The final chapter, so to speak. About your ex-client. The central figure in that little fiction you cooked up for my courtroom."

Somehow Contini kept smiling. "I heard," he said.

"Good, good," the judge said, "just wanted to make sure." He smiled broadly. "Enjoy your lunch," he said. "Mr. Friedland hadn't heard the news, so I was able to tell him. He's already thrown up and gone home."

2

It wasn't until they were in the car and moving that Louella asked where they were going.

"You're half of this wagon train," Calvin answered her, "what do you say?"

"West," she said. "Everybody goes west."

"I've always wanted to see how far this road goes and where it ends up at," Calvin said. He turned the car west on the Jurgens road, passed through the little town, and kept driving. It was one of the long, straight roads that surveyors with no imagination and a vast tolerance for boredom drew across the valley when the land was divided up for farming. It ended finally at another road, this one running due north and south. Calvin turned south and soon found a different straight road running west again. When, ahead of them, they could see it begin to bend to meet the flanks of the mountains, they shouted with relief. It circled a small lake that was dammed to make a reservoir, then narrowed and lost its blacktop as it climbed into the range of hills. They had been driving for almost three hours before they dropped over these hills into a shallow valley that was all but overwhelmed by the mountains beyond.

Louella glanced behind them. "Look!" she said.

Calvin looked in the mirror and then at her, alarmed at the prospect of being followed but seeing nothing behind them.

"There's nothing there," he said.

"That's what I mean," she answered. "What don't you see?" When he didn't answer, she slapped him on the thigh and said, "It's gone. We're free of it. We're out of that godforsaken valley." He stopped the car, and they both got out to look at a landscape that was mercifully small, narrow and overlooked.

She had never left the valley throughout all her life. She had lived in its flat, broad, unrestricting, unconfined space always, and Calvin had escaped it only during the turbulent, unhappy months in the Marines. They had been deceived in the valley's apparent freedom and openness, they had learned; in order to survive, you conformed, you put a bridle on your spirit and you gave up your freedom, and in that they had failed. Joyful exiles, they hugged and kissed each other, feeling like youngsters playing truant.

The road took them to the south end of the small valley, past any sign of life, beyond grazing cattle, until the road tilted up to a shelf of land, where they found the remnants of what had been a resort. The flat, board front of a small hotel still bore a wiped shadow of the name "Pinto Hotsprings Hotel & Spa". A broad porch extended the full width of the building, waiting to connect with other buildings that had never materialized. A small store to one side of it had been refashioned into a house, and a pre-war Ford stood outside this, its black paintwork leached out to a matte gray. On the other side of the hotel a luxuriant stand of willows indicated where one surviving Pinto Hotspring bubbled up, crusted over almost completely with the salts and minerals that had given it a medicinal reputation for a time. A runoff steamed out from under the crust, bordered with orange deposits that coated like rusty snow the clumps of buffalo grass that grew beside it.

A woman in a blue housedress and a long, navy blue

sweater came out of the house when Calvin stopped the car. He got out of the car and looked around him. "Afternoon," he greeted the woman. She smiled broadly but stayed where she was on the small porch of her house. "You sure got peace and quiet up here," he said.

"That's why people come here," she said, "when they do." She had a light, educated voice. Her speech was as clear and carefully chosen as a librarian's, but under it ran a stream of unlibrarianly good humor.

"Have you come to stay?" she asked.

"We're just exploring," Calvin said. "Trying to find a way through the mountains."

"You're going in the right direction," the woman said. "You've left it late in the day, though, with the rain this morning. It was pretty heavy up in the pass." She looked at Louella's baffled expression and laughed. "Come in and have a cup of coffee. I'll tell you about it."

She gave them coffee and cookies at a dining table in the corner of the living room. "Pinto Hotsprings was supposed to be a watering place, back in the gay nineties. It was going to be one of those fashionable resorts that women came to in order to escape the heat of the valley. You've read about that sort of thing, I suppose, they drank some of that disgusting water four times a day, and took long walks morning and afternoon. Their menfolk soaked in a stinking mess of sulphur mud in a little bath house that used to be out back of the hotel. It was all an excuse to be seen to be spending money by other people who wanted to be seen to be doing the same thing."

Louella, always one to ask the question when the lead-up to it has been so well prepared, said, "What happened to it?"

The woman said, "The fashion went the other way, east to the Sierras where there was more scenery, and the Sequoia big trees. Yosemite Valley killed off Pinto Hotsprings. One little sulphur spring can't compete with three waterfalls."

Calvin laughed with the two women, but his restlessness

was evident. The woman glanced at him and said, "I think you'd better wait for my husband. He'll be along shortly. You need to talk to him before you try the pass, you really do, it can be dangerous. The sign up the road says the pass is still open, but the last time a road crew was through here was at least two weeks ago."

Calvin was about to confess that he had no idea where they were or what they were driving toward when there was the sound of a small truck outside. A man came in the back door, while the three waited in the living room for him to come to them. When he did, they could see that he had taken off his boots and put on a pair of moccasins. He had no left arm and he walked with the help of a thick wooden cane.

Calvin felt a rush of blood, and a sweat flush covered his body. Why hadn't he thought of it before? He knew what would come next, and he was not ready for it. "This is my husband, Brian Ellsworth," the woman said, "and I'm Ann." She turned to her guests to listen to their introduction.

Louella spoke up. "We're Calvin and Louella Whitmore," she said.

In the momentary silence that followed, the man's eyes showed no sign of recognition. The woman's smile faltered like a single misfire in a finely tuned car engine, and then she recovered.

"You must be very tired," she said. She looked at them and took in her breath, deciding what to do. "Brian doesn't want to know anything about what's going on," she said. "I listen to the radio every once in a while. Brian, these people have been through a terrible trial. I think they're trying to get away from the excitement it caused."

Brian's voice when he spoke was a thin baritone, the voice of a much older man. "You've come to the right place," he said. "Would you like to look around? Not much time before it gets dark."

Ann said, "I think they planned to go through the pass."

Calvin spoke up, "Well, we didn't really plan anything, but if there was a road west, we thought we'd take it."

"You can't take it tonight," Brian said, "and there's nothing the other side of it, unless you spent the night in your car." It was a decision made, bluntly delivered.

"You don't want to go back, do you," Ann observed. She looked at Louella, who shook her head.

"I'll go light the stove," Brian said.

"You'll stay in the hotel," Ann said. "We keep it up for summer visitors. It's not a bad place, they seem to like it. Some of them have come every year."

Brian led the way to the hotel. He struggled with the two pairs of steps, but once on the hotel porch he moved quickly. The broad door had frosted glass panels with the name of the place spelled out in curled, clear letters. Inside, the lobby and the lounge area were painted in gleaming white. An unused chandelier made up of what looked like a cluster of five small vases holding yellowing candles hung from the ceiling in front of a wide flight of stairs. The large room was lit only in the center, by a single electric light bulb suspended among the vases, and at the top of the stairs a wooden wall had been built to seal off the floor above. A large, cast iron stove bellied out from the wall of the lounge, with a pile of dry wood beside it. It was a well kept relic of a small hotel, one that had had a slightly melancholy air to it even in its heyday.

Ann pointed to the left and said, "Those doors there lead to the room where they used to serve breakfast and tea. That's a bedroom now. Visitors sleep there. The bathroom is through here," indicating a single door beside the stove. "The kitchens and the dining room are at the back of the building, and we've closed them off, like the upstairs bedrooms."

Louella took Calvin's arm and gave it a gentle pull. He said to Brian, "Could we stay here, maybe a couple of nights? We'd want to pay you."

"We'd like your company," Ann said.

Brian added, "Your money will come in handy, too. Every little bit helps."

Ann asked, "Would you like pot roast for supper? About seven? The bath water will take about an hour to heat up, once you get the stove going. Maybe you could give Brian a hand with the stove, Mr. Whitmore, and then he can show you around. Not that there's much to see. I'll show you the upstairs bedrooms, Mrs. Whitmore, if you're interested. There's a servants' staircase at the back that we use when we need to go up there. We've left the old furniture the way it was when we came here. I dust every once in a while. It looks like a movie set up there. You might like to see it."

Calvin was on his knees leaning forward to put the kindling deep into the firebox of the stove when he heard Brian behind him. "You don't bend very well, Mr. Whitmore," he said. "Mind if I call you Calvin?"

Calvin said, "I'd be pleased if you did, if you want to. Maybe you ought to find out more about me first, before you start using my first name."

"I know about you," Brian said. "I'm not so out of touch as my wife thinks."

"It's my wound," Calvin said, straightening himself slowly. "I haven't had much chance to get my exercise for the past few weeks. Hiding out, most of the time. Or else out on show."

"What happened to you? Your back?" Brian said it as naturally as you would ask a person when he last bought a bottle of aspirin.

"Breach fire in a field gun," Calvin answered. "The gun blew up and took away some of my back. It was in training, I never saw action."

Brian looked at his left side. "I did. I was one of the few people evacuated from the Philippines. We came here almost two years ago. I'm getting better. Where are you going?"

Calvin said, "We don't know. Just going, for now. Running away."

Brian said, "There's nothing wrong with that. People said to me you have to face it. Get used to the stares and they won't bother you. Horseshit. I don't know what's so great about the big wide world that I have to be a part of it. It's not very great if it can't do without me. And Ann. This place suits us, we like it here. Ann was a lawyer, almost. She says she might go back to it someday when the men change the rules and give her a chance. I don't know. I want to stay here. Always, for as long as that turns out to be."

Calvin said, "If you were running, like me, would you know a place to run to?"

Brian thought about it for some time while handing sticks of wood to Calvin to be shoved into the firebox. Finally he said, "Not on this side of the mountains. Even here, someone would find you. I'm trying to remember a road that we took once. Ann was driving, maybe she'd remember it better than me. We got to a store out in the middle of nowhere, a store where there wasn't any reason to buy anything and no one around to do the buying. It was a crazy place. We went in there and everything in there was up to date, fresh on the shelves. This old man ran it, and he told us the valleys around him were as full as anyone wanted them to be of people who liked it on their own, and this was their store. The valleys run down the sides of the mountains to the ocean. It was a beautiful place. If we hadn't found Pinto Hotsprings, that's where I'd be. I can show you where it is on a map."

They had opened the curtains on one of the big windows so that the moonlight glowed silvery white across the bed. "It's like a little museum upstairs there," Louella told Calvin. "Ann says the people who owned this place kept thinking times would get better, and they never did. So they locked the door one day and left for good."

Calvin said, "I wonder how much time they wasted waiting for it to get better."

"She said the for sale sign was fifteen years old when they found it, and it probably wasn't the first sign that was put up," she answered.

"I guess we'll be putting up a for sale sign on our place," he said.

"Don't, Calvin," she said, "not yet, please. We've got years of talking to do, but I'm not ready to start yet."

"We've made a good start," he said.

"You're all right again," she said.

"Reckon I am," he agreed.

They spread the map on the table in the hotel lounge. The wicker furniture creaked in the sunshine as it released yesterday's dampness. Ann had brought a dust cloth with her to run round the window frames while they were talking.

"I'd like to see this room again with big, long, white, gauzy curtains," she said. "It's just made for that. They closed the hotel in the winter. It wasn't meant to have those big, heavy drapes that kept the cold and the draughts out. Thank goodness, because we certainly couldn't afford them."

"Well, I don't know," Brian said, "I've got a theory about that. I think the real reason this place was here was for gambling. I think they wanted to start a casino."

"It would have been a good place for one," Calvin said.

"You can just start up a gambling hall any time you want to?" Louella asked.

"I think you could back then," Calvin said. "They could of got away with it for a while, anyway."

Louella said, "Why didn't they then?" She directed her question to Brian, who winked at Calvin and laughed.

"Your pretty wife is very naive," he said.

"About what?" she demanded.

"Where you got gambling, you got gamblers," Calvin said. "Where you got gamblers, you got yourself a racketeer or two, and the other side of the door is a crooked politician with his hand out. I think Brian's hinting that the people who owned this place didn't know who to pay off."

"You've got it," Brian said.

"I'd never have thought of that," Louella said. "And Calvin's supposed to be the innocent one of the two of us." She stopped. "Oh, sweet Jesus, I didn't mean that the way it sounded, Calvin."

Ann said from the window, "You ought to say it more often. You have to start believing it. The sooner the better."

Louella scrambled to her feet and reached for Ann. She took her in her arms and kissed her on the cheek, and Ann hugged her in return.

Brian lifted his cane onto the table. "We're about here," he said.

Calvin studied the map until he found some small black boxes indicating the buildings of Pinto Hotsprings, with the name trailing off beside it. "Found it," he said. "And here's the road going up to the pass. It says San Carlos Pass, 2130 feet. That's not very high."

Brian said, "It's high for these mountains. They shed a lot of mud and shale. There's a rockslide area near the summit that you have to take very carefully. Even in the dry of summer. The air from the valley meets the air from the Pacific Ocean and it makes for pretty severe weather conditions over that small area of mountains."

"Where do you reckon we should go from there?" Calvin asked.

"After you cross over the mountains, the road will run down pretty straight into a sort of side valley of the Salinas Valley, heading generally west. The first chance you get, you turn south again, and you make for a place called Bitterwater, as I remember. Can you find it? I can't lean over to look," Brian said.

"Yeah," Calvin said, "here it is. Hell, Brian, that's a long way down south."

"It's either that or you go to Monterey and down the coast from there," Brian said. "You'd have to go through Salinas to get to Monterey. It's a pretty big place, and they have a daily paper that everybody reads. They look at the pictures, anyway."

"No," Calvin said, ruling that out. "So we go to Bitterwater."

"Then from there you cross the Salinas Valley, and then you go through the west range of these mountains, making for the ocean. When you catch your first glimpse of the ocean, you're about at that grocery store," Brian said. "Those are lousy directions, but it's about as much as we can remember of how we got there."

"Unless it's a foggy day," Ann added, "and you can't see the ocean. I remember it as being a good ten miles from the ocean."

"Maybe even fifteen," Brian said. "Stop there. The old man will help. Be honest with him. You won't be the first refugee he's known."

"Refugee," Louella said. She crossed to Calvin and put her hand on his head, for all the world as if bestowing a blessing.

"That's about right," Calvin said. "You know, a few years back, when we were in the middle of some troubles in Red Branch, I almost missed finding out that this person I met, called the tallest man in the world, Robert Wadlow, he'd died while we were having our riots. And I thought, I wonder who's going to be the next freak that everybody knows about. Turns out to be me."

Louella put her head down, on the verge of tears, and Ann reached out to hold her hand.

Brian's voice and question were brutal. "What killed him?" he asked, and Calvin suddenly remembered he wasn't the only freak in the room.

"That was a funny thing," he answered. "When I first saw him, I thought it was nothing but a big, stuffed dummy, until I saw the way he was afraid of his feet, he was scared all the time about knowing where he was putting his feet. Well, it turned out that he was so overgrown he had to wear braces on his ankles, and one of these rubbed the skin raw and started an infection. It was the infection that killed him. And you know why he come to town? He was advertising for the shoestore. Florsheim shoes. It was almost as if he knew then his feet were going to kill him."

The embarrassment passed, and Calvin added, "Poor guy."

Brian tapped his cane on the map. "This store," he called them to attention. "The old man told me something," he said. "He said that in the old days, when people came west, this was the only way to get down to that part of the coast. They'd come there, and they'd have a look, and then they'd go back to the Salinas Valley to farm and make a living. But the old man says that they never lost the memory of that sight of the coast and the ocean. It was where they really wanted to stay, but they couldn't. Nowadays, some people can."

Ann said, "I guess there's something to be said for progress. Not much, but at least something."

The late light from the west was no longer spilling over into the valley from the heights of the mountains. It was instead a diffused, creamy illumination that came out of the sky spread evenly from horizon to horizon. The four of them sat on the hotel porch wrapped in sweaters enjoying the crisp end of the fall day.

Brian leaned back in his wicker chair so that he could see Ann at the far side of the group. "Honey," he said, "wouldn't now be a good time to open that bottle? The one we've saved?" Calvin's protest was dismissed with a wave of his one hand.

"We'll never drink it ourselves," Ann said. "That's a good idea."

She went into the hotel and came back with a pottery bottle the color and texture of brown stone. It had a black tape across the cork, and this was held in place with red sealing wax that was so old it was crumbling around its edges.

"Can I borrow some glasses from your bedroom?" she asked. Louella went with her to get some.

"What is it?" Calvin asked

"It's a drink called absinthe," Brian said. He pointed out the French name on the bottle, stamped in ink, and the name of the place and producer below that. "It was outlawed in Paris. People who got addicted to it lost their minds. Personally, I think anyone who gets addicted to anything has lost his mind. I thought that's what addiction meant. Maybe I've got it wrong."

"No, you're right," Calvin said. He looked away, then turned to face Brian. "That's the way it took me," he said.

The two women came back with four glasses and a small jug of water. "You're supposed to dilute it to taste," Ann said.

"Now for the story," Brian said. "With me, there's always a story. I don't suppose you've noticed." He picked up the bottle and looked at it again. "We need a corkscrew," he said. "Have we got one?" Ann produced one from her pocket and displayed it in triumph. "Wise guy," Brian said to her. "Now, during Prohibition this hotel was on its last legs. It seems as though the owners thought the only way they could stay open would be to make it into something like a speakeasy. They got bootleg liquor in and let the word get around that there was drinking here. Most of the bootleg stuff during Prohibition came in by boat. Now you may have noticed that we're a long way from the nearest navigable body of water. In fact we're about an equal distance from San Francisco Bay and Monterey Bay, and both of them are a long way away. My theory is that it was too long. I think people would get here, and start the party, and the booze would run out. Okay, I admit that sounds unlikely, but something went wrong, anyway, and it didn't work. They closed down and left a shed full of empty bottles and a few leftovers in the cupboard behind the front desk. The corks had gone from every bottle and the wine had gone to vinegar, all except this."

"That's enough, Brian," Ann pleaded, "we want to try it."

"I'm talking while hoping that someone will do the honors

for me," Brian said. Calvin noticed for the first time the bitterness come into his voice. "I'm no longer equipped to use a corkscrew, you'll notice."

Ann ignored the self pity. "Do you think you could do it, Calvin?" she asked.

The cork was dry and had to be teased out to extract it in one piece. It came free finally, and Calvin handed the bottle to Brian. He sniffed the aroma that came from the bottle and poured a small amount into a glass to examine it against the light. He sniffed again, then poured a few drops of water in and they all watched as the liquor clouded. He added more water and tasted it. He nodded his head and said, "Good, worth waiting for." He then poured the other three drinks. They waited for the toast, while Brian thought about it. Eventually he raised his glass, "The best I can do," he said, "considering the age of this, is 'To auld lang syne'. Here's to turning the clock back. Here's to old times."

Calvin heard the bitterness again, but following Ann's lead, he ignored it. They laughed and raised their glasses, and Louella said, "I never have known what that meant, and it's never stopped me from enjoying a drink."

They tasted, letting the liquor dawdle on their lips before licking it off. It was both musty and fresh on the tongue. They swallowed and waited for the warmth. Ann was the first to comment. "Funny," she said. "It tastes right, but . . ."

Brian drank his down, waited, poured another shot and drank it down without water. Again he waited. Then he started laughing, his laughter turning into a fit that had him gasping for breath. The others laughed with him without knowing why, until his gasps died enough for him to speak.

"No wonder the place closed," he shouted in delight, "there's no alcohol in this stuff, none at all! The unkindest cut of all! They were swindled by their bootlegger!"

When the laughter slackened, Calvin raised his glass again, toasting with more enthusiasm. "You got it right, Brian. To auld lang syne!"

3

They set out early. The pass was narrow, with loose shale filling the edges of the road, collecting behind it heaps of draining mud that could not run off. The slide area, when they got to it, still held firm, although rocks half the size of boxcars looked as if they were on the move. One immense slab of rock hung over the road like judgment. Someone had climbed up to it and painted "Jesus Saves" on its side, either out of religious conviction or the saving grace of humor. They travelled leaning forward as close to the windshield as they could get, looking up past the threatening stone at the uncomplicated, unthreatening sky, longing for the pass to end.

Calvin had an almost overwhelming urge to put his foot down hard on the gas pedal and get through as quickly as possible. He was kept from doing this by reminding himself that one touch on the unstable bank and he would bring down the mountain on them. And how long would it be before anyone would know? The season of recognition was over for that part of the land, and it was ready to be forgotten. They crept out from under the shadows, and stopped in the sun to take in deep breaths.

From there the trip was just as Brian had described, down

in a long decline into a valley that followed a river edged with cottonwood trees, then across some soft, stretching hills to the brown Salinas Valley, and across that to the town of Bitterwater. It was a place that looked as though it had succeeded in living up to its name. A woman with her hair in curlers looked hard at them while they waited at the single stoplight. Calvin realized that she was not seeing them, but she was herself waiting to be seen. Somewhere there was a movie mogul who was destined to drive through Bitterwater and spot a fat woman of about thirty wearing tight jeans and a sloppy shirt, with her hair curlers covered in a purple chiffon scarf and her pink lipstick smeared thickly over her pouting mouth, and he was going to sign her to a contract and make her beautiful, famous and desirable. But not today. They decided to skip lunch. Outside the town they found a narrow road, marked with a yellow and black diamond sign with Dangerous written across it, turning west again.

It was a better road than San Carlos Pass had been, but it was steeper and filled with little jinks that were neither curves nor corners. It was hard on car and driver, as well as the passenger's stomach, and after a couple of hours of this, Calvin thought it was wise to stop. When they got out of the car to stretch, they each felt at the same moment the wind from the west. It carried the sea on it, as on the feathers of a soaring bird. They waited impatiently for the engine to cool before setting off again.

A few miles farther on, the road now falling gradually but steadily as they advanced, they caught sight of what looked like a sheet of shining, silvery metal far off, lightly dented and pounded, the line between it and a cloud bank that stood far out to sea lost in the glare of the sun. Immediately they came to a clearing in a forest of pines and redwoods, with a frame building crowding back against the trees. It was the store Brian had told them of, made from a two room wooden house, with a sharply pitched shingle roof and a porch that ran the width of the building. Through its windows they saw an interior packed and stacked with boxes and jars and cans and bags and packages. Calvin turned the car behind a rank of mailboxes that stood on the roadside, into a small parking lot that had been cut from the woods.

When they got out of the car and approached the store, an old man came from inside and sat down in a chair that partially blocked the doorway. He looked to be over eighty. He was small and slight, but he was strong and he moved like a much younger man. His white hair was long and pushed back from a high forehead. He evidently shaved with a lack of enthusiasm or in bad light, since there were patches of white stubble scattered about his face and throat. He wore a rough but well made tweed suit that had been expensive in its day, and in place of a shirt a blue wool fisherman's sweater with a high neck. All the skin that showed was dark brown, as brown as old leather, making his white eyebrows and blue eyes, that burned into the strangers from behind round, wire framed glasses, look like part of a stage persona. He was in every detail the ancient, eccentric professor.

As they approached the porch the old man smiled, his teeth brilliant white in his wide mouth. The gesture produced a complex of lines around his outsize nose, and his long ears lifted slightly. His voice when he greeted them was high and loud, the voice of a man who had many things to do but could always spare a moment out of courtesy.

"Is there anything that I can do for you?" he said. "I sell only groceries and provisions, I'm afraid. No gasoline." He made no move to go into the store to sell anything.

Calvin felt the reluctance in his greeting. "We stayed with some people in Pinto Hotsprings. They told us about you. We were looking for you, not your groceries."

"Pinto Hotsprings?" the man said.

"The other side of the mountains," Calvin said.

The old man made no move or gesture of recognition. He seemed content to be forever unaware of all that lay on the other side of the mountains. Louella spoke up. "Their name is Ellsworth," she said. "He's a war veteran. He's lost his left arm and was wounded in his legs."

"I remember him, yes, I do," the old man said. He stabbed at the air energetically, putting his finger on the figure in his memory. "They thought about settling down around here, but he had trouble managing the slope. Had a very nice wife. How is he? Is he any better?"

"He says he's improving," Calvin said.

"He said you might help us," Louella said.

"How?" the old man said, showing curiosity but no engagement in the task.

"Mr. Ellsworth called us refugees," she said. "I guess we're looking for refuge."

He looked at Louella with more warmth and interest, then turned to Calvin and studied him. He seemed pleased at the prospect before him. "Sanctuary," the old man said. "An appeal for sanctuary." His face relaxed. "Young lady, behind the counter in the store is a cold box. I'd like a glass of the orange juice you'll find in there. There is also apple juice, very good, pressed from apples just along the coast." He spread his hands and smiled broadly, his ears moving up his head and flattening slightly as he did so. "There is also root beer and cream soda. See if you can find something you and this gentleman would like."

"My name's Whitmore," Calvin said. "This here's my wife. Calvin and Louella."

"I am very pleased to meet you," the old man said. "I'm Harry Stanyon. I recognize you. I know who you are, both of you." He said it as if it was a feat to be commended, and he was pleased with himself. "You need my help."

He got up from his chair and pushed it away from the door, gesturing for them to follow him into the store. When he stood, the heavy tweed suit was reluctant to fit itself to his thin, energetic body. The small, strong man projected from it at each of its openings as if it were only a passingly convenient case to enfold the life and health within it. He was that paradox usually associated with children, an almost dwarfish center of energy that was too large to be contained.

"A house," he said, "first, a house. We have three hours of daylight to find you a house."

They found the dirt road that led off the coast road and up the mountain at a small canyon called Kings Creek, as Harry had described. The road followed the creek, dry at this time of year, staying beside the steep stream bed that had cut its way into the side of the mountain. After a few hundred yards, the road turned left around a hump and entered a tiny valley, circular, about seventy feet in diameter, punched into the side of the mountain so that the ground was almost flat. A low house with a long, sloping roof, hidden from sight from the coast road below, looked out over the ocean. Behind it a few redwoods and pines clumped together, and behind them, up a steeper incline, another stand of trees, denser and larger, broke out along the creek bed and spread over and to the top of the mountain. The dry grass in front of the house, tawny brown in the shadows, was golden in the late sunlight. From the top of the hump they could see the grass like a golden tide sweep its way down to the coast road, then beyond that, all the way to the foot of the mountain, which they thought must have been like its neighbor that they could see to the south, ending in a giant cliff of three hundred feet or more that reared like a stirring animal from the welter of white surf below. At the house, they went up six broad wooden steps to the porch. From there they could see to the north the land bent back away from them, showing the flat sheet of the ocean like a photograph of infinity. As far as they could see to the south the line of the cliffs walled the land against the sea, letting it beat in all its majesty and futility in huge curtains of white that grew out of the surf, shredded against the cliffs, and sank down in white confusion. The vast sky, creating wind and light and color, colluded in the sea's energy, and they felt excitement in the immense peace that possessed the place.

The key to the house was stuck into a crack behind one of the porch railings, as Harry had said it would be. The house was warm and tidy. Except for the empty look of the shelves and cupboards, and the salt stipple on the windows, it did not look vacant.

"What do you say?" Calvin asked. "It's a long way from anywhere," he said. "But it feels safe. What do you think?"

"It's just the two of us again," Louella said, "is that all right?"

"You bet it is," he said. "Come on, let's unload the car."

Harry Stanyon assigned his customers days and times on which to come to his store. Calvin and Louella were given late afternoon, which was early evening in these darker months, on Thursdays. Like everything in Harry's life, there was a ritual to the shopping trip. The three of them meticulously considered what would be needed for the coming week and packed it into boxes, which were loaded into the car. They then looked a week ahead and made a list of what needed to be ordered from the wholesaler when the truck came to deliver this week's orders to the store. Following this, Calvin and Harry would add up the damage, as Harry called the bill, while Louella went through the mail that had been delivered to their box by the road. Since they were his last customers for the day, Harry cooked a supper for all three, letting Calvin pay for the food as part of his weekly bill. If the weather was good and presented no problem for the return trip north to their house, they would stay on, sitting in candlelight, Calvin and Louella drinking red wine, Harry sipping a thin, bitter liquor made of tea, grapefruit juice and ginger root, talking and learning about each other in the black, rich, almost textured nights of that coast.

Harry told them about the other people along the mountains, the other customers whose privacy he protected. Farthest north was a small colony of people who were experimenting with drugs, mainly marijuana which they grew themselves. A man had come there and built a restaurant that balanced on the lip of a cliff above the sea. The restaurant had attracted summer trade and now supported the entire group with jobs and an income. They had little to do with Harry's store in the summer, but they came in the winter. South of them were five houses making up a small colony lived in by a writer and some artists. They were all customers of Harry's. One of these was a sculptor, not a bad one, not a great one either. The writer was famous, but his books, which were published in Europe, were pornographic and as a result he couldn't collect the royalties he was owed. He paid his bill by giving Harry watercolor paintings signed with his famous name. Harry sold them in Monterey or Carmel and gave back to the writer anything they made above the amount of his bill. South of these people lived several members of a family who owned a grove of redwoods that was opened to campers during the summer months. The campers were among his best customers. Their summer money alone was enough to keep him going through the winter. South again were several small ranchers grazing herds of cattle and selling prime timber. Kings Creek Ranch had been owned by one of these.

All along the coast, concealed in the canyons and folds of the mountains, sometimes burrowed into the windy flanks of the slope as near the sea as they dared, were a large number of cabins and houses lived in by people who had their own reasons for leaving the lives they had known and coming to live in a place with a view and few comforts. They were poorer than they had been before, but it was what they wanted. Most of them wrote books and painted watercolors of the sea and the coastline, or tried and failed to paint the sunsets, or wrote music or poetry, or simply looked at the ocean in its moods and colors, and thought.

Harry himself said he needed to be away from a view of the ocean. It was too overwhelming, it interfered with other things that needed to be thought about. He grinned widely as soon as he had said it, punctuating his comment with the white teeth and complex of lines that accompanied each grin. It was a half humorous way of telling them that a serious truth was embedded in the irony.

"You're a farmer, Calvin," he said, "and Louella is a cafe manager. You have kept things simple for yourselves, that's sensible, that's a good idea. Now, I'm not so sensible, in a way. I'm a storekeeper or a grocer, whichever you wish to call me, and I'm also a mystic. I'm very proud of that." He grinned again.

Louella said, "I'll bet you are. What is it?"

"That takes some explaining," he said, and laughed. "That's why I told you. You noticed I like to explain things? Well, a mystic can be called by other names, depending on what his skills are, what the philosophies are that he's investigating. I'm investigating too many to give me any title other than mystic."

"You're a philosopher, then?" Calvin asked.

"Oh yes," Harry answered, "a philosopher, definitely, and other things too."

"Sticking to the philosopher for a minute, here, Harry," Calvin said, "what does he do? How would I know him? Does he do anything for a living?" Calvin had picked up on Harry's technique and was himself only half teasing.

"If he wants to live, he becomes a philosopher and storekeeper," Harry said. "Yes, I think you'd recognize him. But you might turn away from him before you knew more about him. You might do the same to the mystic."

"I don't get that," Louella said. "You said you were one. We're not turning away from you."

"You may feel like doing that when you know more about me," Harry said.

There was a moment of silence before Calvin answered, "You could say the same about us, Harry. You didn't do that to us, we won't do it to you. I don't know why you think we would, or even why we might do that."

"Don't take offense, please don't do that, either of you,"

Harry said. "I think some of what I call my wisdom might frighten you. That's all I mean. My brand of mystic is interested in spiritual health, which is wisdom, and he achieves wisdom in ways that you may think are not the ways of people like yourselves."

"That's your business, not ours," Louella insisted.

Harry didn't answer her. Instead he looked at her intently, and the smile he gave her was a strange one, friendly, but with a warning in it.

"For instance," he said, "take an example, that grove of redwoods above your house. It's one of the reasons I knew about that house. In that grove is something very rare, an albino redwood. A perfectly white redwood, without the slightest taint of color in its bark or branches or foliage. In the old days a few people in Monterey knew about it, because this was the coast where they came to fell timber for their buildings, and someone sometime had found it. It was the old Spanish families who knew about it. The last ones to know were the Castros. One of them wrote a story about it a few years ago, and it was published in a pamphlet in Carmel. Well, after I read it, I searched until I found the tree. They came in a buckboard in the old days, the Castros, on the day before Christmas, and they cut just one bough from the tree, and they took it to Mission San Carlos for the Christ Child. While there was a Castro who was able to make the journey, there was always a bough of white redwood in front of the baby in the nativity scene in the mission church. It sounds like a lunatic idea in a silly story, doesn't it, a white redwood for the Christ child. But I found it."

"I'll have to hunt for it," Calvin said.

"I think you will, someday. When you find it, keep it a secret," Harry said. "If you don't, somebody will come along and cut it down and take it to the museum in Pacific Grove, to stand next to that hideous glass case of stuffed sea otters." He was not lighthearted now, instead serious and almost angry. "Their interest in it would be the same as yours is now, a specimen, a scientific curiosity. The Castros were interested in it because they were Catholics, and all Catholics are superstitious. They were closer to the truth of it than you, being a farmer. Nowadays you farmers are too close to scientists, and you miss the truth. Scientists are ignorant. They search for reality and miss the truth. Scientists and farmers need mystics to see the truth."

Calvin was baffled by what he heard as an insult and sat silent, trying to think what he had said or why otherwise he deserved it.

"Hey! Listen to him," Louella said, trying to tease Harry out of what she felt must be arrogance.

He laughed with them, but he was not fooled. "You see what I meant about turning away from me? Mystics are awkward. We believe everything has a spiritual side. I call it power. More primitive people, like Indians, call it magic."

Calvin flinched as if he had been struck across the face. "What's wrong?" Harry asked him.

Calvin had gone pale. He shuddered. "Think I've got a cold coming, or the flu," he said. "Time to go home," he said to Louella.

On their next Thursday supper visit, Harry turned the conversation once more to his wisdom, as he called it. "I'm still learning. I'll be a shaman, a wise man, someday quite soon, I think. And no one – well, very few people – will know what to do with my wisdom. I'm the sort of person already that you wouldn't have chosen to have anything to do with, except that you need me. As a wise man? Goodness!"

"Hey, hold on, Harry," Calvin said. "We thought we were gettin' along real good with each other. Better than last week, leastways."

"We are, we're improving," Harry answered, "I'm not fooled about what people think of me, that's all. When they get to know more about me."

He leaned forward and pushed the candle in its holder out

of the way so that he could look at each of the young people in turn. "I'm going to keep your friendship. You may not think so now, but I'm going to do that. However . . ." He paused and laughed, while his eyes held them. "I'm going to let you know about me. You have been warned. I won't let you know too quickly, not all at once. I'm starting in a way that will keep your friendship. I'm asking you to be tolerant of me, as my friends." He stopped, then laughed loudly again. "Here!" he said.

He sat down on the floor in the space between two stacks of groceries and crossed his legs, lifting one foot onto the thigh of the other leg so that he was bound into a shape that made Calvin wince with physical pain to look at it. He extended his hands to his knees and turned the palms up, then relaxed his shoulders and curled his fingers.

"I practice yoga," Harry said.

"Is that what you're doing?" Louella asked. She was restraining herself from laughing at the spectacle. The little, brown man in his tweed suit and professorial glasses making himself into a pretzel for an after dinner trick struck her as either deliberately comic or plain loony.

Harry closed his eyes and relaxed his face and jaw. He then took a piece of string out of the pocket of his jacket and put the end of it into one nostril. He breathed deeply, fumbling with the string and working his tongue and jaw as he did so. The end of the string came out of his mouth on his tongue. He took this end in his fingers and pulled the string through and out of his mouth.

Louella watched the process in horror. "What in the world do you think you're doing, Harry?" she said.

"You see, that's what I meant, it's disgusting to you, isn't it? And to someone who doesn't know anything about yoga, it would be, I don't deny that," he said. "It's one of the disciplines I practice. Only one of them. A few weeks ago, if you'd seen me do that, would you have wanted to be my friend? You need a friend, but you're asking yourself, do I need one that badly?" He looked at Calvin. "Do you still want to accept my help?"

"What do you mean?" Calvin asked.

Harry said, "I'm very different from anyone you've ever met. I can help you if you can tolerate my differences. Do you want my help badly enough to let me be strange, as you come to know about me, in my own way?" He paused before adding, "There's another question that follows on that, but I won't ask it yet."

"This is some kind of a test," Louella said, "isn't it. You've been testing us."

Harry nodded. "All along," he said. He unwound his legs and got to his feet, refusing the hand of assistance that Calvin offered, but refusing it politely. "And I'm going to go on testing you. You think about it," he said. "The kind of help I offer is the kind you'll get from an old man who has learned to run a string through his nose into his mouth, in order to help him understand the universe. Maybe you will decide that you don't want that. I think that's the kind of help you need." He smiled. "It's up to you."

Calvin scratched his head and said, "Is there a price tag, Harry? Just so we know?"

Harry shook his head. "Sanctuary, I suppose, if that qualifies as a price. It's a new test for all of us. I don't charge for experiments." He laughed loudly.

Their Thursdays now included a time of tension for Calvin and Louella. They waited for some piece of information, another part of the test, to be given to them. One day Harry was baking brown bread. It was flat and dense, apparently inedible. When Louella commiserated on his baking failure, he smiled at her and said, "That's sacramental bread. Don't worry, I don't expect anyone to eat it except myself."

"Sacramental?" she asked. "When do you eat it?"

He looked at the bread and made a sour face. "I eat very little of it," he said, "only what's necessary. It's pretty awful.

It's better when it has its honey on it. On some days and nights, you see, I celebrate festivals. It isn't the same as religion, but in another way it is. It's as much as most people make religion into, the celebrations. It's the . . ." He broke off as Calvin came toward them. "Times and things of spiritual meaning have to be remembered. Or, let's say, I feel that it's important to me to remember them."

He waited to see that Calvin had moved out of earshot before adding, "I was going to call it magic, but Calvin doesn't like that. Superstition maybe? No – magic. It might only be magic, but it's still there, whether we recognize it or not. I choose to recognize it. That's all."

One Thursday evening the fog which had hovered on the horizon all day moved in from the ocean before Louella and Calvin could get on the road back to Kings Creek, and it was as sensible to stay until darkness as to try to grope a way home through the pearly cloud that had enveloped them. When it was time to go, Louella was cold. Harry took a blanket from his bed and put it over her head onto her shoulders. It had a neatly stitched slit in it for her head to pass through.

"I've seen one of these in Mexican Town," Louella said. "It's a poncho, isn't it? Have you been to Mexico?"

"I wear it as a priest," he said. When she looked alarmed , he laughed and said, "It also keeps me warm, it lies on my bed, there's nothing sacred about it. Wear it."

She considered him and the blanket carefully, and kept it on.

They discussed Harry as they drove home. "How do you feel about him now?" Louella asked.

"I trust him," Calvin answered. "He's a friend, even if sometimes he don't sound like one. I believe him when he says that. Don't you?"

"Yeah," she replied. "We don't know much about friends, of course." She felt safe to add, in the darkness, "We've been wrong about friends before."

It was some time before Calvin spoke again. "He's got a secret life, of course," he said. "That makes him different."

"That's not true," Louella answered. "It's only secret because we don't know enough about it to ask about it."

"Or we're too embarrassed about all that stuff to know what to say," Calvin corrected her.

"That's the same thing, Calvin," she insisted.

Her reply struck home. "Hey now," he said, "you know, that's right. I think old Harry's beginning to teach us things without us even knowing it."

"I wouldn't put it past him to have that in mind," Louella said. She removed the mild sarcasm from her voice when she added, "He just about warned us that was what he was going to do. And when we were ready, he would help us."

Louella had admired a carving of a bird several times. It stood on a high shelf in the corner of the room that passed for Harry's kitchen. Each time she asked about it, he said he would tell her and changed the subject. She was drying dishes when she glanced up at it and said, "Come on, Harry, what's so mysterious about a bird? Tell us about it."

"It's not mysterious, only embarrassing," he said. "It was foolishness, I guess. Maybe arrogance. I carved that bird to remind myself that some things I plan, you know, some ideas I have, are less than inspired."

Harry was squirming, but Calvin was not going to let him off the hook. "We're waiting," he said.

"Well, I'd always wondered about St. Francis and the birds. Calling them by name, wearing them like clothes, all that. My experience with birds, especially wild ones, is that they're by nature cautious, they're vulnerable, they have to be cautious or they die. And St. Francis lived at a time when men slaughtered birds just the way they do now, maybe not by shooting them, but it was still slaughter. So it wasn't likely that birds would think that a man, even St. Francis, was just another kind of bird, or some equally innocent creature. I decided that the only way St. Francis could have controlled those birds, if the stories are true of course, was to control their feed. He would have to be the only source of food for them."

He took down the carving and looked at it. "So, I trapped a few finches, the brown ones that come in flocks when the seeds are ripe in late spring. You'll see them next year. I don't approve of trapping anything, but I did it. Well, I forced them to eat from my fingers, then they had to eat by standing on a finger and pecking food from the palm of my hand, and so on. In the end I tried doing what some mother birds do, and I chewed up food and kept some on the end of my tongue to let them eat from it."

"Harry!" Louella choked. "Ugh!"

"It was nice, very natural, in its way," he said defensively. "They would perch on a finger and I'd raise them up to my chin, and they would feed from there."

"This is beginning to sound like a joke I heard once, about a high diver at a circus." Calvin was laughing as much at Harry's discomfort as at the story. "What's the punch line?" he asked.

Harry turned to him, embarrassed, but his determination surfacing now. "Something had never occurred to me. We see live birds, and we assume they're healthy. We don't read their faces for illness, or for pain, the way we do with humans." He dipped his head suddenly at Calvin, looking into him with his keen eyes, and then as quickly looked away. "It seems that birds are more like us than I knew. One of them was sick, later it died, in fact, and it passed its disease on to me. So much for an assumption of a perfect state of nature, I suppose. We live and learn, if we live long enough."

Diverting the subject from himself, Harry teased, "What happened to the high diver at the circus?"

Calvin had understood the reference to himself. "Huh?" he said. "Oh, you don't want to hear that."

"Yes, I do," Harry insisted.

"Lordy, lordy," Louella mourned in mockery. "You've never heard a Calvin story, obviously. You've got a treat coming."

"Well," Calvin said, "maybe it's like your bird story more than I thought. There was this high diver in a circus, and he started by diving fifty feet into fifteen feet of water, and people thought he was great, but he decided he wanted to be not just great, but the greatest ever. So for the next year, every week he pushed his platform up another five feet and cut down the water level by a foot a time. He got so he was diving into five feet of water from a hundred feet up, and people agreed, he really was the greatest.

"He used to do his circus act in the afternoon and again at night, and in the morning he'd practice it. He was funny about his practise, though. This was always in secret. He'd perform in front of big crowds, but there wasn't no one allowed to watch him when he was practicing. Well, one morning he went off for his secret practise, and when he came in for lunch he was all wrapped up in bandages and walking with crutches. Everybody crowded around and wanted to know what happened, but he said it was embarrassing and he'd only tell his story once, to everybody at the same time, out at his secret practise place.

"After lunch they all trooped out there, and when they got there and looked around, they saw this big ladder going up so high it made you sick to look at it, and down below where the tank of water used to be was what looked like a big dish rag. This high diver stood there and told everybody to look carefully at this, because there was a lesson they had to learn. He said the ladder was a hundred and twenty-five feet high. He could dive from that high into no water at all, just that big damp rag. He said he was sure no high diver would ever do any better. He was sure to be the greatest ever. That's what he wanted.

"Well, somebody asked, of course, if he was so great, what in hell went wrong? And he said, 'I forgot you can go too far. I was all right with the rag when it was wet,' he said, 'but when I wrung it out, I was finished.' "

Harry laughed with them but stopped quickly. "I know what you're saying, Calvin," he said. "We understand each other. This is different. This time it is for a friend, and that makes it different."

They talked one evening about the possibility of running the Kings Creek property as a small ranch again. Without their realizing it their talk became confident and optimistic, with Harry explaining how other ranchers along the Big Sur managed their land. It suddenly struck both Calvin and Louella, almost at the same moment, that they had a future again, at least a tentative one, and that this was bound up with Harry. He was part of their plans.

Calvin felt, just as suddenly, bold. He said, "You started to ask us a question one time, Harry, and then you held it back. You think we're ready for it yet?"

"Probably," Harry said and grinned. "I'll take a chance that you're ready." He collected his thoughts and clasped his hands together. "Let's see now, I believe I asked if you were prepared to allow me to be strange in my own way, and still trust that I was your friend."

"Yeah, that's right," Calvin said, "that's what you were saying. Then you said there was another question that ought to be asked. You mind asking us? We'd like to pass all of your tests." He corrected himself. "We'd like to know if we pass all your tests, I mean."

Harry smiled. "It's not much of a test, not yet." He said, "It's only a very simple question – Will you let me be tolerant of you in the same way, by telling me about your own strange ways? Confidence – and that's all friendship is – works both ways. You have a lot to tell, that a friend ought to hear."

When he laughed, Harry opened his large mouth and let out a piercing cackle of a sound. It was the sort of laugh that needed open spaces. Within the confining walls of his store, sitting around his table, his laughter was painful to hear. When he was the third party in any argument between Louella and Calvin, the observer or sometimes the cause, his defense was to laugh, drowning with noise whatever was at issue so that it was obliterated, forgotten.

Louella was slow to recognize it as a tactic, and Calvin was even slower. She challenged Harry on it one Thursday when he had avoided a clumsy question from Calvin by laughing it away. "You do that on purpose," she accused him. "You just blast us out of the way with that laugh of yours." She could not have explained why she added, "You can tell you've never been married."

He was instantly sober. "Oh, you're wrong there, Louella, I was married for more than thirty years, we had two sons." He tried to lighten his mood. "You're right about the laugh. It works very well, doesn't it," he said, and he laughed again.

"Are you a widower?" Calvin asked, when Harry's laughter had died.

"I don't really know," Harry answered. "Maybe one of my sons will find me one of these days and let me know what I am, domestically speaking."

There seemed nothing that could be said to untie the knot of feelings in his voice, when he added, "After all that time, thirty years plus, it turned out we didn't want the same things out of life. Isn't it strange that two people, well, four people in the end, could live together and grow apart?"

Louella said, "It's not strange to us."

"No," Harry said, "you learned about that too, didn't you."

It was the first indication they had had that Harry knew more about them than they had hinted at or the newspapers had revealed. The knowledge disturbed Calvin. Yet he felt the rush of a kind of comfort that Harry was finding out things for himself, that he was reading their minds and souls behind their protecting faces. It was a relief to know there was someone who could penetrate some of their mysteries, even though they were still guarding them. An alarm bell rang, welcoming the intruder.

His face showed what he felt, both the alarm and the relief, and Harry read it as always. When it was time for Louella and Calvin to go, as the three of them crossed the porch, Harry put a hand inside the crook of Calvin's elbow, holding him back by the gesture rather than by the force of it. Calvin stopped as if held in iron, and Louella paused on the steps to see what had happened. The light from inside the store made the three of them silhouettes, and when he spoke, Harry's voice came from a small, black cutout of a man.

"It's almost time," he said. "Don't be afraid of it."

They came to do the week's shopping at Harry's on the last Thursday of the year. Calvin had begun adding up the damage when there was a shout from Louella, who was standing by their mailbox with a letter in her hand, waving as if she was trying to set a new record for semaphore signalling. The farm had been sold. The last link with Red Branch was broken. Calvin whirled her into the air when she told him the news, and carried her into the store.

All the time that the damage was being settled and supper eaten, the young people chattered to each other like house sparrows. Harry was left out, unnecessary, but his face showed only a reflection of their joy. As they sat over coffee, he broke into their celebration and said to them, "Well, a chapter is closed. It's ended. Red Branch is history now, and you're talking about some of it." He looked closely at them in turn, examining them. "Not all of it, though. How are you going to make your new start? It's almost a new year, there's no better time."

Calvin pushed himself back from the table, and Louella began to comb at her hair, now mouse brown except at the ends, with her fingers. They were suddenly very sober, and there was anger in the air.

"We'll talk it all out when we're ready," Calvin said. His tone and his face excluded Harry. Louella, however, studied the table top and did not join in his rejection.

Harry persevered gently. "This is a new year coming," he said again. "Start it like a really new year." The other two remained silent. "I know enough about you now." He said it quietly and soothingly, petting them with his incongruously high voice. "I'll help you. Let's start tonight."

Calvin sat strained and twisted in his chair, prepared to flare into anger. Louella looked at him, uncertain of his mood and afraid of a rash decision. They sat where they were, nevertheless. Neither of them was willing to be the one who by standing up to leave would deny the offer of help.

Harry saw this and smiled his most expansive smile. He got up and turned his back on them, as if discounting that a walkout might conceivably come. He brought out three glasses and got a bottle down from a high shelf in a cupboard where he kept it among his spare sheets and blankets. "This is something very special," he said. "This is a wine to celebrate with. I think we'll celebrate tonight. Only the first, tender blossoms from the wild apple trees go into this. This is eight months old now, ready to drink and at its best."

When he had filled the glasses, he lifted his own and offered a toast. "To truth," he said. He waited for their response.

The two younger people lifted their glasses warily, but they drank to truth. Louella said, "The last time we drank a toast it was to auld lang syne, for old times' sake." Her remark failed to break the tension, and Calvin sat stiffly in his chair, leaning heavily on his forearms and staring at his glass.

Harry turned his glass in his fingers, admiring the shapes and colors in the patterns thrown onto the table by the candlelight as it passed through the glass. "I'm an old man living on the farthest edge of a continent," he said. "Behind me are millions of people, millions of lives. It stands to reason that I know something about them, seeing how long it took me to get here. Something about the lives of those people, I mean. Including your lives.

"Are you ready?" he said. "That's the only question. That's what you are wondering. I think you are. I don't think I'm wrong." He said it as if he read it in the colors of his glass. He looked up then and smiled in reassurance. "Don't be afraid. You sit there, Louella, on that side of the table. You sit at the end, Calvin, not facing her but facing me."

"What are you doing, Harry," Calvin asked, "putting me on trial?" His voice was husky. The old sense of being a victim came at him again in a sickening wave, and his voice was harsh even to his own ears.

"In a way, yes," Harry admitted. "A more honest trial than you got before."

"What do you mean?" Calvin challenged him angrily.

"They let you lie by not making you testify," Harry answered.

Calvin drew in his breath as if he had been struck. He looked at Louella and moved his hand to the back of his chair, looking for her to support his desire to get up and leave, but she sat where she was.

Harry said, "I'm not your judge. I'm your friend. I'm a person that you learned to tolerate, and therefore to trust. Before you could love me as a friend, you had to learn to trust me. Trust me now. You have to be healed, both of you, and I can help you. I can."

He paused before continuing, "I sit like the buddha, sometimes all night. I stand on my head to meditate, in order to clear my mind. On certain nights of the year I dress in sandals and that blanket over there and go up to the top of the mountain to call 'Om' in a loud voice and eat wild honey on unleavened bread. It sounds pretty comical. That is my way of worshipping a God who means life to me, and who is unknown, means nothing, to you. I have found places in the forest that have the power of a whole spiritual universe in them. When I am in one of those places, I don't know or even recognize any other existence. At times like that, if you were to see me, I think I wouldn't be recognizable as a creature of this world. That is my way to wisdom.

"I know what other people, people from outside, would think of me if they knew me. They would regard me as a freak. They would see the richness of my life, the spiritual life that they know nothing about, as something so strange in their eyes that it would seem deformed. Something that is extra, refined, outside the pattern of their ordinary lives would look to them like a curse, and they would cross the road to avoid me. Before you were my friends and learned to trust me, to love me, you would have felt the same. Now you know something very different. Here on this mountain, among his friends, this freak is merely a wise man. And the beginning of wisdom is honesty.

"Truth. That is where I am asking you to begin. It is time for you to make a beginning. You, Calvin, tonight, and Louella will see and follow you. Trust me."

Calvin stared at him. He wanted to revile the old man, to denounce his interference and take Louella by the hand and storm out of the place. Inside another part of him there remained, however, the bleak landscape, dry and untenanted and scraped by a sour wind that droned remorses, and remained and would remain until he spoke of it, he could no longer deny it. A feeling of great relief came over him and his anger vanished. Harry saw it and smiled. He sat forward, urging Calvin with his support, and waited for him to speak.

"All right. I was born without a mother or a father," Calvin began. "I grew up knowing something was wrong and always knowing it was me that was wrong. My mother didn't want me, she hated the sight of me. The man who called hisself my daddy always said everything was my fault, and he was right. Talk about a freak, you're looking at one, a real one. It was wrong for me to be born. It wasn't just a mistake. It was wrong. It was an evil. I grew up knowing that. If you're nothing, there's no place for you, anywhere you look. But you're stuck with being alive. I had nineteen years to hate being alive.

"Well, I met Louella, and she showed me how things could be different, and for a few months things really were different. I got to be one of the good guys, men depended on me, I did good things for them. All along, though, when I looked at the people around me, the men that belonged somewhere, I knew they would shit on me for what I was, if they knew. And I looked at the men I grew up around, the Whitmores, and I knew I disgusted them, made them sick inside because of what I'd come from. Now here I was trying to be like the real men.

"People who didn't know what I really was picked on me to be a leader, and I had to be hard and look mean. I had to be tough, I had to pretend to be like some God damned gunfighter come back to make everything come out right. I had to walk around and swing my jeans like my pecker was itching to get out every second of the day and night. I had to be like the blackhearted, whiteheaded Whitmore men who pretended to me that nothin' was wrong. You kep' goin', that was what I was supposed to do, that was the way real men behaved, and you beat the shit out of anyone who got in your way. Whatever you felt about yourself inside, you put it to one side, and you took it out on anybody that got acrost you.

"Then my real father was killed, and I found out. He was some kind of a – I can't say what because I don't know a name for it, and it's best I don't. When I found out who he was, when I understood what kind of a man would be my father in the way he did, I understood what I had known inside myself all along, I understood what made me sick to think about. Whatever it is, it's in me too. You understand that? Whatever it is, I've got it, from that man. I think that maybe one time it was something that wasn't wrong, but it was twisted and made into something purely evil. It killed two women and three children, and him too, and now it's killed another man, and it's all but killed the two of us. And it's still in me."

Calvin had begun his confession pale and strained. Now he was calmer, but his breath came rough and heavy, as if he had to walk hard through difficult terrain in order to find the words he wanted, which kept evading him.

"There was this trouble in the town. They called on me to be the hero. They chose me. I did my job, and people still think it was a great thing I did, bein' hard and tough, and thanks to me a lot of people were hurt, and scared, and a boy ended up dead. But people said I was a hero. I didn't know if they were right, or if what I thought inside myself was right. What I knew was that to do that for them, to hurt people, I had gone to the evil inside me, the evil my father gave me, and I had used it. I thought I used it in the right way at first, and then I knew that was lying to myself. What's born in me – " He took a deep breath. "What's born in me is death." He leaned forward and put his hands to his sides, pressing into himself the strength to continue.

"Louella helped me put that out of my mind, but it was there, and it still is. In the war, when the war come along, I wanted to say to people that I knew what death was, because I carried it with me, and there was no good to it, and no good to come out of it. I knew that. And yet, people would look at me, and they'd wonder why a man like me, one that had stood up and been a hero when they thought they needed one, how that man could stay at home when there was enemies to be killed. I didn't have the courage to tell them the truth about me, or about death. I didn't mind the idea of going into an army. It sounded like the sort of thing that would get me out of that backwater town leastways. The killing, though. I heard them bringing back Richie Thomas all shot up. I saw Karl in that truck. I saw my mamma's arm coming out from between the two-by-fours reaching out for my sisters, and what she wanted was to kill them because they were his.

"Then Herman come along. He was a nice guy, I liked him. Too nice. He wanted to do everything to make it easy for me to leave farming and go to killing. Herman didn't have a reason for what he was doing. He never did have a reason for what he was doing. He was a funny guy, and I didn't realize how funny until it was too late, because he seemed just so ordinary. But he was an extra in life, there wasn't no hole or place for him. He said once that they'd taken away the magic for Indians, and there wasn't anything in its place, and he was still an Indian. I guess you'd understand that, Harry. He wanted things to change, any old way, just change to see what would come out of it. For him, of course. We had a saying for it, when we was kids. Herman fished in muddy water. So he decided he'd get rid of me, by making it easy for me to go. He made Louella think that the two of them would be just being kind to make the decision an easy one for me. It was his way of getting Louella to let loose of me. Louella meant well. In his own way, Herman meant well too – well, he didn't mean anything against me, me personally, not too much. It was just that at the end of it, something new would be there, a new chance for him. He wanted that. A new chance for him, without me around, and with Louella. When I saw what he was up to, and Louella didn't, it drove me crazy.

"Everytime he took another job off of me, to make it easier for me to leave, I hated him more, but I owed him more thanks. I didn't want to go, but going was the only way to stay the Calvin that I'd turned into in the eyes of the town, the one that had a little bit of pride connected to him. The little tin soldier of an American hero, the one carrying the gun. It broke me in two. I needed my pride, what I could scrape together of it, because that was all I thought I had. And at the same time I didn't want to be a killer again, the other side of me wanted to find a way to keep what my father put into me down, beaten down, drowned. Jesus Christ! The black dog, that's what it was all the time! Anyway, it took the manhood out of me. I hated Herman for that too. I couldn't love my wife, and here he was, always smiling and saying never mind, everything's all right, it's going just fine. It wasn't fine, it was all going wrong.

"In the end it wasn't the war, it was Herman. He drove me away for the reason I didn't have any answer to, he made it easier to go than to stay. I spent nights and nights awake the whole night hating him, using him to try to learn to love the idea of going to war and killing again. And in the end it worked. He won.

"So then I went, and this big, stupid son of a bitch Dumbo got in my way, and ended up dead, killed, because he hated me so much. Maybe he could see I was a fake all the time. Maybe he could see I'd carry the wrong sort of death with me, even in a war. And that killed Dumbo, and fixed me up for the rest of my life. Oh, Jesus, I had some crazy ideas then. I thought I'd paid it off, that maybe the part of me that was torn off would take away the evil with it. The dope found it, though, the evil. I listened to it again. I decided I had to kill Herman. I was so weak, I couldn't stand up to what I knew about myself, I had to do what real men did, I had to kill the man who'd taken my wife away from me to prove to people I was what they thought I ought to be. That's what people would expect of a real man. That's what they would expect of Calvin Whitmore. And I did it. I killed Herman because I was too weak not to, because I gave in to the death in me. And I knew all along Red Branch would make me a hero for doing it, even if they turned around and sent me to the gas chamber. And I wanted that too. I wanted to be executed. Wiped away. Finished. I wanted to sit in that gas chamber and think those green walls were beautiful, and watch that pellet fall down into that bucket of acid, and smell those almond blossoms, and die.

"All of it finished and done with, that's what I wanted. All but one thing. I never stopped loving Louella. I never wanted that done with. Ever.

"I was guilty. That court got it all wrong. I'm guilty as sin. That's why I'm running away."

He stopped. "That's enough," he said, "enough for now." Calvin shuddered and looked at the ceiling, as if gazing at the surface of a pool from its depths. He turned then to face Harry. "I guess you know what you're doing, Harry. I didn't want to tell that, because I'm scared of only one thing, I have been all along, that Louella will leave me for it." Calvin kept his eyes on Harry, unable to swing them to the side of the table where Louella stared at him, her mouth open behind her hand. His body eased, and he dropped his eyes and lowered his head onto his arms.

Harry had shared Calvin's struggle, his thin body rigid and wracked in sympathy, pushing Calvin with his physique as well as his will. Now he wilted, as drained as Calvin.

Louella had not visibly breathed during Calvin's confession. The cigarette between her fingers was dead. Now she shook herself awake and unnecessarily stubbed out the cigarette in the scarred ashtray. She looked at Calvin as if something familiar had changed shape, considering the body of this strong man fallen at her feet. She had been crying without sobbing, her eyes running tears without hindrance, and now her wet face gleamed behind the candlelight. She wiped it on her sleeve and looked at Calvin with clearer eyes. Her face now reflected her concern for her husband, tempered still with the shock of the experience. She got to her feet and went around the table to him, approaching warily as if he were to be disturbed only with caution, first stroking his slumped shoulders, then leaning over him and cradling his head to her breast, pulling it to her until he straightened up and responded to her reassurance.

Harry slowly smiled. He lifted his arms onto the table, turned his palms upward and relaxed his fingers. Slowly the relaxation spread up his arms, into his body, through his shoulders and neck. Slowly, slowly, so slowly that the movement seemed both prolonged and sudden, his eyes closed and his face was at rest.

When he spoke, it was if his voice came out of a room nearby. "I am one man, Calvin, so are you. Men were not made to a pattern, unless that pattern is infinity. Each of us mirrors the universe, a universe that includes both the bad and the good, in which the only true sin is to deny that we are spirit by denying that we have a need to reply to the spirit in us as much as to the animal. Find it, the spirit in you, the one thing that cannot be taken away from you, and you will be healed."

They did not sleep that night. To begin with, the young people could not have moved from Harry's table for an earthquake. The immensity of what they had done, the breadth of the step that had been taken, shocked them into submission to the advice and direction of their friend. They waited without speaking until Harry was ready to talk. At last his eyes snapped open, and then he was on his feet and himself again, tending to their needs like the keeper of their lives and souls.

"We will proceed carefully with your healing," he said. "We'll start with soup." He bustled around his tiny kitchen, reaching for things and lighting the stove. He spoke with great urgency, the words flowing from him, impelled by a joy that showed itself in his face.

"It will have to be done in my way, of course. You agree?" He paused in the stirring of the soup, waiting with the ladle in his hand for them to accept that his recipe was the correct one. When they nodded, he smiled and measured out the soup. As he put it on the table and sat down to eat with them, he continued, "You will find it embarrassing, sometimes at least, I warn you. A little bit too strange now and then. However, I can't believe you don't realize by now that getting to know my ways is part of the cure. You do, don't you? Both of you?"

He put his spoon down on the table and waited for a clear sign from each of them. They nodded when they saw what was expected of them. Satisfied, he picked up his bowl and began eating his soup, slurping it with relish. "I wonder if confession is as exhausting for a Catholic as it is for us heathen," he said. "For the priest, too."

He got up from the table and found some of his unleavened bread, breaking it into chunks and putting it on the table near the candle. "Possibly this is the one time my sacramental bread has been put to its real use," he said, cackling at the top of his voice and dropping pieces of his bread into their soup bowls. "Soak up the soup with it. I think it will be good this way," he said.

Wiping out his soup bowl with a piece of the bread, eating and speaking at the same time in his excitement, he continued, "Remember now, I have always said to you, you don't have to believe in any part of what I am doing. All you have to do is to accept that this is my way, it is part of me."

He picked up the soup bowls, empty now, and absent-mindedly stacked them on the floor at his feet. "You are my friends. You have learned to accept me for what I know myself to be, now let me work for you in my way, even if it is strange to you."

He looked at Calvin and Louella, who sat speechless, exhausted by the experience of the night and now pummelled by Harry's rush of words. "Do you have any idea what I am saying?" he asked. He laughed and clapped his hands in his delight. He got to his feet and went behind first Louella and then Calvin, taking them by the shoulders and wrapping his arms around them, pressing his stubbly cheek to theirs and laughing deafeningly into their ears. "Do you have any idea how excited I am that I am going to be able to help you?"

He moved to the widest space in the crowded room, tumbling the soup bowls with his feet as he did so. Moving them aside with a few swipes of his feet, he folded himself to the floor like a collapsible mannequin, into the yoga position they had seen before. As he did, his mood changed from elation to one of quiet assurance. "You will heal yourselves," he said. "You will be whole. There is light at the end, you'll see. Excuse me now."

*

"Well," Louella had said to Calvin, "it's all harmless, I guess."

Harmless. Finally, something harmless. Calvin felt his heart sing with the assurance that he had not harmed Louella with his confession. His willingness to walk naked in the light of day on the first day of his life, to reveal his secret to her, was harmless. How did he know that? How did he know that something had happened between them that bound them together beyond their understanding? What was it that told him that? Was it the same thing that had compelled him to tell his story against his conscious will? Was it conceivable that he was not a hollow man after all, that Harry had already found for him that thing that couldn't be taken away from him, when what he had wanted was to have everything taken from him? Was this the beginning of wisdom as Harry promised, when what it felt like was the beginning of life? He was excited beyond reason, filled with hope, and the gray curtains of despair lightened as he looked at them, searching them eagerly for a shadow or silhouette to indicate what might lie on the other side of them.

Now they sat wrapped in their coats and a blanket. They had walked down the dry, steep slope from their house to the edge of the cliff. There at the end of the world, they sat watching light begin.

"I always wanted to do this," Calvin said, "be at the end of the land, as far as a person could go, and watch what happens when the sun comes up behind me."

"What did God do first?" Louella asked, then tried to answer her own question. "I always forget that you don't know anything about it. I remember he separated chaos from something. Was it water? Or was it light?" She was very tired, and her mind slipped over the surface of her memory.

"I don't know anything about it," Calvin answered. "I wasn't allowed to have a religion. For pretty good reasons."

She was intent on remembering and didn't hear him. "I think what he did was shine a light into chaos. He shone a light into chaos, like holding up a floodlight to see what to do to sort everything out. Then he started making the world." She paused and pressed her temples with her fingers. "I'm too tired, I can't remember now. Someplace along the way, though, he created man. I used to think man was created because God was so proud of the world when he got it done that he had to have someone to show it off to. But with man he got things wrong, in spite of being God, and then man messed everything up. Maybe, I thought, he shouldn't have wanted to show off."

Louella laughed quietly to herself at her memories. "When I said that once in Sunday School, the woman who was teaching us came down on me like one of those people the Israelites were always fighting. There wasn't an ass's jawbone handy or else she'd have used it. She said I was talking sacrilege and God didn't need to have a reason for anything, especially creation, and I ought to have brains enough to know that it was the serpent that made things go wrong. I thought blaming everything on a talking snake was so dumb that I laughed, and she got really mad then. She was only a clerk at Penney's, I don't know how she knew that much about God. Maybe she didn't. Maybe I was right."

"Come on now, keep your eyes open," Calvin said. "There's plenty of time to wonder why God bothered with man." He turned her head, holding it in his two hands from behind. "Talk about creation, watch there, the way the light's just starting to divide the land from the sea. Looks like it's coming from nowhere, or else all the way the other side of creation. There's a beginning of blue already. Who knows, maybe that's the first blue that was ever made. Maybe we're seeing it all begin."